In Range

Ven'Thyl Saga Part I

Fables of J

Contents

Chapter 48: *Human History and Teleportation Circles* 1
Chapter 49: *Gryphon Helvi'Ett* 12
Chapter 50: *The Capital City of Ven'Thyl* 22
Chapter 51: *Persistence and Opportunity* 32
Chapter 52: *The House of Ven'Thyl Part 1 (Welcome)* 43
Chapter 53: *The House of Ven'Thyl Part 2 (Members)* 51
Chapter 54: *The House of Ven'Thyl Part 3 (Head of the House)* 61
Chapter 55: *Unexpected Morning* 73
Chapter 56: *The Noble Houses* 82
Chapter 57: *Shooting and Styles* 92
Chapter 58: *Rivaled* 101
Chapter 59: *Drinks from a Stranger* 112
Chapter 60: *A Fall and a Challenge* 123
Chapter 61: *Material Promises* 132
Chapter 62: *Reveals and Plans* 140
Chapter 63: *Whereabouts Part 3* 148
Chapter 64: *Trinity Tattoo and Skill Creation* 163
Chapter 65: *Magic Archer and Complicated Love* 171
Chapter 66: *The House of Ven'Thyl Part 4 (House Treasury)* 179
Chapter 67: *Partial News and Trinity Ritual* 191
Chapter 68: *Hand-to-Hand and Swordsmanship* 205
Chapter 69: *Archers' Playground* 215
Chapter 70: *The Millennium Dungeon of Blood* 226

Chapter 71: *Combat Test Part 1* 236
Chapter 72: *Combat Test Part 2* 247
Chapter 73: *Calm Before the Moon* 256
Chapter 74: *Crimson Moonlight* 268
Chapter 75: *Combat Test Part 3* 276
Chapter 76: *Limbo* 287
Chapter 77: *Remorse and Guilt* 296
Glossary 309

Chapter 48
Human History and Teleportation Circles

"Psst…wake up…" her voice whispered to me, "Jude, wake up… let me show you my favourite spot in the hospital..."

"Ughhh… it's like the middle of the night… can't you show me later?" I asked, too tired and lazy to wake up.

"Don't be like that, Jude… You don't wanna miss the view tonight…" she said, being her usual persistent self.

"Ughhh...fine! You know I'm blind, right? Showing me—"

But when I decided to reluctantly wake up, I realized I wasn't where I thought I was, but actually in the open field where Odelia and I made camp for the night.

"Was I being too much of a bother, Lord Eyes?" Odelia timidly asked, thinking she did something wrong.

"Huh, no… I just thought I was somewhere—never mind," I said, shaking my head to wake myself up. "Were you trying to wake me up?" I asked, fully sitting up.

"Kind of, my Lord," she said as she pointed her finger up to the clear night sky, "I did not want you to miss out on such a rare sight."

Unsure what she was referring to, I looked up to see a very visible shooting star quickly streaking across the night sky.

"Woah, I haven't seen a shooting star since I was child!" I exclaimed, pleasantly surprised by the sight.

"You make it sound like it is over, Lord Eyes."

Then suddenly an almost identical one came flying across the night sky in a different direction.

Fables of J

"This has been occurring for the last few seconds," Odelia explained, as another one came flying right after.

"What the hell? Is this normal?" I questioned, in awe of the shooting stars lighting the night sky every few seconds.

"Not particularly, though this is not the first nor the last time this event will be witnessed," Odelia informed me. "Tales tell us it is the Twin Goddesses playing a game with the stars, but those same tales tell us it is also their way of sharing a sign to the people of Novus."

"A sign?" I repeated, not knowing.

"A warning of times to come," Odelia answered, "which has caused the people to name the occurrence, the Bouncing Stars of Warning."

I chuckled at the childish name, and asked Odelia, "You wouldn't happen to know what those times to come would entail, would you?" wanting to prepare myself for what's to come.

"Sadly, I do not. Though I can tell you it may be related to the Five Great Heroes," she mentioned.

"Oh? Why's that?" I asked curiously.

"This year will mark the millennium since their disappearance, and one would think the Twin Goddesses' favourite champions would receive some sort of memorial celebration, especially since they have shown us a sign this close to the date," Odelia figured.

"So their warning isn't necessarily a bad thing then?" I said, feeling slightly relieved.

"Not entirely. But if the Twin Goddesses are planning something, then it is more than safe to assume Gom is as well; and I am sure whatever it is, it will not be as pleasant as the Twin Goddesses," Odelia said with concern in her voice.

"Gom? Didn't Sister Maebel mention that name before? And it sounds like this 'Gom' person can oppose the Twin Goddesses, does that mean they're also some type of God too?" I wondered to myself, noticing that the shooting stars had finally stopped appearing.

"Now that the Bouncing Stars of Warning have gone, you should return back to sleep, my Lord. We will be arriving at Leon in half a day's travel, and Ven'Thyl by day's end. I would not want you to be too exhausted when you finally return to your rightful Kingdom for the first time in your young life."

Ultimately agreeing with Odelia's sentiment, I tried to sleep soundly again, but my memories left me restless through the night.

Both of us preferring not to waste too many days on unnecessary travelling, Odelia and I agreed to travel non-stop for two and a half days straight, only taking short breaks for food and water, or resting for the night. All the while I slowly continued to level up my movement Skills when I had the Stamina and Mana to do so.

Sprint increased by 3 Levels.	Archer's Dash increased by 2 Levels

During our travels, we mostly passed through heavily forested terrains, but there were a few grasslands, rolling hills, and rocky river creeks along the way. Though to my surprise and disappointment, we didn't run into a single real monster, only occasionally seeing forest animals like deers and rabbits, and a few already eaten or rotting carcesses. I asked Odelia about it during one of our breaks, and she explained to me that the monsters have learned to steer clear of well traveled routes—like the one we were using—as they would most likely be hunted by adventurers if they were spotted.

We also passed many travelling merchants, a handful of horse caravans, and multiple adventuring Parties; though we always kept our interactions brief as we were in a rush, and because the people couldn't exactly trust two elves suspiciously speeding through the roads. And I did take note that I didn't see a single Player amongst the people we passed, and it made me wonder if Lavie and the others already made it Leon.

Coming up to the edge of the cliff, I pantingly asked, "That's Leon?"

"It is, my Lord," Odelia answered, resting on a boulder nearby, "What do you think? Is it what you expected?"

Fables of J

"More or less," I said, catching my breath and walking right to the edge to get a better view.

From where I stood, I had a perfect view of a massive split field of farmlands ahead of us, currently being attended to by multiple farmers. Directly between the farmlands was a long, wide dirt road that led up to the massive gates and walls of the city—at least 30ft in height. The walls were built in an enormous semicircle around the front of Leon, while the backside of the city was covered by a vast ocean or sea behind it, also having a familiar barrier—that was practically invisible—creating a border around the whole outside.

The city itself was pretty much exactly how I expected it to be, as it was clearly divided into 4 distinct semicircle layers, with the deeper ones being elevated higher than the others, and countless distinctive buildings spread throughout the city layers. The first layer was clearly the city's slums, the second was the middle class where there seemed to be a lot of business, the third being much more high class and well structured, and the fourth was a beautifully built and isolated castle overlooking the entire city. And with my farseeing and keen eyes, I could barely spot 6 indistinguishable giant marble statues spread along the long road leading directly up to the castle; with one extra large statue standing tall right before the castle entrance.

Pointing to the castle, I said, "I assume that's where the Tyrant lives?"

"Indeed. As well as the other members of the Royal Family of Leon," Odelia confirmed, strangely looking elsewhere.

"Wait, if there's a Royal Family of Leon, does that mean there's also a Royal Family of Sya?" I suddenly suspected.

Odelia gave me a puzzled look, and said, "Truly sire, your lack of knowledge never seems to end. Maybe I should be teaching you history instead of archery," she laughingly suggested.

"Why not both?" I replied, not minding the idea of learning more about the world. "But that's a discussion for later. Now what's with having two royal families? And why isn't the royal family of Sya in control of the Kingdom? They must be better than the Leons, right?"

Happily indulging my genuine interest, Odelia said, "I am unfamiliar with exact details of human history, but from what I recall, the two families were actually once united as one when the great Leon and Sya married—together creating a central capital city where the town of Asheton currently resides."

"Huh? What happened then?" I asked..

"After their disappearance and some years later, the two heirs separately led the branches of the Leon and Sya families to a devastating dispute over the rightful ruler of the Kingdom. A dispute that quickly turned into an all-out civil war which resulted in the complete destruction of the capital city and central lands, only leaving ashes in their wake, and splitting apart the two royal families once again."

"And somehow the Leons became the ruling family of the kingdom?" I asked, trying to figure out how.

"They did," she said, explaining, "the rule was overwhelmingly seized during the First Trinity War, when the dwarven and elven kingdoms declared war on the human kingdom, believing they were greatly weakened after their recent taxing civil war. Though it was then where the royal family of Leon proved themselves as the stronger of the two families, leading their armies to simultaneously protect both borders from the invading forces for an entire year, and through their great feat gained the immense support of the people at the time."

"The First Trinity War? It must be one of the major wars Odelia mentioned a few days ago, but I better not ask her about the details, she already thinks I don't know anything," I thought to myself.

Odelia continued, "Since then, the Royal Family of Sya has been relegated to being called the lesser of the royal families, as they could never really overcome the raw destructive power of the royal family of Leon, but that hasn't stopped them from voicing their desires to challenge the Leons' reign. Though these last few years they have been strangely silent about their desires to rule, and rumour has it that the Tyrant has been forcefully suppressing them with something, but with what, I am not sure."

"Interesting... that was very informative, thank you, Odelia," I said, thinking, *"Maybe I should visit Sya in the future. Sounds like I might find a really important Quest there to help the human kingdom."*

"It is my pleasure to inform you, my Lord. Now shall we go?" Odelia asked, gesturing to a path leading down the cliffside.

"Lead the way," I said, following her down the narrow cliffside path.

While we walked through the farmlands on the dirt road to the city, I said to Odelia "So... which part of the city is the teleportation circle in?" not knowing from just the view earlier.

"Oh my, my Lord. I am really starting to question who has educated you until now," Odelia said, shaking her head in disappointment; then saying, "Remember I said the public TC is outside of Leon—as all of them are—so we are actually heading over there." She directed my attention to a stone building far north of us.

"Wait, why is it so far away?" surprised by the great distance from the city.

"It is a precaution to avoid certain individuals running into the city to hide, as well as to prevent any invading armies from appearing at the city's doorsteps," Odelia explained.

"There has to be teleportation circles inside the city, right? Couldn't people just teleport to one of those?" I figured.

"They could, but they would first need to know the runes of the circle they are teleporting to, otherwise they would not be able to."

Odelia then explained to me that the teleportation circles inside the major cities were all privately owned, heavily guarded and monitored, and that even the right to own one was only reserved for the highest and most trusted ranks in the cities.

Most of her words were lost to me though when I heard that you need to know the runes to teleport, making me think, *"If knowing the runes is basically essential to be able to teleport, there must be records or writings of them somewhere then,"* as I remembered how the runes on the teleportation circle in Castle Creedmor were way too complex to only go by memory. *"And if that's the case, I wonder if you can buy them, and if not maybe I can borrow them."* I was slightly amused by the thought.

Spending about another half an hour on the north road, we finally arrived at a large, stone brick building, and I noticed it was very simple in design. Almost like a large barn made of stone, the building had a completely wide and open entrance, with a few dozen people entering and exiting it every few minutes. Unfortunately for us, there was a long line up for the people entering, and we had to stand behind a merchant with a cart selling different types of food—about 20th in line.

Seeing the merchants exiting the building holding papers, I curiously asked, "I don't need some type of identification, do I?"

"No, we should be fine." Then she noticed why I was asking. "Those papers are only meant for people who are travelling with a lot of cargo, to ensure there is no smuggling of illegal goods, otherwise we should only be stopped if you are wanted in the kingdom. You are not wanted are you?" Odelia asked, making sure before we entered.

"No, are you?" I asked back, moving up in line.

She chuckled at my reply, ignoring it and saying, "Good, now we only need to pay 5 Gold each and tell them our destination, then we are golden."

"5 Gold?! That's a steal!" I reacted enthusiastically, "I can't believe the Adventurer's Guild was asking for 100 Gold to use their teleportation circle."

"That is expensive, but it does allow one to enter the city directly if needed to, and without needing to be seen and checked at the gates," Odelia pointed out. "Depending on the person, those reasons could be worth the cost."

"I never thought about it as a direct line into the city—Wait, did you just say checked at the gates? Do I need to worry about that when we get to Ven'Thyl?" I asked, moving in line again.

"Not really, as I will be the one vouching for you, and the guards at Ven'Thyl are only really suspicious of other Races, or really shifty looking folk," she replied, staying beside me in line.

Fables of J

"Well that sounds racist," I said in disappointment of the elven kingdom.

"Sadly it is, but the other kingdoms' guards will also do the same," Odelia said sadly.

"That's even more disappointing to hear." We were now about 9th in line.

She then came closer and whispered, "If you were King, I more than believe you could change how our kingdom would perceive the others, and that would be a welcomed start." She stared at me hopefully.

"Hmmm…no, thank you," Odelia looked extremely disappointed to hear my answer, but trying to cheer her up I said, "Don't worry so much about the Kingdom, I think I know of a way to make it better in the future."

She suddenly perked up, looking utterly intrigued by my words, "Ooh? What did you have in mind, my Lo—" catching herself from saying Lord with people around.

"I'm not entirely sure about the details yet," I answered truthfully, "but what I can say is that I have to find something really important to the Kingdom."

"Something important to the Kingdom? What are you trying to find, maybe I can help you?" she said, offering her services.

"No offense, but I doubt it. What I'm searching for is something that has been missing for a long, long, long time." My words seemed to cause Odelia to greatly wonder to herself.

I then heard someone shout, "Next!" as I finally noticed that we were now inside the building.

The inside was a huge open space, built out of stone brick floors and walls, and in the center was a long, divided counter with one person for each of the six sections—each section having multiple people and merchants lined up in them. There were also two heavily armoured guards standing at each end of the counter, and I could see that they had different names but were both **Lv.35**. Then on the left side of the space, guarded by four heavily armoured guards that were all **Lv.27-30**, was a sign that hung above a dark chamber that said 'Arrivals' and every now and then the chamber lit up and a few people and merchants would come through it. On the right side of the space was also a dark chamber guarded by another four heavily armoured guards, but this time they were **Lv.29-30**, and the sign above said 'Departures.' I then let out a little laugh when I realized what this place reminded me of. and saw the people heading to the right showing the guards a small slip of paper before heading inside the occasionally lit up chamber.

We heard another worker shout again, and Odelia said, "It is our turn L—Eyes," catching herself again as she led me to an unoccupied counter.

Seeing us approach, a middle aged woman wearing a maroon coloured uniform said to us, "Two tickets?"

Odelia noddingly replied, "To Ven'Thyl please," then counted the Gold for the worker who held her hand out for the payment.

"It's on me, Odelia," I said, quickly taking out the 10 Gold needed from my Inventory and handing it over to the worker.

"That was not necessary, my—" she stopped herself from talking.

"It's okay, I've got a lot of Gold," I assured her.

After counting up the coins, the worker began to search for something behind the counter, and said, "Here it is, two tickets to Ven'Thyl," sliding to us two slips of identical paper and then gesturing to the right. "You may make your way to 'Departures' now."

Following Odelia to the right, I took a look at the paper she handed me, and saw that it was a simple piece of paper that said 'Ven'Thyl' in the middle, with a complex runic circle surrounding the word. Looking at Odelia's ticket, it also had an identical runic circle, and I thought, *"Isn't this what you need to know to teleport?"*

We then showed the tickets to the guards and they let us pass into the dark chamber.

Spread evenly around the edges of the chamber was a semicircle of six huge alcoves, each having large teleportation circles within them that were a good distance apart to allow any merchant carts or carriages to have space to move. There were also a few hooded individuals attending to and activating the circles, all **Lv.50-52**, with the one exception being a **Lv.65** person.

9

Fables of J

"Is being Lv.50 what it takes to get the Teleport Skill? And what's with the much higher Lv.65?" I wondered, as Odelia seemed to be waiting for a specific person to call us, seeing how she ignored the others calling.

Waiting for about 2 minutes, a hooded person with a dark blond, greying beard finally called us over, and Odelia grabbed the ticket from my hand and handed it to him. Reading the runes on the paper, the man spoke to us with a deep and raspy voice, asking, "How's Drune doing? And who's the kid?"

"You know you live a lot closer than I do, Gryph. Why don't you just go visit and ask him yourself instead of asking me the same question every time I come here?"

Realizing Odelia knew him, I took note of his name—**Lv.65 Gryphon Helvi'Ett**—and thought, *"Seems to be an old friend of Odelia and Drune's."*

"Unlike you and Drune, I actually age, you know? My body isn't what it used to be," Gryphon said, massaging his shoulder.

Odelia rolled her eyes at him, "You are making excuses again. We both know you could go there anytime you wanted, and your body is completely fine," she patted him hard on his shoulder.

Gryphon huffed at her words, then changed his attention onto me, "Does Drune know you're bringing a young elf to Ven'Thyl with you?" he smirked, "Maybe I should go visit him, then I can tell him all about this."

"Go right ahead," Odelia said, smirking back, "Drune will tell you all about the greatness of this young elf; about what he has done for the both of us, and what he will do for our k—" I covered Odelia's mouth knowing what she was about to say.

Taken back by our interaction, Gryphon looked me over intently, questioning, "Greatness? He just looks like an ordinary young elf to me, what greatness could he have?"

Slightly irritated from his condescending tone, I smiled and said, "My name's Eyes, but no need to introduce yourself, I already know who you are."

"You know who I am?" Gryphon's right eyebrow raised, "There's no way Odelia or Drune would ever reveal who I am, right?"

"Never. And as far as I can recall, Drune and I have never even spoken about you to Eyes," Odelia confirmed to him, giving me a curious look.

"Ouch, not even a mention about one of your oldest friends, huh?" Odelia shrugged at his words, as he said, "So tell me then young elf, who is it you think am I?"

I smirked at him, and said, "From what I can see right now, you're Gryphon Helvi'Ett, correct? Currently Lv.65?"

Gryphon's smug expression quickly diminished, turning very sour and serious; then with a sudden, surprising burst of speed, he pressed his forearm against my neck, pinning me against the back of the alcove, asking "Who are you!?"

Chapter 49
Gryphon Helvi'Ett

Pressing his forearm harder into my neck, Gryphon reiterated, "I won't ask again, who are you?" and as I struggled to breathe, Odelia hastily came up from behind him, grabbed his shoulders and threw him away from me.

Catching me in her arms, Odelia worriedly asked, "Are you alright, my Lord?"

Coughing and rubbing my neck, I said, "I think so..." trying to catch my breath.

"Odelia, what are you doing!? Are you really protecting him after he said my true name?" Gryphon angrily questioned, stomping towards us.

Positioning herself in front of me, Odelia spoke with the same cold and serious tone she used in the barracks prison, saying, "Gryphon, calm down." At the same time she readied herself to reach for her bow to show she was truly serious. "I do not know how he knows of your true name, but I cannot allow you to threaten or hurt him any further—even if you are an old friend."

"What are you talking about? This isn't like you, Odelia. Just who is this elf?" he stared daggers directly at me.

When Odelia noticed that the other people in the chamber were all drawn in and attracted to the sudden commotion, she said to him, "I cannot say, there are too many listening ears here," nodding for him to look around.

Turning to see all the eyes in the chamber on us, Gryphon nodded back and cupped his hands together saying, "**Barrier**," creating a small, see-through dome in the space of his hands. "**Silence**." As he then blew

In Range – Ven'Thyl Saga Part I

a purple coloured magic into the dome—giving it a purple hue—and pulled his hands apart to cause it to expand to the size of the whole alcove.

"There, they can't get in and they won't hear us. Now tell me what's really going on, Odelia," he demanded.

"Always so quick to act. We could have just left the building, you know?" Odelia mentioned, relaxing her stance and explaining the whole situation about me being the heir to Gryphon.

Listening to the whole story, Gryphon's anger calmed and he surprisingly became nonchalant, saying, "Odelia, that's impossible, and I can't believe you're still on this after all these centuries. We already know the great King Ven'Thyl never had children. You're just believing what you want to believe, and I especially can't believe Drune got roped into it too."

"Actually, the great King Ven'Thyl did have children, and grandchildren," I corrected him, remembering that there were still two descendants alive somewhere.

"I told you he was the heir," Odelia smiled, while Gryphon seemed to be more than skeptical about it.

At that moment five guards came knocking at the dome, shouting something to us that we couldn't hear at all, "I think we're in trouble. What are we gonna do now?" I asked them.

"I wonder if I'll get fired for this," Gryphon said, ripping the tickets and causing the runes to manifest from them and travel into his head, "Too bad, this job paid really well, even if it was extremely boring."

"If you believe in the heir, I am sure he can find you another high paying job when he becomes the king," Odelia smiled again.

Rolling my eyes at her, I refocused my attention back to Gryphon who was now beginning to mumble a long incantation to himself; and as he did so, runes floated out of his mouth into the surrounding space, with the runes on the ground slowly lighting up by the second. After a minute of speaking the incantation, Gryphon announced, "**Teleportation!**" and the whole teleportation circle erupted with an intense blinding magic light.

Fables of J

Covering my eyes from the intense light, I suddenly felt the ground beneath me disappear, causing me to feel as if I was falling; but just as quickly as it disappeared, I suddenly felt the ground reappear beneath me again. Right afterwards I heard Odelia say, "You may uncover your eyes now, we are already here."

"Odelia, was that his first teleportation? How can you truly believe that he's the heir?" Gryphon asked, but Odelia quickly shushed his words.

Uncovering my eyes, I found that we were standing in a similarly structured chamber as the previous one, but instead of stone brick floors and walls, everything was simply made out of wood. However this chamber was quite a bit larger than the other, seeing a total of 18 teleportation circles inside, as well as no one attending to them. Curious, I asked them, "Why are there 18 circles here? And why isn't anyone attending to them like before?"

"Look at him, Odelia, he doesn't even know that," Gryphon said, shaking his head.

"You will sadly learn he does not know much," Odelia replied, giving me a teasing look before answering, "It is because we are in the Arrivals chamber, Eyes. There needs to be more circles here because people can come from all over the continent, and the circles are not attended to because people just arrive here and do not get teleported here."

"So I suggest you get out of the circle before someone teleports onto you," Gryphon mentioned, as I noticed they were already both standing outside the circle.

Quickly running myself over to them, I followed Odelia and Gryphon to the central chamber where people bought their tickets. Looking around, everything was pretty much the same, except for the structure being made out of wood, but I did notice that the guards here were all significantly higher level compared to the ones at Leon—all ranging from **Lv.45-50**. They continued to lead me outside the building, and I looked back to see that it wasn't actually a building that we were in, but three hollowed out giant trees that grew into each other, and to my surprise they still seemed alive and well—seeing the bright green leaves on their branches.

Abruptly stopping just outside, Gryphon said, "Well it was fun catching up, Odelia, but I can't blindly trust this suspicious elf like you can, so I'll be going now."

"Will you not come back to Ven'Thyl?" Odelia asked. "How long has it been since you left?"

"Left? Hah! You know very well that I didn't choose to leave, as you should know what would happen if I returned," Gryphon spoke with sadness in his voice. "I'm not accepted there..."

Knowing much more than I do, Odelia expressed a face of pity to Gryphon, but she suddenly dragged the both of us behind the building, and said, "Silent barrier the area again."

Not questioning her, Gryphon repeated the same magics he casted earlier, creating a purple dome around us again.

"Listen to me, Gryph. I am telling you he really is the Heir," she pointed to me. "Things in Ven'Thyl will surely change for you, Drune, and everyone else when he finally takes his rightful place on the throne."

"Your house is always so hopeful when it comes to the missing Heir. It's very admirable," Gryphon smiled only a little.

"I don't understand the problem here. I thought Humans and Dwarves were allowed in Ven'Thyl. How exactly is he not accepted there?" I asked, trying to figure out the situation.

"The other Races are allowed, but this is not a situation entirely about Race," Odelia clarified. "And regardless of how he calls himself or even looks, Gryphon is not Human."

"Oh, I just assumed since he was aging and looked like one," I curiously observed Gryphon's pretty human appearance to me. "So does that make him a really old elf then?"

"Why'd you go telling him that? And I'm not old," he stated, "I'll have you know, I'm actually younger than both Odelia and Drune," pulling his hood down to fully expose his aging face, his short blonde greying hair, his sapphire blue eyes, and his pointed ears. "She's wrong though, I am human, but I'm also an elf."

"I see, you're a Half-Elf then," I figured, then thinking, *"I just assumed they weren't a thing because there wasn't an option to pick one in the Tutorial."*

"That's right, I'm a Half-Elf, and we're even more ridiculed and discriminated against than the Dwarves in Ven'Thyl," he said, putting his hood back up to cover himself.

"Why's that? Aren't you Elven too?" I questioned.

"I told you, Gryph, change will come," Odelia pointed at me again. "Our future King believes that you, a Half-Elf, is Elven too."

Gryphon scoffed at her words, "Tell me when change is already here, until then I'll be going elsewhere."

"Wait," I said, stopping him for a moment, "Have you decided where you're headed to?"

"Probably somewhere in the Human Kingdom again for work. People are always looking for useful Mages like myself," he looked at me with curiosity. "Why do you ask?"

"I just so happen to be one of those people," I smirked, explaining. "I need someone who I know can be trusted to stay and use the teleportation circle in my castle, and you seem like the perfect person, considering Odelia seems to trust you enough to tell you the truth about me."

Gryphon chuckled in disbelief, "You have a castle?"

"Oh, what a fantastic idea, Lord Eyes!" Odelia gushed, loving my idea, "With Gryph there, I can spend even more time with Drune and come back to Ven'Thyl right away!"

"He really has a castle?"

Odelia excitedly nodded yes.

"Drune will also be in the town nearby if you ever wanted to visit him, so what do you say? " I eagerly waited for his response.

"This is too much right now, I'm still at the part where you have a castle," Gryphon said, trying to wrap his brain around the idea.

"We started off on the wrong foot, Gryphon, but if Odelia and Drune truly consider you a trusted friend, that's really enough for me," I said, sending him an invite to be a Resident. "Don't overthink it too much, accept my offer. Odelia and Drune already have."

In Range – Ven'Thyl Saga Part I

The same confusion about the invitation that Odelia and Drune had also came to Gryphon, who then looked to Odelia for an answer.

"Gryph, you may not trust him after learning he knows of your true name, but know that Drune and I already do. And if that is enough for you, then accept. If it is not, then decline," Odelia gave him a slow trusting nod, and Gryphon nodded back.

"It is enough, but I better not regret this, Odelia," Gryphon then said to me, "But before I accept, I want you to know that I only work for 100 Gold a month. That should be nothing for someone who owns a castle," he smirked mischievously.

"Gryph, you know that is way too much, and I know for a fact the Mages working at the TC only earn 50 Gold a month," Odelia stepped in.

"100 Gold?! Even 50 Gold is a lot more than I expected," I then decided to ask, "What about all the public teleportation circles, do you know all the exact runes for them?"

"Of course not, I've only ever bothered to memorize 3 of them after all," Gryphon mentioned.

"And you want me to pay you 100 Gold a month? I don't think so," I shook my head.

"Hey, no one knows all the runes," he stated, "and you only really need to know 1 from each of the 5 major cities. Anything more is redundant—plus the cost for even just one of them is absurdly high."

"Here's my offer then: 20 Gold a month, free castle lodging, and I'll get you all the runes for the public circles, maybe even some other ones if I come across some," I offered him.

"All of them?! You know that the True Runes cost 1,000 Gold each, right? Meaning it would cost well over 100,000 Gold to have all of them," he then gestured to my appearance, "and I don't think you're that rich to be able to spend 100,000 Gold like nothing, especially since you're only offering 20 Gold as my pay."

"Wait, how much Gold!?" I exclaimed, "What about the tickets, can't you just use the runes for them? Or what about copying the ones on the ground in the Arrivals chamber?"

Fables of J

"Wouldn't you think everybody would know the runes and bypass the TCs then? And the tickets are just a one time use shortcut that us teleporters use to speed up the teleportation. Once ripped, they become useless pieces of paper," Gryphon continued to explain, "they only give us a general idea of the location being teleported, and help guide us to an available circle nearby. And the runes you are suggesting to simply copy, are all hidden with powerful illusions casted on them centuries ago. You couldn't see their True Runes if you tried."

"If you can buy these 'True Runes' for 1,000 Gold outright, there must be a record of all them somewhere then, right? So where are they?" I inquired curiously.

"There are, but they're kept and guarded by incredibly powerful Mages," Gryphon informed me, "mages who selectively choose who can buy the True Runes from the Transport Towers in the different cities."

"Lord Eyes, I hope you are not planning to steal those said runes," Odelia looked at me with concern. "The Mages at the Transport Towers are all at least of a Grand Wizard Class, and are far more powerful than Gryph over here."

"Hey!" Gryphon shouted, feeling offended.

"Even I would struggle to fight them," Odelia stated, worried about what I was planning to do.

"Struggle, you say?" I laughingly smiled at her, "That means you would still beat them, yes?"

"Of course I would, Lord Eyes," she proudly proclaimed, "no silly Mage Class could ever beat the greatness of a Trinity Archer, let alone any of the other Classes."

Gryphon rolled his eyes, saying, "Odelia, your archery elitism is showing again," but she ignored his comment.

"Don't worry, Odelia, I won't be personally stealing anything from anyone. It's not my forte," I assured her, while Gryphon looked at me skeptically again. "So do we have a deal, Gryphon?"

"Hmmm..." Gryphon hummed loudly, thinking over the decision, "the pay's a bit low, but I guess I can manage it. Especially if you're planning to obtain all the True Runes of the circles."

I then received a notification.

> **Gryphon Helvi'Ett has accepted your Invitation, and has become a Resident of your Homestead.**

"I guess we have a deal—" but my words were cut short as Gryphon suddenly began to freak out.

"Wh-What's happening? What did you just do to me?" he questioned, "Why do I feel so much stronger? And what is this new Skill?"

I immediately recognized it as the crown's effect and the Return Home Skill.

I saw that Gryphon's level changed to **Lv.70** from the Lv.65 it was earlier, and asked myself, *"Does the crown somehow affect people who don't swear their loyalty to me? Is it really just because I hired him to work for me?"*

"Drune and I also had the same experience happen to us, Gryph. We also became stronger and received the same Skill, even skipping 5 whole levels instantly," Odelia said, pausing for a moment, "Gryphon, I am telling you, he is the one we have been waiting for..."

"It's...impossible..." Gryphon seemingly began to second guess what he thought was true.

"It's not impossible, but I will tell you that I'm not the 'one' the elves are waiting for," I firmly stated.

"W-What does that mean?" Gryphon asked, left in confusion.

Ignoring his question and changing the subject, I handed Gryphon his 20 Gold for the month, and explained to him where the Return Home Skill would send him. I also told him about Goblex who lived and worked in the castle, and warned him not to accidentally kill him.

"You got all that?" I asked.

Gryphon nodded, saying, "I think so, but just who are? Are you truly the heir?"

"I thought I told you when we met, my name's Eyes, and until the foreseeable future you'll be working for me from now on," I said, giving him a wink and a smirk. "Now make yourself acquainted with Castle

Fables of J

Creedmor, and I'll tell Drune to meet up with you there and help you settle down," I told him, sending Mako a message.

> **Mako Nomura**
>
> Can you tell Drune that his old friend Gryphon will be waiting for him at the castle?

While I waited for a response, I listened to Gryphon asking Odelia, "Will this new Skill really teleport me to a castle? All without needing to draw or be in a teleportation circle, or even speaking the incantation?"

"Amazing is it not?" Odelia replied.

"It's revolutionary! I have to witness this in person right now!" Gryphon then announced, "**Return Home**!" and in an instant, a blue coloured magic enveloped him entirely, then in a blink of an eye he was gone—causing the dome around us to disappear with him.

Odelia sighed, "Always so quick to act, he did not even say goodbye to us."

"Damn, I never got to ask why he was so worried about me knowing his true name. It didn't seem like being a half-elf had anything to do with it, and I would ask Odelia but it doesn't feel like she should be the one telling me. I guess I'll have to remember to ask him when I return to the castle," I thought, as Mako responded.

> **Mako**
> I told Drune and he was super happy to hear that.
> By the way, are you in Ven'Thyl yet? Drune was asking.
>
> Not yet, we got distracted by the friend, but I think we're at the outskirts of the city, just outside the teleportation circle.
>
> **Mako**
> Okay, I'll let him know.

> Oh and I forgot to tell you before you left because of Rayna's crazy party, but bring me back a souvenir.
>
> Sure thing, I'll keep an eye out for something you'll think is interesting.
>
> <u>Mako</u>
> Thanks, gotta go.

Seeing that I was finished, Odelia asked, "Are you ready to go, Eyes?"

"So ready," I said excitedly.

"Then this way," Odelia said, leading me back to the front and showing me a long, heavily forested road.

Chapter 50
The Capital City of Ven'Thyl

A NOTE FROM FABLES OF J

I wanted to write the other languages in other fonts, but I decided to just stick with the default Open Sans since there aren't a good variety of font types for other possible languages, and the ones available aren't very good.

So technically all the conversations in Ven'Thyl are spoken in Elvish, unless stated otherwise, or if it's Odelia personally speaking to the MC.

Following the straight dirt road, we passed by many travelling merchants, traders, caravans, and groups of people all heading the same direction. Though it was great to hear their passing greetings, I did take note that mostly everyone we talked to was an elf. A handful of the people we passed humans, and none of them were dwarves whatsoever. Letting that fact slip by, I also realized we were in an extremely dense, overgrown, and tall forest. Not even comparable to the one surrounding Asheton, the forest here was so dense and overgrown that I couldn't see anything past the first layer of foliage and tree trunks, and the trees seemed to only get taller as we continued down the road—starting to reach well over 100ft in height.

After about half an hour, I saw the foliage and trees in the area begin to thin out, and in the distance—past the forest—was a vast body of water. As we got closer, we arrived at a large clearing that was connected to a short land bridge leading across to an enormous peninsula; which amazingly had trees the size of skyscrapers evenly spread throughout it. There were also two twin towers on either side of the bridge, made completely from two thick, hollowed out, branching trees, with some building structures and platforms built into the trees itself, as well as onto the thicker branches of the trees.

In Range – Ven'Thyl Saga Part I

Observing the towers closer, I could see about 15-20 guards patrolling up and down each of the trees, all wearing the same sharp, dark green armour with silver engraved etchings; but some wore hoods, while others wore helmets that matched the design of the armour. The guards on the higher branches had either a bow or a staff as weapons, while the lower ones had mostly a bow paired with a sword or daggers, but a handful did just have a sword or a spear paired with a shield. In addition to all their names being different, their levels equally differed from **Lv.40-50**.

When we reached the lineup of people waiting to go across, I took notice of the 10 heavily armoured guards on the ground—5 on each side of the bridge—in a similar but bulkier armour design as the ones in the tower. Built like absolute tanks, these large guards wielded equally large tower shields in one hand—with a silver branching tree engraved onto each of them—and long silver spears in the other; as well as slightly curved swords sheathed on their waists. They ranged from **Lv.50-55**, and seemed to be ones in charge of screening people for both ways of passage onto the bridge.

Turning to Odelia while we waited in line, I asked, "Is that all really the city Ven'Thyl? Because if it is, it must be at least 3x the size of Leon just seeing it from here, and that's not even accounting for how far it goes back..." gazing at the peninsula which only got wider the further back I looked.

"It is. Everything ahead of us is the city of Ven'Thyl," Odelia answered, gesturing ahead, "and in terms of the sheer amount of land it occupies, Ven'Thyl even gives the dwarves' mountain cities a run for their coin."

"Wait, does that mean the rest of the Elven Kingdom is behind us?" I glanced back.

"Well of course, we are—" Odelia suddenly came to a realization, "Oh no. Do you not even know that we are in the deepest and furthest part of the kingdom, Eyes?"

"Well now I do..." I said under my breath.

Odelia sighed and began to tease me, "Would you like me to teach you geography as well as history? Or shall we start with math? In fact, do you even know how to speak Elvish? How about we start with the alphabet?"

"Haha, very funny, but I'll have you know I can speak Elvish. Along with any and all other languages, even the monster ones," I confidently stated.

"Oh really? Allow me to test you then. After all, everyone in Ven'Thyl mostly only likes to speak in Elvish." Clearing her throat, Odelia began to speak in Elvish, "If you can understand me, can you answer me how many Elven races there are? And if you cannot, you must promise to take your rightful place as the...thing."

"Easy, it's 3. And no I will not," I replied to her.

She tilted her head at my answer, and said, "You are truly baffling, Eyes, but your Elvish was perfect. Now since you claim to speak all other languages," she suddenly switched languages, "may I hear your Dwarvish?"

"Sure. Is this enough? Or do you want to hear more?" I simply asked her.

"Wow, your Dwarvish is even better than mine, and I have studied for decades. Drune would be so surprised," she appeared genuinely shocked. "I am sure the Dwarven Kingdom will truly appreciate you negotiating in their native tongue when that future time comes."

I smirkingly rolled my eyes as a guard called for us in Elvish, "Come forth." He seemed to recognize Odelia, "I've seen you leave at the start of every month for over a century now, but this is the first time I've ever seen you bring someone back with you, Odelia."

"I'm sure you saw the stars last night. Things are changing, Nai," Odelia grasped his forearm as they greeted each other, and I saw that he was **Lv.55 Nai Gysse'Yrr**.

"It would seem so," he said as he then leaned down to get a better look at my face. "He's pretty young, doesn't even look to be 50 years of age yet. And from the wary look he's giving me, adding to the fact I don't recognize his face at all, he must not be native-born, correct?"

"As insightful as ever, Nai," Odelia complimented him, "and you're correct, he wasn't born in the kingdom."

In Range - Ven'Thyl Saga Part I

"I thought so, but what's his reason for coming here? Or more like, what's your reason for bringing him here?" Nai inquired, tapping his finger on the chin of his helmet.

"He's my new student," Odelia answered, "and though he may be lacking in a lot of general knowledge he should really know, I bore witness to the incredible kingdom changing potential within him," winking at me as she said that, "so I made the decision to personally bring him here to train with me in Ven'Thyl."

"A student? Really?" Nai looked surprised, "I heard from Mother that you gave up teaching after, you know…" whispering, "your last student exposed your secret marriage to Drune."

"Last student? Is that why Drune was so happy to hear Odelia was gonna teach again? I wonder what happened?" I thought to myself; then deciding, *"But I shouldn't ask her about it, Odelia will tell me if she wants to."*

"Are you saying you're starting to teach again?" Nai asked.

"Indeed. But stop mentioning things that happened 109 years ago. And this student right here," she suddenly pointed to me, "he'll be unlike any student I've ever taught before!" proclaiming, "I'll nurture and mould him into the greatest archer in all the lands, and I know that when he finally becomes recognized, he'll change the Kingdoms!"

"Uh-huh, settle down," Nai said, trying to stop Odelia from making a commotion. "And you guys are free to go ahead now," hastily setting us off onto the land bridge.

Proceeding across the bridge in relative silence, I took the time to peer over the thick branch railings built near the edges, and saw that we were at least 200ft above sea level—watching some of the waves crash into the rocks below. Then turning my attention back ahead of us, I spotted two more twin towers built at the other end of the bridge, and finally took notice of the barely visible barrier surrounding the entire peninsula.

Turning to Odelia to ask a question, I stopped myself when I saw that she was looking a bit sad, and thought, *"Is it because of what that Nai guy said about her last student? Was being exposed to marrying a dwarf really that bad?"*

25

Fables of J

"Go ahead and ask, I can hear you loudly thinking about what you heard about my last student," Odelia said, noticing my stare.

"Was it that obvious?"

Odelia nodded.

"Look, I won't go out of my way to ask about your last student, because frankly I don't care about them… especially since they seemed to have betrayed you." Her nose crinkled for a split second. "if you decide to tell me, then I'll gladly be here to listen. But if you decide not to, then my life will still keep going unbothered by the fact. My uncle used to tell me that whenever I was upset about something and didn't want to talk."

Odelia suddenly perked up, exclaiming, "You have an uncle?! Where is he? Are you blood related?" She looked around for the area to be clear of people before whispering, "Do you think he would want to be the heir?"

I laughed at her complete mood change and continued onwards.

"Eyes, you did not answer me!" she shouted, quickly catching up and pestering me about it.

Reaching the other end of the bridge, there were even more guards stopping and inspecting people before they entered; but these ones were all **Lv.60**, while the ones patrolling the towers were **Lv.55-60**.

"Jeez, these guards are even higher than the first ones," I thought to myself, *"I wonder if the other cities have guards this high level?"*

Then as we came up next for the inspection, the guard simply informed us, "There was a merchant earlier trying to smuggle in a large shipment of Bliss into the city. We've been asked to carefully inspect everyone as a precaution, but you two are good. You can go on ahead."

Odelia just nodded and walked by, but I looked back as we passed by and saw that only the humans were really the ones being inspected—and a few sketchy looking merchants—while the elves were mostly allowed through after less than a minute of talking with the guards.

"I see the problem, Odelia," I said, following her on the downward sloping path. "I haven't even really entered the city yet and I've already seen a glimpse of racism. I just hope I don't see more of that."

Odelia frowned, "Sadly, I cannot promise that you will not see more, but I will try my best to help you avoid seeing those situations in the future." She then smiled and gestured her hand forward. "Anyways, allow me to present to you your rightful new home, the capital city of Ven'Thyl."

Beholding everything before me, I was left completely captivated and in awe of the sight; speechless from the pure natural beauty of the land. It was a sprawling city that seemed to be endless; massive in size and expansive in reach, nature perfectly integrated itself into almost every nook and cranny of the city. Though I was overwhelmed on where exactly to look first, I could clearly see that the city was split up into three sections: a lower, a middle, and a higher section.

"It may be a lot to take in for your first time, but I am sure you will get to know Ven'Thyl quickly," Odelia assured me.

"It's not just a lot, it's too much," I said to her, while I explored with my eyes. "Leon looked pretty massive from afar, but compared to Ven'Thyl, it's nothing."

"Well it would need to be," Odelia said, explaining, "Ven'Thyl is the only major city in the Elven Kingdom, and is almost where all elves in the kingdom choose to live, therefore it boasts the highest population amongst the 5 major cities. For the other kingdoms, their populations are generally split between their two major cities; Leon and Sya for the humans, and Beldra and Nobren for the dwarves."

Though while Odelia spoke, my eyes chose to follow the long sloped path down. It led me to a massive lower central area that seemed to be in an even more massive crater, and was the only part of the city that I could see without any of the giant trees. In the middle of it all was a round clearing of a large streaming pond of water, with multiple branching streams flowing throughout the whole lower area, which all originated from a wide waterfall at the other end of the crater opposite us. This lower area was very heavily shaded, covered by the shadows of the giant trees surrounding the top of the crater, and only having small sections of sunlight shining through. It also had a lot of clumped up buildings with natural foliage growing around them, with the buildings having varying size and design, and thousands of people moving all along the crowded streets.

Watching me observe the city, Odelia mentioned, "We call that whole lower area the Roots, Eyes. Named after all of those roots over there," pointing to the edges of the crater where some of the roots from the giant trees could be seen poking through the crater walls. "In the Roots you can find almost anything and everything you can think of from weapon and armour shops, to taverns and inns and much, much more. It is the central hub of Ven'Thyl where a lot of the population resides and works in—as most of the city's business is done there—and it is also where you can find the Adventurer's Guild if you were wondering." She pointed to an area on the left side of the crater. "The Roots is also where you will find most of the Dark Elves, as we find it more comforting for our eyes in the heavy shade."

Focusing my attention to the area above the crater next; I found the buildings built up there were designed very similarly to each other, having very sharp structures and curved roof designs. They were built into or around the base of the trees, and were much more spaced out than the building in the lower area.

Pointing to it, I asked, "What about that area?"

"That area is called the Soil, and it is the largest of the four areas, spanning to the whole rest of the peninsula; which is also connected to the Trunks—referring to any area between the halfway point of the Sky Trees and the Soil." I looked slightly up to see the multiple buildings protruding out of the trunks of the trees.

"Roots, Soil, and Trunks, huh? Not very imaginative naming if you ask me," I said, chuckling to myself a little.

"Well, the areas do not really have official names. The people have just started to call them as such to help differentiate the areas from each other," Odelia justified.

"I see. Then what can I find in the 'Soil' if business is done in the Roots? I can only see the beautiful Elven buildings from here." I glanced at the other buildings spread along the top of the crater, and at the grand looking bridge that arched right over the wide waterfall.

"It is largely a residential area throughout, but there are exceptions like the City Guard Barracks to our right."

I looked over and saw a large building built entirely into the closest giant tree, with a constant flow of guards entering and exiting the place. I also spotted a few dozen guards training in an open field next to it.

"Or the Mel'Jra Stables to our left."

I turned the other way and saw a very wide, fenced off building, which seemed to be where all the wagon and carriage travellers' first stop was—seeing multiple workers come out carrying the goods they brought towards the Roots.

"God, this place is big, and I'm only at the entrance," I thought, feeling even more overwhelmed.

Bringing my attention back ahead of us, Odelia pointed past the waterfall, and said, "If you travel farther back and deeper into the Soil, you will eventually reach the Rich Soil where most of the wealthy choose to live, as it has larger homes and more space to be free in. It is also where you can find the Ven'Thyl Academy, the three Noble Houses, and Castle Ven'Thyl. But only House Fre'Nddare and House Baen'Mtor really reside in the Rich Soil."

Simply nodding at everything she was saying, my eyes wandered to all the daunting trees towering around the whole area of the Roots, and were amazed by their skyscraper-like size—standing at least 300ft tall. Each of them had multiple structures built into and around their trunks, from houses, balconies, standing platforms, spiral walkways, and even some sort of pulley elevator. Even reaching up to the unbelievable heights of their branches, they were all connected by a series of different crossing rope bridges—on multiple levels of the trees—that continued to parts that were blocked from sight by treelines, and which never crossed over the huge gap of the Roots.

"What you are seeing is the Tops—or the Crown if you would prefer," Odelia said, noticing me taking interest in the trees. "You will mostly only find more housing up there, but there are a few unique and specialized shops set up in the Sky Trees closest to the Roots. And who knows, you may even find something interesting up there." She then pointed to the right of the waterfall. "The Tops is also where the last of the three Noble Houses resides, House Helvi'Ett."

"Helvi'Ett? Isn't that—"

"It is…" Odelia turned silent.

Allowing the silence to hang in the air, I thought to myself, *"Now I get it. Gryphon is from one of the Noble Houses, and I could probably guess having a Half-Elf in one wouldn't look so good for them in the kingdom,"* as I concluded, *"They probably disowned him and forced him to leave the city. Must be why he has such a problem with me knowing his real name, but maybe I should talk to him about it when I meet him again,"* Then breaking the silence, I said, "Odelia, you never said where you live. Is it somewhere in the Roots like the other Dark Elves?"

"Sadly, no," Odelia sighed. "We live in the Tops."

"We?" I repeated.

"The other members of House Ven'Thyl, of course," Odelia said with a smile.

"Oh right, I forgot there were others," I said, remembering she was part of a House.

"Would you like to go to the House and meet them? You may also get a good rest there since we have been travelling for days now."

While I thought about it, Odelia then suggested, "We may also go exploring the city first if you would like? Maybe go shopping for new armour and clothes for you since you have been travelling shirtless under that cloak of yours?" pointing to my stomach that wasn't covered by the cloak.

Fixing the cloak to cover myself, I said, "Both ideas sound great, but I think I'll choose—"

Before I could say, someone loudly yelped behind me, and before I could look back and see what happened, I suddenly felt someone come crashing into my back, the force of which caused me to go crashing face first right into the ground, tumbling down the sloped path, and ending up with the person weighing on the top of my back. Both of us groaned in pain.

Odelia quickly ran over and attended to me, "Lor—Eyes, are you alright?"

"Uhhh… I've got to stop running down these slopes with these heeled boots on."

I then felt the person get off me, and apologize saying, "I'm really sorry about that. I hope I didn't injure you."

Odelia helped me back to my feet, and yelled, "What kind of fumbling fool are you? Do you think—"

Suddenly, Odelia strangely ran directly behind me, pulling her hood down and covering her face.

"Not again, how is it she always runs into me?

Chapter 51
Persistence and Opportunity

After shaking my head from the daze, I saw the most beautiful elven girl standing worried before me; her fair face dirtied by some smears of dirt, her long brown hair turned a mess from the tumble, and her emerald coloured eyes earnestly looking at me with concern.

"Again, I'm so incredibly sorry," she apologized, bowing her head slightly, "I should've been more careful running down the slope without watching my steps."

"It's fine," I told her, taking notice of the extremely shiny choker necklace she wore, "no need to apologize..." focusing on the transparent spherical crystal in the center and the three different coloured lights floating within the choker: green, blue, and violet.

She sighed in relief, saying, "Oh, thank the Goddesses you're not angry." As she then tried to wipe the dirt off the dark leather armour she wore, she also checked on the two sheathed blades strapped horizontally on her lower back, and turned her ankles to examine the heels of her leather boots.

Then a man suddenly came running down the slope towards us, politely insisting, "Please stop being so reckless, milady. Look at the incident you caused again."

"I know, I know, I'll try to be more careful, Jhan," the girl replied, dismissing his concern.

"Please do better than try, milady. Your family has a reputation to uphold," the man said.

Seeing the man's face closer, he appeared to be slightly older than the girl—as much as an elf could look older—and had short, styled up, brown hair. He wore a simple brown robe with a light blue ringed pattern on all the edges, accented by a light blue scarf wrapped around his neck, and a staff with a simple wooden crescent design on his back.

The man then turned to us, pulling the sack of coins from his waist, saying, "Please accept this as an apology, and I hope it's enough to keep quiet about this small incident," he said, presenting the coins to me.

Pushing the coins back to him, I said, "No worries. Keep the coins, I'm sure it was just an accident anyways. Besides, it was my fault for standing in the middle of the road, I was too distracted from my first time being in Ven'Thyl."

"Your first time? Then I welcome you to the great city of Ven'Thyl, and wish for you a splendid stay," the man then turned to the girl, saying, "Now we should probably be on our way, milady, we promised to return—"

"Wait!" the girl shouted, slowly walking towards me and trying to get a look at Odelia—who for some reason continued to try her best to use me as cover, "I thought I recognized her voice," telling the man, "Jhan, it's her...it's Master Odelia!"

I heard Odelia whisper behind me, "Damn..."

Grabbing the man's attention, he peered at Odelia behind me and was taken back in surprise, "Oh! I'm sorry I didn't recognize you, Lady Odelia!" deeply bowing his head towards her.

Reluctantly stepping out from behind me, Odelia said, "Aahhh... what a coincidence to have met you here, Jhan, young Lady Fre'Nddare."

"Fre'Nddare? Isn't that one of the Noble Houses?" I recalled.

"A coincidence—no, more like fate, Master Odelia," The girl smiled brightly, "and I thought I told you to stop calling me that. I don't want to be addressed the same way my sisters and mother do, for I'm clearly not as old as they are."

"I shall stop addressing you as such when you stop addressing me as your Master; as well as insisting every time you see me to be your archery teacher. There are far more capable and willing Trinity Archers who could teach you in the city. Your father for example," Odelia suggested.

Fables of J

"You know well and good that Father has no desire for teaching and is way too busy with the Council to ever have time to train me properly," the girl mentioned, "and you're right, there are plenty of willing Trinity Archers who could train me at my request, but everyone knows none are more capable than you and Father."

"I think there are a few," Odelia smugly smiled a little.

"You can't even say that with a straight face, Master Odelia," she pointed out, "and even if there was someone equally as capable, only you and Father were the ones grandfather ever accepted to train as his students, and are the only people left in the whole Kingdom who can reliably perform the Tri-Fusion Ritual without fail."

"Her grandfather trained Odelia? And what's this about a ritual?" I wondered, continuing to listen.

"Jhan, please stop her," Odelia urged him to step in. "Ever since you told her that story when she was 5, she's been bothering me for over 15 years now, unlike her siblings who gave up in less than 2 years."

"I'm once again terribly sorry, Lady Odelia," the man apologized, "but you know as much as I do, the young Lady does as she pleases, and nothing I or anyone else could say would change the fact."

Odelia sighed, "I know..." then said to the girl, "Young Lady Fre'Nddare, I'll tell you once again, I retired from teaching over a 100 years ago, and I've no desire or plans to return to teaching whatsoever."

"That's news to me," I thought, quietly listening to Odelia continue.

"You'd do better to earnestly start your archery training with another, or the public and other Houses will continue to question House Fre'Nddare—even more so the longer you continue to prolong your training."

"She's right, milady, the people—especially the other Noble Houses, still heavily question your father for allowing you not to attend Ven'Thyl Academy when you were of age. It'd be best for the House that you became a Trinity Archer as quickly as possible," the man agreed.

"Not unless Master Odelia's the one teaching me," she stubbornly stated.

In Range – Ven'Thyl Saga Part I

"But, milady, I truly believe you could be the first to accomplish the feat again. Even with a late start to your training, your talent is still unmatched!" the man claimed. "Becoming a Trinity Archer before reaching the age of 100 hasn't been accomplished since Great King Ven'Thyl first did so all those centuries ago. You would be known in the Kingdom as a 'one-in-a-millennium genius,' and would surely bring House Fre'Nddare all the accolades that come with it," the man looked to rejoice at the thought. "Doesn't that sound amazing to you, milady?"

"Not even a little bit," she answered, completely uninterested, still only focusing on Odelia who tried not to make eye contact with her.

What the man said confounded me. I instinctively spoke to Odelia, asking, "Does becoming a Trinity Archer really take that long? Please say no."

All three of them looked at me in shock, as if they seemed to forget that I was even there, and then Odelia looked to have realized something.

"Oh right, the stranger I crashed into," the girl said, staring at me with curiosity. "You seem to be quite close with Master Odelia, though if I recall not many are...Do you mind introducing yourself, stranger?"

But before I could answer, Odelia covered my mouth and strangely panicked, "He's nobody! Ummm... just someone I met on the way back to the city, and... I'm escorting him because he asked me to show him the way to an inn."

"Is that so?" the girl chuckled, pointing to Odelia's hand covering my mouth.

Quickly removing her hand, Odelia whispered to me, "Oh, please do not tell her why you are here."

"Now that you can speak, mind introducing yourself?" the girl asked again, waiting curiously for my answer.

Keeping Odelia's words in mind, I responded, "Before I tell you, isn't it polite to introduce yourself first before asking who I am?"

"You don't know who I am?" the girl was taken back by my cluelessness.

"Milady, he said it was his first time in the city," the man reminded her.

Fables of J

"And I'm a bit clueless since I was born outside of the Kingdom, so I genuinely don't know who you are, but should I?" I asked, pretending not to know from their names above their heads: **Lv.20 Myeyl Fre'Nddare**, and **Lv.50 Jhan Ilzt**.

"Perhaps, but it's a pleasant change of pace..." as she then unexpectedly brought her face towards mine and stared directly into my eyes.

"Uhh...is something wrong?" I asked, moving my head back a bit.

"No. I just have a feeling telling me I don't like you very much," she said, making me wonder why as she then gestured to Jhan, saying, "This is my personal vassal and close friend, Jhan, but if you ask me he's more like my babysitter."

"That last part was unnecessary to add, milady," he showed me a quick bow before introducing himself, "Jhan Ilzt, currently a vassal of House Fre'Nddare, nice to meet you."

"He's about what I expected from someone watching over a noble, and he seems as insistently loyal to the girl as Odelia is to me."

"And I'm Myeyl, but I'd prefer to be called Mye. Or maybe Yeyl?" she introduced herself too.

"She however is not what I expected from a noble, and knowing that she skipped out on the academy and archery lessons only makes her more odd to me."

"Do not call her either of those things, and please always address her as a Lady," Jhan requested of me.

"You don't have to listen to him. I know I don't," Myeyl said, playfully smiling at Jhan. "Now it's your turn. Who are you to Master Odelia?"

Glancing over at Odelia, I saw that she appeared to be nervous about what I was gonna say, and I quickly thought, *"I know Odelia said not to tell her, but this could be a great opportunity to make friends with one of the Noble Houses."* Though I decided to say, "It's nice to meet you two, Jhan, Lady Myeyl. My name's Eyes, and I'm actually just a friend of Odelia's husband."

"Oh, I understand why Lady Odelia was trying to keep you quiet then," Jhan said, making his own conclusions.

In Range – Ven'Thyl Saga Part I

"I don't. I've never gotten to meet Master Odelia's husband, what's the big deal?" Myeyl questioned.

"Good thing you don't listen to me or the gossip about Lady Odelia, milady," Jhan said, reminding her, "Don't you remember the time when I told you that Lady Odelia was married, and then you kept asking more about it?"

"Oh, is that it? I can't believe you'd think so low of me, Master Odelia. You don't have to hide that you're married to a Dwarf, it makes no difference to me," Myeyl assured Odelia.

Surprised by how easily they were misdirected from my true identity, Odelia smiled and said, "Then I thank you for your understanding, young Lady Fre'Nddare."

"Does that mean you'll be my teacher then?" Myeyl asked, still optimistically hoping.

"Nope," Odelia answered bluntly, but not accepting that answer, Myeyl pleaded and begged Odelia to reconsider.

Quietly observing their relentless back-and-forth, I took notice of how close Odelia really was to House Fre'Nddare. Not only did Myeyl and Jhan always address her respectfully, but Odelia didn't actually look to be all that bothered by Myeyl asking her to be her Master. I also recalled the fact that Myeyl's grandfather trained both Odelia and her father, and if they trained together that would likely make them friends or rivals of each other, which would create an even closer bond with the house and Odelia.

Their undeniable connection was too strong to ignore, and I decided to go against Odelia's wishes, thinking, *"I'm sorry to do this, Odelia, but this will all be for the Kingdom you wish for. The noble houses are too valuable of a resource to let slip past simply because you won't accept students other than myself. They could ultimately help me find the missing descendants. And after hearing how close you are to them and how open-minded Myeyl and her father are, House Fre'Nddare is the perfect noble house to befriend first."*

"Pleeeeease!" Myeyl begged again.

"Umm...no," Odelia rejected again.

Interrupting them, I asked, "Odelia, may I speak with Myeyl in private for a moment?" gesturing my head for her to take Jhan away.

"Wh-What about, Eyes?" Odelia nervously asked, unsure and worried about what I wanted to talk to Myeyl about.

"I just want to offer her an opportunity," grinning mischievously at Odelia and giving her a wink, causing her to look even more nervous—now sure about what I wanted to talk about. "Are you not going to let me speak with her?"

I showed Odelia a serious look so she would agree.

Odelia let out a great big sigh, "Of course you can, Eyes," reluctantly dragging Jhan away by his robe's collar—catching him off guard by her strange reaction towards me.

With the two of them walking quite a distance away, Myeyl asked, "How did you do that? Or more like, why did Master Odelia willingly listen to you?"

"Beats me," I shrugged, "maybe she just likes me more than you."

Myeyl gave me a questioning look, "So what's this opportunity you want to offer me?"

I smiled and told her, "First, why don't I tell you who I really am, and why I'm here in the city with Odelia," Myeyl suddenly looked intrigued in what I had to say. "I'm Odelia's new student, and I'm here because she personally invited me to train with her in Ven'Thyl."

"What?!" Myeyl loudly exclaimed, shocked by the news, "Why would—" when she looked over at Odelia in the distance, she saw Odelia avoiding her glance—already knowing what I just said to her, "How? I've been asking her for years and she's only ever rejected me!"

"The how doesn't really matter, but the opportunity I'm offering does," I said, and Myeyl eagerly waited to hear what I said next. "Let's just say I could convince Odelia to let you be her student too. What would you give me to have such a great opportunity?"

"You can!? Really!?" Myeyl sounded extremely hopeful. "I can give you anything and everything my Noble House Fre'Nddare has to offer, you name it! So just please help me convince Master Odelia to let me be her student too, and I'll forever be indebted to you. I promise on the name of my noble house!" she said as she tightly gripped and held my hands together.

After she pleaded to me, I couldn't help but smile when I saw a new quest pop up, thinking, *"Bingo, there it is."*

Quest

A Stubborn Persistence:

Find a way to help the headstrong Myeyl convince her only desired teacher, Master Odelia, to accept her as a student, all before Myeyl turns 100 years in age.

Reward: Myeyl Fre'Nddare is forever indebted to you and will offer anything her Noble House can give.

Failure: Myeyl will never become a Trinity Archer, and she never reaches her full potential.

Time Limit: 80 Years

Will you accept:

Choosing 'No' will lead to automatic Failure

[Yes] or [No]

"What a weirdly long time limit… Does the System actually expect us to be in this world for that long?" I wondered to myself; then thinking, *"If I have 80 years to complete this quest, does that mean Myeyl is 20 years old? I guess that means we're the same age then,"* I realised, as I gladly accepted the Quest and called over Odelia and Jhan back to us.

"Eyes, you did not, did you?" Odelia asked, already seeming to know my answer.

Fables of J

"I did," I chuckled, telling her, "Accept Myeyl as your new student. And no you can't object."

Odelia let out another great big sigh, "If that is what you wish, Eyes, consider it granted."

"Wait, are you really agreeing to accept me just like that, Master Odelia?" Myeyl asked, being surprised yet thrilled at the same time.

"Lady Odelia, I don't understand. After all this time you always refused, but you're listening to this young man here without questioning?" Jhan questioned, appearing completely baffled by the situation.

"Is there a problem, Jhan? Is this not also what you wanted?" Odelia asked him.

"No problem whatsoever, Lady Odelia, but knowing you it simply seems... out of character," Jhan replied, carefully observing me. "Just who is this young man that you value listening to? And why do you strangely switch to Common when you speak to him?"

"I cannot say. But know that he'll be known to the whole Kingdom in time," Odelia gave me a smile, then turned to Myeyl and said, "I'll truly accept you as my student, Lady Myeyl, but as your Master, I simply request you to call me Odelia from now on, is that clear?"

"Absolutely!" Myeyl agreed with the brightest smile on her face, "Thank you, thank you, Odelia! I can't tell you how much this means to me. How long I've waited for this day to come!" she said, quickly giving Odelia a tight hug.

Smiling, Odelia said, "It shouldn't be me you're thanking, Lady Myeyl," she then gestured to me, "he should be the one receiving your thanks. After all, without him I would've still refused you for years to come."

Releasing Odelia from the hug, Myeyl looked at me and said, "It's Eyes, right?

"That's right," I confirmed.

"Well Eyes, whatever it is you ever find yourself in need of, I swear I will use all of House Fre'Nddare's power and influence to provide it," she promised to me. "I will forever be in your debt, thank you."

In Range – Ven'Thyl Saga Part I

She held her hand out for me. I gladly shook Myeyl's hand, and said, "I'll hold you to that."

> **Quest Completed**
>
> **A Stubborn Persistence has been completed.**
>
> **Reward: Myeyl Fre'Nddare is forever indebted to you and will offer anything her Noble House can give.**

"Can we start my training now, Odelia? Can we?" Myeyl enthusiastically asked, too happy and eager to stay still.

"No, not yet," Odelia stated, "I still have to get Eyes acquainted and settled into the city, and it may even be a week before we can actually train."

"A week?!" Myeyl exclaimed, "I can't wait that long, I'm too excited now!"

"Yeah, I have to agree with her, Odelia. I don't want to wait a week for my training either," I agreed with Myeyl. "I'd prefer to start as soon as possible, maybe even tomorrow if we can."

"See? Eyes feels the same way," Myeyl added.

"Is that what you wish for, Eyes? To start training tomorrow?" Odelia genuinely asked.

"Yes, please," I answered, telling her, "That was going to be my choice between going to the house and exploring the city anyway."

"Well, alright," Odelia smiled, "how does tomorrow morning sound?"

"Yes! And we can even train where Father and Odelia trained!" Myeyl excitedly suggested to me.

"Oh... actually, I thought we'd be training separately," I said to her.

"Why would you think that?" Myeyl asked.

"There's no way I should tell her it's because she's lower level and hasn't even trained in archery yet," so I instead said, "I just thought we were in different leagues."

"What's that supposed to mean?" Myeyl sounded offended.

Fables of J

"I believe he meant that you're from a Noble House, milady," Jhan clarified, "while he of course is a commoner—a city outsider at that."

I raised a finger to stop Odelia as she didn't seem to like that description of me.

"Oh, if that's what you meant, don't worry about it," Myeyl smiled brightly, not caring about our statuses. "After all, we're the same. Fellow students of Odelia."

"Wow, that's great to know..." I said, thinking, *"I may not want to train with her because she might slow me down, but her seemingly open-mindedness about Odelia being married to a Dwarf and being alright that I'm a commoner makes her a pretty good person in my book, and definitely the most perfect person I could've befriended."*

Coughing loudly to get our attention, Odelia said, "Actually, I'll be deciding whether you two will be training together, though I think we will visit House Fre'Nddare tomorrow morning. At which point I'll assess both of your skills and determine whether or not you're on the same archery level as each other. I'll plan your training according to your different results."

Impressed that Odelia actually took command of us, I decided to listen and said, "Sounds good to me."

"Me too!" Myeyl happily agreed. "And I can't wait to see Father's reaction when I tell him about today. He always told me you would accept eventually if I just didn't give up. And today you did, Odelia."

"Haha... Goddesses, I hate him so much sometimes," Odelia laughingly stated. "Can't even be bothered to train any one of his children, and instead sends all who wish to come begging to me."

Myeyl laughed and said, "Yup, but unlike the others I never gave up, and for that I get to be trained by the greatest teacher in all the Kingdom—Odelia the Trinity-Maker!"

A NOTE FROM FABLES OF J

Not that it really matters, but Ilzt is spelled with an **i** first and an **L** second.

Chapter 52
The House of Ven'Thyl Part 1 (Welcome)

As we waved Myeyl and Jhan goodbye, Odelia made sure no one was around and then whispered, "I cannot believe you, Lord Eyes. I mean, I will already have my hands full teaching you. How could you force me into teaching Lady Myeyl as well?"

"Oh, you're not really angry, Odelia. But I will say I'm sorry for forcing you to accept her without telling you my reasoning," I apologized. "Even so, don't act like you can't teach us both, Miss 'Trinity-Maker'."

"Simply an exaggerated epithet bestowed during my time as a professor," Odelia explained dismissively, "Though back to the topic at hand, I would love to hear your reasoning, my lord."

"It's pretty obvious, isn't it? Having a member of a noble house indebted to me can only be good for us. And Myeyl's desperate desire to be your student was the perfect opportunity to make that happen," I divulged to her.

"Ahhh… I see. What a splendid idea, my lord," Odelia nodded in agreement. "You are already planning to increase your influence within the kingdom."

"Huh? What are you talking about?" I asked, not following.

"For your rise to the throne, of course."

I rolled my eyes again as she continued, "You will undoubtedly need at least one of the noble houses' support to truly bring change upon the kingdom, and even more so to lead it once again into a flourishing prosperity—as it once had during the Golden Age of Novus," Odelia relished the thought. "I really should have thought of the idea myself,

Fables of J

but from now on I will try to come up with more ways to find support for your inevitable coronation, Lord Eyes."

"Okay, you keep thinking that," I shook my head at her grandiose delusion. "Let's just hurry up and head to House Ven'Thyl. I want to rest for the day and get to tomorrow's training as fast as possible."

"As you wish, my lord. Follow me," Odelia said, leading me back up the path I tumbled down and towards the stables she mentioned earlier.

Passing the stables and getting a closer view of the large fenced off field, I took notice of all the creatures kept inside—eating grass, drinking water, and lazing around. There were, of course, the multiple different breeds of drafting horses, as well as elk, camels, and reindeers; but what caught me by surprise were the large rams, birds, lizards, and beetles along with them. Intrigued by their uniqueness, I focused and saw their names as: **Ram**striders, Giant Eagles, **Axe**beaks, **Giant Lizards**, **Desert** Lizards, and **Sand Scarabs**.

"Wow! Those must be the animals they use for traversing the land," I figured, as we quickly passed them by and arrived at the base of the nearest Sky Tree.

Standing at a wooden station beside the tree, I saw a single Elven man, dressed in a bright yellow vest, manning a series of levers connected to ropes and a platform leading all the way up the tree. Without speaking a single word to each other, Odelia handed the man 10 silver coins and he passed her back two of the hooped ropes tied to the multiple wooden posts.

"Here, Eyes," Odelia said, passing me one of the ropes and gesturing for me to stand in the designated area beside her. "Now whatever you do, do not let go."

"Huh…?" I suddenly saw the man pull one of the many levers and almost immediately my feet left the ground—skyrocketing upwards by the tug of the rope. "What the hell?!" I shouted to Odelia beside me. "Is this even safe?!" I asked, tightening my grip around the rope.

"Very!" Odelia shouted back, "Only about 250 accidents happen every year, and only about half of them turn out to be fatal!"

In Range – Ven'Thyl Saga Part I

"Half?! Are you crazy?! That doesn't sound safe at all!" I looked at the ground rapidly shrinking the higher we went, while Odelia simply laughed at my worry. Though before I knew it, we'd already reached the top where the ropes ended, and did so in under a minute.

Hanging just out of reach above a wooden platform where another wooden station stood, Odelia, without hesitation, swiftly swung herself from the rope and landed onto the platform below. "This is where most accidents happen, Eyes!" she shouted, grinning mischievously at me, "If you miss the platform you will surely fall and most likely die!"

Not falling for Odelia's obvious goading tease, I confidently swung my legs to gain momentum and leaped from the rope—safely clearing the gap between to the platform. Landing beside Odelia, I asked with a smirk, "Was that your way of punishing me for the Myeyl thing?"

Odelia smiled, "Not entirely, but I did quite enjoy the worried look on your face. The Express Ropes are the fastest way up the Sky Trees—taking less than a minute to arrive at the top—though they can be slightly dangerous if the ropes and mechanisms are not regularly maintained by the workers." She gestured to the woman wearing a bright yellow vest manning the station up here.

"And the other ways?" I inquired, following her around the tree.

"Well there are the People and Cargo Lifts," she said, pointing to rectangular platforms a few people waited on. "Though their speeds heavily depend on the amount of people or cargo they carry." She then pointed to a door built into the tree. "And there is always the classic flight of stairs you can choose to climb, which is actually a great way to exercise everyday."

"Hah, with the size of these trees, no thanks," I said, following Odelia onto a stable, long rope bridge leading across to a different Sky Tree. However I started to lose myself staring at the beautiful view of the city from above, and the equally beautiful elves we walked by.

"Are there any elves that aren't good looking? Because I haven't seen any yet," I asked.

"I guess that depends on your tastes. Speaking for myself, I do not find elves that particularly attractive like most people do," Odelia revealed.

"Does that mean you find me ugly?" I jokingly asked.

"Uhhh… no, of course not!" Odelia began to stammer. "Yourrr...beauty knows no match, Eyes!"

"My beauty knows no match? Jeez Odelia, I didn't know you were such a bad liar," I said, amused by her reaction.

"I am sorry, Eyes," she said, assuring me. "I promise that I am only a bad liar when it comes to non-important things, so please do not lose your trust in me."

"I doubt I could ever lose my trust in you, Odelia."

My words caused her to smile, yet all I could think was, *"But I'm not sure you'd feel the same if you found out who I really was,"* as I continued to walk with that thought in mind.

Continuing from bridge to bridge, and tree to tree, we passed many buildings and shops in the Tops, which mostly confused me. I couldn't tell whether some of them were one huge building taking up and spanning the whole tree, or just multiple separate buildings taking up the same tree; as they didn't all have doors or platforms to enter from. I leaned towards them being separate buildings when I saw multiple different looking elves entering the same doorway, and thought of them as very much like apartment complexes. But before I knew it, we arrived at a Sky Tree standing right at the edge of the peninsula—about 6 trees away and left of the Roots—and with the sun finally beginning to set in the horizon.

"This is it. This is my home. And hopefully yours, Eyes, " Odelia voiced proudly. "Welcome to the House of Ven'Thyl!"

Carefully observing the tree in front of us, it didn't look much different than the other trees, except that the top seemed to have something up there—as the thick branches holding the leaves above the trunk left a large open hole to the sky. Other than that, there were a few structures, balconies, and windows built into and protruding all along the tree—a few above the level of the double door entrance, but the rest being under the platform level we stood on.

Genuinely curious, I asked, "This isn't all our house, is it? We share it like the other Sky Trees, right?"

"Not at all, Eyes. This Sky Tree is purely owned by House Ven'Thyl, bought by the founders of the house over nine centuries ago," Odelia stated.

"Over 900 years?! This place is ancient!" I thought, as I then said, "I assume all the founders passed away, yes?" Odelia nodded yes. "Then who's leading the house? Don't tell me it's you?"

"Thankfully I am not the head of the house, but in the future I hope it will be you, Eyes," Odelia answered. "Though as of right now that title is held by the oldest member and matriarch of the House—Verana Ven'Thyl."

"You're not the oldest member? Wait, I don't even know how old you are, Odelia," I realized.

She simply smiled and said, "Now let us head inside, the others are probably already home," ignoring my question as she went ahead and walked up to the entrance.

Walking up with Odelia, I tried to read the cursive engraved letters above the door, but I couldn't as they were spelled out in what I assumed to be Elvish. Too embarrassed to tell Odelia I couldn't read Elvish, I decided to focus on the ivory inlaid wooden doors, which I noticed to have very similar runes to the ones the stronghold entrance had. *"Does it need the—"*

"To fulfill a promise to a friend after his departure on their odyssey," Odelia whispered to the doors in Elvish, "in search to inform his eccentric and elusive loves."

Instantly the runes on the doors lit up green and we could hear the locks inside unlocking, until finally the doors swung open inwards.

"That was clearly the words to unlock the doors, but what an unusual phrase they chose..." I thought, heavily pondering the words.

Though pulling me out of my thoughts, Odelia tugged me inside and shouted, "Verana! I'm home! Where are you!"

Having lost my train of thought, my attention was drawn to the welcoming sight of a very cozy and rustic wooden-styled home, somewhat reminiscent of cabins in the other world. But suddenly stealing all the attention, an almost perfectly ageless woman turned the corner and entered the large open room—wearing a well-fitted light blue dress and a white apron over top.

"Well someone's excited to be back. Welcome home, Odelia," she said, drying her hands on her apron before giving Odelia a welcoming hug. "How's Drune doing? And I see that you brought a guest with you."

Leaving me speechless from her smile alone, I noticed the slight wrinkles around her mouth and eyes—on her otherwise flawless, fair skin—as well as her loosely braided, greying blonde hair, and thought, *"I can tell she's on the older side for an elf, but my god is she still drop dead gorgeous."*

The rest of her facial features were still very sharp and defined, and her clear sky blue eyes still brightly captivating, only really making her appear to be in her late 50s or early 60s.

"Drune's fantastic, Verana, but is everyone home yet?" Odelia eagerly asked.

"That's great to hear, and I better make more food for dinner now that there'll be two more mouths to feed," she said, walking away from us. "Would you mind closing the doors for me, young man? And welcome to our home!" Odelia followed her while I closed the doors behind us and they magically locked themselves again.

Catching up to them in a large kitchen room, I walked in to the woman telling Odelia, "Aelthar finally had a day off today so he's been sleeping in his room for most of it. As for Shurtyrr, he just got home before you did, and should be freshening himself up and waiting in the library. Amariina on the other hand still hasn't returned from the TCs yet, but she said she should be arriving before dinner time."

"Oh, if I'd known Ama was working today I'd have asked her to send us here right away, and I wouldn't have had to run into Myeyl Fre'Nddare again," Odelia mentioned.

"Still avoiding and rejecting her?" the woman asked while chopping some vegetables.

"Apparently not anymore," Odelia said, telling her, "My student here heavily persuaded me to accept her request, and we're actually going to be training together starting tomorrow."

In Range – Ven'Thyl Saga Part I

The woman immediately stopped her chopping to look at Odelia, "Is that who this young man is? A new student? And are you saying that you're going to be teaching again?"

Odelia nodded yes and they exchanged smiles to each other, "Well this is a cause for celebration! I better cook up your favourites then. Now why don't you go show your new student around the place, I'll call for everyone when dinner's ready."

"Okay. Thanks Verana, but after dinner I've even bigger news all of you need to hear!" Odelia replied back, guiding me to the next section of the house, leaving the woman wondering what Odelia had to tell.

While Odelia guided me around the House, I mentioned to her, "I only heard 4 other names excluding yourself. Does that mean there are only 4 other members in House Ven'Thyl?"

"Uhhh... Well there used to be more in the past," Odelia hesitantly replied, showing me to a whole floor of bedrooms.

"How much more? And what happened to all of them?" I curiously inquired, peeking a little in each room.

"Over 100 more at the houses' peak, though most of them have passed away from old age, while others have died in dangerous places searching for clues about the missing descendants. And disappointingly some have simply given up that a descendant ever existed, cutting ties and quitting the house all together," Odelia chuckled at the thought. "Oh, how wrong they were to have given up on you, Lord Eyes," she said, leading me up another flight of stairs.

From just the quick passing of the 3 floors above the entrance floor, I learnt that they were all basically the same, being just a series of empty and unused bedrooms; opposed to the floor we entered on, which was more of a traditional home, with a giant kitchen, an even larger dining room, and a huge living room that took up half the floor. Odelia also explained to me that the floors were counted from the top to the bottom because the lower floors weren't all bedroom floors.

"Verana occupies the 2nd floor to herself, while the 3rd is mine, leaving this whole 1st floor to yourself if you'd like? It even leads to Verana's beautiful garden on the rooftop for some late night sightseeing," Odelia informed me, pointing to a door at the end of the hallway.

"You don't all live on the same floors? Which floors do the others stay on then?" I asked, more curious about that than seeing a garden.

"Well there are very few of us. Why waste floors that can give us a lot of personal space to ourselves?" Odelia rationalized, leading me back down the floors.

"I don't know how it works, but have you ever considered inviting more people to become members of our House to make it thrive more?" I suggested. "Or is there like some type of test that people have to take and they just keep failing to get in?"

"Hahah... no, no test," Odelia stated, amused at the thought. "You see, House Ven'Thyl is not really a house that aims or cares to be recognized within the kingdom. We simply wish to find and serve the heir, for the kingdom's greater good. Though there is no test to become a member, one would still need to be recommended by one of the current members, and then somehow gain Verana's approval as the head of the house. But there has not been any new members since the time Ama joined 80 years ago."

"She says 80 years like that's not a long time, but I guess elves have a different perspective of time. CJust how old is Odelia?" I kept wondering, as we arrived at a door on the 5th floor.

Odelia loudly knocked, shouting, "Ael! Wake up and get decent for dinner! And come introduce yourself!"

Behind the door I could hear the floor loudly creaking as a person walked towards us, replying in their low deep voice, "O'de, you're back already? And what's this about introducing myself?"

A huge, intimidating, and heavily sweating muscular man then opened the door for us, standing at least 7ft in height and barely fitting through the door frame, "Oh? Who's this?"

Chapter 53
The House of Ven'Thyl Part 2 (Members)

With his intense, curious stare, I couldn't help but observe his full head of dark, buzzed hair, his strong, defined jawline, his stunning green eyes, and the black piercings on both ends of his eyebrows.

"Come on, Ael, I said to get decent," Odelia sighed. "You didn't even bother to put on a shirt," she pointed out that he was only wearing simple, brown trousers and was completely shirtless—showing off his large, well defined muscles, and a series of scars and tattoos all over his body.

"Give me a break, I was working out," the man defended himself, taking a second to put on the cloth shirt that was on top of some heavy weights in the corner of the room. "Besides, I didn't expect to be introduced to anyone in front of my room, and if I'd known that it was a young man that looked like this... I would've freshened up first." He gave me a wink as he checked me out. "But it's strange that you brought someone to the house. Is he joining us? Did Verana already approve?"

"Yes to the first question, no to the second, but I know she will," Odelia stated confidently.

"Really? Why's that?" the man asked, being intrigued.

"I'll explain everything after dinner," Odelia said, dragging me away. "Oh, and take a bath. You reek!"

"Yeah, yeah!" the man replied. "I guess we'll just get introduced to each other later," he said to me, giving me another wink before closing the door.

"Do not mind him, Lord Eyes. I promise that he is not usually that way all the time," Odelia assured me.

"It's okay, it wasn't a bother. But just how many floors do we have left to go?" I asked, walking down another flight of stairs.

"In truth only six, but we do not have to see them all if you do not wish to, Lord Eyes," Odelia then decided to skip the 6th, 7th, and 8th floors as they were just filled with more bedrooms—the 6th being Shurtyrr's, the 7th being Amariina's, and the 8th apparently being the house's baths.

"I think I remember Verana saying Amariina wasn't here yet, but why didn't we knock on Shurtyrr's room like we did with Aelthar's?" I asked, bringing up the point as we headed onto the 9th floor.

"That is because our Shur is deeply in love with our Ama, and always waits for her to arrive on the 9th floor when she has work," Odelia explained.

"Are they together then?"

"Sadly for the both of them, Ama recently got engaged to a wealthy House, though I cannot recall the name right now."

"Didn't you say Ama joined the house 80 years ago? If Shur is deeply in love with her, why didn't he make a move before she got engaged? Or did he get rejected?"

"Their love story is long and complicated, but the gist of it is that Shur lied to Ama about what he did for a living, and when she found out she hated him," she summarized for me. "She has been cold to him for 75 years now."

"75 years of the person he loves hating and being cold to him, only for her to get recently engaged to someone else, and he's still deeply in love with her?" I couldn't imagine how that must have felt. "How... depressingly heartbreaking."

"Indeed they are," Odelia agreed.

But curious, I asked, "What was he doing for a living then? I can't imagine how a job could've made her hate him so much."

"Well you see, Shur works in the markets in the Roots, more specifically... the black market," she revealed the fact to me.

"The black market?!" I exclaimed, now slightly more intrigued in their love story. "But just because Shur works in the black market

In Range – Ven'Thyl Saga Part I

doesn't automatically mean he's a bad person, right? So why did Ama have such a problem with it?"

"It is because Ama associates the black market with the bad memories she has of it from her past, and the horrible time she spent as a slave sold many times in the Human Kingdom—that was until I was able to free her and the other slaves from a slave auction," Odelia explained. "And that is the reason why all of the house went along with not telling her about Shur and his work. However she did eventually find out in time, and she was extremely furious at the house, even threatening to leave, but ultimately she forgave everyone except for Shur."

"Why didn't Shur just stop working in the black market then? Or why didn't the house encourage him to quit? Especially if all of you already knew what happened to her."

"It is complicated..." she said again. "At the time, Shur truly believed he found a lead about where the last known location of a descendant was, and he needed to use all his underground connections to follow it up. We could not just give up that chance lightly. But sadly, as it always does, the lead turned out to be a dead end." Odelia then showed me a warm smile. "Though it would seem things turned out quite alright with you here now."

"Wait. Go back. Do you remember anything about that lead?" I questioned Odelia intently.

"Not personally. Shur kept it pretty private from Ael and I, but he should have recorded the details about it in the library," Odelia answered, surprised by my eagerness. "Though I do not exactly know where he put those records."

"It may be nothing, but a lead is a lead, and I've got to start my search somewhere." I thought to myself, asking, "Where's the library, and can you show me right away?"

"Of course, we are already headed that way. However, may I ask why you are so interested in a lead from decades ago? I am sure you were not even born yet, or were you?" she second guessed herself as she looked me over.

Fables of J

"I told you I was looking for something, and that lead may help me start my search for it," I said, walking a little faster down the stairs.

"Are you sure you do not want to tell me what you are looking for? I will gladly help you find whatever it is, you know?" Odelia offered, as we finally arrived at the bottom of the stairwell where a double door entrance stood.

"I'll consider it if I can't find anything," I pushed the two doors open and was greeted by the smell of papers and books.

Entering the room, I immediately realized that the whole 9th floor was one giant, round, two-storey library; and that we stood on the second storey. Walking over to the balcony railing, I had a perfect view of the handful of spiral staircases evenly spread throughout, the bookshelves all along the sides of the first and second storey, as well as the even rows of them on the first storey—with a couple bookshelves that had fallen over. There were also a few desks, tables, chairs, and stepping stools spread all throughout the space. But directly in the center of the library, on a slightly elevated stone platform, was a now very recognizable teleportation circle on the ground.

"Who are you?" a voice asked, as a man with long damp brown hair walked out from behind a bookshelf, holding a bouquet of purple and white flowers in his hands. But before I could answer him, the runes on the teleportation circle suddenly began to glow brightly, and they caused him to completely ignore me, as he focused his attention on that.

A moment passed and a contained pillar of light erupted within the teleportation circle, and a hooded, robed woman came stepping on through the quickly dissipating light. The man immediately presented the bouquet of flowers to her, and she surprisingly took them, though she didn't speak a word or even look at the man. She then jumped up in excitement, shouting, "O'de, you're back!" as she unexpectedly flew through the air straight towards Odelia and gave her a hug. "When did you get back? And why didn't you look for me at the TCs?"

"I just got back a few hours ago," Odelia informed her, "and I didn't know you were working today."

Releasing Odelia from her hug, the woman looked at me and asked, "Who's this? Another one of Ael's 'friends'?" judging my shirtless attire with her eyes. "He doesn't look like Ael's recent types, but maybe it's changed again, though who can keep track with him?"

"I was wondering the same thing, O'de," the man added, somehow appearing beside me—sitting on the balcony railing.

"I'll introduce him to everyone after dinner, but I was just showing him around the house," Odelia told them, smiling in amusement.

"A new member?" the woman openly wondered.

"Not exactly. But don't worry about that for now, just go help Verana with dinner," Odelia instructed.

"Alright, but tell me about your trip later," the woman listened, rushing up the stairs and secretly smelling the gifted flowers as she did.

"Interesting…" I thought.

"I'll leave you to your tour then," the man tried to leave but was stopped by Odelia's arm.

"Actually Shur, I need you to show us the lead you found 75 years ago," Odelia told him.

"75 years ago? W-Why would you want that? Verana told you and Ael it was a dead end, remember?" He then quickly changed the subject. "Wait, if you're letting him see the records, does that mean he's actually joining the house?"

"Maybe. Just hurry up and show us please," Odelia demanded politely.

"Okay, okay, it's over here," he said, leading us past a few bookshelves and stopping to grab a certain book at the very bottom of one. "It's this one, but Verana gave me strict instructions to tell you and Ael that neither of you are allowed to read it without her permission."

"Huh? Why not?" Odelia questioned, shocked by the fact.

"She didn't say that to me, so…" I easily grabbed the book from the man's hands as he was too distracted by Odelia's interrogating stare.

"Hmmm..." Odelia loudly hummed at him, but the man kept his mouth shut. "Fine! To think you would still keep secrets from me even after I've worked so hard to help you with Ama."

"Yet she still hasn't spoken to me in over 75 years, and her wedding is basically only two and half months away… What do I do, O'de?" the man asked desperately.

Fables of J

Not all too interested in their absolutely crazy conversation about how to sway Ama's feelings with a Love Potion, or how exactly they were gonna sabotage her engagement and or wedding with outlandish schemes, I simply took the book to an empty table and opened it up—shocked at the realization.

After a few minutes of flipping through all the pages in the book, I couldn't help but laugh at myself. "Haha… of course everything's written in Elvish." I grabbed a few random books from the nearest shelf, and found they were all written in Elvish too.

"I might actually need to start learning Elvish if I ever hope to read any of these, but at least I can see—"

I was suddenly interrupted by the sound of a bell audibly echoing throughout the whole library.

Odelia and Shur seemed to recognize the sound, and Shur left for the stairs while Odelia walked over to me explaining, "That was Verana's bell. She rings it to let us know when dinner is ready, and it can be amazingly heard on all floors of the House." She then inquired, "So, did you find something to help you with what you are looking for, my Lord?"

"No… But unrelated to anything, you wouldn't happen to have some type of translation dictionary, would you?" I half-heartedly asked. "Or maybe know if there's some leads written in Common somewhere?"

"Well this whole library is made up completely of the records of past members searching for the descendants over the span of 999 years, so I am sure there are a few written in Common, but do not tell me you cannot read Elvish, my lord?" Odelia looked worried when she saw my reaction to her question. "Oh no. What am I going to do with you, Lord Eyes?"

Trying to move past it, I commented, "999 years of searching and nowhere close to finding any descendants. That's insanity, you know?"

"Some do call our house that, but it is all for the prosperity of the Elven Kingdom and its people. Though fortunately we can stop looking now." She smiled at me again. "Now are you ready for the feast I am sure Verana prepared for us?"

"Actually, if it's alright with you, I'd prefer to stay here and look around for a bit. Is that okay?" I said, asking to be excused.

"Are you sure? The other members might get a bad impression of you if you decide not to eat with us when you have just arrived."

"If they're anything like you, I doubt it," I stated confidently. "They won't mind a single bit when they find out who I am."

"That is true, when they come to know who you are, they will also dedicate themselves to you—like I have," Odelia proudly claimed. "I guess I will simply have to introduce them to you later then." She waved me goodbye as she left up the stairs.

Waiting a few moments and now seemingly left all alone to my own devices, I said to myself, "Time to collect the rest of them."

Activating the **Eyes Of A Seer**, I began to thoroughly search all the bookshelves in the entire library for any hint of Significance I could see glowing from any of the books' pages—stacking and piling any I found around a desk off to the side of the library.

After spending the next hour painstakingly scouring the thousands of books in the library, I only amassed a total of 246 books; but nearly half of them had less than a page glowing with Significance, even less had more than a page, and only a handful appeared to be much more significant than the others.

"I think that's all of them," I said to myself, sitting down on the chair within the stacked pile of books—slightly tired from carrying all the surprisingly heavy books.

While I rested for a bit, I suddenly heard a series of faint footsteps rushing down the stairs, and a few moments later I saw the 3 people I met earlier come bursting from the library doors—followed by Odelia and Verana who entered behind them.

"He's over there!" the muscular man directed them, vaulting over the railing and recklessly charging towards me. On the other hand, the robed woman flew in the air straight towards me, while the long haired man swiftly ran on top of the bookshelves, and Odelia and Verana simply took the spiral staircases like normal people.

Fables of J

Then as they all stood in front of me, everyone except for Odelia said, "Thank you!" and another Quest popped up when they did.

Quest Completed
Once A Teacher Always A Teacher has been completed:
At the request of the family who deeply love her, help them find a way to convince Odelia to willingly start teaching once again.
Reward: Immense gratitude from all current members of House Ven'Thyl.

"Why'd I only get this now. Didn't I convince her to teach me a while ago?" I thought, then figuring, *"I guess they're the Quest givers so maybe that's why it didn't complete earlier? But isn't their gratitude redundant after they find out I'm the Heir?"*

Odelia stepped forward and explained, "Verana told the others that you are my student, and they all wanted to thank you for some reason."

"It'd seem he'd prefer to speak in Common if Odelia is doing so," Verana noted to the others, stepping forward as well—now without the white apron she wore earlier. She then clarified in Common, saying, "We have been trying to get her to teach again after the incident with her last student, but she always refused, claiming she never wanted to teach again. So imagine how overjoyed we were to find out that you are her new student."

"We are very thankful that you helped O'de decide to teach again," Ael also spoke in Common—now wearing a tightly fitted cloth shirt.

"If you ever need anything, we can all find a way to help in our own different ways," Shur offered in Common, with his long brown hair now dry and very voluminous, making me realize he was quite a good-looking guy.

"O'de is our family, so no request you could ask for would be too much to show you our thanks," Ama continued in Common as well, no longer hidden by her hood—showing her beautiful face, piercing blue eyes, and her short blonde hair tied up in a simple high ponytail.

"That includes staying for as long as you would like," Verana generously expressed, "but is there something you need help with right now?" She gestured to all the books I piled up. "Odelia informed us you are searching for something related to the missing descendants. Is there something in particular you have in mind?"

But before I could respond to their thanks and Verana's question, Odelia suggested, "All of you should formally introduce yourselves to him first. I am sure it will greatly help him to know what exactly we can offer to help with."

"Great idea, Odelia. I will go first," Verana volunteered. "I am Verana Ven'Thyl, head of House Ven'Thyl, and I may be old but I do have a lot of influence and connections in high places within the city. I am also a top-notch Healer if you ever find yourself in need of healing."

"She is like a mother to all of us," Odelia added, and the others nodded their heads in agreement.

"I am Aelthar, but my friends call me Ael. You can call me Ael too if you want." He gave me another wink. "As for what I can do… I am one of Ven'Thyl's 10 Guard Captains. I overlook half of the Roots, but I can help you get away with things in other sections if need be."

"A possibly corrupt Guard Captain? How useful," I thought, listening to Shur speak next.

"Ael, you're gonna make us look bad when I tell him I work in the black market there—"

We all quickly noticed Ama visibly cringing at the words black market, but no one chose to address it, including myself.

"Uhhh… you can call me Shurtyrr, or Shur for short, whichever you prefer. I mostly deal with rare and smuggled goods. I am able to obtain almost anything you need, but that does not mean I am not well connected to the other parts of the—market."

"I wonder if he can show me around the black market sometime? I'd love to see what I can buy there," I thought, showing Ama attention next.

Fables of J

"I'm Amariina, and I may not be as useful as the others, but I can freely teleport you to any of the other Kingdom's TCs if you'd like."

After they all finished introducing themselves, I took a second to read their levels and name: **Lv.59 Amariina Ven'Thyl**, **Lv.63 Shurtyrr Ven'Thyl**, **Lv.82 Aelthar Ven'Thyl**, and **Lv.94 Verana Ven'Thyl**.

"Holy shit these guys are high level, and they haven't even gotten their bonus for following me yet! But what the hell's up with Verana? Why's she so significant?" I wondered to myself, staring at the golden glow of Significance radiating all out from Verana.

Subsequently they all stared back with a look of intrigue on their faces, and Odelia said to them, "I noticed the Ocular Skill he uses too, though I do not know exactly what he sees with them when he stares at us like that, but I assure you he has no ill will towards us."

"She's noticed my Seer eyes this whole time? Maybe I should start being careful when I use them then. I wouldn't want people I can't trust seeing them."

"Lord Eyes, I think it is your turn to introduce yourself," Odelia smiled, suddenly kneeling down and causing the others to be utterly confused about what was happening.

"I guess so, it's only polite." Standing up from the chair, I finally pulled my hood back to reveal myself. "My name's Eyes, and it's nice to meet you all. I'd like to thank you for accepting and allowing me into your house," I said, though the whole room just stood in silence.

Everyone except for Odelia appeared to be stunned and speechless from my reveal, their faces strangely mesmerized at the sight of me standing before them. Then slowly coming back to their senses and acknowledging who I was, they all immediately knelt down alongside Odelia, announcing in unison, "The heir to the elves has finally returned!"

Chapter 54
The House of Ven'Thyl Part 3 (Head of the House)

"We of House Ven'Thyl humbly kneel to you, our king, and solemnly swear our unquestioned and undying loyalty to you and your divine bloodline!" they all declared, cheering and rejoicing with each other.

I actually found their genuine happiness to be extremely infectious, filling me with a sense of joy from all their ecstatic and cheerful expressions; but at the same time I felt a sense of guilt from the illusion that I knew I was. Shortly after they made their declaration, everyone except for Odelia began to freak out in a familiar way. Odelia and I both recognized what was happening, and I let her explain to them what it was.

"It is nothing to be alarmed about," she told them, "It is simply the effect Lord Eyes has on people who swear their servitude towards him, and it is proof that he is truly the one we have been searching for… The heir and king to the elves!"

Calming, they all looked up to me from their knelt positions, and I could see their eyes filled with such awe and admiration for me.

"Oh no, four more Odelias," I thought, wondering what I should say to them. Clearing my throat, I said, "Again, my name's Eyes, so please just call me that, okay? Meaning no over the top titles like calling me king, alright?"

Odelia stood up and clarified to them, "What Lord Eyes means to say, is do not let the Elven people and the other kingdoms know of his existence, for he claims he is not yet ready to ascend to his rightful place as king."

Fables of J

"That's not what I—" I got cut off by Aelthar aggressively standing up to Odelia's face.

"O'de, why didn't you tell us sooner!" he shouted in Elvish. "You let me look like a fool, flirting and being shirtless in front of our king!" he blamed her.

"If you looked like a fool, Ael, that's all on you. Don't blame me for your own foolishness," Odelia replied, smugly chuckling at Aelthar.

"You should've at least told everyone else, O'de!" Shurtyrr added, inserting himself into their conversation. "Our king probably thinks less of us after we didn't even recognize who he was when we first met!"

"Oh, boohoo. You're an illegal smuggler, Shur, how much less could he think of you?" Odelia responded, not backing down from Shurtyrr's point.

"You even let me embarrassingly call him one of Ael's 'friends' earlier, O'de!" Amariina angrily jumped in. "How am I supposed to live down the fact that I thought our king was a Roots' whore?"

"I doubt you will," Odelia wickedly laughed at Amariina. "Now out of the four of us, who do you think will be his favourite?" she asked the others. "The sexual and corrupt Guard Captain? Maybe the illegal smuggler? Or how about the one who thought he was a Roots' whore? But personally, I think it'll be his perfectly normal and loving archery teacher." Her laughing at all of them made Aelthar, Shurtyrr, and Amariina began shouting an earful at her; but Odelia didn't back down and shouted back at the rest of them—starting a huge, loud, and petty fight amongst themselves.

"What the hell did I get myself into?" I asked myself, trying to ignore the four of them. Turning my attention to Verana—still kneeling down before me—I immediately noticed the tears falling down the side of her face, so I knelt down and asked, "What's wrong, Verana?"

Trying to suck the tears back up, Verana said, "Forgive me, my king, I should not have let you see me in such a state, and cause you to worry about an old woman like myself."

"There's nothing wrong with that," I assured her, "but why are you crying?"

In Range – Ven'Thyl Saga Part I

"Do not worry, my king, these are not tears of sadness, but tears of joy." Wiping the tears from her eyes, Verana explained, "it has been almost a whole millennia since the disappearance of the great King Ven'Thyl, and in all that time, House Ven'Thyl has never been able to find any of his descendants, the only rightful heirs to all elves—that was until today." The others finally stopped arguing to listen to Verana speak. "I have been in House Ven'Thyl since the day I was born, as my mother and her father before her were members too, and it has been 597 long years since my birth—299 of which I was the Head of the House."

"You don't look a day over 60," I complimented her, while thinking, *"She really must be significant if she's lived this long."*

Verana smiled and continued, "I am unsure how much longer I will live, and I always thought I knew who I had planned to replace me when I am gone, but today has changed everything..." She paused to take a moment to look at each of the other members, and stood up to say to them, "I have said all this to say that I am officially relinquishing my title as the Head of House Ven'Thyl to another, naming you as my one and only true successor, my king." The moment Verana finished speaking, I was hit by a barrage of new notifications before I could even process what she just said.

Quest Completed

The Head Of House Ven'Thyl and the bonus Hidden Quest has been completed:

Greatly build up your standing within the House, earnestly gain the respect of the majority of the current members, and convince them to nominate and support you as the next Head of House Ven'Thyl.

Somehow earn Verana's impossible trust to become her only choice as her true successor to the House of Ven'Thyl.

Fables of J

> **Rewards: Gain the reluctant acceptance of the other current members who voted against you, and the ownership of all the House's property for becoming 'The Head Of House Ven'Thyl'.**
>
> **Hidden Rewards: Gain the full acceptance and obedience of all other current members of House Ven'Thyl, and the respect of individuals who still hold the house in high regard.**

"Another Quest I didn't know about, but most of the rewards are kind of redundant since they'll already listen to me," I thought to myself, already reading another notification.

> **You have gained the Title: [A Member Of House Ven'Thyl]**

> **A Member Of House Ven'Thyl: Officially accepted as a member and part of House Ven'Thyl, you proudly take up and inherit the house's name to yours. Joining another House, Family, or Clan will remove this Title if you cannot persuade your multiple allegiances.**

> **Your Name has now been changed from 'Eyes Thalion' to 'Eyes Thalion Ven'Thyl'.**

"Wow, it just completely forced a name change on me. I didn't even get a choice to say no," thinking, *"This is gonna annoyingly bring so many Players' attention to me later,"* as I read the next title.

> **You have gained the Title: [The Head Of House Ven'Thyl].**

In Range – Ven'Thyl Saga Part I

> **The Head Of House Ven'Thyl:** Though not recognized as an official Elven House, the previous Heads of House Ven'Thyl have always been held in the highest regards as potentially one of the most powerful individuals the Elven Kingdom has to offer, and you carrying on their legacy will be no different.
> **+100 to All Stats.**

"What the fuck, +100 to all stats?!" I exclaimed in my head, completely surprised by the title's amazing bonus, *"I don't think the System accounted for the crown's effects correctly, cause I'm pretty sure this title shouldn't be something a Lv.24 should have if the Head of the House is potentially one of the strongest in the Kingdom. I'd probably guess that you're supposed to get this title around Lv.80 or something, considering Odelia and Aelthar were probably the next in line to be the successors."*

"Is there something wrong with what Verana said, my Lord?" Odelia asked, noticing me thinking hard.

"Not at all, I was just thinking," I replied, trying to read some of the other notifications.

Your Homestead has gained the Feature: [Multiple Estate]	Your Homestead has gained the Settings Feature: [Divided Estate]	Your Homestead has gained the Settings Feature: [Estate Restrictions]

"Well, I hope you know that I fully support Verana's choice of making you the next Head of the House, and that you should not worry that Aelthar and I are upset for not being chosen, right Ael?" Odelia nudged Aelthar to respond.

"I agree completely with Verana's choice, my Lord," Aelthar stated wholeheartedly, "and I know Shur and Ama feel the same," as both Shurtyrr and Amariina nodded their heads vigorously.

Fables of J

"Okay, okay, I understand how you guys feel, but just let me think for a second, alright?" They all nodded and knelt quietly, so I tried to figure out what these notifications meant.

> **Multi Estate:** Having obtained a second place to call your own, isolated from the first, you(Owner) and the Residents can now specify which Estate to teleport to when using the 'Return Home' Skill. You can only ever own a maximum of 3 Estates at a time, but can merge Estates together when the lands overlap.

"Wait, this is broken! But I think it's almost impossible to merge this place with Castle Creedmor considering how far away they both are from each other."

> **Divided Estate:** Land within your Homestead is all equal, but there is only so much power that can go around, giving you(Owner) the choice of how the Homestead's Perks should be shared between Estates

> **Estate Restrictions:** You (Owner) can now selectively specify which Residents are allowed to enter in which Estate, also limiting their 'Return Home' choice.

"I don't exactly get what this all means, but I guess I should check out the Menu," I thought, opening the Homestead Menu.

Homestead	[Settings]
Owner:	Eyes Thalion
Level:	1
Estates:	[Castle Creedmor], [House Ven'Thyl]

Perks:	[Aura Of Allurement], [Barrier Of Protection]
[All] Residents [Invite]:	Drune Stoneheart, Goblex, Gryphon Helvi'Ett, Hestyat Creedmor, Mako Nomura, Odelia Ven'Thyl
[All] Guests [Add/Requests]:	None
[All] Intruders:	None

I noticed nothing much changed about the Menu, except for the new Estate category; and that I could choose to see which Residents, Guest, and Intruders were in which Estate. Though I did notice when I clicked each Estate that I had the options to **Merge** and **Relinquish** them. I didn't bother testing them, seeing how I could already guess what they did, and just moved on to the Settings.

Settings

Homestead Access: [Closed]

Targeted Allurement: [All(No Bonus)]

Divided Estate: [50%(Equally)]

Guest's Maximum Time Access: [24 Hours]

Barrier Notifications: [On]

Request Notifications: [On]

Request Access: [Everyone]

Request Ban List[Add]: None

Estate Restrictions[Add]: None

Fables of J

Playing with the Divided Estate settings a little, I learned that I could specifically choose how much any one Estate could be affected by each Perk, but noted that I could only ever give 90% of any Perks' power, leaving the remaining 10% to the other Estate—ultimately I decided to keep it at the default 50% for now. I didn't really have much to do with the Estate Restrictions setting since I trusted pretty much every Resident I had, but out of respect for House Ven'Thyl, I decided to restrict anyone who wasn't part of the House for now.

> **Estate Restrictions [Add]: [Drune Stoneheart], [Goblex], [Gryphon Helvi'Ett], [Hestyat Creedmor], [Mako Nomura]**

Then finally looking at all the members still quietly waiting for me to be done thinking, I gave them a brief explanation of what was gonna happen, what was gonna appear in front of them, and what they could do with the Return Home Skill; and right after sent all of them an invitation to be a Resident. While they were surprised and read the invitation, I told Odelia, "I restricted Drune, Gryphon, and Mako from teleporting here out of respect for House Ven'Thyl, but I can remove their restrictions if you want?"

"No, that is completely fine, Lord Eyes," Odelia said, unbothered by the fact. "I already have the convenience of Gryph teleporting me back to the TCs, and that is already way more than I could ever ask for."

"The TCs? But there's a teleportation circle here," I pointed out. "Why would you teleport there?"

"Well... I am not allowed to," Odelia whispered, giving a subtle glance to Verana. "She only gives us permission to use the House's TC if you can both remember the True Runes and use the Teleportation Skill—which only Ama and herself can do."

"Tell you what, as my first action as the new Head of the House, I give you full permission to use the teleportation circle here," I whispered back. "But only if the reason is related to Drune, and if you make Gryphon promise to keep the runes a secret, okay?"

"Lord Eyes, you are too kind," Odelia smiled brightly. "Thank you."

In Range – Ven'Thyl Saga Part I

> **Verana Ven'Thyl has accepted your Invitation, and has become a Resident of your Homestead.**
>
> **Aelthar Ven'Thyl has accepted your Invitation, and has become a Resident of your Homestead.**
>
> **Shurtyrr Ven'Thyl has accepted your Invitation, and has become a Resident of your Homestead.**
>
> **Amariina Ven'Thyl has accepted your Invitation, and has become a Resident of your Homestead.**

They all accepted as expected, but what wasn't expected was another new notification popping up.

> **Congratulations, you (Owner) and the Residents have fulfilled the Requirement to Level Up your Homestead! The Homestead is now Level 2 and gains the [Natural Thriving Growth] Perk.**

"What the hell happened? And what Requirement did we fulfill to Level Up the Homestead?" I still wondered as I read the new Perk.

> **Natural Thriving Growth [On/Off]: Gradually expanding the lands of your Homestead, nature and the environments within begin to develop and grow in richness. The lands' expansion, development, and growth multiply per experienced Homestead Level.**

Even though it seemed like a pretty good Perk, I decided to turn it **Off** for now as there was no way to control the Perk's automatic expansion, and I didn't want to worry about dealing with any possible problems it could bring. My stomach then audibly growled—having not eaten anything since morning—and Verana immediately offered to cook me dinner. Having already skipped the dinner she cooked earlier, I couldn't say no and accepted her offer, and we all walked back up the floors.

After finishing all the food Verana quickly cooked up for me, I said, "Thank you for the delicious food, and I'm sorry for making you work so hard, Verana."

"You are welcome, my king, but there is no need to apologize," Verana replied, dismissing my apology. "I will—No, we will always be at your service." The other members sitting around the large dining table nodded in agreement.

"Thank you, but you don't have to be," I told them. "Like Odelia said earlier, I don't want others to know I'm the 'heir to the elves', so if you have to call me whatever over-the-top title you choose, only do so in complete privacy—and that includes gestures like kneeling to me."

"Umm... may I speak, my Lord?" Shurtyrr raised his hand and I gestured for him to go ahead. "You may already be known..."We all looked at Shurtyrr to elaborate. "There have been some interesting rumours going around the bl—market the last few days," catching himself for Amariina's sake. "The rumours were all basically about multiple sightings of a descendant of Ven'Thyl appearing in a human town called Asheton."

"Wow, words travel fast. Those rumours must've come from the elves who saw me wearing the uncovered crown," I realized. *"I wish I knew being the elven royalty was actually important earlier, I could've stayed hidden more."*

"What?!" Aelthar exclaimed, slamming his hands on the table. "Why are you just bringing this up now?!"

"Think for a second, Ael. That is the town Drune is currently in, remember?" Shurtyrr reminded him. "I thought I would wait for O'de to come back and tell us if the rumours were true or not. And how true they were," he smiled towards me.

"Thanks for letting me know, Shur, it was my fault for exposing myself," I said, and he bowed his head accepting my thank you. "Anyway, continuing from what I was saying; Odelia said it was because I said I'm ready to be king, but in truth it's because I don't want to be king," Odelia sighed in disappointment, while the others were utterly shocked and asked why; but when Verana started to speak, they all listened.

"Your choice is your choice, my king. I completely respect it, and will gladly continue to serve you regardless if you ascend to the throne or not. But if you could, could you at least tell us why that is your choice?" Verana inquired endearingly.

"They might just keep bothering me if I don't tell them some semblance of the truth," giving in, I said, "The reason is simple... it's because I'm not the rightful heir to the elves... I'm not the next in line for the throne."

They all loudly gasped in shock and disbelief of the revelation—even Odelia was taken completely by surprise.

Amariina spoke first, and asked, "Are you saying there's another heir somewhere, and that they're next in line ahead of you, Lord Eyes?"

"To be more precise, I believe there's at least two of them," I divulged.

"At least two?!" Aelthar repeated, then asking Odelia. "Did you know about this?"

"Of course not, how could I hide such a fact?" Odelia denied, still flustered by the news. "After all, Lord Eyes is the only descendant we've ever found in 999 years of searching, and in all honesty, he really just found me."

"There's no way she could've known, Ael, we barely even believed there was one descendant left, let alone three or more of them," Shurtyrr rationalized.

"May we ask where the other descendants are, lord Eyes?" Verana kindly asked, changing how she addressed me.

"That's the problem. I don't know where they are, and that's what I was trying to look for in the library—clues about their whereabouts," I told them honestly, but their faces looked so disheartened to learn that the rightful heir to the elves was still missing. Trying to lift them up a little, I said, "Even though I technically don't know where they are, I do know that they're somewhat safe somewhere, and that you'll just have to believe me on that," remembering that there wasn't a time limit or

Fables of J

failure option in their Quest, meaning they probably aren't gonna die anytime soon. "So I assure you, when we do find them wherever they are, they will happily ascend to their rightful place on the throne—bringing with them the prosperous change you all expect for the betterment of the Elven people and our great kingdom!"

Their faces brightened at the glorious thought, and I left them to discuss with each other as I picked a random room on the 1st floor to crash in.

Chapter 55
Unexpected Morning

A NOTE FROM FABLES OF J
Sorry for no Chapter update last week, was really busy.

An alley somewhere in Asheton...

"I can't believe Kyra accepted such a simple request in the middle of nowhere," a hooded dwarven man complained, holding a half smoked cigar in his mouth. "I mean, verifying a clearly fake rumour is so boring, and I kind of feel bad for the guy we have to kill."

"Stop complaining, Ignus," a hooded elven man replied, carefully watching the people walking by the alley, "and no you don't, you heartless bastard."

"Haha... I said kind of," Ignus replied back, exhaling the cigar smoke through his nose, "but at least the payment for such an easy Request is unbelievable, so maybe it's not all bad, right Lefan?"

"Stop babbling and tell me what you found on your side of town already," Lefan said, relaxing and leaning back against the alley wall.

Holding the cigar in his hand, Ignus relayed, "Only thing I found was that the target in question is a good-looking elven man with longish black hair and emerald coloured eyes—so basically a general description of any Wood Elf with black hair," and then he asked, "You think I can bail on this Request without getting in trouble again? You and Kyra are more than enough to handle and kill a random guy, right?"

"Go right ahead. I'll just watch Kyra beat the living crap out of you again for leaving another Request early," Lefan answered, not caring.

"Hmmm... what'd you find on your side?" Ignus quickly moved on from the idea.

"Nothing much. The target seemed to only frequent a blacksmith shop in the market, and the big inn in the town square, but I did find out where he and his Dark Elf companion likely left for," Lefan informed him.

"Aww, seriously? Our target must really be a nobody then, if all we needed to do was ask the locals about where to find him. So it begs the question, why go through all the trouble to personally request us from the Underground?" Ignus brought up.

"Who knows," Lefan shrugged, figuring, "maybe the Request-Maker thinks all the sudden rumours are actually true? Or maybe they want us to make sure it isn't true?" Then he told Ignus, "They probably think the elves finally getting a king will not only put the Tyrant on edge about the Kingdoms' Truce, but also your Mountain Queen."

"Well when you put it that way, maybe this Request isn't so boring," he said, holding the cigar back in his mouth again, "now imagine if the rumours do turn out to be true. You think Kyra would be okay with the idea of kidnapping a king for ransom? I mean the Request's payment will be nothing compared to what a Kingdom could pay us, you know?"

"Ignus, you're absolutely insane... but you do make a solid point," Lefan considered the idea, "except you know Kyra would never accept, she's too... Kyra."

"Yeah..." Ignus exhaled some smoke again.

"What wouldn't I accept?" a hooded woman suddenly asked, silently walking into the alley, "And what's 'too Kyra' supposed to mean?" she sounded slightly offended.

"N-nothing, Kyra!" Ignus panicked, surprised by her sudden appearance. "And being 'too Kyra' is a compliment, right Lefan?"

"Uh-huh. But forget all that. How'd collecting info at the Guild go?" Lefan asked, quickly trying to change the subject.

Kyra narrowed her eyes and glared at the two of them, but she relaxed and said, "I got a lot. And I think I have an idea of where our target is, but I need you two to tell me exactly what you found to confirm it all—be very detailed."

She slowly grinned as both Ignus and Lefan both told her what they found out, "Perfect, it's exactly what I thought."

"Uhhh... care to share?" Ignus and Lefan both looked clueless.

"It literally happened yesterday, how could you two already forget?"

They both tried to remember, but Kyra just sighed at them, "You dunces, remember the incident we heard about Leon's TCs yesterday? A Wood Elf man, a Dark Elf woman, and one of the Teleporters?" she reminded them.

"Oh yeah, I guess they do match the descriptions we were given here," Lefan remembered.

"I don't think I was sober enough to remember that, but you think it was really them?" Ignus asked.

"I knew you two wouldn't bother speaking with the guards, but I did, and they told me the woman's name is Odelia, and apparently she lives in Ven'Thyl; added with the fact that the pair here left for Leon and the pair at the TCs bought tickets to Ven'Thyl, and it all points to them being the same people," Kyra concluded, taking account of the descriptions she's heard from both places.

"Urgh, how annoying," Ignus reacted in disgust, "I hate that city. It's too massive, and if we're looking for an Elf there, it could take weeks, maybe even months."

"Maybe, but maybe not," Kyra grinned again, making Ignus and Lefan curious about what she meant,. "I talked to the Branch Leader in town, and he more or less confirmed that the target is a member of the Guild."

"Does he go by something? And did you get what it is?" Lefan inquired.

"No,. You know they never tell us the names of other members, even if they do know them—but, he did let it slip that the target is a Platinum Rank Adventurer."

"A Platinum?!" Ignus exclaimed, "I was expecting this Request to be a breeze, but he must be kind of strong if he's a Platinum. Now here's hoping he puts up a good fight," he smiled, anticipating the encounter.

"Does that mean we're headed to Ven'Thyl right away, Kyra?" Lefan asked.

"We… are," She answered hesitantly, explaining. "Even with the information we have on the target, it'll still be hard to find him in that city, so might as well start searching while the trail is still hot. And it'll give me a little time to plan a strategy around how strong he could be, as well as a few plans just in case we have to deal with any extra companions accompanying him."

All nodding in agreement, they all travelled back towards the Adventurer's Guild.

***

"Lord Eyes… Lord Eyes… It's time to wake up, my Lord," I heard a soft voice call to me, "umm...I'm sorry my Eyes, but O'de asked me to wake you up at this time." I felt someone gently shaking me awake. Slowly opening my eyes, I was met by the lovely sight of Amariina, who then nervously greeted me, "G-good morning, Lord Eyes!"

Yawning and sitting up, I greeted her back, "Good morning to you too, Amariina."

"You remembered my name, thank you my lord," Amariina replied gratefully, "and Verana told me to cook you food while they're gone, so if you're hungry, breakfast is ready for you downstairs."

"Of course I remembered, but where did they all go?" I curiously asked, standing up from the bed.

"About that… there was a small incident that occurred quite early in the morning while you slumbered, Lord Eyes," Amariina shyly mentioned.

"An incident? What kind of incident?" I raised my brow in curiosity.

Amariina explained, "Late last night, around 500 city guards arrived and surrounded the whole house, even blocking the entrance in the Soil—with 5 of the 10 Guard Captains all coming to knock on the Tops entrance."

"Wait, what!?" I yelled, losing my morning grogginess immediately, "500 guards and 5 guard captains doesn't sound like a small incident at all, what the hell happened!?"

"Well as O'de tells us, you somehow made that incredibly powerful barrier around the whole tree—all without any of us noticing, and it was immediately reported to the city guards. And as expected for such a suspiciously powerful barrier to appear out of nowhere and without warning, the guards angrily demanded an explanation from the house right away," Amariina informed me while she guided me back down the floors.

"Oohhh... I didn't even consider how my Barrier appearing in the city would be such a problem. That's my bad," I thought to myself; then asking Amariina, "Is everything alright then?"

"I... believe so," though she didn't sound too sure, "but it all depends on how Verana, O'de, and Ael clear up the issue in the courts." She then pointed out one of the small windows in the stairwell. "A few hundred guards did leave after their shifts were done, but they were all replaced by the morning guards."

Seeing a passing glance of all the countless guards along the Tops' bridges and platforms, I asked, "If the guards are still here, does that mean making a barrier around the house was illegal?"

"Not entirely, but one would usually need the approval of both the Tribunal and the Noble Council first. For it's nearly impossible to create such a permanent barrier without the many powerful mages the kingdom could call upon to do so," she detailed the process to me.

"If it's not illegal, what's the problem?" I asked, reaching the 4th floor.

"I believe that the guards were forced to investigate the sudden barrier as none of the top mages in the city were in any way connected to creating it, and they cautiously—but justifiably—assumed it may be an enemy attack coming from inside of the city," she rationalized.

"Makes sense. I should've told everyone about it yesterday so they wouldn't haven't been so surprised in the morning," I said, sitting at the dining table full of different foods, *"It really was my fault for not telling them."*

"To be honest, Lord Eyes, we all would've still been as dumbfounded and astonished as we were this morning," Amariina claimed. "Well except for O'de who said she's seen an even more monstrous barrier created by you," she said, respectfully sitting herself a few chairs away, "and even Verana noted she's never seen such a powerful barrier created by a single person, let alone one that can rival Ven'Thyl's barrier and one which was also created in an impossibly short amount of time without our noticing."

I simply nodded and ate my food while she continued, "As a mage myself, I cannot fathom it at all. After all it would take over a hundred high-level Mages to create such a permanent barrier, and it would surely take days of unyielding focus to complete it all—but for you to accomplish such a feat alone... is honestly a little demoralizing as a Mage."

I thought she was going to be sad from what she said, but Amariina simply stared at me with a huge amount of awe and admiration.

Ignoring her unusual stare, I thought to myself, *"I better tell all the house to keep quiet about me creating the barrier, if they haven't already spilled it wherever they are. Wouldn't wanna bring even more attention to myself now that I'm the Head of the House,"* I thought, continuing to eat my breakfast, with Amariina joining in too.

After we both finished eating, there was still plenty of food for the others when they got back, but Amariina then informed me she had to leave for work soon. Telling me that if I needed something to just ask 'the guy' who hadn't left yet—in fear that the guards would arrest him—as she quickly ran off down the stairs. Then wanting to get a better look at the situation outside, I walked over to one of the curtain covered windows and partially peeked through them.

"There really are a lot of them, and they're all pretty high level," I noted, seeing the hundreds of **Lv.40-60** guards blocking all the areas connected to our House.

Deciding that there wasn't much I could do except wait for the others to return, I went down to the 6th floor and knocked on a few doors until I found Shurtyrr's room. I asked him whether or not there were any rules for using the baths on the 8th floor, and he let me know there weren't really any except for showing common courtesy while in them. Honoured that I remembered his name, Shurtyrr happily guided me down to the baths, leading me to a narrow corridor with two large double doors opposite each other—left for the men, and right for the women.

In Range – Ven'Thyl Saga Part I

Showing me into the men's side, we entered a changing chamber where Shurtyrr explained that the baths were just through the next doorway, as he then excused himself and closed the chamber's doors for me.

Removing and putting everything I had on in my Inventory, I walked through a longish doorway and entered a massive, steamy bath chamber. Unlike the previous chamber, or any other of the floors above that were made of wood; this entire chamber was basically all made up of chiseled, natural stone, with foliage and vines hanging all along the pillars and walls of the place.

It was all very reminiscent of some sort of traditional bathhouse, with several smaller pools of steamy hot water sectioned off on the sides, and one giant pool that occupied a large space in the center. However this chamber was slightly dark, only being illuminated by a few dim light crystals on the pillars and walls, and an unexpected small tree standing on a flat, rock-bordered island in the center of the giant pool.

The tree was the centrepiece of the chamber for a reason, as all its leaves uniquely gave off a faint, colourful glow from each of them, and the moment one would fall off from its branches, it would increasingly grow in brightness—perfectly floating above the water with the rest of the fallen leaves, all helping to beautifully light up the center of the chamber with a rainbow of colours.

Stepping down the stairs into the center pool, I dove straight into the soothing hot water, and thought, *"This is just what I needed,"* feeling the not-so-ordinary water wash all the dirt clean from my body as I resurfaced for air. Then, while I soaked my body in the water, I noticed that I had multiple unread messages from both Global and Mako—all sent during the time I slept. Reading over Global's messages first, they were all just her questioning how my name changed, if I meant to do so or did something to do so, and if it was somehow related to the city of Ven'Thyl; though I didn't answer a single one, as I responded.

Fables of J

> ### Global
>
> ...
>
> Is it somehow related to the Elven capital city of Ven'Thyl?
>
> If you want answers, bring me something that you'd think would be useful for me to know, or maybe something that I'd find interesting. Until then, it's my little secret.

Not caring to wait for a response, I skimmed through Mako's messages next, but it made me slightly worried so I carefully read it again.

> ### Mako Nomura
>
> Eyes, I was working overnight on finishing up my new sword, and somehow an elven man wearing black leather armour entered the locked up shop asking about a man with your description. I freaked out at first, but I only told him that you just bought armour here and never really talked to us, always leaving right afterwards. I couldn't ask Drune about it since he's still at the castle visiting his friend, but I'll let you know what he says when he comes back.
>
> Little update: When I returned to the inn to have some breakfast, I saw the same suspicious man talking to Rayna. After he left, I asked Rayna what they talked about, and she said that he was an old friend that wanted to reunite with you and asked where exactly he could find you. But Rayna only told him that you left town westward, and that she didn't know where exactly you left for.

In Range – Ven'Thyl Saga Part I

> I don't know if you actually know him or not, but he definitely didn't look or act like any of the Players I've seen in town, so you better watch your back just in case, Eyes.

"I haven't met many people, but if he's specifically looking for someone that looks just like me, maybe he also heard the rumours about a descendant being in Asheton? Ideally he's just another dedicated fanatic like House Ven'Thyl are, but if he's not... I better get on with my training when Odelia gets back," I thought, sending a response to Mako.

> Thanks for letting me know, and for covering for me. I'll remember to bring you back something extra special from Ven'Thyl.

Closing the Menus, I slowly submerged my whole body into the hot pool waters again, and felt every inch of my body relaxed and soothed the further down I sank. Then before I knew it, I was suddenly no longer in the waters of the pool, and instead found myself floating in the golden space of the Seer—with an ocean of eyeballs drifting all around, and the quick-moving visions of the future right behind them.

Having leveled up Seer's Visions Skill quite a bit since the last time I've seen the future, the passing images and memories were noticeably much more clearer this time around. And although there was still plenty I couldn't see, I valued and noted everything I could see. From the various different individuals I looked to be meeting ahead, to the multiple training sessions and Skills I was going to receive; but a single future instantly undermined and overwhelmed everything I saw.

My heart dropped as the future brought back all too familiar memories I thought I had completely suppressed and finally forgotten. A future which foretells me being absolutely devastated and weeping over another lifeless body of a person I care about. The future unmistakably presented the horrible sight of Odelia tragically dying in my blood-soaked arms.

Chapter 56
The Noble Houses

    I returned in a panic at the bottom of the pool, reaching for the seen future I didn't ever want to be fulfilled, and heavily gasping for air as I resurfaced from the waters.

    "No... Not again..." I angrily slammed my fists onto the water's surface at the thought of the possibility. "I won't let it happen... I can't..." I slammed the water again as a promise to myself. Though completely startling me, a sudden sound of knocking came from behind, but I was quickly relieved to see it was just Shurtyrr standing in the doorway.

    "Please excuse my intrusion, Lord Eyes," Shurtyrr bowed as an added apology, "you were not answering to my calls from the previous chamber, so I worried the Waters of Tranquility dangerously caused you to accidentally fall asleep within them—though I am glad to see that is not the case."

    Brushing my wet hair back out of my face, I took a deep breath and calmed myself, saying to him, "Thank you for worrying, but what were you calling for me?"

    "I wanted to inform you that Verana and O'de have returned from the Courts, and with the guards beginning to disperse from around the House, I can finally make my way over to the Roots," he replied. "If you are in need of me again before the sun sets, Lord Eyes, you may find me staying in the biggest restaurant at the center of the Roots. Simply tell the owner that you wish to have a drink with the Poisoned Sapling, and he will gladly escort you right to where I am," he bowed once more before promptly leaving me alone in the baths.

    "A drink with the Poisoned Sapling? Is that like the password to enter the black market or something?" I wondered, stepping out of the pool and drying myself off in the changing chamber.

In Range – Ven'Thyl Saga Part I

Arriving back on the 4th floor, I found Odelia and Verana eating the leftover food Amariina and I purposely saved for them; though when Verana saw me approach the dinner table, she immediately stood up and pulled out the chair at the head of the table for me. I told her that it was unnecessary to treat me like that, but she insisted nevertheless, and so I complied and sat down at the head of the table.

"Shur told us that you visited the baths. Were they to your liking, my Lord?" Odelia asked, having cleared her plate.

"Too hot? Too cold? I would be more than happy to adjust the temperature if you would like, Lord Eyes?" Verana gladly offered.

"No need. The baths were absolutely perfect, and I wouldn't change a thing—but that's besides the point," I said, asking, "What happened with all the guards and stuff? And is the house already in trouble with the city on my first day as the head of it?"

"It is nothing to worry about, Lord Eyes," Odelia assured me, explaining, "We ingeniously smoothed out the whole situation by throwing Ael completely under the bridge, revealing that he was the one who claimed the personal responsibility of informing the other captains, the tribunal, and the council of the barrier; as he was our house's court representative."

"Okay… but if there's nothing to worry about, why isn't Aelthar here then?" I pointed out, remembering Shurtyrr never mentioned Aelthar being back.

"Well, he does have work today, but I assume the real reason is because he is currently being heavily scolded and reprimanded by the other captains and the head captain at the barracks regarding irresponsibly not reporting such a notable matter beforehand," Odelia figured, while Verana took a sip of some tea.

Their seemingly nonchalant attitudes towards the whole situation caused me to relax a little, but I asked to make sure, "So everything's really okay?"

"It is, Lord Eyes," Verana reaffirmed, "for this is not the first time our house has been in trouble with the city, nor do I expect it to be our last."

Fables of J

Odelia nodded in agreement and continued, "We may be an unofficial house, but Verana and Ael together are highly respected by many throughout the city, and are not so easily condemned for many of their questionable actions—which helps protect the house from incidents much like the one we had today."

"Hmmm... I've already heard you refer to our house as 'unofficial' multiple times now. Why? From what I've gathered, almost all of you have some sort of influence within the city, so why are we an unofficial house?" I questioned, curiously.

Odelia let Verana answer, and she explained, "After the First Trinity War finally ended 799 years ago, the Council of the Noble Houses discreetly convinced the surviving members of the tribunal to wrongly strip our house of official recognition, as they surely feared us at the time for being far superior in power and influence than their own noble houses." She elaborated, "For the elven people had come to recognize our house's pivotal role in protecting the kingdom's armies from the countless dangerous monsters they encountered during the 50 long years of the war; as well as the ones who volunteered to clear out the many dungeons that sprouted up during that time."

"Slaying monsters and clearing dungeons. Sounds like I have more in common with the house than I thought." Although I felt more connected to the place, I still wondered about the present, and asked, "Does that mean I should be looking out for the noble houses then? Or do they no longer consider us a threat to them anymore?" I recalled that Odelia didn't seem to have any real issues with House Fre'Nddare yesterday.

"Actively avoiding them is unnecessary, my lord, but you may find most of all the different members to be variously pretentious and entitled in their demeanours—which I know may lead you to avoiding them anyway," Odelia assumed, already understanding me a little. "And as for our house being considered a threat, well..." She looked at Verana who finished taking another sip of her tea to speak.

"I would not fixate on how the noble houses perceive of us, Lord Eyes," Verana advised, "for most of them will always resent our house's ability to show that any can stand equal to them, regardless of blood."

Nodding in understanding, I left the table and allowed them to finish their breakfast without my distraction.

Waiting for Odelia outside of the house, I felt the slight chill of the cold morning air on my slightly damp hair—under my hood—and on my shirtless body under my cloak. "**Dark Red**," I said to myself, changing the Cloak Of Colours to be a warmer colour than green. Then, while I took in the view of the city in the morning and our house's new barely visible barrier, I remembered I wanted to send Lavie a message and opened up the Menu.

> **Lavie en Rouge**
>
> Hey, do you think when you have down time you can make me some ordinary clothes? I'll even pay you what you want for them?

To my surprise she replied right away.

> **Lavie**
> Sure, I was already planning on making some for myself and Dream anyway, but did you have anything specific in mind?
>
> Not really, just like sweats and t-shirts to sleep in or something, cause I don't think any clothes this world has would be more comfortable than those.
>
> **Lavie**
> Got it, but it'll take a few days to make them, you know?
>
> No problem, I'll tell you how we can meet up later when you're done with them.
>
> **Lavie**
> Alright, I'll message you when they're done then

Fables of J

Closing the chat with Lavie, I also remembered I wanted to send a message to Tobias.

> **Tobias Casper Grim**
> Hey, I want to hire you for an ongoing job. Are you interested?

Waiting about a minute, Tobias replied.

> **Tobias**
> A job? What kind of job?
>
> I want you to find and steal any and all of the records for a teleportation circle's True Runes, from wherever you can find them. Be it from the Transport Towers, the Guild, or anyplace else records of the True Runes are kept.
>
> **Tobias**
> Never heard of these "True Runes" before, but stealing them shouldn't be too hard for me, after all I can pass through any wall with ease.
>
> Well I wouldn't be so sure about that.
>
> **Tobias**
> What do you mean?
>
> I called it an ongoing job because I don't think you're a high enough level to complete it yet, as I'm pretty sure the people guarding the records must be at least Lv.50+. Specifically the Transport Towers that likely have multiple Lv.60+ Mages guarding them, which I know their magics can hit a ghost regardless of their form.

Remembering that Odelia mentioned they were stronger than Gryphon, who was Lv.60 at the time; as well as that Goblex stated that magic can fully harm ghosts.

> **Tobias**
> That sounds like a whole lot of unnecessary trouble, why exactly do you want this done? And what's in it for me?
>
> I want it so we can have a convenient way to travel, for knowing the True Runes of a teleportation circle can provide the means to be able to teleport almost anywhere around the world, free of charge. So consider the job for your own benefit, as well as our Party's. Plus I'll pay you for each one you bring to me.
>
> **Tobias**
> I'll have to do some research on how dangerous this job could actually be, but I'll let you know if I want to accept it.
>
> Fine by me, I didn't expect you to accept the job so easily anyway.
>
> **Tobias**
> I'll get back to you with an answer in a few days.

Happy enough Tobias is even considering the job, I suddenly received a new message from Mako.

Fables of J

> **Mako Nomura**
>
> Drune is back, and when I told him about the suspicious man, he said that it is very likely to be an assassin hired to kill you. He also told me to warn you to be very careful and not to underestimate assassins, as it's very likely there's more than one after you, and explicitly stated to inform Odelia about this right away.

"I guess it is true what they say. Uneasy lies the head that wears the crown," I thought to myself as, almost right on cue, Odelia walked out the doors of the House.

> Thanks for letting me know, and tell Drune thanks for me too.

After closing the Menu, I was about to warn Odelia about the potential assassins, but my mind vividly remembered the future, and I questioned myself, *"What if that's the reason she dies? What if I'm the reason? Knowing how unbelievably strong she is, there can't be another way... If I tell her, I'm sure she's gonna do everything in her power to protect me no matter what, even if it means sacrificing her own life for mine, and I can't let that happen."*

I mentally apologized to her as she raised her hood to hide from the morning shine. *"Sorry Odelia, but I'll deal with the assassins myself. You're not gonna be another person I lose in front of me."*

"I am sure Lady Myeyl must already be eagerly waiting for us to arrive, so shall we get going, Eyes?" Odelia delightedly asked.

"Yeah, definitely. But where exactly are we headed to?" I inquired, following her lead.

"Well if you look over there in the distance," she said, pointing to the far left of us, "you will see where Ven'Thyl Academy stands at one corner of the peninsula."

I could faintly see a white stone, massively large, and enormously tall building structure over in the distance.

In Range – Ven'Thyl Saga Part I

"But on the complete opposite corner of the peninsula is where the noble houses reside, and that is where we will be headed today." She simply pointed in the direction ahead of us blocked by the tall treeline.

"I think you mentioned you were a professor before, right? Does that mean you taught at the academy?" I asked, not letting the topic slip by as we rapidly dropped down the tree by the Express Ropes.

Odelia hesitated to answer, "...Yes, and it was very fulfilling to teach and see all those talented students grow and develop, but that was a very long time ago…"

"I assume Myeyl and I are too old to be accepted as students, right?" A part of me kind of wanted to attend.

"Not entirely, but for the likes of you two, I could not see either of you gaining any benefits you would not already gain from being personally taught by myself. Well, maybe it would do you some good to attend the children's classes, Eyes," Odelia playfully teased, as we reached the bottom of the tree.

I smirked at her cheeky remark, kind of agreeing with my lack of knowledge, but all I thought was, *"That's too bad, but maybe I'll get to visit the academy some other time then,"* as I continued to follow Odelia's lead through the Soil.

Walking a few minutes down a nice stone road, I noticed that all the houses in the area were much nicer and larger than the ones closer to the Roots, but the houses and trees around us became scarcer the further down the road we went, and eventually I couldn't see any at all. However, once we arrived at the end of the road, I found us standing right in the middle of an intersection leading to 3 very different and distinct noble houses—each with a faint barrier surrounding them, each with their own unique orchards, and each fenced off from one another.

To my right was an orchard of black spiky trees, with crimson leaf tops, and red liquid oozing from the branches and leaves—dripping and staining the ground red. And right in the center of it all was a simple and small building made from dark grey wood, with a dark purple roof, and black tinted windows. I also took note of the two **Lv.50** Dark Elves guarding the fence entrance, and two more guarding the building's entrance—all wearing a uniform black and purple coloured armour.

Seeing me underwhelmed by the noble house, Odelia commented, "It may look like nothing from aboveground, but House Baen'Mtor is a house that consists entirely of Dark Elves, and so they have chosen to construct their great manor completely belowground." She pointed directly below their land.

I nodded and thought, *"I wonder if it's as massive as that one,"* while I looked to my left at the only Sky Tree in the whole area.

Ignoring the four **Lv.50** guards at each of the entrances of this house too—with their uniform white and blue coloured armour—I took more interest in their orchard of birch-like trees, which had no leaves whatsoever, but did have mana that I could see flowing within them. Then moving on, I also ignored their very similar, small, whitish wood, and blue roofed building at the base of the tree; and instead looked up at the tallest Sky Tree I saw in the entire city.

It had an expansive multi-floored mansion sitting on top, with separate buildings spread throughout the different levels of the tree, and all with the same white and blue colour scheme. It also looked to have much more branching and thick branches all along the trunk, giving the mansion more than enough space to build all around the whole tree top; and I could even see that there were parts of the mansion blocked from sight because they were built above the leaves.

"That is House Helvi'Ett," Odelia informed me, with a bit of a sour expression on her face, "and most of them truly embody their High Elf stereotypes, as they even snobbishly live above the other noble houses, and both figuratively and literally look down upon them."

Seeing a silver lining, I said, "You're saying most of them are snobbish, but that means there's some that aren't, right? So what are the chances of me meeting a non-snobbish Helvi'Ett?"

"Very unlikely," Odelia replied bluntly, telling me, "even Gryphon cannot help being snobbish at times."

Then we both suddenly heard someone yelling for us, "Odelia! Eyes! You're here!"

We turned to see it was Myeyl running towards us, with Jhan closely chasing after her. She wore the same attire she wore yesterday, but now added a fully stocked quiver on her back, and a wooden longbow with strangely thick limbs. Before Odelia and I could even say hello, Myeyl already grabbed us both by the arm, and eagerly dragged us towards the large manor.

"Now where have you two been? I've been waiting since dawn for you to arrive, you know?"

"I did plan for us to arrive earlier, but I had to deal with an unexpected situation," Odelia explained, allowing herself to be dragged along.

Letting myself get dragged along too, I focused ahead at the orchard of ordinary looking trees that seemed to move unusually, as if strong winds were currently blowing through them, even though it was clearly a perfect, windless day today. There was also the large and wide 4-storey manor straight ahead; built with simple brown wood, a few stone supports, a dark green roof, and in a symmetrical U-shape towards us.

"So these are the three noble houses of the elves…" I thought, giving each of them a glance one more time. *"Now I wonder how they'll react when I eventually bring missing descendants here?"*

Chapter 57
Shooting and Styles

A NOTE FROM FABLES OF J

Sorry for not updating the Chapters the last few weeks, I got a severe case of covid and only just felt like myself again.

As we passed the guards at the fenced gate entrance, they gave each of Myeyl, Jhan, and Odelia a nod of acknowledgement, but only looked to have taken note of my face.

"Odelia really does have a good connection with the house if even the guards are acknowledging her."

But surprised that Myeyl was dragging us completely around and behind the very wide manor, I mentioned, "I don't know where we're going, but wouldn't it have been faster to go through the inside and then head back out?"

"It would've, but some of my siblings are very jealous that I'm being trained by Odelia exclusively, and I want to keep it that way," Myeyl mischievously smirked. "If we went inside, they might just privately beg her to replace their trainers, but if we stay outside, their pride won't allow them to beg where they could be seen by others."

"Sounds like you have a pretty big family, but there's no way there's enough of you to occupy this whole manor, right?" I asked, slightly curious about the number.

"Of course not, there's only ten of us, you know?" but she noticed that I didn't know and elaborated, "Besides Mother and Father, there's also my four elder brothers, my three elder sisters, and finally myself; not to forget each of our vassals, like Jhan here, or the multiple other loyal servants and guards who are happily housed here.

"Wait, you have seven older siblings?" I was shocked at the number, "That means you're the youngest, right? And I assume one of them is going to be the next Head of the House?"

"That's right, and it's my eldest brother Thereyl who's next in line to be Head of House Fre'Nddare," Myeyl informed me, with a slight look of admiration on her face. "He's the most competent, talented, and decorated out of all of us siblings; he's even achieved the amazing feat of becoming a Trinity Archer at his early age of 105."

Shocked by another unexpected number again, I thought to myself, *"Wow, that's a crazy age difference if Myeyl's only 20 years old! And if it took the most talented member in their family 105 years to become a Trinity Archer, how long is it going to take me to accomplish it?"*

"That's untrue, milady," Jhan suddenly interjected, "I truly believe you're the most talented out of all your siblings, even compared to young master Thereyl."

"Pfft, don't believe him, Eyes. I'm definitely not more talented than Thereyl, but I will agree that I'm much more talented than any of my other siblings," Myeyl confidently stated, as we finally arrived at the back of the manor.

Right in front of us was a large and beautiful stone courtyard, but what really stood out to me was a large stone gazebo at the very end of the courtyard—overlooking the endlessly vast, blue sea past the edge of the peninsula. Though what also stood out to me was a larger, slightly elevated, and circular stone platform right in the center of the courtyard; with thick 30-foot tall stone pillars bordering around the platform, and multiple straw dummies on the edges of the platform.

While I was being dragged towards the stone platform, I glanced back at the manor as I felt multiple people inside beginning to watch us, and vaguely saw about 30 people currently doing so from the different floor windows. Most of them looked like they were servants or guards, but a few seemed to be vassals like Jhan, as they each stood beside four individuals hiding and peeping behind the window's curtains; though there were another three individuals that watched freely, not caring to hide from sight.

"Don't worry about them, Eyes, it's just mother and my siblings," Myeyl said, noticing them as well. "I'm sure they'll get fed up watching me finally get trained, and will soon leave after they get too jealous of the sight."

"What about your father? Doesn't he want to watch you get trained?" I asked, trying to ignore the stares from the windows.

"He did, but there was apparently an emergency call for the council this morning. He's probably stuck dealing with whatever it is," Myeyl explained, as I looked to Odelia who nodded that it was definitely about our barrier, "but I'm sure it'll be over quickly if it isn't anything important, and then I'll happily introduce him to you when he gets back."

"It would be an honour to meet the Head of House Fre'Nddare," I graciously replied, giving a little bow to show I was being respectful.

Then as we stepped onto the stone platform, Myeyl noticed that I didn't carry a bow or a quiver, and asked, "Do you need me to ask Jhan to go fetch you a spare bow and quiver from inside, Eyes?"

"Oh, thank you for offering, but I already have both right here." I pulled both Infinity and Shame out from my Inventory and surprised all 3 of them by the random appearance of the items.

"H-How did you do that!?" Jhan questioned. "That was unlike any spatial magic I've seen before, and I didn't even see the moment you casted, or the space you stored them in? It was like they appeared from nothing..." He seemed to lose himself in thought.

Odelia curiously looked at me while Myeyl exclaimed, "Who cares about that!" as she stared intently at my bow, "Is... is that a bow Odelia handcrafted, Eyes?"

"Uhh... I think so? You said this was the first bow you crafted, right Odelia?" I asked her, making sure.

"Indeed it is," she replied simply.

"Hey, that's not fair, Odelia! You're already picking favourites!" Myeyl pouted.

"I'm not picking favourites, Lady Myeyl," Odelia assured her. "Eyes simply already owned the bow before I ever met him."

"If you think it's unfair, do you wanna borrow it for training today?" I offered, presenting Shame to her.

Myeyl instantly became ecstatic, "Really?! You'll really let me borrow it?!"

In Range – Ven'Thyl Saga Part I

"Well yeah, we're just training, so feel free to try it out," I said, gladly handing over Shame to her and thinking, *"Even though she still owes me for helping get her accepted as a student, I should still try my best to get completely on her good side."*

"First you help me become Odelia's student, now you give me the opportunity to wield our teacher's handcrafted bow; your kindness towards me is just unending, Eyes. Thank you." she showed me such a stunningly beautiful smile as she handed me her bow to use. However, shaking my head from her beautiful sight, I decided to look at the Stats for the surprisingly heavy longbow she handed over to me.

Fre'Nddare Longbow
Uncommon
Attack: 230
Requirement: Lv.20, Str 110

"Wow, this bow is almost as good as Shame in terms of Attack, but too bad it doesn't have the Effect and +25 Strength Shame has."

Then as I lightly tugged on the bowstring, I was surprised to feel that it was actually slightly harder to do so compared to Shame, *"Interesting... Odelia's bow already had a pretty heavy draw weight, but this bow's is somehow heavier. I wonder if it's because of these unusually thick limbs,"* I carefully inspected the total make of the bow as Myeyl did the same for Shame.

Loudly clapping her hands to get our attention, Odelia said to us, "Now that you two have your bows sorted out, why don't I go ahead and evaluate your archery skills. But first..." She turned to speak to Jhan, "I need you to do me a favour and silence this whole platform for the remainder of the lesson, and I ask that you remain outside for the entire duration, Jhan."

"Of course, Lady Odelia," Jhan readily accepted; then pronouncing the word "**Silence**" and creating a slightly larger purple dome around the whole platform area and walking himself right out of it.

Curious, I asked, "Why silence our training? Is it supposed to be secret or something?"

"I was wondering the same thing," Myeyl added, then mentioning, "I've never seen my siblings' teachers make such a request when they were training out in the open, so is there really something we're learning in secret, Odelia?"

She chuckled at the both of us. "There's no secret here. It's simply the environment I prefer to privately teach students in, as it very much reminds me of how I once learned from my own Master," she said, leading us to one end of the platform.

"Grandfather taught you and father this way? I wonder why father never mentioned such an odd training method to us?" Myeyl questioned out loud.

"Probably because he didn't want to tell you and your siblings that Master only preferred the silence so that others wouldn't hear him yelling at your father and me for making all our mistakes," Odelia then seemed to reminisce at the memories.

"You don't think we're gonna get yelled at, do you?" I whispered to Myeyl.

"I'm not sure, but now that I think about it, I heard Odelia was once the strictest professor in the whole Academy, so I wouldn't put it past her," Myeyl whispered back.

"You know I can hear you both, right?" Odelia glared at us and we immediately shut our mouths. She then shook her head and sighed with a grin. "Why don't you both show me what I'm working with? Shoot a few arrows at the dummies on the other side, and let me examine how well you both naturally shoot with a bow."

Not wanting to be the first one to get yelled at, we both quietly nodded at Odelia's instructions and lined ourselves up with a dummy on the other side of the platform—I estimated it was about a 50m distance away.

In Range – Ven'Thyl Saga Part I

    Confidently straightening my stance and pulling an arrow from my quiver, I thought, *"With a longbow at this distance, it'll be a piece of cake."* In one smooth motion, I nocked the arrow, drew the bowstring back, raised the bow up in front of me, and held the bowstring to my anchor point beside my mouth; then using the arrowhead as my guide, I carefully aimed at the dummy's head, and released the arrow flawlessly. While I listened to the arrow fly and the bowstring rubberbanding back in place, I instantly knew I didn't like shooting this bow whatsoever. I could already tell it was way too heavy to reliably keep stable while aiming, and the vibration it had after being shot was unusually intense; but nevertheless, I still watched my arrow pierce the center of the dummy's chest.

    "Wow, fantastic shot, Eyes!" Odelia sounded genuinely impressed. "Fre'Nddare bows are notoriously difficult to shoot, yet your form was perfect, and your arrow true."

    "I could tell. But I've been doing this for years, and all I need is a few shots to get used to how it feels and I'll be good with any bow," already drawing another arrow and readying another shot.

    "I see..." Odelia noted, watching me shoot my second arrow right next to the first, "I was always curious about how good of an archer you were ever since I saw all those dead goblins at your… 'home', but now I think I'm beginning to understand just how you slayed them all." Slightly grinning, she looked over to Myeyl who was trying to perfectly nock her first arrow correctly.

    "She looks exactly like an amateur at a local shooting range," I thought, observing her shakily draw and aim my bow, releasing the shot soon after. *"Huh, it really does seem like she hasn't been taught any archery before, but at least that means she's a blank slate Odelia can perfectly mould into a fine archer."*

    Then to my surprise, the arrow struck the right in the center of the dummy's head and Myeyl cheered, "I hit it!"

    "Woah, she hit a 50m headshot on her first try! Now was that just beginner's luck, or was that the talent Jhan was talking about?" I wondered, releasing my own shot and creating a tight grouping of arrows.

"How was that?" Myeyl excitedly asked Odelia.

"It was very impressive, Lady Myeyl," Odelia lightly applauded. "Although, we'll still need to work on your stance and form, as well as how to properly breathe; but all in all you did great, so keep shooting."

And she did just that, getting better and better the more she shot; though not wanting to be outdone, I did so too.

After about an hour of alternating shooting hands every couple dozen arrows, my proficiency finally leveled up again.

> **Archery proficiency increased by 1 Level.**

Soon after Odelia stopped us. "That's enough. Go ahead and retrieve all your arrows." And as we did so, she loudly asked, "Now do you two have a preferred Archery Style you wish to train in first?"

"Mmmh… I've been using dual-blades ever since I was young, so I think I'd prefer the Combat Style," Myeyl answered first, already knowing the choices.

"And you, Eyes?" Odelia asked me next.

"Uhhh… I don't know any of them," I answered truthfully. "Maybe knowing a little summary could help?"

"Hold on, you don't know the 3 Archery Styles?" Myeyl questioned in disbelief, "I mean how can you even call yourself an elf if you don't know that?"

"Hey, give me a break. I was born outside the kingdom after all." But I could tell Myeyl was still judging me in her head.

"Apologies, Eyes, I forgot that fact. But allow me to explain." Odelia walked over to us to educate me. "There are 3 types of Elven Archery Styles: the Dark Elves' Close-Combat Style, the High Elves' Magic-Wielding Style, and the Wood Elves' Long-Range Style—or Combat, Magic, and Range Styles for short. And as tradition, aspiring Trinity Archers would usually start by training in their own Races' Style first, but in the last 250 years we've shifted into the idea of allowing one to choose the Style they prefer to train in first—pioneered by yours truly of course," she proudly claimed.

"Okay, well is there one that's stronger than the others? Or maybe one you suggest to learn first?" I inquired, genuinely interested to hear Odelia's opinion.

"There's no one style stronger than the other, even though you might hear people claim otherwise, or see peoples' natural affinity for a particular style display a sense of superiority. In truth they are all equal, and when one finally reaches the Trinity Archer Class, they come to understand that as well." Odelia made sure Myeyl understood that too before continuing. "And as for my suggestion… I say you choose the style you lack the most in—to help balance your flaws in combat. Or you could choose the one you have the most affinity for, like Lady Myeyl—it'll greatly increase your immediate combat strength, and help you get used to and learn your first style faster. But ultimately, it's really up you, Eyes."

"I've always been a fast learner when it comes to archery, so I don't think needing to learn faster will be a problem, but I still don't know what to choose? Combat, Magic, or Range?" While I contemplated the 3 choices in my head, I asked Odelia, "Do you think you could show me an example from each Style? It would really help me decide."

"Of course I can, but may I have permission to break the pillars a bit, Lady Myeyl?" Odelia asked politely.

"Definitely! Break all of them if you want!" Myeyl happily suggested, anticipating a firsthand demonstration from her Master.

"Then may I also have an arrow?" Myeyl immediately passed Odelia one. "Well then, the first style I'll be demonstrating is the Range Style. It specializes in precise and accurate long distance shots, controlling and multiplying your arrows, and can be used at such distances that your enemies will only be able to see the arrows piercing straight into them." Odelia then walked to the base of a pillar away from the manor, in the direction of the water, and aimed her bow diagonally up at it. "This Skill is called Piercing Shot, and it's one of the later Skills you'll learn when training in the Range Style, so watch carefully."

Not doing anything out of the ordinary, Odelia simply fully drew her bow, and released the arrow at the pillar a moment later; but as

Fables of J

Myeyl and I both carefully watched, we immediately noticed the arrow suddenly begin to spin at incredible speeds in the air. Then the moment the arrow made contact with the pillar, it completely drilled a hole straight through the solid stone, only leaving a clean arrow-sized hole left behind. Though not stopping, the arrow kept flying upwards over the water, and disappeared from sight in the clouds above.

We both applauded in amazement, and Odelia explained, "Piercing Shot may not be as damaging compared to magic-type Skills, but the usefulness it has against heavy armour and dense structures truly makes up for it. The Skill should be used when physical attacks are needed rather than magical ones."

"That's not damaging!?" I exclaimed to myself. *"She just drilled a hole in a solid stone pillar with a regular arrow like it was paper, how much stronger could other Skills be?"* I became excited at the thought.

"Another, another!" Myeyl demanded, wanting to see more.

But as Odelia was about to show us another Skill, she suddenly stopped herself and looked past Myeyl and I; smugly smirking while she asked, "Is the council going to make trouble for us, Zebey?"

We then heard a smooth voice respond behind us. "Maybe, but everything should be fine for now—well besides the other two deciding to send a few undercover guards to keep watch on your house."

Recognizing the voice, Myeyl quickly turned around shouting, "Father, you're here!"

Chapter 58
Rivaled

A NOTE FROM FABLES OF J

I didn't know how to properly split this Chapter with the previous Chapter, so this one turned out to be a longish Chapter.

Hearing Myeyl call the name "father," I immediately turned around to see a gorgeous elven man with longish, finely styled, chocolate brown hair walking towards us; dressed in a surprisingly simple white cross-string shirt, black trousers, and black boots. We were about the same height and build, but I was slightly taller, and he was slightly more built, though I could tell he had a natural regalness about him—something I obviously didn't have.

"So that's Myeyl's father? Well I can definitely see where she gets her looks from," I thought to myself, seeing their family resemblance—with their same emerald coloured green eyes, their exact shade of chocolate brown hair, and their very similar facial features.

"That I am, my little emerald," he replied to Myeyl, telling her, "I just got back from the council meeting, but after I changed my clothes, I was informed you were still training in the courtyard, so I thought I'd come to observe. Now what did I miss?"

"Well Father, we simply spent a few minutes showing Odelia how well we could shoot, but she was currently showing us a demonstration of each of the archery styles to help Eyes decide what he wanted to train in first," Myeyl explained to him.

The man then turned towards me and looked me directly in the eyes, saying, "So you're Odelia's mysterious new student..." He stared as if he was trying to read me. "Eyes, is that correct?"

"That's correct, Lord Fre'Nddare," I answered, while giving him a deep bow to show my respect, "and may I just say it's an honour to meet you, as well as to be invited into your beautiful home." In the corner of my eye, I saw Odelia twitch at my words and actions, but she stopped herself from exposing me.

"Much more polite than I expected from someone who I was told claims to be an outsider, but I'm sure that's not the only reason Odelia accepted another student after all this time." He circled me while he talked. "Speaking of which, I heard that you're the main reason my dear little emerald was finally accepted by Odelia as her student, is that true?"

"I mean it is true, but I wouldn't say I'm the only reason she was accepted, Lord Fre'Nddare," telling him, "Odelia may hide it, but if she didn't actually want to train Lady Myeyl in the first place, she wouldn't be here right now doing so."

"Hmmm... I wouldn't be so sure about that, for I've known Odelia longer than any other—including her house or her husband," he claimed, sounding so sure of himself, "I know exactly just how headstrong and steadfast she can be, so I wouldn't have even been surprised if she never accepted Myeyl as a student for decades."

"Wow, he does know her," I thought to myself, remembering how the time limit for Myeyl's Quest was 80 years, *"but it's strange to think he knows Odelia longer than Drune or the house."*

He then seemed to have thought of something, and said, "I can save what I have to say until after, but for now why don't I personally demonstrate the other archery styles for the two of you?"

"Really, Father!?" Myeyl shouted in excitement.

"Of course. It would be an honour to see your skills firsthand, Lord Fre'Nddare," I said, bowing to him again.

"I thought you didn't want to affect or influence any of your children's training, Zebey?" Odelia asked, smugly crossing her arms.

"I don't," he responded. "I've always wanted them to find their own way of doing things—a path they alone choose, and they alone walk. That's why I allowed them to choose to attend the academy or not, but in this case, Myeyl is special." He smiled at Myeyl and she smiled back. "As you know, she was the only one who chose to not attend the academy, so I think a little of my influence will be good for her. She is behind on her training after all, no thanks to a stubborn somebody," looking at Odelia as he said so.

In Range – Ven'Thyl Saga Part I

Ignoring his gaze, Odelia gestured for him to go ahead, saying, "Be my guest, but I've already shown them the Range Style, so why don't you show them the Magic Style next?"

"Oh, I'd love to," he said, smugly smirking at Odelia while he stood in the center of the platform and faced towards the waters.

Then the moment he raised his empty right hand, Odelia explained, "The Magic Style is the most versatile and imaginative of the three styles; allowing one to alter and enhance their arrows in all sorts of different ways. But to truly embrace and master the style, one must essentially learn to physically manipulate and wield their mana to a point at which physical bows or arrows are no longer needed."

When she finished speaking, we suddenly watched a blue bow begin to take form in the lord's hand; and taking only about ten seconds to do so, the bow took the shape of a simple longbow design, and was completely made out of pure mana.

"I didn't see him do anything out of the ordinary, but maybe I should be looking a lot closer to see if I can figure out how it works." I then changed to the **Eye Of An Elder Cyclops** and saw the constant steady flow of mana focused into each of his hands. *"Looks like he's fully controlling all the mana inside of him and emitting it out of his hands, but I'm sure it's not as easy as he's making it look."*

We watched him easily form a mana-arrow as he drew the bowstring of the mana-bow—though strangely the tip of the arrow was round and circular.

When Odelia saw the arrow was fully drawn, she continued to explain, "One of those ways, in particular, is the most basic Explosive Arrow Skill, and it is almost exclusively used to cause widespread destruction on the battlefield."

And as soon as she finished speaking, the arrow was released with such surprising force that my hood was almost blown right off from the wind pressure alone. Barely following the rocket of an arrow with my eyes, it flew straight past the stone pillars of the platform—cracking the ones it passed near—and soared right over the vast waters. A moment passed, and when the arrow reached about 500m away, it abruptly exploded into an enormous light blue coloured dome. Soon after we all got hit by the immensely strong shockwave of the explosion, so much so that Myeyl and I had to brace ourselves to not be knocked over, while some of the cracked pillars dangerously toppled over. Yet simply standing tall, Odelia and Lord Fre'Nddare smugly smirked at each other.

"What the hell was that?! It was like a giant bomb just went off! How is that considered a basic Skill?!" I questioned, quickly reverting my eye back to normal while they weren't looking.

"Apologies. It's been a while since I last shot an arrow," Lord Fre'Nddare explained, "so I may have used too much power on that one." He relaxed his hands and made the mana-bow dissipate away.

"You definitely did, but you knew what you were doing, Zebey," Odelia smiled, shaking her head at him.

"That was amazing, Father! I always knew you were powerful, but not that powerful! And to think my teacher is someone just as equally powerful!" Myeyl exclaimed, staring at both her father and Odelia with admiration.

"I don't know if I would say she's equally as powerful—almost as powerful is more like it," Lord Fre'Nddare confidently stated.

Odelia loudly exhaled, "Zebey, don't even start. We both know it's the other way around, or do you want to come and prove otherwise?"

After a brief staredown, they simply jokingly laughed at each other.

"Well maybe they were equally as powerful, but I wouldn't say that anymore," briefly using the **Eyes Of A Seer** to compare **Lv.85 Odelia Ven'Thyl** to **Lv.80 Zebeyeyl Fre'Nddare**, *"but it's interesting to see that Odelia doesn't even refer to him by his full name, and instead uses a nickname. Looks like they really have known each other for a long time."*

"Why don't you allow me to demonstrate the Combat Style, okay Zebey?" Odelia asked, already holding her bow in one hand and her sword in the other.

"I don't think you were really asking, but go ahead. I didn't bring out my bow or sword anyway," Zebeyeyl mentioned, while stepping back a little.

Positioning herself a few meters in front of a dummy, Odelia explained, "The Combat Style is the fastest of the three styles, focusing mostly on close quarter fighting—whether it be with your arms and legs, a weapon of choice, or a sturdy bow." Then barely following her movements, I watched Odelia swiftly dash towards the dummy, go into a slide, and break the wooden post the dummy stood on with a sliding kick. As the dummy fell towards her, Odelia extended her other leg straight upwards, kicking and sending the dummy incredibly high in the sky, as she jumped up right after it.

In that split second she floated in the air slightly above the dummy, Odelia quickly shouted, "This next Skill is very advanced, but I can't let you show me up in front of my students, Zebey!" Her bow and sword then began to glow with a purple aura around them, and with incredibly fast movements, Odelia swung her sword in a flurry of slashes at the dummy, slicing it up into little tiny pieces, and leaving only the head intact. She finished by shouting, "**Earth Piercer!**"

As soon as Zebeyeyl heard those words, he panicked, quickly grabbing Myeyl and me and throwing us right over his shoulder. He then jumped into the air as high as he could, and shouted back, "Warn me next time! And hold back a little, will you!" But Odelia had a wicked smile on her face.

We then watched the purple aura around her bow and sword intensify as she brought the hilt of the sword to the bowstring—almost as if it was an arrow—and in one smooth motion drew the bowstring back; though as she did so, all the purple aura rapidly flowed right into the sword, as it was then released straight down at the dummy's head she'd kept intact. Easily piercing through the straw, the sword went flying directly into the center of the stone platform, and explosively crashed and embedded itself deep into the ground, leaving only the very end of the handle exposed. With the bird's eye view we had, we could see all the damage that single attack caused—basically destroying the whole platform into countless perfectly shattered stone pieces, causing all the already damaged stone pillars to fully collapse, and even causing Jhan outside to stumble and fall from the sheer impact of the attack.

While we fell back down, I was simply amazed at their display of strength, thinking, *"These two are insanely strong! Is this what the*

Fables of J

power of two Trinity Archers can do? And can I be just as strong when I become one?"

"That was absolutely incredible!" Myeyl shouted, hopping off her father's shoulder and running over to Odelia.

Also getting off, I said, "Thank you for saving me, Lord Fre'Nddare," though when I tried to bow, he stopped me.

"There's no need for that. And please, call me Zebeyeyl—well at least in private training like this," he smiled.

And as we watched Myeyl shower Odelia with praise and compliments, I decided to compliment him too, saying, "Your Magic Style demonstration was equally as impressive, Lord Zebeyeyl."

"I'm glad you thought so, Eyes," as he then directed his attention to my back, "but I noticed that you carry quite a unique looking quiver on your person, and I've been dying to ask if you could perhaps share where you found such an item?"

"Uhmm… I guess you could say it was a gift from a beautiful goddess," I truthfully told him, smirking because it was technically true.

"A goddess, you say? Well, I guess beautiful women do seem like that sometimes," he replied, not taking my words in a literal sense, "I also wanted to point out that my daughter carries Odelia's first bow, is it yours?"

"It is. Is something wrong with that?" I questioned.

"Not at all. It's just that I haven't seen that bow in over 250 years…" Zebeyeyl seemed to get nostalgic as he looked at the bow from afar.

"250 years?!" I exclaimed to myself, *"They don't even look a day over 30, so just how old are these two?"*

Finishing reminiscing, Zebeyeyl turned back to me, and said, "The more I think about it, the more I find your quiver very alluring to me. So if you don't mind, may I see?" Not wanting to refuse his request, I happily handed over Infinity to him; and he examined it with the same fascination, intrigue, and mannerisms Odelia did when she did so in Asheton.

After thoroughly examining the quiver, Zebeyeyl handed it back, asking, "I believe you're staying at House Ven'Thyl, are you not?"

"How does he know that?" I wondered, responding with, "I am."

In Range – Ven'Thyl Saga Part I

"Then have you already joined their house?" he asked, curiously.

"Uhhh… I guess, in a way I have, but why do you ask?" I asked, curious why that would matter.

"In truth, I have this strange feeling that there's something different about you...." He examined me with his eyes. "And if that quiver you're carrying is what I think it is, it means that you're no ordinary person for owning it, and I am more than sure Odelia came to that very same conclusion when she decided to accept you as her own student." Zebeyeyl then gestured a hand out towards me, saying, "Knowing those facts, I cannot help but to offer you an exclusive opportunity to join the Noble House Fre'Nddare—one as my personal vassal, and two as my first ever archery student."

Quest Completed

A Noble's Impression and the bonus Hidden Quest has been completed:

Find a way to greatly impress the Head of House Fre'Nddare.

Demonstrate amazing archery ability to Zebeyeyl Fre'Nddare, and have him acknowledge your incredible potential.

Reward: An invitation to become a Vassal for House Fre'Nddare.

Hidden Reward: Accepted as Zebeyeyl Fre'Nddare's first ever archery student.

"I… I don't know what to say," I stammered, unsure how to respond to the offer and the Quest, *"What do I do here?"*

"Say yes of course, what else is there to say?" Zebeyeyl smiled, confident in what my answer will be, "You may even consider it my personal thanks for helping Myeyl be accepted as Odelia's student if that makes you feel better—or perhaps my personal belief in your clear potential to become strong and invaluable to a Noble House."

"Your offer sounds great, Lord Zebeyeyl, but I've already joined House Ven'Thyl, and I'm already going to be taught by Odelia. I just don't think I can get out of either of those situations that easily, so I'm sorry to say, but I'll have to decline your very generous offer," I said, thinking, *"Especially since I'm the head of House Ven'Thyl, and I could never face any of the house again if I just abandoned them to join a Noble House."*

Zebeyeyl let out a little laugh, "Haha… If that's all you're concerned about, don't be worried. I can personally resolve all those matters in a single day, have you join my Noble House soon after, and get you settled into the Fre'Nddare Manor in no time. So, what do you say?"

"I wouldn't be so sure about all that," but before I could respond to Zebeyeyl's insistence, Odelia came rushing in front of me and aggressively pushed him away from us.

"Sorry, but I couldn't take overhearing your blasphemous conversation any longer, Zebeyeyl." Odelia's voice and expression became very serious. "Know for one that Eyes is off limits, for he already plays an integral part of House Ven'Thyl, and we would never allow him to be a mere servant of any house—noble or otherwise."

Taken back by Odelia's sudden seriousness, Zebeyeyl looked concerned and said, "Wait outside, Myeyl. Now."

Confused by the abrupt mood change, Myeyl reluctantly listened to her father anyway and left the silenced area to where Jhan stood. Composing himself, he calmly addressed Odelia, "I haven't heard you speak to me like that in decades, Lia, and you never call me by my name. So tell me, what's wrong?"

"Lia? I've heard Drune and the House call her O'de, but I've never heard Lia before," I thought to myself, wondering about the name.

"Is there a problem in House Ven'Thyl? Or maybe with Lady Verana's health?" Zebeyeyl inquired, sounding genuinely concerned over either.

In Range – Ven'Thyl Saga Part I

Covering her mouth with her hand, Odelia said, "No, there's nothing wrong, Zel. I was simply slightly irritated by the lack of respect you were showing to Eyes since you met, and the reversed roles you were about to place onto him as a vassal of your house."

"Lack of respect? Reversed roles? What are you talking about, Lia?" Zebeyeyl questioned. "And wait, this isn't about you being angry at me for attempting to steal your student from you?"

"Of course not," Odelia assured him, "if Eyes wishes you to teach him, then who am I to stop his wishes. You are my equal after all, and I wouldn't trust anyone else but you to take my place to ensure he reaches his full potential."

"Well, clearly there is something wrong if you're hiding your mouth from being read, so what really is it?" he insisted.

"Look Zel, I don't have permission to tell you anything yet, but if you really wish to know, come to House Ven'Thyl later and ask the new Head of the House yourself," Odelia informed, still covering her mouth. "He'll tell you why Eyes cannot join your own, and why he's not fit to be anyone's mere vassal."

"Woah, Odelia must really trust him if she's willing to tell him about me. They must've really known each other for a long time if that's the case."

Hearing that fact, Zebeyeyl now looked shocked and also covered his mouth to speak. "A new head? Who? When? Why?"

"Like I said, I don't have permission to say," Odelia stated.

"No wonder you covered your mouth…" Zebeyeyl then recalled, "Wait, is that why a barrier suddenly appeared around your house?"

Odelia stayed quiet.

"Well besides that, there should be no one in your house who could replace Lady Verana so easily—be it in the city or the kingdom for that matter; and I always believed you or Captain Aelthar would be next to succeed Lady Verana, but your secrecy tells me otherwise."

"I'm sure you and everyone else saw the Bouncing Stars Of Warning, Zel. We are at the cusp of great change, but I assure you at least one of those changes will be for the better," Odelia snuck a wink towards me as she said so.

"Hmmm... you know, it's still a horrible idea to go there. Your house hates the nobles, and being seen there will only cause more people to question my house's decisions," Zebeyeyl reasoned.

"Well, don't be seen then," Odelia smugly stated, removing her hand from her mouth, "like old times."

"Like old times, huh? You know those old times always got us in trouble with Father, right?" Zebeyeyl also removed his hand from his mouth.

"They did, but remember that time when Master chased us all around the city for hours?" Odelia happily recalled.

"How could I forget, we almost died when he started shooting arrows to slow us down, remember?" Both their moods brightened from the memory and they began laughing together after reminiscing about another tale.

Seeing that they were both distracted reminiscing about the past, I snuck out of the silenced area and walked towards Myeyl and Jhan.

"I think that's it for training today," I said, disappointed I didn't learn anything, but glad to have experienced some of Odelia and Zebeyel's power.

"I thought as much. I mean they did basically destroy the whole back courtyard," Myeyl said, pointing out how the shockwaves of their attacks ravaged the entire courtyard. "Oh, here's your bow back by the way. It was great to use, even for a little bit." We exchanged our bows. "So, did you decide on a style you want to start training in?"

"Umm... I'm pretty confident in general archery, so I think I'm leaning towards Magic or Combat to learn," I said, contemplating the two choices.

"If you pick Combat we can train together. What do you say?" Myeyl suggested.

"Sounds tempting, but I don't think I could keep up with your... talent, Myeyl. So maybe I'll just go with Magic," I decided, thinking, *"I have a strange feeling I would end up as her punching bag if we trained in Combat together."*

"Too bad, I might've even shown you a few tricks I learned with the dual-blades," she proudly claimed.

In Range – Ven'Thyl Saga Part I

"That is too bad, but I better get going now." I said, noting that Odelia and Zebeyeyl were still talking, "you know, before Odelia notices I left and follows me everywhere I go."

"Oh, I know the feeling." Myeyl gave Jhan a funny look, but he continued to mind his own business. "Well, I guess I'll see ya later then, but don't be afraid to come visit."

I gave her a wave as I left the same way we entered from.

After I left the mansion grounds, I immediately sensed that I was being followed. However, I couldn't tell exactly where they were without letting the person know I noticed them following me.

"Seeing how they followed me right after I left, it's probably just someone sent from Myeyl's house to keep an eye on me," I thought to myself, walking along the paved path towards the direction of the Roots. *"I was gonna go check out the black market today, but with someone following me, I guess I'll go on another day. Don't wanna add more suspicion to myself,"* I thought, continuing my way to the Roots.

Chapter 59
Drinks from a Stranger

Standing on the grand bridge built over the large waterfall overlooking the Roots, I looked below and thought, *"I'm still being followed, and with all these people around, I really can't tell who's following me or how many there are."* I then casually looked over the crowds of people crossing the bridge. *"I could really use some armour just in case I get attacked, but I could probably wait. They just seem to be following for now."*

Turning back to the Roots, I remembered the area Odelia pointed to for the Guild's location and looked for a building that stood out.

"Good armour will cost a lot, and I still have to pay Gryphon in the following months, not to mention paying for the clothes Lavie makes and Tobias' future work..." Peeking in my Inventory, I saw that I only had **677 Gold**, **98 Silver** and **65 Copper**, and thought, *"Looks good, but I don't think this will last as long as it looks."*

I then spotted an unusually large building and knew that it was the Guild. *"Now I wonder what kind of Requests I can do here? Ideally ones that can help me Level Up too."* I then crossed the bridge and found a staircase leading down to the Roots.

Making my way through the Roots, I found that the city was vibrant and full of life, and seemingly very peaceful at the moment. I saw families walking together, children playing on the streets, couples holding hands, and the occasional pair of guards patrolling around. All three types of elves were present here, but I'd guess half of them were Dark Elves, while the other half was split between High Elves and Wood Elves. I quickly lost myself in the intertwining streets of the Roots, finding myself walking through a series of alleys, countless homelike

In Range – Ven'Thyl Saga Part I

buildings, a variety of different weapon and armour shops, and by a few smaller inns and taverns.

With the help of some locals giving me a few directions, I finally found myself standing in front of the largely overgrown stone and wood building that I saw from the bridge. It had the words "Adventurer's Guild" hanging right above the two double door entrances. The building was three storeys tall, as opposed to the two storeys of the one in Asheton, but it looked to be twice—maybe three times the size. Walking up to the doors, I was about to push them open when they instead opened themselves. A hooded dwarf opened it from the inside, with two other hooded people walking through it first. I politely stepped out of their way and let them all pass.

As they walked by, I heard one of them say, "Maybe that's him?"

"Can you be serious, you said that about everyone inside," another responded. "Half of them weren't even Wood Elves."

Walking through the doors after them, I barely heard a woman say, "Doesn't matter, we can check again tomorrow. Besides, there's still plenty of places to look for him." The doors then closed behind me.

"They seemed to be looking for someone. Can't be me right? Maybe I'm just getting paranoid because I'm being followed right now." Not giving it a second thought, I stared at the giant Guild Hall.

The Guild Hall was huge, and I was able to count well over 200 different adventurers right off the bat; all wearing and carrying different sorts of armour, weapons, and gear. While I watched them walk around, conversing with each other, it was the first time since I arrived in Ven'Thyl that I saw all three races; but about 75% of the adventurers were still elves. Other than that, the hall had tables filled with people all around, with a large bar on the left serving food and drinks; and on the right side of the hall were four large notice boards surrounded by constantly moving adventurers grabbing the countless pinned requests, and Guild workers struggling through the crowd to place more. There were also stairs on the left and right leading to the second floor balcony and space which wrapped around the hall, and unlike the Guild building in Asheton, which had only one door in the hall, this building had several doors placed everywhere. Then at the opposite end of the hall

Fables of J

was a long semicircle counter where all the requests were taken in, manned by about a dozen Guild workers, all wearing the same uniform black suit clothing—I noted that workers were all Elven, and so were the people manning the bar.

Taking a seat at a recently vacant table, I covered my right eye and observed the levels of everyone in the room through my fingers. I couldn't tell if they were Guild workers, but the people working at the bar were all **Lv.24-28**, with one **Lv.36** who seemed to be in charge of the bar. The ones that were clearly Guild workers however were all **Lv.55-60**. The adventurers on the other hand were pretty diverse; I could see some **Lv.10-20**, most being **Lv.21-49**, and a few dozen **Lv.50+**. The highest being a **Lv.68** man named **Morril Blake**, wearing a bright suit of metal armour, a white tabard with an emblem of an open palm holding gold coins, a horned helmet that covered his whole face, and a massive, dark blue crystal bladed greatsword on his back. He was accompanied by a party of four other **Lv.66-67** people; all with their own unique armour, gear, and weapons and all having the same emblem of an open palm holding gold coins on their gear. They all made their way out of the hall after deciding on a request together.

Not noticing him approach, a dark elf man suddenly placed a mug of ale in front of me and sat down across the table. "I saw you eyeing up everyone in the hall, and the Avarices seemed to have caught your attention, slowpoke," he said, taking a swig from his mug of ale.

"Slowpoke? And where did he come from? I don't remember seeing him around the hall, and I didn't even sense him watching me. The only people that left or entered the hall were those Lv.60s just now, so where did he come from?" I wondered, surprised by the sudden appearance of the man.

The man continued, "Seeing your face when you saw them, I could tell that you're a new adventurer, right? But I haven't seen you around here before, so tell me, what's your name, slowpoke?"

Before I answered, I took a look at his name and level with my covered right eye, and was shocked at what I saw, *"**Lv.71 Cyspar Baen'Mtor**! There's no way I met another member of a Noble House!"*

I thought, staring at the man's amethyst coloured eyes, his long flowing silvery white hair, and the fresh cut on his lower lip.

"You gonna answer me, slowpoke, or are you just gonna stare at me all day?" he asked, taking another swig of ale.

As he tilted his head back to finish up his drink, I saw an old, large horizontal scar on his partly exposed chest. When he looked at me again, I said, "Eyes. My name's Eyes."

"Well, slowpoke, drink up," he gestured to the mug he put in front of me, and seeing that he was waiting for me to drink, I decided to quickly chug the whole mug down. Smiling, he cheered, "Now that's what I like to see!" With some ale spilling from the corner of my mouth, I chugged it all down. "Great job, slowpoke!"

Wiping my mouth, I said, "Thanks, but why are you talking to me? And what's with calling me slowpoke?"

"It's because I've been waiting for you to arrive, slowpoke," he smiled knowingly.

***

An hour earlier...

"Ouch!" Cyspar grimaced, touching the fresh cut on his lip, "What happened to pulling our punches, Ther? It was only supposed to be light sparring, remember?"

"That was light," Ther chuckled as she walked up some stairs, "and you should've been able to dodge it anyway."

"Well, I got distracted by my new hot maid who came in," Cyspar explained, following Ther up the stairs.

"Then it's your fault you got hit then."

They laughed and both made their way up the floors and left through the front doors of House Baen'Mtor. Instantly, they both noticed an unrecognizable hooded man leaving House Fre'Nddare; along with a few others from the house secretly following.

"I recognize the vassals, but who's the other one?" Cyspar asked curiously.

"I don't know, but I remember Myeyl saying Lady Odelia was training her today..." Ther replied, wondering about the person too.

"Woah, that's a big deal! Why didn't you mention that earlier?" Cyspar exclaimed, surprised by the fact.

"Ehh, I forgot," Ther shrugged.

Cyspar sighed, "Anyway, that doesn't look like Lady Odelia to me. And whoever it is, your siblings seem like they really want to find out."

"I know…" Ther thought for a second, before saying, "Go follow him too. Tell me what you learn when you come back. I'll go check with my house if they know anything there."

"You got it," without hesitation, Cyspar suddenly disappeared and they went their separate ways.

Cyspar was completely unseen the whole time, by both the hooded man and the vassals tailing him—following them all the way to the Roots. Though when he heard the man ask for directions to the Adventurer's Guild, he thought to himself, *"Thank the goddesses I know where he's going. I was getting so bored following him around. Now I'll just have to wait for him at the Guild. Here's hoping he doesn't take too long."* Cyspar then headed directly for the Adventurer's Guild.

***

"So you've been following me since I left House Fre'Nddare too?" Then I thought, *"Wow, I really never sensed him at all, unlike the others. He must be really good."*

"I have, and I know we just met, but can you tell me why you were at House Fre'Nddare?" Cyspar inquired, while drinking some more ale.

"You expect me just to tell you for nothing? I don't even know who you are?" I said, wanting to see if he would offer me something.

"You're right, but what if I tell you all about that high-rank party you were staring at?" Cyspar offered. "Will you tell me then?"

"No thanks," I bluntly refused, telling him, "Guessing from what you said earlier, they're probably from a Guild Faction called the Avarices or something, but what I'm really interested in is who you are?

In Range – Ven'Thyl Saga Part I

Or more like, why you seem to be familiar with these 'Avarices', and why you're interested in what I was doing in House Fre'Nddare?"

He raised an eyebrow at me, and said, "I thought you might just be a newbie copper who didn't know anything, but I think I underestimated you." He gave me a little smirk.

"No, you were right to think that. I only joined the Guild about a week ago, but if you're not gonna tell me who you are, we're done here." I got up from the table.

"Wait," he said, and I stopped to listen, "a week ago you said? I don't believe that for a second. With your attitude, I would have guessed you were a veteran." Letting out a sigh, he pulled out a dark metal Guild bracelet from his pocket and placed it on the table to show me. "I go by Cy in the Guild, and I'm familiar with those Avarices because I'm a high-ranking adventurer too. So could you answer my question now?"

I stared at the bracelet trying to figure out what rank it was. *"It doesn't look like the adamantite I've seen before, so is that mithril or orichalcum?"*

"Wait, are you really just a newbie? Why are you staring at my bracelet like you don't know what it is?" Cyspar questioned.

"Like I told you, I've only been in the Guild for a week, I don't know what all the ranks look like yet," I told him, honestly.

Cyspar laughed loudly, drawing the attention of a few adventurers, "Haha… I like you, slowpoke. Want another drink? It's on me," he then grabbed his bracelet from the table and got up to grab us some more drinks.

Seeing his full body when he stood up, I saw that he was wearing a long, collared, hooded black coat that reached down past his knees. The coat was sleeveless and left completely open, exposing his arms and shirtless torso, and showing off his extremely well defined muscles. He also wore matching black pants and boots, and dirtied cloth wraps around his hands and forearms. All his clothes looked pretty simple in appearance, but I could tell they were well crafted from the little bit of shine they were giving off; though what stood out to me was that I didn't spot a single weapon on his person.

"Why not? I'll take another." I got up to take him up on his offer. "Just let me go look at some high-paying requests first."

"Ooo, about that. I don't think you'll find any," he gestured for me to follow.

"And why's that?" I asked as I followed him through the crowds of adventurers. I noticed that people got out of his way as he walked, and thought to myself, *"He must really be a high rank if people are moving out of the way for him, or maybe it's because they also know he's from a Noble House?"*

While he led me to the bar, he explained, "Most of the high-paying requests right now are being held hostage by either the Elvenkind, the Greenwood Striders, or the Avarice Faction. They'll only give you a request if you pay them a fifth of the reward upfront, or if they somehow deem you worthy to be a member." He then ordered two more mugs of ale and they were quickly passed over to us.

"That doesn't sound very fair," I said, taking a sip of mine.

"It's not, but what can you do?" Cyspar shrugged.

"What about you then?" I inquired. "You don't seem like you belong to any of those factions, how do you get work?"

"We ask politely, of course," he smiled mischievously. "The Guild knows what my party is capable of, and the other factions don't want any problems."

"He has a party?" Wanting his help, I asked, "Wanna help me get a request then?"

"I don't know... you still haven't answered my question from earlier."

"Oh, that's simple. I was only at House Fre'Nddare because my archery teacher wanted to train there."

"No way! Are you saying Lady Odelia is your Master?" Cyspar exclaimed quietly.

"She is. Do you know her?"

"I've never directly spoken to her, but she partially trained my older sister and cousins."

In Range – Ven'Thyl Saga Part I

"Looks like Odelia isn't just connected to one Noble House. What a teacher I got!" I then asked again, "So, what do you say? Wanna help me get a high-paying request?"

Cyspar thought about it for a moment, and said, "Sure, I like you enough. What rank you looking for?"

Pulling out my own Guild bracelet from my Inventory, I said, "Anything around Platinum is good." Cyspar looked surprised, staring at me up and down. "I know it's hard to believe, but I actually did join last week, even if my rank is Platinum already."

"It's not your rank that I'm surprised at, it's your whole person."

I gave him a confused look, and he elaborated, "Before you arrived, three Underground assassins were asking around for someone who fits your exact description, and who just so happens to also be a Platinum Rank."

"Three assassins?! Two I probably could've taken, but three just sounds like trouble!" I now felt more concerned than I was before.

"Did you happen to arrive from Leon recently?" Cyspar questioned.

"Yeah, yesterday. And I already knew about the assassins, but I didn't expect them to be here already. I thought I still had at least a few days." I tried to remember the faces of the people I passed at the entrance, but their faces escaped me.

"I can't believe you knew assassins were after you and you still accepted a drink from a stranger—not once, but twice." Cyspar let out an amused chuckle. "You either have a lot of guts and confidence in your abilities, or you're incredibly naïve and ignorant to how dangerous assassins and their methods can really be."

"Maybe a little bit of both, but now that I know they're here, I should be more careful from now on." I then lost myself in thought. *"They're here faster than I expected, and I know I'm not ready yet, but what to do, what to do, what to do…"*

Interrupting my thought, Cyspar said, "It's none of my business, but here's a little heads up because I like you, slowpoke: one of them had a Titanium bracelet on, and it's safe to assume the other 2 companions are also the same rank. Seeing how they're all one rank above you, it might be best for you to stay low for a while and not go

Fables of J

on a request that could lead them straight to you—I mean the people here are already spreading the news they saw you here today."

I could hear some faint whispers around the hall about me.

"The assassins will definitely be coming back here to check for you again, and this time, they'll know exactly who they're looking for."

"Damn, that means I can't get more money until I deal with them." I scowled in annoyance, and said, "I better get out of here then, but thanks for the heads up, Cyspar. Hope we can meet again after I deal with them."

"Likewise. And good luck, slowpoke! Oh, and if you make it out alive, drinks are on you!"

Giving him a thumbs up, I made my way out of the Guild Hall and ducked into an alley nearby.

Waiting for a moment when nobody passed by, I then activated **Return Home** and thought, *"House Ven'Thyl,"* and in a blink of an eye I found myself standing on the teleportation platform in the library.

Sitting down at a table, I thought about the whole situation. *"How do I deal with three assassins by myself? I could always ask the House for help? But what if that's the reason I'll end up holding Odelia in my arms..."* Unsettled, I got up and walked around the library. *"If they're strong enough to injure Odelia, who's to say no one else in the house would be in danger because of me... I'll just have to deal with them myself, and any other assassins sent after them."* I then rushed up the stairs to check if Odelia was home so I could actually learn something today.

***

Outside of the three Noble Houses…

"So?" Ther asked, wondering what Cyspar learned.

"I like him. Seemed like a pretty good guy to me..." Cyspar answered, looking back to see if he was followed.

"I'm sensing a but."

"I don't think it's anything, but I introduced myself as Cy to him, but when we said our goodbyes, he called me Cyspar," he informed Ther.

"Interesting, what else?" Ther became intrigued.

"Not much. He goes by Eyes, and apparently he's one of Lady Odelia's new students, like your sister," adding, "Oh, and he's a Platinum adventurer."

"That's what Father and Lady Odelia told me too, well except the adventurer part," Ther confirmed. "Though strangely, when Lady Odelia heard he left the manor grounds, she immediately went rushing to look for him. And when Father and I were alone, he told me he wanted to make him a vassal in our house."

"Woah, seems like the Underground isn't the only one who wants him."

"The Underground?" Ther repeated.

"Yeah, some Titanium assassins came asking around for him at the Guild earlier," Cyspar relayed.

"Even more interesting…" Ther appeared even more intrigued. "Father told me he's from outside the kingdom, so I thought he was a nobody, but if Father wants him to join the house, and he's someone who's being hunted by some assassins, my mind has changed about him."

"You're not thinking about recruiting, are you?" Cyspar looked worried at the idea. "I mean he's only a Platinum, and besides carrying our supplies, how much is he really going to help there?"

"We all know we need someone we can trust. Who better than someone Lady Odelia trusts?" Ther reasoned.

"I guess, but—"

"The big Factions are all bringing 9-10 Parties each for the Dungeon Raid; do you really think me, you, and Lua will be enough to even survive that bloodbath?"

Cyspar stayed silent.

"But look, we don't have to decide right now. I'm sure Lua will have plenty to say after being locked up in her house for two whole months."

Fables of J

"She definitely will, and I guess the raid isn't for another three months anyway, so maybe you have a point."

"I always do. Now we just have to wait and see what this 'Eyes' does."

"What do you mean?" Cyspar wondered, unsure what Ther meant.

"I mean how he plans on surviving three Titanium assassins." Ther sounded eager to find out.

Chapter 60
A Fall and a Challenge

"Aww, come on, Odelia. Don't be mad," I said, following her to the other end of the library.

"I am not mad, my Lord, just disappointed you left me," Odelia expressed, opening the doors and leading me further down the floors.

"Oh, don't be like that. I was only gone for like an hour or two. And besides, I met an interesting person while I was gone."

Odelia's ears perked up, "And who would that be?"

"Cyspar Baen'Mtor."

"Cyspar? I have not seen him since he was a little boy," Odelia recalled. "Well I hope your exchange with him was pleasant at the least."

"It was. He offered me drinks at the Adventurer's Guild."

"At the Adventurer's Guild?" she repeated, piquing her interest. "Now that I think about it, I did hear he was an adventurer with Thereyl and Lualaf as his other party members."

"Who are–" But before I could ask about his other party members, my attention was distracted by two solid stone and metal doors with intricate magical runes written all over them, "What's this?" I asked, redirecting my question.

"Oh, that is just the 10th floor," Odelia casually answered, continuing past them.

"Woah, woah, woah, I'm talking about why is it magically sealed off?" I said, pointing it out. "The other floors weren't like this?"

"Oh, my mistake, Lord Eyes. It seems like I forgot to inform you." Odelia apologized with a bow before explaining, "The 10th floor is the house treasury, and for that reason alone makes it the most secure floor in the whole House as it holds countless valuables within its walls."

Fables of J

"Like?"

"Coins and treasures that have been collected for centuries to fund the house, a myriad of items and gear recovered from past members who have fallen in the search for the descendants, and from what I hear, a miscellaneous collection of peculiar relics and artifacts," she informed me.

"Sounds like everything I need!" I thought to myself; eagerly asking, "Would you mind opening the doors for me? I'd love to see the treasury in person."

"Sadly I cannot, Lord Eyes. Only the Heads of the House knows how and is able to open them, along with being the only ones even allowed to enter the treasury in the first place," she said, telling me, "However you will still first need to ask Verana to show you how to open them, otherwise the runes will reject even *you* from entering them right now."

"Too bad..." I said, thinking, *"If the coins and treasures are meant to fund the house, maybe I shouldn't take any, and I should probably treat the items and gear the same if the previous owners are fallen past members; but I should still ask Verana to show me the treasury some other time."*

"Shall we continue, Lord Eyes?"

I nodded and she led me down even more stairs.

When we finally reached the bottom of the stairs, we arrived in a small, dimly lit room; old weapons racks all along the walls, dull and rusted weapons scattered on the floor, unused targets and straw dummies piled up together in a corner, and a single wooden door on the opposite side the room.

"Pardon the mess in the storage room, my lord, it has been quite a while since any of us have been down here," Odelia apologized. "I will make sure it is cleaned for next time. But for now, onto the last floor of the house." We headed for the opposite door and she gladly opened it, saying, "Welcome to the 11th floor: the training chamber."

When I walked through the door, I was blasted by the heavy scent of soot and dust in the air, but I found myself standing on a small railing-less platform overlooking a large, cylindrical stone brick chamber. Spread all along the walls of the chamber were multiple targets with varying degrees of damage; some with old scorch marks, others with holes made from different thrown weapons or arrows, and a few dozen that were completely burnt black or destroyed. Looking down I guessed we were at least 50ft high, and looking up there was another 50ft more above us. But looking back down on the ground of the chamber, I could see multiple target dummies with similar damages to the ones on the walls—all with the addition of a few large slashes and bisected targets.

There was very little of the walls that weren't scorched or not covered in soot, but the parts that weren't showed me small and intricate runes written all throughout the bricks.

"Must be runes to protect the walls from being damaged," I figured, seeing the walls—besides the cover of soot—were completely fine and undamaged.

Embarrassed by the state of the chamber, Odelia apologized again, "I am so sorry, Lord Eyes! I did not know the floor was in such a state! It is so rarely used anymore, but I will ensure it gets cleaned up for the next time we train here!"

"It's fine, Odelia. It doesn't bother me, as long as I can still train here." I then pointed to the single door on the ground opposite us, and asked, "By the way, where does that go?"

"That is the Soil entrance, my lord. But it too is rarely used anymore," she stated, "for the others and I do not wish to deal with the hassle of climbing up the stairs."

"The house only technically has 11 floors, but the Sky Tree itself is still well over 250ft tall, and that means a whole lot of stairs," I thought, then asking, "Okay, now how do we get down from here?" as I didn't see any stairs or ladders leading down.

"It seems the training ropes have been incinerated, but you can try climbing down the walls if you would like," Odelia suggested, pointing out how the brick walls were designed to be climbed on. She then handed me her bow and without hesitation leaped from the platform. Though holding her bow for the first time, I took a quick look at it as she fell.

125

Fables of J

Odelia's Pride

Epic

Attack: 1190

+230 Strength

+200 Magic

+170 Agility

Effect: Increases damage by 1.5% the closer you are to the target, up to 45%.

Requirement: Lv.70, Str 700

"Odelia's Pride, huh? If Shame was the worst bow she created, Pride must be the best bow she created. But what are these ridiculous looking Stats on it? Are all Lv.70 weapons like this?" I wondered, turning my attention back to Odelia.

Watching her fall down 50ft, she landed perfectly into a roll and got up like it was absolutely nothing to her. Dusting herself off, she shouted, "If you are scared, I can always just catch you, Lord Eyes!"

I scoffed at her and thought, *"50ft is a long way down, but maybe it isn't so bad if Odelia can do it. Plus, it could be a perfect time to check out the fall damage here."*

Making up my mind, I threw down her bow to her and followed her lead, jumping from the platform and readying myself for the impact. The fall was quick, but when my legs made contact with the ground, I suddenly heard a loud cracking and breaking in my ankles and knees; and when I tried to follow it up with a roll like Odelia did, I ended up slamming my body hard against the stone brick ground, all culminating in me losing a third of my Health instantly.

"Ahhhhh!" I yelled out, feeling an intense aching pain coming from all over my body. "Fuck that was a stupid idea!"

Odelia immediately came rushing towards me shouting in a worry, "Lord Eyes!" but quickly trying to ease the pain, I started to spam multiple **First Aids** on myself. Odelia seemed surprised as I did so, "Lord Eyes, how are you healing yourself? What Skill are you using?"

"What? It's just First Aid. Didn't you learn it when you were a Ranger Class too?" I questioned, still flustered from the pain—casting more **First Aids** on myself.

> **First Aid increased by 1 Level.**

"Of course not. Learning Skills is different from person to person, so in general two people of the same Level and Class could have completely different Skills from one another," she elaborated. "For example, I used a Skill I created called Earth Piercer at House Fre'Nddare earlier, but even after a century of mimicking me, Zebey still has not completely learnt it from me yet—it is the same for me with his equivalent Sky Piercer."

The pain made it hard to fully grasp everything Odelia was telling me, but I watched my **Health** slowly return to full and the pain began to subside. *"My legs would've shattered if I had a normal body, but good thing it isn't."* Sighing in relief, I slowly got up to check if I was truly okay, and with a little movement in my legs, I knew I was alright.

Odelia was still rambling, "Even so, I have never met an Archer Class who has learnt the First Aid Skill before, so it is truly amazing you know it, my lord. And if I recall correctly, usually only Beastmaster Rangers tend to learn the Skill in the wilderness—they use it to heal themselves and their beast companions in combat."

"A Beastmaster?" My ear perked up at the thought.

"Yes, though none choose to live in the city as their beasts do not fit very well with a domesticated lifestyle."

"Awww, having a beast companion sounds fun. Kind of makes me wish I picked a Ranger." Changing my thoughts, I said, "Odelia, you said learning Skills is different for each person, right?" She nodded. "Then can you tell me if any of my other Skills are out of the ordinary?"

"It would be my pleasure, my lord," she gladly expressed, giving me a little bow. "I have been looking forward to experiencing the true extent of your abilities for quite a while now."

"Then let me show you," I said, as I then drew Shame and then shot a **Power Shot** straight at a charred target dummy.

Odelia looked unimpressed, telling me, "Power Shot, the first Skill any Ranger learns, but becomes very obsolete when compared to an Archer's Piercing Shot."

"Okay, then how about this," I casted **Turning Arrow** and shot it directly at Odelia.

Unflinching to my attack, Odelia's head followed the arrow as it curved around her body and hit the dummy directly behind her. "Turning Arrow is a fundamental Range Style Skill; it takes years to learn and master it, but when one does master it, your arrows will never miss a target you do not want them to." She turned back to me with an impressed expression on her face. "How did you learn it at such a young age, my Lord?"

"Well technically the System just gave me the Skill when I was showing 13 some trick shots, but I guess I can't say that to Odelia." Instead I answered with, "My uncle was a bit of a show off when it came to archery, but when I saw something he could do with a bow that I couldn't, I spent all my time annoying him until he gave in and taught it to me too, and that's pretty much how I learned everything I know."

"He must have been some great teacher," Odelia smiled warmly.

"I guess he was…" Shaking my head of the sad thought, I continued to display my other Skills.

When I showed Odelia **Spread Shot**, **Leaping Shot**, and **Rapid Shot**, she didn't look as impressed as before. "Spread and Leaping Shot are useful Combat and Range Skills, but they are pretty standard and common to learn as Skills go. On the other hand, Rapid Shot is a fundamental Combat Style Skill as it is essential for fighting and shooting in close quarters, and is quite the relief for me that we can cross it off so early on."

I then showed her **Twin Arrow** and **Arrow Shower**, and the impressed expression came back to her face—with a little bit of disbelief. "Lord Eyes, are you really not a Range Style Archer already? Turning, Twin, and Shower are all fundamental Skills of the Range Style; they all need years of learning and practice to be as good as you have shown me, yet your age very much contradicts that fact."

"Uhhh… I'm pretty sure I'm not a Range Style Archer. I mean I did only turn into an Archer Class last week." But the question floated in my mind, *"Am I already a Ranged Style Archer? I don't think so? Shouldn't the System have told me if I learnt a Style? Or maybe it'll even change my Class to tell me?"* though I was clueless to the answer.

"That cannot be right. Have you been lying to me, my Lord?" Odelia questioned, seeking the truth.

"In this particular case, no," I told her truthfully.

"Hmmm… just how old are you then?" she wondered curiously. "At first I believed you were in your 20s or 30s, but you must be at least in your 60s if you learned and developed those Skills to that extent."

"Believe it or not, I think I'm the same age as Myeyl," I said, thinking, *"There's no way I could imagine being as old as 60."*

"That is unbelievable. And I think you might be telling the truth." She then looked at me closely. "Without knowing you and judging only on your Skills alone, I would have guessed you were a Range Style Archer training in Combat on the side, though the only thing I have not seen you do to confirm the fact is shoot a target from 500 meters away."

"500 meters?! That's almost impossible to shoot a target that far!" I exclaimed, remembering the old world's record was under 300m.

"Not for a Range Style Archer," Odelia stated, "that much is required."

"Are you saying I'll become a Range Style Archer if I can do that?"

"From what I have seen from you, I believe so. For one only truly needs the Fundamental Skills and the Required Feat to really be classified as a specific style archer," she informed me.

"If that's the case, why'd I hear it takes over 100 years to become a Trinity Archer? Couldn't it be done way before then?" I questioned.

Fables of J

"It may be a surprise to you, my Lord, but regular people are not as talented as you seem to be. And besides the struggles everyone faces with a particular style, ultimately combining and utilizing the three styles perfectly to succeed the Trinity Trials proves to be the most difficult for everyone who takes part, with failure resulting in many stagnating their growth for years to come."

"The Trinity Trials? Sounds interesting," I thought, excited at what they could be.

Odelia then mentioned, "Not even the so-called 'Noble geniuses' could accomplish such a feat, and they do not even compare to the progress you have already made, Lord Eyes."

"Would Myeyl's brother be one of those 'Noble geniuses'?"

"If you are referring to Thereyl, yes he would be considered one; along with Cyspar Baen'Mtor and Lualaf Helvi'Ett."

"No wonder they have so much power in the Guild, they're all from Noble Houses, but it does sound like they're pretty strong," I noted to myself.

"Though do not worry about being compared to them, Lord Eyes. You are clearly greater than them already," Odelia tried to assure me, "and if you were to learn your first style this year, you would be the first in history to accomplish such a feat at your age—not even the Great King Ven'Thyl accomplished that! He only learned his first style when he was in his 40s, or so the history books tell us."

I laughed in amusement, "Haha... When I heard that it took over 100 years to become a Trinity Archer, I actually got worried for a bit and thought it might take me a few years, but knowing I basically already have one style down, I'm even more confident that I can learn all the styles in a month."

"My oh my, confident, are we?" Odelia then looked to have gotten a great idea in her head, and asked "Do you think you can back your words up, Lord Eyes?"

"Definitely," I stated confidently, "but what are you talking about?"

"I challenge you to learn all three Archery Styles before month's end, or otherwise announce yourself to the city as the Heir to the Elves and rightful king of the kingdom during the Eve of the Five Heroes Festival!"

And like that, a new Quest suddenly popped up.

Quest

Odelia's Challenge:

Learn all 3 Archery Styles (Close-Combat Style, Magic-Wielding Style, and Long-Range Style) before the end of the current month.

Reward: ???

Failure: Be forced to announce yourself to the city of Ven'Thyl as the Heir to the Elves and rightful king of the kingdom during the Eve of the Five Heroes Festival.

Time Limit: Until the end of the month.

Will you accept:

Choosing 'No' will lead to an automatic Failure.

[Yes] or [No]

Chapter 61
Material Promises

"What the hell is this? This can't be a regular quest, right? It's so tailored to me." Then I remembered the messages the System gave me in Dayla's office.

> **Unexpected outcomes have been detected.**

> **Analyzing unexpected outcomes and all previous outcomes...**

> **Creating all new alternative outcomes for the future...**

"Is this one of those alternative outcomes?" I wondered, reading the Quest again. *"But why is it another quest that basically gives me no choice? I mean if I say no, I'll just be forced to expose myself to the city. And why is the Time Limit so vague? How am I supposed to know when the month ends? It could be tomorrow for all I know? This quest feels like it's so unfairly stacked against me that I might even think the System is trying to force me to be king too."*

"What do you say, Lord Eyes, do you accept my challenge?" Odelia eagerly waited for my answer.

"I don't know, could you tell me when the month ends first? Or how about when it started?" I replied, already knowing I had to accept.

"If you know, you might not accept," Odelia smirked, mischievously.

"Oh great, that means it's already close to ending."

I then asked, "Could you at least tell me what I get for completing your challenge?" really wanting to know the Reward for the Quest at least.

Odelia put her finger on her lip and thought about it, "Hmmmm… How about my bow?" And then the Quest Reward changed.

> **Reward: Odelia's Pride**

"Tempting, but useless until I reach Lv.70, and I doubt I could reach that anytime soon," I reasoned, rejecting the offer.

"Okay, okay, then how about my sword?" Odelia suggested, changing the Quest Reward again, "It is a lower level than my bow, and I know its creator would be honoured for you to wield it."

> **Reward: Twilight Blade**

"Looks like I can negotiate the reward before I accept the quest, but I wonder if I can do it after accepting too?"

Rejecting the offer once again, I said, "From what I remember, it's around the Lv.60s, and that would make it have the same problem as the bow, so I don't want it either."

"Then I am out of ideas, Lord Eyes. I do not have much left to offer you that the house will not already be willing to offer you freely." Odelia looked slightly sad and disappointed that I rejected all her rewards.

Feeling sorry, I said, "Okay, how about this… if I complete your challenge, I want you to find me either a unicorn horn, a dragon heart, or a phoenix feather."

"Lord Eyes, I know those are the materials Drune asked you to collect for your armour, but those materials are Legendary in rarity and nearly impossible to find," Odelia tried to reason.

Fables of J

"Well let me ask you this, Odelia," smiling, I asked, "what's harder to find; an heir to the elves, or a unicorn horn?" I continued before Odelia could answer. "How about a dragon heart or a phoenix feather compared to a person who's confident enough to take up your clearly unfair challenge; which would be harder to find?" Odelia stayed silent. "What I'm trying to get at is that none of those materials are as rare as me, now are they? And don't you think doing something impossibly amazing like learning the 3 Archery Styles in under a month be rewarded as such?" Odelia then just stared at me in awe, "What? What's wrong? Why are you looking at me like that? Is it too much of a reward to ask for?"

Odelia gave me a gentle smile, and softly said, "I truly hope you fail my challenge, Lord Eyes. And I accept your terms."

With that, the Quest Reward changed one last time.

> **Reward: Odelia's promise to gift you whichever material she obtains first (Dragon Heart, Phoenix Feather, or Unicorn Horn)**

"I don't know what's going on in her head, but I'm glad she accepted," I thought. Finally accepting the Quest, I said to Odelia, "Hey, I'm sure I only have a week or two at best, so you better not teach me wrong just so that I fail your challenge, alright?"

"Though the idea did cross my mind, I would never hinder your potential to become a Trinity Archer, my lord," she assured me, making me believe her words. "And besides, you somehow succeeding in learning the three styles by month's end would not only greatly boost your status and respect around the city, but it may also in a sense confirm your legitimacy to the throne."

Before I could respond to that, she declared, "So you have my word, I promise I will only ever teach you with my absolute best efforts, Lord Eyes."

Truly believing her, I excitedly said, "Then let's get started!"

"If that is your wish my Lord, then let us start. Now, did you decide on which style you wish to learn first?" she asked.

"I was thinking of magic, but seeing how I'm almost done with range, maybe I should just finish it first? What do you think?" asking for her opinion.

"If you wish to try the 500m shot, we will have to leave for an area outside of the city, my lord," she informed me. "It is a place where traditionally most people practice the shot, as there is a cleared out section of trees there, and shooting inside the city has caused people to be arrested for some… unfortunate accidents."

"It does sound pretty dangerous to shoot an arrow that far away, but I've been wondering if I could use a Skill to help me with it?"

"You may. However, if you do not accomplish the feat with your own ability, you may never be able to learn such a valuable Skill as Sniper Shot."

"Interesting…" Then a thought popped up in my head. *"I thought it was weird that I haven't learned any new Skills since I turned Lv.20, but maybe I just have to learn them on my own from now on?"* Noting to myself, *"I'll remember to ask the Party if they learned any new Skills when they leveled past 20, it could just be me that hasn't."*

"So, do you intend to leave the city to try the shot, Lord Eyes?" Odelia asked. "We should still have two to three hours of daylight left if you want to go right now?"

"Nah, if that's all I need to do, I can save that for last," I decided, wanting to minimize the risk of encountering any assassins. "Oh, and I just remembered I still have one more Skill to show you."

"You have more to show?" Odelia looked surprised.

Drawing my bow again, I casted **Charged Arrow** and only put **50 Mana** into it—not wanting to damage the training room. Once the arrow fully charged, I shot it straight through an already damaged target dummy; but when it made impact with the walls of the chamber, it looked like the mana around the arrow was completely absorbed by the wall's runes, causing the ordinary arrow to ricochet onto the ground.

"What was that?" I asked out loud, wondering what kind of runes those were.

"I should be the one asking that, my Lord." Odelia had a look of disbelief on her face, telling me, "Only High Elves should be capable of manipulating their mana at such a young age to learn the Wield Mana Skill, yet how is it possible for you to have done so and even already learned Charged Arrow too?"

"Is that what the Skill to make arrows is called, Wield Mana?" I inquired, noting how useful that would be to learn.

"That is correct; having the control to wield your mana to your own will, as if it were a bow you held, or an arrow shot," she said, explaining, "It is one of the most difficult and advanced—yet fundamental Skills of the Magic Style. As well as the cause of many to fail ever fully mastering the style. But with it, anything you imagine can become real." Odelia then questioned, "Did your uncle somehow teach you that too? You even seemed to precisely control the mana infused into your Charged Arrow, which of course needs years of experience to properly control as you did."

"My uncle didn't teach me any of that, I just leveled up and learned the Charge Arrow Skill," I told her honestly. "I didn't even know you're supposed to learn Wield Mana Skill first. Is it weird that I still don't know it?"

"What?! That is even less possible!" Odelia exclaimed. "One should learn Wield Mana before using a Skill that uses it, should they not?"

I shrugged at her question, not knowing what to tell her.

"Well I am not even quite sure what I should be teaching you now. You truly keep breaking all of my expectations."

"Thanks, I think? But why don't we start with the Wield Mana Skill then? You told me it was too advanced before, but how about now?"

"Lord Eyes, with your seemingly insurmountable talent and potential, I doubt there is anything I could not proudly teach you." With a bright smile, Odelia began to teach me the Wield Mana Skill.

Spending the next two hours training, I first listened to Odelia explain the visual image I should have of my mana flowing inside of me; but after not being able to imagine it after a few minutes, I decided to cover one eye and secretly use the **Eye Of An Elder Cyclops**. When I did so, there was no longer a need to imagine, as I could now clearly see the general flow of the mana—and not just inside me or Odelia, but also the entire chamber.

Telling Odelia I already got the visual image down, she then moved on to demonstrating how to control the mana to your will, and I kept a keen eye on her mana and how it flowed through her body. Though when I tried to imitate what she did and what I saw, I failed, and failed, and failed again. With all my efforts, my mana would just not budge—unmoving and resisting my will. I wasted another half an hour failing to do anything, but Odelia continued to happily encourage me, so I continued to try and continued to fail.

Then suddenly after taking a short break, I got the brilliant idea of watching my mana while I casted Charged Arrow, and it was just what I needed. Seeing and feeling how exactly the mana should move within me gave me such a clarity on how to accomplish it. In a sense, mana was very much like the flow of blood; it pumped and travelled throughout the entire body, and I simply needed to find a way to raise the amount it pumped—like when using Charged Arrow—and draw it out of my hands. I tried a few different methods, but ultimately I figured out raising my heart rate worked the absolute best, causing the mana to rapidly flow throughout my body. I was about to attempt drawing it out, but a message suddenly appeared in my face.

> **Zebeyeyl Fre'Nddare has Requested permission to be a Guest at your 'House Ven'Thyl' Estate:**
> **[Accept] or [Decline]**

I turned to Odelia who was attentively observing me, and said, "I think we should stop for now. Zebeyeyl is here."

"He is? He must be waiting at the door then," Odelia made her way to the door on this floor and headed into a small corridor.

I followed her through and raised my hood again to hide the crown, thinking to myself, *"At least I made progress. Now all I need is a few more hours and I think I can learn it."*

We then arrived at a much nicer door than the one before—one with many locks and magic runes like the doors on the 4th floor entrance, but this had a single round window to see outside.

Fables of J

Seeing a hooded Zebeyeyl standing outside the window, Odelia spoke the Elven phrase she said the last time, "To fulfill a promise to a friend after his departure on their odyssey, in search to inform his eccentric and elusive loves." The door then magically unlocked and opened itself. "Good thing you came to this door, Zebey, I saw a lot of guards watching the Tops entrance."

"I know, I saw them too, that's why I headed for this one," Zebeyeyl replied. "Now can you get the one who controls the barrier? I still need permission to come in."

"No need, he's already here," Odelia gestured to me.

Zebeyeyl looked confused and stared at me, "Are you saying Eyes controls this barrier? Why?"

I answered for her and said, "I do control it, but why don't you come inside first." I accepted Zebeyeyl as a Guest and he walked straight in. Odelia quickly closed the door behind him and it magically locked itself again, she then led us back through the way we came but Zebeyeyl kept staring at me in confusion.

Stopping in the center of the chamber, Odelia said, "It's best we speak here, I don't want the others to know that I asked you here."

"Wait, I thought you asked me here so I could speak with the new Head of House Ven'Thyl? Why would we not go up?" Zebeyeyl questioned.

"I did ask you here for that reason." Odelia smiled and gestured to present me. "Here he is, the recently appointed Head of House Ven'Thyl, the presumably named Eyes Ven'Thyl."

"Presumably?" Zebeyeyl shook his head in disbelief and looked even more confused, "Is this some strange new ruse or joke, Odelia? Why'd you really bring me here?" he questioned, not believing her at all.

"This is no ruse or joke, Zebey. Lord Eyes is the new Head of House Ven'Thyl." Relaying to him, "Even Verana herself chose to loyally kneel and personally appoint him as her rightful successor."

Zebeyeyl read Odelia's dead-serious face, but he still couldn't comprehend the idea, saying, "None of that makes any sense. Why would someone as great as Lady Verana choose someone who hasn't even been to the city before? Surely you or Captain Aelthar would be better suited—even Shurtyrr would be, would he not?"

Odelia hesitated to speak, but said, "First I need you to swear that whatever you hear today will not leave this chamber."

"What? Sure, I swear I won't speak of what is spoken," Zebeyeyl promised, holding his right hand across his heart.

"No, Zel, I want you to swear on the Dreadful Oblivion," Odelia told him.

Zebeyeyl stared at her shocked, "Lia, are you being serious right now? There's no way this is something to swear on Father's bow for, is it?"

"Trust me, Zel, it is," Odelia seriously expressed.

Knowingly trusting her, Zebeyeyl nodded and said, "Fine. I swear on Father's Dreadful Oblivion bow that I will not speak of what is spoken here." He then demanded, "Now tell me."

Before she did, Odelia turned to me and asked, "Will you allow me to tell him, Eyes?"

Having already thought about it, I said, "For all I know, the disappearances of the other descendants could be very much related to the Noble Houses. Are you really sure we can trust the head of one with my secret, Odelia?"

"Truthfully my lord, our house has always been suspicious of the Noble Houses with the disappearance, but we have never found any evidence alluding to such.

"Lord?" Zebeyeyl repeated, wondering to himself.

Odelia continued speaking, "And though I do not trust the entirety of House Fre'Nddare—or any of the other Noble Houses for that matter; I can say that I have complete trust in Zebeyeyl, maybe even more than some members of our own house." She sounded genuine.

Shrugging at the idea, I put my trust in Odelia's decision, and said, "Go right ahead then, you have permission. Just keep it down while I'm focusing, will you?" She nodded and I left to the opposite side of the chamber to continue training.

Chapter 62
Reveals and Plans

"I said she could tell him, but he probably won't really believe her if I don't show him the crown I'm wearing," I thought to myself, hardly being able to focus while listening to their conversations.

"Lia, it's been over nine centuries since King Ven'Thyl disappeared, why must your house still believe in something that clearly doesn't exist?" Zebeyeyl questioned. "If only your house would stop with these delusions, it would still be considered equal to the Noble Houses."

"They're not delusions, Zel," Odelia refuted, sounding slightly irritated. "What we believe is actually true, and Lord Eyes is proof that it is."

"He should only see me as a normal person like everyone else, but it was a good thing I decided to put my hood up before he saw me." I slightly pulled the hood more over my face just in case.

"Not a single descendant in all those centuries has ever claimed the throne, or has even been found for that matter; why would one only just show up now?" Zebeyeyl argued.

"I don't claim to know their reasons, for it is their reasons to keep," she said, glancing over to me. "But I'm telling you, Zel, he is our future king," Odelia proudly stated with strong belief in her words—Zebeyeyl on the other hand continued to argue otherwise.

"With that Quest I got earlier and Odelia's words just now, it seems like she still believes I'll be king even though she already knows I'm not the rightful heir. Maybe it's just the crown's influence over her, but maybe she just doesn't believe we'll be able to find the other descendants," the thought brought real doubt about the difficulty of the Bloodline Quest for the first time.

After an hour of them loudly arguing with each other, and myself continually making tiny bits of progress while I listened, we then heard the echoing sound of Verana's bell ringing throughout the chamber. Momentarily stopping their dispute, Odelia said, "Dinner is ready."

"Then I better make my way home in time for my own dinner." Zebeyeyl then walked over to me say, "I don't know how you were able to convince House Ven'Thyl that you're a descendant and the heir, or how you convinced Lady Verana to name you her successor; but nevertheless, I'll concede to the fact that you're the new Head of House Ven'Thyl, and congratulate you on earning such a highly respected title."

"Thanks?" I said, unsure if I should be thankful.

"With that being said, you should know that the other Noble Houses will surely try to destroy and belittle your house's reputation further if and when they learn Lady Verana is no longer the head. Especially if they learn she's been succeeded by someone who is… to put it lightly, not her equal," Zebeyeyl warned, sounding reasonably sincere. Advising me, he added, "It may be best to use Odelia as a false head who can compare in power and ability, or perhaps Captain Aelthar who can compare in name and reputation—better yet, use Lady Verana herself as the false head."

Surprised by his genuinely good advice, I suspiciously asked, "What's in it for you? Won't House Fre'Nddare just do the same as the other Noble Houses?"

Zebeyeyl let out a little chuckle. "You can be assured I will never intentionally cause harm to your house." He gave a quick glance to Odelia who stood away watching us, and whispered in my ear, "Truthfully, I don't wish to be targeted by her fury."

"Odelia has fury?" I quietly replied curiously.

"Oh, you've no idea the hassle and turmoil she's put me through. She once even almost destroyed—"

"Zel, we are in the same chamber! Do you really think I can't hear you speaking ill of me behind my back?" Odelia angrily stomped over towards us.

Fables of J

Zebeyeyl covered his mouth and whispered extra quietly, "See what I mean," and then spoke normally again, "Well anyway, it was nice truly meeting you, Eyes Ven'Thyl. Or should I say, the new Head of House Ven'Thyl?"

"Likewise, Zebeyeyl Fre'Nddare," I replied back, "and I think I'm beginning to see why I hear people question your decisions."

He simply smiled and said, "My offer from before still stands, but I eagerly look forward to seeing your future within the city, Eyes."

When he turned around to head back to the entrance, I caught a faint glimpse of a small purple tendril sticking out at the nape of his neck, but it got quickly covered up when he put his hood back on.

"What was that?" I asked myself, closely observing Odelia lead Zebeyeyl out of the chamber—noting they spoke to each other normally, *"Strange, maybe I'm just seeing things?"*

Changing my attention, I looked up at the platform 50ft above me and wondered how exactly I wanted to reach it. There was always the simple choice of climbing the jutted out bricks on the walls, but I figured while I was here I should test out the extent of my mobility Skills.

First I tried using **Leap Shot** on the spot to see how high I could jump, but I was only able to get 30ft in the air. Next I tried combining **Sprint** and **Leap Shot** to get some extra speed, and it significantly increased the height I was able to jump—adding about 10ft to it. Luckily, as a surprising hidden effect of Leap Shot, I softly landed back on the ground, feeling absolutely no impact from a dangerous fall from that height. It was assuring to know I had a Skill that could seemingly negate fall damage, and knowing that fact let me confidently try some dangerous ways to reach the platform.

While I failed a few more times to reach the platform, Odelia finally returned and saw what I was doing, offering to just bring me up to the platform. Refusing the offer, I tried one more time and positioned myself slightly closer to the platform; using **Sprint** to get some speed, I followed it up with a **Leap Shot** right after—heading purposely into the chamber wall a bit away from the platform—then as soon as I made contact with the wall, I looked up above me and instantly used **Leap Shot** again, propelling me straight upwards.

In Range – Ven'Thyl Saga Part I

Rising above the height of the platform, I realized my wall jump angle was slightly off, and I was about to fall and miss the platform completely. Quickly reacting, I used **Archer's Dash** to close the distance and barely got a hand on the ledge of the platform. Then as I tried to pull myself up, Odelia suddenly came skyrocketing up over me and easily landed herself onto the platform, applauding my amusing effort. She gladly helped me up and we both decided to head up for dinner, and though my mobility testing didn't go according to plan, I was at least happy in learning different ways to use my Skills.

Walking up the floors, I asked Odelia something I thought Zebeyeyl said was strange, "Hey, Odelia. Zebeyeyl said you compare in power and ability to Verana, but that Aelthar compared in name and reputation. Does that mean you're stronger than Aelthar, and just as strong as Verana?"

"Ummm... contrary to his appearance, Ael is more tactically brilliant than he is strong, if you would believe it."

I couldn't believe it, but Odelia seemed to be telling the truth. "Many of the guards even call him the Untouchable Wind, as not even the other guard captains can land a clean strike on him during their monthly open-challenge duels."

"Where'd he get all those scars he had then?" I asked, remembering he had quite a few of them.

Odelia strangely hesitated to answer, but said, "Let's just say a few of them were from me, the others..."

Noting her strange reluctance to say, I changed the topic, "I get you're stronger than Aelthar, but how does Verana compare to the two of you?"

Snapping back to her senses, Odelia said, "Verana? She is in a whole other realm. Ael and I do not even come close to the power she can call upon."

"Huh? From what I saw you're both below her Level, but the gap in power can't be that big, can it?" I remembered that Odelia was Lv.85, Aelthar was Lv.87, and Veretha was Lv.99 after swearing loyalty to me.

Fables of J

"How would you know our Levels?" Odelia gave me a questioning look.

"Uhh... secret?" I smiled, nervously.

"You seem to have a lot of those, Lord Eyes," Odelia said, curiously looking at me. She then continued, "Anyway, Levels are not the only thing that determines one's strength and power, as the Skills they develop and grow play a big factor in that matter—not to mention the basis for it all: their Class. Zebey only compared me to Verana because the true potential of a Trinity Archer rivals—and in some ways is greater than Verana's Astral-Body Mystic Class."

"An Astral-Body Mystic?" I repeated. "Never heard of it."

"Not many have, as Verana is only the second person in the entire history of the world to have ever obtained the Legendary Healer Class, rightfully inheriting her the title of Star Caller," she said. "But do not be mistaken by its name, an Astral-Body Mystic is no simple healer, for it even surpasses my own current abilities."

"That's some praise, but if Verana is only the second person to have the Class, who was the first?" I questioned while continuing up the stairs.

"Well, that would be the one who made it Legendary in the first place," but Odelia sighed when she saw I had no clue who that was, and said, "The person of which was of course the Great Queen Sya, the Caller of the Stars."

When we arrived back onto the 4th floor, we entered the dining room and were greeted by a feast of all sorts of delicious looking food; and patiently waiting for us around the table was Verana, Aelthar, and Amariina.

"You know you guys don't have to wait for me, right?" I said, sitting myself at the head of the table.

"We know, Lord Eyes, but we want to," Verana said, already generously placing food onto my plate.

"But it looks like we're missing someone, where's Shurtyrr?" I asked, though the moment I mentioned his name, Amariina showed an upset expression on her face.

The others noticed too, and Aelthar said, "I-I heard there was trouble in the market today, so maybe he is just busy with that? Yes, that is probably it, and it must have been more trouble than I first thought."

Aelthar was clearly trying to cover for Shurtyrr, but to my right I noticed a slight grin on Odelia's face, and then I remembered part of their conversation that I couldn't help overhearing in the library yesterday.

"Here's the final part of the plan. Avoid Ama at all costs, up until the day of the wedding," Odelia instructed Shurtyrr. "That means no more waiting for her in the library, and if you just so happen to cross paths, ignore her existence and walk the other way."

"What! No way! That's not a plan!" Shurtyrr exclaimed, refusing the idea. "How is that in any way going to help me convince her to stop her engagement and not get married?"

"Shur, just trust me. Ama will definitely acknowledge her feelings for you after she realizes exactly how much she enjoyed seeing you show your love to her everyday for the last 75 years; and not to mention when she realizes just how much she's been taking it for granted when you do not."

Shurtyrr let out a big sigh, "Fine, I'll do what you say. But if this doesn't work, I'm quitting the house!" reluctantly agreeing to Odelia's plan.

"Oh, don't be so dramatic, you worry too much. It'll definitely work... probably," Odelia kind of assured him.

"Hmmm..." Shurtyrr irritably hummed as the sudden dinner bell interrupted him.

"Well I don't know if their plan is working, but she's definitely upset about something," as we all watched Amariina aggressively stabbed the food she ate with her utensils. I then thought, *"I wonder if I'm invited to the wedding? I've never been to one, but I'd love to see if their plan works or not. Maybe I'll even get to see them cause a scene there?"* I ate my food while thinking of the chaos that could happen at the wedding.

Fables of J

***

In the Noble Council Room…

Zebeyeyl easily pushed open the two giant doors leading into a tall, brightly lit chamber and walked right through. In the center, was a triangle shaped marble table with two figures sitting there, waiting for him. Finding his way to the last empty seat, he demanded to know, "Why was there another emergency meeting called today? Did something else happen?"

"Depends. Can you inform us what you were doing in House Ven'Thyl?" an old Dark Elf man asked.

Zebeyeyl smiled and said, "I was simply visiting my old friend Odelia, why—"

A purple magic unknowingly struck him, halting his speech and movement, and putting him in a general state of stasis.

"Why do you even bother, Lord Baen'Mtor?" an old High Elf woman questioned. "You know as well as I, simply controlling his mind is far easier to know what we want."

The man sighed, "I know, you're right, Lady Helvi'Ett. But I guess a part of me just wishes House Fre'Nddare would finally return to being on the Noble House's side again."

The women sighed also, "I wish for that too, but it would seem Lord Fre'Nddare is going to continue following his father's footsteps in opposing us." She then began to smile. "Though at least now we can control Lord Fre'Nddare, unlike his father before him."

"Well his father was one of our Kingdom's Heroes in the Second Trinity War after all," the man stated.

"That's ancient history now, Lord Baen'Mtor. You should look more into the future; our houses' future—one where they're finally united together and ruling the kingdom."

"Are you sure announcing the engagement on the Eve of the Five Heroes Festival is a good idea? We haven't even informed our grandchildren of the arranged marriage yet, and you know how much trouble those two can be."

"We're too close to accomplishing our goals to consider the grandchildren's feelings about the marriage, but if it comes to it, a little bit of persuasion always does the trick." A purple magic swirled around her finger tips and floated right into the back of Zebeyeyl's head. "Now tell us, Lord Fre'Nddare. What really occurred in House Ven'Thyl?"

Chapter 63
Whereabouts Part 3

A NOTE FROM FABLES OF J
This Chapter and the next 2 are on the longer side.

Knocking on the door, Odelia loudly asked, "Lord Eyes, are you awake yet? May I come in?" After not getting an answer after a few moments, Odelia knocked again and entered the room. "Pardon the intrusion, Lord Eyes, but you asked me to wake you up early for… training."

When she entered the room, she found that it was completely empty. *"Did I get the room wrong?"* Odelia questioned herself, quickly searching the other rooms on the 1st floor. *"Could he have already gone down to train?"* She headed back down herself after not finding Eyes anywhere on the 1st floor.

Seeing Verana already cooking breakfast in the kitchen, Odelia said, "Good morning, Verana. You wouldn't have happened to see Lord Eyes this morning, would you?"

"Good morning to you too, Odelia," Verana greeted her back, "and no I haven't; though shouldn't he be in a room on the 1st floor?"

"I thought so too, but I couldn't find him in any of the rooms," Odelia relayed, slightly worried as it was already the third time Eyes had disappeared on her.

"I see…" Verana then recalled, "Well, he did come back downstairs after you showed him where he could rest last night—he offered to help me with the dishes. I tried my best to refuse, but he insisted on thanking me somehow for all the delicious food the last few days." She smiled at the fond memory and told Odelia, "What an honour it'll be to serve such a humbly benevolent king in the future."

"I agree, but after he helped you with the dishes, did he go back upstairs?" Odelia inquired.

"No, no he didn't," she said, remembering, "He actually said he would train for a few more hours and then head back up after he was tired."

"If you didn't see him this morning, he must've fallen asleep in the Training Chamber," Odelia figured.

"Lord Eyes must be already pushing himself too hard." Verana sighed at the thought. "I know you said it was for him to announce himself as the heir, but why challenge him to accomplish such an impossible task?"

Odelia grinned mischievously. "The kingdom knowing of Lord Eyes' existence, or Lord Eyes taking an impossible leap closer to becoming a Trinity Archer—it's a win-win for our house and the kingdom either way, is it not?"

"In a sense. But still, don't you think it's a little too impossible of a challenge? Unfair to Lord Eyes perhaps?" she said, reminding Odelia, "Even Aelthar and Amariina agreed when they heard the challenge last night."

"Hmph!" Odelia scoffed, telling Verana, "I don't believe Lord Eyes would agree with that statement, as I truly believe he thinks he can accomplish it. And with the incredible progress I've seen he's already made, I might've been inclined to actually believe him if he had more than two weeks until month's end."

"I just hope Lord Eyes doesn't get too discouraged when he fails at the end of the month," Verana stated, finishing preparing a tray of breakfast for Eyes. "Anyway, from your experience, how long will it really take our lord to become a Trinity Archer?"

"To be completely honest, Verana, I do not know," Odelia told her honestly. "Lord Eyes is already skies above anyone I've taught or experienced before—greater than Zebey and I, greater than Master, and possibly even greater than the Great King Ven'Thyl himself."

Verana was stunned in disbelief after hearing such high praise from Odelia, but that disbelief quickly turned into delight—a delight that Eyes would be an impossibly great king someday. She then handed the

Fables of J

tray full of breakfast to Odelia and went back to cooking for the rest of the house with an even brighter mood on her face.

When Odelia finally arrived at the door leading to the Training Chamber, she suddenly heard a loud yell coming from the other side and quickly opened to find out what happened.

***

> **You have learned the Proficiency: [Wield Mana]**

> **Wield Mana: Physically drawing out and manipulating your Mana, you form and wield it to your own will. Cost is the amount of Mana drawn out. Damage based on Magic and Skill Level, and Manipulation Control based on Intelligence and Sense.**

"Yeahhhhh!" I yelled out, heavily panting and falling to the ground from the exhaustion. "Fuck...that was way harder than I thought it was going to be… How long did that take me?" I watched my **Mana** slowly recover from **0** as I heard the door on the platform unexpectedly slam wide open.

I reactively reverted my **Eye Of An Elder Cyclops** and saw Odelia rushing through the door. "Are you alright, Lord Eyes! What was that yell!" Oddly, she carried a tray of food in her hands.

"Wait, is that breakfast? Does that mean it took me all night to learn one Skill? Oh, that doesn't sit well with me at all. If I assume the end of the month at the earliest is a week away, I need to really pick up the pace if I'm going to complete the Quest in time." I then shouted to Odelia, "Everything's fine! But I'm so ready to move on!"

Odelia looked surprised as I watched her create a rope made of mana—attached to the platform—and used it to carefully slide down to the ground. "I never took you for a quitter, my lord, but you cannot just give up after not even a single full day of training yet." She completely misunderstood what I meant while she placed the food onto a small table she quickly manifested with her mana.

"No, I'm not a quitter. What I meant was—"

"Good! And I know you confidently said you understood what I explained and showed you yesterday, but you should know it is hard for everyone to grasp the idea of a new Skill on their first day; especially one as advanced as Wield Mana."

I tried to clear up the misunderstanding, but Odelia continued lecturing me. "Wield Mana takes years of learning to feel and control the rough flow of mana within one's self, as one cannot see or imagine it perfectly in the beginning. But do not be discouraged, my lord, keep trying and I am sure you will make great progress someday."

After she finished talking, I bursted out into laughter.

"What? What is so funny?" Odelia asked.

I settled down but couldn't help smugly grinning at her. "You hurt me, Odelia. How could you ever underestimate me like that? But if there's one thing you should learn about me, it's that when it comes to archery, there's nothing I can't do."

Imagining the image of a simple short bow, I could feel the little bit of mana I recovered slowly begin to move through my body and into my left hand; and drawing it out, that very image of a simple short bow began to form exactly fitting into my hand.

"I don't know about you, but I think I'm more than ready to move on to the next Skill." My **Mana** drained back to **0** and caused the short bow to dissipate into nothing.

"Th-That... is impossible..." Odelia was left almost speechless.

"Well, I only just learned it before you got here, so it was actually pretty hard, but I wouldn't say impossible," I said, thinking, *"Although I would've failed again if I didn't make that sudden breakthrough an hour ago."*

"But... but... how can that be?" Odelia questioned, still in shock.

"I don't know, a whole lot of hard work?" I shrugged off her shock, "But it does seem like it took me all night if that makes it any better?" I picked up and ate a slice of a delicious purple fruit from the breakfast tray.

Fables of J

"It does not, my lord." While Odelia tried to come to terms with the possibility, I hungrily ate my breakfast and checked up in the Top 10 Chat.

Top 10

Lavie
Does anyone know where Dream is? She hasn't replied to any of the messages I sent her.

Xian
I think I heard other Players somewhere say she's pretty young, so are you sure she's not just avoiding you because you're being overbearing or overprotective?

Lavi
First of all, Dream loves me; and second, we were supposed to meet up today before I left for the Dwarven Kingdom to complete a new Quest I got, but she just never showed up.

Tobias
Strange, the boy wanted to meet up with me earlier too, but he also never showed up to our meeting place.

Lavie
Is Faust missing too?

Tobias
So it would seem.

Xian
Didn't you all go to the same city together? What if the two of them are just spending time with each other?

In Range – Ven'Thyl Saga Part I

> **Tobias**
> Doubt it.
>
> **Lavie**
> He means they got into a little fight before we got here, which in turn made us arrive in the city separately, and I don't think they've made contact with each other ever since.
>
> **Xian**
> Well I know I'm the only other person who left Asheton so far, and since I don't know, I think it's safe to assume the others wouldn't know either.
>
> **Tobias**
> I honestly couldn't care less, and after seeing what they can do by themselves, I'm more than sure they'll be fine wherever they are.
>
> **Lavie**
> You're probably right, but I can't help but worry.
> Oh, and if anyone else is reading this and you know where they are, send me a message

"Aww, man. How could they let our Party fall apart like that? And why are they both missing?" I then moved on to yesterday's most recent messages.

> **Essex**
> Hey, here's a little warning. I think there's something going on with the monsters and animals outside of Asheton.
>
> **Casino**
> What do you mean?

Fables of J

> **Essex**
> My friend and I are travelling somewhere far away, but we recently came across a monster called a Zombie Deer.
>
> **Da Vinci**
> (O.O) ?
>
> **Casino**
> Like a literal zombie?
>
> **Essex**
> That's what it was called, and apparently they're the real kind. You know, the ones that eat brains, goes around infecting people, and causing zombie apocalypses.
>
> **Da Vinci**
> (•_•)
>
> **Casino**
> I can't tell if you're joking or not.
>
> **Essex**
> No, I'm being completely serious. My friend and I even incinerated it to limit the chance of scavenger animals getting infected, but he said that if a deer was turned, it's very likely other animals and monsters are also infected in the area.

"Uh oh, that's not because of me, is it? I'm pretty sure all the ones I killed should be behind my barrier, right Goblex?" I wondered if Goblex actually disposed of all the bodies properly.

> **Omega**
> You got me interested, where do I find them?

Casino
Well, look who came to talk.

Essex
I wouldn't go out looking for them without knowing a sure way to cure yourself, Omega.

Omega
I can handle myself.

Essex
It'll be Asheton's problem anyway, so I guess I don't care. We saw it Northeast of town, but my friend tells me animals in the area tend to travel clockwise around the forest.

Omega
Got it, thanks.

Casino
Just hold on a minute, what am I gonna with my plans for Asheton then?

Essex
Sounds like a 'you' problem.

Casino
Wait, at least tell me how to deal with them? Or better yet, about this cure you know of?

Essex
They're zombies, don't overthink it. Plus I'm sure they won't be much of an issue with our abilities, don't you think?

Fables of J

> **Essex**
> Oh and about a cure...
> Good News: My friend thinks he knows exactly how to make one, and I can definitely make sure it turns out correctly (we even have a sample of the zombie virus we took for research purposes).
>
> **Da Vinci**
> \(^.^)/ !
>
> **Casino**
> Great! Whip some up and I'll make sure to pay you accordingly.
>
> **Essex**
> Bad News: Besides that fact that we're long gone from Asheton now, my friend just thought of quite the interesting experiment to help me complete my current Quest, and I'm feeling very much inclined to help him with such.
>
> **Da Vinci**
> (X_x)
>
> **Casino**
> If y'all already far away, I guess I'll just have to take my chances here.
>
> **Essex**
> Yup, and good luck!

"I'm not sure how many Healer Class Players actually have the Cleanse Skill, but I know it'll be a problem if a bunch of Players get infected and bring the virus into Asheton without a cure," I thought. "I really don't want that to happen. There's good people there."

In Range – Ven'Thyl Saga Part I

Deciding to prepare some countermeasures, I first tried contacting Mako, but after she didn't reply, I figured she was busy and left her a warning and some instructions. Then knowing Global had the biggest voice and influence in her World Chat, I contacted her next and informed her on the potential situation.

> **Global**
> See how that could be a problem?
>
> **Global**
> I get it, but when I want something from you, you ghost me; and when you want something from me, I'm just supposed to say 'Yes, what is it, Eyes'?
> You know that's not how that works.
>
> Yeah, yeah. What do you want then?
>
> **Global**
> Answers to some gnawing questions I have.
>
> You get 3.
>
> **Global**
> Deal!
> What did you do the night of the Goblin Attack to have leveled up so high?
>
> I became the First Giant Slayer. Next.
>
> **Global**
> Hey, no vague answer or I'm not helping!
>
> Fine.
> I asked the Guild for a hard Request, and they sent me out to go scout a Giant Monster in the forest heading towards Asheton. Then the next thing I know, I found myself giving the Giant a funeral pyre.

Fables of J

> Global
> Sounds like there's more to that, but I'll leave it alone for now. Now next question:
> How'd you change your name, and what's the relation with the Elven Capital?
>
> For trying to make me answer two questions in one, all you get is a simple answer.
> Just go find a way to join a House, Family, or Clan in the Kingdoms.
>
> Global
> That was fair, but let me think about my last question carefully.

"What a pain. Why does she have to be so information hungry? But maybe I should start lying to her?" Though I quickly squashed the idea, *"Nah, knowing the type of person she is, she'd probably find out somehow and end up being an unavoidable problem in the future, and that doesn't sound like something I wanna deal with."*

> Global
> Okay, I've decided.
>
> And?
>
> Global
> I contemplated on whether I should get more info for the Players about you owning a whole mountain range and barrier that protects it, or about my personal interest on that incredibly strong NPC(Odelia) who seems to care a lot about your wellbeing; but I think I'd rather start from the very beginning.
>
> What?

In Range – Ven'Thyl Saga Part I

> **Global**
> There's something that's been bothering me ever since the end of the Tutorial. When we were shown the Tutorial Rankings, it specifically showed us the Top 10 first, but when the Administrator gave out the Awards, he stopped at the Top 100. Now I thought that was very strange, I mean why stop at 100, why not award the Top 10 and 1st Place too, right?
> I thought nothing of it at first, simply dismissing it as their design choice; but after I heard a rumour about Dream (the only known person appearance wise from the Tutorial Top 10) fighting together with a pink cat monster, it really made me think. Shortly after, I heard the other strange rumours of unknown Players with unique abilities that not a single other Player had, and like a truck it suddenly hit me. The Top 10 did get awarded, but that fact was completely hidden from the other Players.

"She's too smart and too curious for her own good, but I guess it was only a matter of time until someone found out," I thought to myself before responding to her.

> Stop monologuing and ask your question already.
>
> **Global**
> Sorry, it's a bit of a habit of mine.
> Now tell me, what exactly did the Tutorial Top 10 get as their Awards?
>
> > I'll give it to you, Global, you're a smart one. But let me ask you this, are you sure you really want to know? If I tell you the truth and the others find out, some of them could come after you, and I know for a fact 3 of them are already on the Player Killer Rankings.

Fables of J

> **Global**
> Being an info broker in both worlds is not easy, and I more than know the dangers that come with the trade; how do you think I ended up here?
> So yes I am sure I want to know, now answer my question.
>
> Alright, if that's what you want to know.

I then revealed to Global that the Top 10 in the Tutorial were actually all awarded before we arrived in the Waiting Hub, and that we were all presented with a completely Unique Subclass to choose from.

> I can't speak for everyone else, considering I placed last and was only left with one option to choose from, but just so that you don't bug me in the future, my Subclass is a Seer.
> Make of that as you will.
>
> **Global**
> Fascinating! Knowing that alone is causing my brain to explode with so many other questions, not to mention there are 9 other Unique Subclasses that give out abilities.
>
> Okay, it's my turn now.
>
> **Global**
> Oh right, yes. What do you want me to do?)

***

Somewhere in a corridor full of cages underneath the capital city of Leon…

"So, what do you think? She'll go for a lot, right?" a scarred man hoped, expecting to get a lot for a young Elven girl.

In Range – Ven'Thyl Saga Part I

"Looks like you roughed her up a bit, but nothing a little healing won't fix," a clean-shaven man noted, writing something down in his ledger.

"Yeah, she put up a pretty good fight, but after I took down her strange pink pet, she was much easier to deal with," the scarred man proudly stated.

"A pink pet?" the clean-shaven man questioned with interest.

"Yeah, I wanted to capture it too, but it suddenly disappeared. So I think it was actually just some type of summoned familiar," the scarred man figured.

"Oh well, but back to the girl." The clean-shaven man opened the cage door and entered where an unconscious, dirtied, bruised, and chained up Dream lay. "Now that I'm getting a closer look at her, she's really young. Good catch!" The scarred man smiled after hearing a good start to the appraisal.

"I'm not sure about the three tattoos I see, as most buyers tend to avoid already damaged or marked merchandise, but other than that, I think she'll be at least a B-grade slave," the clean-shaven man estimated, writing that down in his ledger. "Now, why don't we see what else she's hiding under those clothes..." Though just before the clean-shaven man could even lay a finger on Dream, a sudden bolt of lightning struck him right in the back and caused him to scream out in pain, "Gaahhhh...!"

The scarred man immediately drew his blades. "Who's there?!" But when he turned around, there was no one there.

"Hey, you fucking slave trading pieces of shit! Over here!" The voice came from the cage right across Dream's.

"What the hell? Did someone bring in a Mage without locking them up with Mage Shackles?" the scarred man questioned, dodging another sudden bolt of lightning from the opposite cage.

"Maybe you fucking slave traders are all just dumbass pieces of shit!" Another bolt of lightning was sent flying out of the cage.

Recovering from the bolt of lightning, the clean-shaven man angrily came stomping to the other locked up slave. "If you were smart, boy, you would've kept being a Mage secret! You might've even found a way to eventually escape, but now—gaahhhh...!" he screamed again, as a point-blank bolt of lightning struck him through the bars of the cage.

Faust loudly laughed, "Hahaha...! Like I said, dumbass pieces of shit! You want some too, ugly?" The two men then nodded to each other and backed away from the cage. "Awww, that's it? The big bad slave traders already had enough?" They didn't respond and instead just left elsewhere. However after a few moments passed, Faust suddenly heard many voices and footsteps, and turning the corner of the corridor was about 20 armed men angrily approaching his cage.

"Oh, shit! Maybe I provoked them too much!" Faust thought to himself, seeing all the men ready to beat him inside his cage. *"These pieces of shit are lucky I came here for a reason and can't kill them just yet. And I don't know how Dream ended up here too, but at least I got all their attention off her."*

Faust then proceeded to willingly accept their ruthless beating of him—bringing him to the brink of death. Then they restrained him with new Mage Shackles, and left him to rot until later beatings.

Chapter 64
Trinity Tattoo and Skill Creation

A NOTE FROM FABLES OF J
The Chapter ended up being too long, so I split it, and now it's a bit short.

Closing the Menu, I finished up the rest of my breakfast, and Odelia randomly asked, "May I see and touch your back, Lord Eyes?"

"What? My back? Why?" I asked, completely caught off guard by such an odd request.

"I feel that you are doing things that should be considered impossible at your age," she said, while already walking behind me. "Though seeing and touching your back will reveal the truth and answer all my questions."

"I mean I guess you can." I completely removed my cloak to show her my bare torso. "But I don't know what you think you'll find back there."

Odelia's slightly cold hands then touched my back and almost seemed to be searching for something.

"There… there is no trace of them." She removed her hands from my back and covered me back up with my cloak again. "They are not there at all, however feeling your skin does confirm your young age to me." Odelia walked back in front of me and this time looked carefully at my front torso—tapping her finger on her lip.

"Hey, could you at least tell me what you're looking for? What isn't there at all?" I inquired, wondering what she expected to find.

"I thought you may have been lying about your age and not knowing a style already, as well as hiding your tattoos with Invisibility

Fables of J

Magic; but there truly does not seem to be anything on your back or your front," Odelia replied, still tapping her finger on her lip.

"Tattoos? Why would I have those?"

"It is required after learning a style to be marked with a special tattoo on part of your body—traditionally on the back or the front, and usually given to you by the Trinity Archer who taught you," Odelia explained, "Yet I found no signs or the basic marks on your body whatsoever, which could only mean you truly do not know a Style."

"Well, I told you so—Wait, does that mean I have to get tattooed later!?" I exclaimed, feeling slightly anxious about getting a tattoo.

"Many have tried forgoing the Trinity Tattoo, but those who do have severely hindered or halted their ability in becoming a Trinity Archer entirely," Odelia warned me. "And in the best cases of making that terrible choice, one would still add 50-100 more years to their already long training. The Great King Ven'Thyl created the Trinity Tattoo for a reason; the technique and the magic imbued within each part of the tattoo will help suppress any already learned styles from overwhelming the ones unlearned, as well as eventually guiding one to combining the three styles in unison, and greatly enhancing one's progress in becoming a Trinity Archer."

"Adding 50+ years to training is a no go, so I guess I've got no choice. I just hope it doesn't hurt too much." I then brought up, "That means you should have them too, right Odelia?" She nodded yes. "Then can I see them?" I asked, curious about what they'd look like.

"Of course, my lord. Just give me a moment." Odelia, without hesitation, began unlacing and loosening her black leather chestpiece in front of me, and I immediately turned away to give her some privacy. When she was done, she said, "The overall design differs from person to person, depending on who created each part of the tattoo, but the overall structure is the same for everyone."

Slowly turning around, I saw Odelia facing away and holding her breasts, as she then moved her partly braided hair to the front and revealed her back to me.

Tattooed on Odelia's smooth grey skin was a full back tattoo made almost completely with white ink—making it visually prominent on her

In Range – Ven'Thyl Saga Part I

darker skin tone. Surprisingly, it moved and rotated in a circle on her back. *"Woah, I've never seen a tattoo move before, but man does it look cool,"* I thought to myself, looking at the fine details of the tattoo.

The tattoo was pretty simplistic in its design, consisting of three defined isosceles triangles—one blue, one green, one violet—and 3 layers of runic circles encircling them. Pointing outwards and connecting the other two points in the middle, the triangles were contained in an outer layer of runes, with another layer of runes at the halfway point of the triangles—though never overlapping onto them—and lastly an inner layer that circled the space in between. But sticking out like a sore thumb, a poorly drawn sword was directly in the center of it all.

"Mine and Zebey's Trinity Tattoos are quite basic in design compared to others," Odelia informed me, "for Master was very traditional and strict in his teaching, which of course included any additional personal designs we wanted. Though we were able to eventually convince him to allow us one; mine a sword, and Zebey's a bow." She pointed to where she thought it was.

"I don't want to sound rude by insulting my master's master, but have you ever thought your master was just a bad drawer? And maybe that's why he didn't want to add any personal designs?" I figured, not understanding how one could draw a simple sword so poorly.

Odelia let out a little chuckle. "Yes, Zebey and I came to that very same conclusion when we saw each other's sword and bow. So in hindsight, maybe it was a good thing Master only allowed one personal addition."

I nodded in agreement. "Oh, you can put your chestpiece back on by the way. I got a good look at it," I said, turning away again.

While she did so, Odelia said, "I hope learning that does not make you worry about your own eventual tattoo, my lord. I promise I am quite a decent artist, and give my students all the additional designs they wish. Which I thought might be in a few decades, but witnessing you accomplish something I thought was impossible, it may be much sooner than I could have ever expected."

Fables of J

"Should I think of a design to add to my tattoo? Or maybe I should stick with the basic one? I mean it didn't look half bad?" I contemplated the choice, but hearing Odelia turn back around, I thought, *"But that doesn't matter right now, I still got to focus and learn the three styles first,"* as I looked forward to learning more Skills.

My mornings were spent with Odelia teaching me the many other Skills in the Magic Style, though she explained to me that I only needed five out of ten for her to consider me a Magic Archer. Then when she left to go train Myeyl in the evenings, I spent the rest of the time secretly figuring out exactly how to learn all the Skills I was shown, as I would never willingly miss out on something related to archery. And knowing my own greedy obsession could cause me to fail the Quest, I made sure to utilize the same method I used to learn Wield Mana.

The Eye Of An Elder Cyclops allowed me to clearly see Mana and Magic, but that alone wasn't enough; what I needed was to see more. So using the Subclass Skill 'Seer's Eye Sacrifice'—a Skill I completely forgot about—I was able to sacrifice the abundance of goblin eyes I've collected to enhance the visual powers of the Eye Of An Elder Cyclops—one minute per eyeball. And what it gave me was complete visual clarity in how exactly the mana inside my body could be manipulated to achieve the results I wanted.

Dedicating the next few days solely on training and learning—only taking short breaks to eat or bathe—I returned back to my archery obsessed self, only capable of thinking of how to be a better archer and how to learn all archery techniques I could. My archery obsession was what always drove me to accomplishing something great, something impossible, and this time was no different. Time quickly passed by, and before I knew it, 3 days had already passed and I learned all 10 Skills Odelia taught me.

In Range – Ven'Thyl Saga Part I

> **Ensnaring Arrow:** Conjure two strands of Mana on the tip of an arrow, and ensnare the first target you hit. Cost 100 Mana. Ensnare and Strand Strength/Length based on Magic and Skill Level, Number of Strands increases by 2 per Skill Level.

> **Explosive Arrow:** Compacting Mana within the tip of an arrow, it immediately explodes on impact. Cost 150 Mana. Damage and Explosion Radius based on Magic and Skill Level.

Though after I learned the last Elemental-Type Skill, a new message appeared.

> **Skill Creation**
> Having learned all the possible Elements for an Elemental-Type Skill, you are given the choice to perfectly combine all the Skills into one and create a whole new Skill, or leave them as they are and develop them to your own desired preference.
>
> Will you create a new Skill:
>
> *Choosing 'Yes' will cause you to lose the following Skills: [Lv.1 Fire Arrow], [Lv.1 Ice Arrow], [Lv.1 Lightning Arrow], [Lv.1 Stone Arrow], [Lv.1 Wind Arrow], [Lv.1 Poison Arrow], [Lv.1 Light Arrow], [Lv.1 Dark Arrow].*
> [Yes] or [No]

"Oooh! I can create a new Skill!" The idea excited me, though I noted, "But if I leave them as they are, it says I can develop them to my preference—whatever that means." I heavily contemplated the two options for a few minutes, but I ultimately came to the conclusion that there must be a good reason the message popped up, and that leveling one Skill will be a whole lot easier than 8 of them—especially since I haven't even learned the other styles' Skills, or even fully leveled up the ones I already had.

> **Combining previous Skills...**

> **Creating new Skill...**

> **You have learned the Skill: [Element Arrow]**

> **Element Arrow:** Imbue an arrowhead with a chosen Element, and gain the partial Effects and Damage-Type it's associated with. Gain a bonus Elemental Damage equal to 5% of the Arrow and Weapon's Attack. Choose from: [Fire], [Ice], [Lightning], [Earth], [Wind], [Poison], [Light], and [Dark]. Cost 125 Mana. Damage based on Element, Magic, and Skill Level; Effects and Status Chance based on Intelligence and Skill Level, Bonus Elemental Damage increases by 5% per Skill Level.

Fire - Burning hot, ignites flammables, and has a slight chance of causing the 'Burning' Debuff.	Ice - Chillingly cold, sharpens arrows, and has a slight chance of causing the 'Freezing' Debuff.

Lightning - Shockingly erratic, strikes anything near, and has a slight chance of causing the 'Stunned' Debuff.	**Earth** - Solidly heavy, strengthens arrows, and increases penetration and impact.
Wind - Gaseously light, unaffected by wind, and increases speed and distance.	**Poison** - Venomously damaging, degrades Vitality, and has a slight chance of causing the 'Poisoned' Status Debuff.
Light - Blindingly bright, illuminates everything, and has a slight chance of causing the 'Blinded' Status Debuff.	**Dark** - Dreadfully gloomy, weakens Sense, and has a slight chance of causing the 'Hexed' Status Debuff.

"Huh, it really did just combine them. Now I wonder what the actual difference is…" But I was clueless, as I didn't even bother reading the Skills I forgot since I was too focused on only learning them as fast as possible. "Well I'm sure I'll find out later," I figured, deciding to head back up and rest for the night.

The next morning, Odelia expected to start our 4th day of training, but when I claimed I already learned 5 out of the 10 Skills I needed, she of course asked me to show her proof. Then to prove to her that I did, I decided to pick **Ensnaring Arrow**, **Explosive Arrow**, **Element Arrow (Fire), Element Arrow (Ice)**, and **Element Arrow (Lightning)**; and with the display of my already learned Skills, Odelia simply stared at me speechless.

Fables of J

"Good thing, I only decided to show her 5, or who knows how she'd react if she found out I learned all 10."

I asked, "That's all I needed, right? Five out of the ten fundamental Skills, and the Required Feat of learning Wield Mana?"

"Y-Yesss..." Odelia stuttered, still baffled.

"Then that's one style down, two more to go!" I cheered loudly, taking one step closer to becoming a Trinity Archer.

Chapter 65
Magic Archer and Complicated Love

A NOTE FROM FABLES OF J
This is also a bit of a short Chapter.

"Lord Eyes, in normal circumstances it would take a person 20 or more years to learn everything you have shown me so far—10-15 if one were a genius talent, or had great affinity for the style. So I simply cannot even begin to fathom and comprehend how you were able to learn all that in **only three days!**" Odelia paused to calm herself. "And to be honest my lord, I find your talent to be so overwhelmingly frightening that it makes me question my own talent and ability when I compare myself to you… and whether I should really be the one teaching you..." She sounded so disheartened.

Quickly thinking of a way to reassure her, I enthusiastically said, "What are you talking about, Odelia? You're the only one who could teach me! The only one who's qualified, and the only one I want!"

Odelia smiled slightly.

"Teaching and learning isn't done alone, now is it? I'm only learning as fast as I am because I have such an amazing teacher—or should I say master?"

Odelia's slight smile turned into a small giggle.

"Here's what I think; she's the best master in the entire city! No, the entire kingdom! Not that either. More like the best master in the whole entire world!"

And with that her small giggle turned into a happy laughter.

Fables of J

When her laughter calmed, Odelia said, "Thank you, Lord Eyes. I will always remember your encouraging words when I feel down on myself."

"Anytime... Master Odelia." I chuckled at the sound of calling her Master, then eagerly asked, "Now what's next?"

"Well as you are now equivalent to a new Magic Archer, I think it is unbelievably already time to create the foundation and first part of your Trinity Tattoo, my lord." When Odelia finished speaking, a large notification appeared out of nowhere.

> **2nd Class Promotion**
>
> **Meeting the required conditions to become a 'Magic Archer' Class, you are now eligible to obtain a 2nd Class Promotion before meeting the Required Level for the 2nd Class Choice, and will greatly benefit your next potential Class Progression Choice.**
>
> **Will you accept the 'Magic Archer' Class Promotion:**
>
> ***As you have not met the Required Level for the 2nd Class Choice, you will not gain the 2nd Promotion Stat increase until the Required Level is met.***
>
> **[Yes] or [No]**

"Wait, if I'm reading this right, doesn't this mean I just need to level up to get a Magic Archer as a Class Promotion? And won't some other people just get the same Class by also leveling to the 2nd Class Choice? Why am I working so hard for it then if I could just be doing some leveling instead?" I asked myself, starting to question my decisions. *"The next potential Class Progress Choice better make my effort worth it,"* I thought, clicking "Yes".

> **Congratulations, you have been promoted to a 'Magic Archer' Class!**

You have gained the Title: [A True Magic Archer]

You have learned the Skill: [Magical Arrows]	You have learned the Class Proficiency: [Magic-Wielding Archery]
Magic-Wielding Archery proficiency increased by 13 Levels	Magic Arrows increased by 1 Level

A True Magic Archer: Learning the Magic-Wielding Archery Style from someone who's already fully Mastered it, you obtained the power with your own ability and effort, and are acknowledged as a True Magic Archer. +33 Magic and Intelligence.

Magic Arrows: All the arrows you shoot are now magical, and deal an additional 5% of your Magic as bonus Magic Damage. Bonus Magic Damage increases by 5% per Skill Level, Skill level based on Magic-Wielding Archery Level.

Fables of J

> **Magic-Wielding Archery:** One of the Three Pinnacle Styles of Elven Archery; Magic-Wielding provides the Versatility, Concentration, and Imagination needed to become a Trinity Archer. Complete Mastery is required for combining the styles, but unbalanced Mastery will result in overwhelming the others and erasing their progress. Skill Level based on Skill Levels of the Magic-Wielding Style.

"The Skill and the Title bonus are great, but what is this Proficiency? Does it actually erase progress of the other styles?" I then recalled what Odelia said about the Trinity Tattoo. *"Ah, no wonder she said it would suppress the learned styles before, but if I already leveled the Skill up 13 Levels, I should probably get the Trinity Tattoo as soon as possible."*

Seeing Odelia patiently waiting for me to be done thinking, I said to her, "Sorry, I was in my head, Odelia. But what were you saying about my Trinity Tattoo? Am I getting it now?"

"No, I did not mean right now, my Lord." She chuckled at the misunderstanding. "In truth, I am completely unprepared. You clearly took me by surprise this morning; so I will ask you to give me a day to find, buy, and prepare the supplies and Magic Ink needed to create the tattoo."

"A day? Isn't there a way to speed that up? Or could you at least teach me another Skill from a different Style before you go?" I questioned, not wanting to waste my already limited time doing nothing.

"To answer your first question; no, no there is not," she said. "The materials and supplies will be difficult to find and obtain from the shopkeepers on such short notice, and the preparation for it all will take at least 3 hours to complete." Odelia then replied to my second question. "And about teaching you another styles' Skills… First of all, the other styles do not translate well from one another, so teaching one would not be much help, even with your amazing talent. And second, I think you need to take a day off, my lord. I heard for the last few days you have only taken short breaks to eat and bathe, and return straight back to training down here right after." She began lecturing me, "You should not push yourself too hard. You need rest. You need sleep. You need—"

"Okay, okay, stop. I get it. I'll take the day off, but only because I'm so confident I'll win anyway," I reluctantly agreed to her suggestion.

In agreement, we took the day off of training and left for the Roots to go get the supplies. Odelia let me know she was only going to buy enough for the foundation and first part of the tattoo, but I instead told her to buy enough to create the whole thing, and she finally opened up to the idea that I might actually be able to learn all three styles by month's end. Though while we shopped for the supplies, I realized they were quite rare to find, and that when we did track one down, Odelia had to haggle for an unreasonably long amount of time for the shopkeepers to even consider selling it to her.

Getting easily bored by the process, I used Shurtyrr as an excuse to leave Odelia on her own—having not seen him the last few days—and left to go find him in the Roots instead. Following Odelia's instructions on where exactly to find him, I found myself standing in front of a large, busy, purple restaurant with an unreadable Elven name—in the center of the Roots like Shurtyrr told me before. Strangely enough, Odelia didn't seem to be worried about me going to visit Shurtyrr in the black market alone, and that made me feel assured she thought I would be safe inside.

Confidently entering inside, I easily found the owner talking to a waiter and told him, "I wish to have a drink with the poisoned sapling."

He simply gave me a nod and led me down a flight of stairs in the back of the restaurant. When we reached the bottom, the owner unlocked the door and gestured for me to go inside as he went back up the stairs. Preparing myself for the horrors I could see in the black market, I slowly opened the door and went inside.

"Wow... I was expecting the black market, but this is just sad." All I saw was a drunkenly sleeping Shurtyrr laying on a table, spilling wine bottles in each hand, and ten already empty bottles surrounding him—with plenty more on the ground.

Fables of J

"Shurtyrr?" I called for him, but he just responded with a sleeping groan. Walking more inside the room, I realized it was simply a plain old restaurant cellar where they stored the food and drinks of the place. "Shurtyrr, you alright?" I poked him in the cheek while he mumbled something about Amariina. "I guess you are, but what was that about Amariina?"

As he continued to mumble to himself and I took a look around, a new Quest randomly popped up.

> **Quest**
>
> **Complicated Love:**
>
> **Shurtyrr has pleaded for your help in finding a way to resolve his love for Amariina; whether it be finally letting his seemingly hopeless love for her truly go, or her finally accepting his love unconditionally and wholeheartedly.**
>
> **Reward: ???**
>
> **Failure: Certain outcomes will result in Shurtyrr, Amariina, or both leaving House Ven'Thyl.**
>
> **Time Limit: 25 Days**
>
> **Will you accept:**
>
> *Choosing 'No' will lead to an automatic Failure.*
>
> **[Yes] or [No]**

"What the hell is this!?" I shouted to Shurtyrr, who just continued to drunkenly sleep. "Why is every Quest our house gives me basically an ultimatum? And why is this one so horrible? I mean how is both of you leaving the house even an option?"

Having no real choice I accepted the Quest.

"You should've at least asked me when you were awake and sober, Shurtyrr," I muttered, helping him up from the table and carrying him on my back. "Now I hope you know I'm gonna ask for a ridiculous reward when I finish this Quest, you hear me?"

Thinking of how I should bring Shurtyrr home, I said, "You better hope this works, 'cause I'm not coming back if it doesn't." I activated **Return Home** and thought, *House Ven'Thyl.*

Instantly teleporting back to the house library, I was pleasantly surprised to see Shurtyrr came back with me. "You're lucky, and you even helped me figure out I can at least bring one person with me."

Carrying Shurtyrr up to his room, I purposely caused a ruckus in front of Amariina's room when we passed it, and she came out wondering what it was.

"What's all the—Shur!" she exclaimed, unable to hide her concern. "Lord Eyes, what happened to him?" She touched his face to check if he's alright.

"Oh, it's nothing serious, he just drank himself to sleep." I couldn't help smiling as Amariina helped me carry Shurtyrr to his room. Then as I laid him on his bed, I told her, "But I think he might have a heart problem in a few weeks."

"A heart problem!? What? Why?" Amariina asked in concern, sitting herself down beside Shurtyrr to check his chest for any problems.

"You know why, Amariina." I stared directly at her. "Because the love of his life is going to get married to someone else."

"Oh…" Amariina reluctantly distanced herself from Shurtyrr, saying, "I'll go get Verana, she'll make sure he's alright. If you'll excuse me, my lord." She quickly tried to get away, but I stopped her.

"Wait. You're not excused," I said, making good use of my authority. "I'll go get Verana, you stay here and take care of Shurtyrr."

"But—"

She tried to object, but I stopped her again with a simple gesture for her to stay put. Before leaving them alone, I gave a quick glance back, and saw Amariina smiling warmly as she gently caressed Shurtyrr's sleeping face and moved his long messy hair out of the way.

Fables of J

Happy with that sight, I went to go find Verana, but she was already smiling and gesturing for me to follow her down the stairwell. When we passed the 8th floor, Verana finally said, "Nice work, my lord. Those children make love so unnecessarily complicated."

"I don't know why, they clearly love each other," I said, following Verana down to the 9th floor.

"They do, I just hope they finally figure it out—with a little help from our house, of course." Verana gave me a smile and a wink, and led me all the way down to the 10th floor treasury doors. "Odelia tells me you wish to enter, is that correct?"

"I do," I answered honestly.

"And as you should, for the new Head of the House needs to be recorded inside." Verana put both her hands on the stone doors, and all the magic runes began to move in unison, before promptly lighting up green and disappearing from the stone.

"That does it."

And with a little push, Verana completely opened both doors, and I was immediately blinded by the sheer shining brightness of everything inside.

"Now, after you, my lord."

Chapter 66
The House of Ven'Thyl Part 4 (House Treasury)

A NOTE FROM FABLES OF J

Thank you to all the longtime readers still reading, and though the next few new Chapters might still be similar to what you have already read, at least the story will now continue!

"Oww… oww.. .ouch!" I yelled out, laying flat on my stomach. "Can't you be a little bit more gentle, Odelia?" I asked, wincing in more pain.

"Please endure, my lord," Odelia asked politely, "and stop fidgeting so much, will you?"

"Oww…! Maybe I'm talking nonsense here, but isn't there a less painful and modern way of tattooing, Odelia? Oww…!" I squeezed my forearms to ease the pain.

"No? Unless there is a new method I do not know about?" She painfully made small cuts into my back with a needle. "Now hold still," she said as she then lightly, but painfully hammered the Magic Ink directly into the cuts.

"I'm just gonna throw out an idea here—ouch! Think about a magical tool that's made up of tiny needles that can inject the ink into the skin for you—maybe call it a tattoo… mechanism or something," I knowingly suggested.

"Well if one is invented, I will openly consider trying it," she said, continuing her traditional way of tattooing.

As I winced in pain again, the others tried to cover their amusement, and I said, "Actually, forget the idea, I'd rather know why everybody's here watching this! Don't you guys have anything else better to do?" I

Fables of J

asked, questioning Aelthar, Shurtyrr, and Amariina's unwanted attendance.

"Sorry Lord Eyes, Ael unwillingly dragged me here. I was not even aware of Odelia's challenge until this morning," Shurtyrr defended himself, completely sober now—as opposed to yesterday's drunkenness.

"Well, it is not everyday we get to witness history being made, my lord," Aelthar smiled, looking the most amused by my pain. "And do not believe what Shur said about being dragged here, he happily came with us after hearing what was happening."

"True," Amariina added, carefully observing Odelia's detailed craftsmanship, "and who wouldn't want to see your Trinity Tattoo being created, my lord? You are our Head of the House after all."

"Hmmm… can you at least not laugh and look so amused while you guys watch? This tattoo really hurts, you know?" They all agreed but I could still hear them giggling to themselves—even Odelia giggled a little.

"Do not mind them, Lord Eyes. They are just happy to witness such a momentous occasion," Verana said, entering the room and bringing me some soothing tea. "And I hope this will soothe you after your sudden collapse in the treasury yesterday."

"Thanks for the tea, Verana, and I told you I was fine. I was just… tired," I assured her and everyone else. "Now what I really need is something to distract me from the pain."

"Oh, if the pain is a problem, allow me to erase it for you." Verana placed her right hand on the top of my head and a strong white magic emitted from it; then before I knew it, all the pain completely disappeared and a message popped up.

> **You have been affected by the Status Buff: [Pain Nullification].**

"There; you will no longer feel pain for 24 hours, which is plenty of time for Odelia to finish everything she needs to do today," Verana stated, sitting down with the others and taking a sip of her own tea.

In Range – Ven'Thyl Saga Part I

"You're amazing, Verana!" I complimented her. "Thank you!"

"My pleasure, my Lord," Verana accepted my thanks.

Now that I felt no pain, only the sensation of something tapping my back, I relaxed and took a look at that buff.

> **Pain Nullification: Both a blessing and curse, your body will no longer feel pain whatsoever, giving you the opportunity to break through the physical limits of your body and feeling none of the painful consequences.**
>
> **Duration: 23 Hours, 59 Minutes, 38 Seconds**

"Interesting, that means even if I break an arm I wouldn't feel it, but if I get cut and start bleeding out, I also wouldn't feel it. That is a blessing and a curse."

Then, suddenly interrupting my thoughts, Amariina said, "By the way, Lord Eyes, you entered the treasury yesterday, right?" Aelthar and Shurtyrr also looked curious about it.

"I did. What of it?" I replied, curious why they were interested.

"Then, if we may ask, what was it like?" Amariina inquired eagerly, with Aelthar and Shurtyrr also eager to hear. "Verana never tells us what's inside, or even lets us see a glimpse of it."

I looked to Verana for permission to tell them, but she simply nodded a gesture that it's completely my choice to do so. Not really having an issue myself with revealing what's inside, I openly told them everything I saw inside the treasury yesterday.

A day before…

Before I even entered, I completely suppressed the effect of the Eyes Of Goblinkind, as even receiving the partial benefit blinded me from the bright shine of everything inside. However when I did enter first, I was still kind of blinded by the endless mountains of different coins, jewels, gemstones, and treasures piled up in the large, brightly lit square chamber. A chamber where everything was stacked so high that

Fables of J

the piles of treasures touched the ceiling, but which left three narrow paths to different arched doorways leading to other unknown chambers—one on the left, one on the right, and one straight ahead.

Entering after me, Verana said, "This is the coffer; it is where all the funding for the house is collected and stored, along with being the members' personal bank if they wish it to be."

"Th-this place is unbelievable!" I was in complete awe of the ridiculous amount of treasure in this one chamber. "H-how much is this all even worth? Can't be less than a million, right?" I asked, extremely curious about the potential amount.

"Hmmm... let me think," Verana said, actually thinking about an answer.

While she did so, I ran my hand through the nearest pile of coins and thought, *"Holy shit, they're loaded! I knew they'd have something good in here if they locked it up so tightly, but this is more like a dragon's hoard than a treasury—and this is only the first room!"*

Verana finished thinking and calculated, "If we get a decent price for the jewels, gemstones, and treasures; and convert any Platinum, Silver, and Copper to Gold; I estimate everything would total to around 250-275 million Gold."

It didn't hit me right away. "Umm, excuse me? What did you say?"

"Well if I am being honest, my lord; with Shurtyrr's connections to the black market, and my connections to certain people in the city, the real estimate would probably be nearing 300 million," Verana corrected herself.

"........." It took a second to process her words. "What?! 300 million?! 300 MILLION GOLD!?!"

"Yes, though you could also convert it to 3 million Platinum if you would prefer?" Verana suggested.

"Wait, wait, wait. Why the hell does the house have 300 million Gold sitting around here for?"

"I told you, my lord, we use it to fund the house."

"Huh? We use 300 million Gold to fund the house?" I reiterated, knowing that's very much not true.

"Well yes, at least a portion of it," Verana clarified. "We mostly use it to buy daily supplies or hire people to repair something in the house if needed, but when a promising lead about the descendants comes along, sometimes a little bribe works wonders in loosening lips."

"That's it? What about using it for other ways, or maybe personal reasons?"

"As you are now the Head of House Ven'Thyl, you may choose to use the house fund however you see fit." Verana kindly smiled, but added, "However, I would advise not using it for trivial personal reasons, for centuries of blood and sweat have been spent obtaining such an incredible fortune, and it would be so disappointing to see it all go to waste." Her voice became slightly stern towards me for the very first time.

"Damn it, she's trying to guilt me into not selfishly using it for myself, and it's kinda working." I then asked, "If it's a fortune collected for centuries, does that make our house the richest in the city?"

"I am not sure about the richest, though I would say we are up there with House Ar'Baste and the noble houses."

"House Ar'Baste? Never heard of them. Are they important or something?"

"Slightly. They do own all the banks in the city after all."

"Oooh, no wonder they're rich."

"But if you only found out about them now, then you must not know that Amariina is engaged to the eldest son of the house, right?" Verana revealed to me.

"Oh no…" I said, already thinking of ways that could be an issue.

"I see you already understand what that means."

"I do..." I sighed. "You think they'll cause trouble if we convince Amariina to break off the engagement or mess up their wedding?"

"Most certainly, my lord," Verana grinned, having already come to terms with that possibility. "Though the trouble might become more troublesome if we wait until the wedding, instead of privately dealing with the matter beforehand. The embarrassment House Ar'Baste would feel in front of the noble houses in attendance would definitely anger them more, especially when it relates to our house."

Fables of J

I sighed again, thinking, *"I hope convincing Amariina will be as easy as I think it is. I really don't want to deal with more trouble than I have to when it comes to this house stuff."*

Moving on to the rest of the treasury, Verana led me to the right chamber first, but when we entered I realized it was just a single curved hallway—simply called the armoury. As the name suggests, it was a place filled with countless pieces and sets of armour and weapons, easily accessible on stands and racks all along the walls. And while we continued to follow the curved hallway, I placed my hand on as many items as I could, and learned that almost everything here was unbelievably ranging from Lv 50-90+ in all rarities except for Legendary—most even had specific Class requirements to use them. However I did eventually come across something that was clearly far better than the rest, and even though I sadly would never be able to use it, I still took the time to admire the glorious armour and matching double-bladed sword.

Crimson Dawn Azure Dusk Armour Set

Legendary

Be it the warmth of the dawn or the chill of the dusk, and you will prevail. But be it the horizon of twilight, and you will conquer.

+1000 Strength and Magic
+1000 Agility and Stamina
+500 Vitality, Intelligence, Endurance, and Sense
+50% Total Physical Damage Reduction
+50% Total Magical Damage Reduction

Helmet Effect: Unlocks the Skill 'Horizon's Call'.

Chestpiece Effect: Fighting in direct sunlight engulfs you in a shroud of fire, fighting in direct moonlight shields you in a shroud of ice, and fighting in direct twilight envelops you in a shroud of invisibility.

Pauldrons Effect: Reflect 25% of Physical Damage received during the day, reflect 25 % of Magical Damage received during the night, and reflect 50% of All Damage received during twilight.

Gloves Effect: Armour Piercing increases by 25% during the day, Magic Piercing increases by 25% during the night, and Armour and Magic Piercing increases by 50% during twilight.

Chausses Effect: Stamina Regeneration increases by 25% during the day, Mana Regeneration increases by 25% during the night, and Stamina and Mana Regeneration increases by 50% during twilight

Boots Effect: Immune to Fire Damage during the day, immune to Cold Damage during the night, and immune to Fire and Cold Damage during twilight.

Set Bonus: At the start of dawn the armour becomes crimson, increasing Strength by 50%, but decreasing Agility by 25%. At the start of dusk the armour becomes azure, increasing Agility by 50% but decreasing Strength by 25%. At the start of twilight the armour awakens, increasing Strength and Agility by 50%.

Requirements: Any Elven Race, Lv.100 Godly Blademaster, Str 1,000, Mag 1,000, Agi 1,000, Sta 1,000

Can only be worn as a full set.

Fables of J

> ### Dusk 'Til Dawn
>
> **Legendary**
>
> *The difference was once night and day, until day and night became the difference.*
>
> **Attack: 4000**
> **+1000 Strength and Magic**
> **+1000 Agility and Stamina**
>
> **Effect: Damage with the crimson blade 'Dawn' increases by 25% during the day, damage with the azure blade 'Dusk' increases by 25% during the night, and damage with the double-bladed 'Dusk Till Dawn' increases by 50% during twilight**
>
> **Bonus Effect: Wielding 'Dawn' and 'Dusk', or 'Dusk Till Dawn' while wearing the 'Crimson Dawn Azure Dusk' Armour Set doubles the Swords' Effect.**
>
> **Requirements: Any Elven Race, Lv.100 Godly Blademaster, Str 1,000, Mag 1,000, Agi 1,000, Sta 1,000**

"What absolutely broken items! I love it!" I thought, carefully looking over the Stats of both, *"I guess that's what makes it a Legendary Lv.100 armour and weapon, but the required Class of Godly Blademaster sounds pretty broken too."* I then recalled 13 being at **Lv.1000** and thought, *"But if that's all a Lv.100 Legendary can amount to, how do the Guides ever expect the Players who want to return to be able to kill them? They actually probably know we can't, but I'm sure there'll be people dumb enough to try at least."*

"I wondered if this would catch your eye, my lord. And it seems to have done exactly that." Verana stood beside me to admire the gear too. "I am sure this is unknown to you, but this armour and sword once belonged to the First Head of House Ven'Thyl."

In Range – Ven'Thyl Saga Part I

"I should've guessed it was someone that special, these were the only things I saw that were above a Unique Rarity so far," I pointed out.

"They are also the only thing that has yet to be passed on since the Founders have long gone," Verana mentioned, "for no one in the history of the house or the kingdom have ever been worthy of claiming them for their own."

"Wait, are you saying it's okay to give them away if someone can use them?"

"Of course. It was the First's wishes to pass them on in the first place, and so we must respectfully uphold those wishes until they are fulfilled by us, or someone else who comes along."

"Sounds like a pain, but doesn't that also sound like the start of a—"

Quest

One Who Is Yet To be Worthy:
To uphold the First Head of House Ven'Thyl's wishes, you must find someone worthy of claiming 'Crimson Dawn Azure Dusk' and 'Dusk Till Dawn' as their own.

Reward: ???

Will you accept:

[Yes] or [No]

"Ugh, I just knew it was another one. Well at least this one doesn't look too bad." I accepted it right away, but I decided to ignore it for now since it didn't seem like there was a rush to complete it.

We walked through the rest of the armoury, but there wasn't anything else that could compare to the Crimson Azure gear. Though Verana did let me know I was allowed to do as I see fit with the rest of armour and weapons in this place, as they too also could be passed on to others, but lucky for me there wasn't a Quest to find all of them new owners. Then surprisingly, when we reached the end of the hallway, we

Fables of J

ended back on the opposite side of the coffer chamber, as the armoury seemed to be one big loop around the whole treasury.

Leading me to the last chamber, Verana informed me, "This is the vault; and it is where we keep the scrolls, tomes, potions, accessories, relics, and artifacts our house has found or created," as she gestured to the many shelves of items in the large round chamber. "And yes you can take stuff from here too if you would like—I can already hear you wondering, my lord."

"Oh, then don't mind if I do," I said, picking up a very useful scroll I spotted on the nearest shelf.

"Anyway, please come and sign your name in the Founders' Registry first, Lord Eyes," Verana politely asked, walking to a stone pedestal directly in the center of the chamber where a large blackened book and quill floated in place. "When you do so, the runes on the treasury door will allow you to open them on your own."

"That's it? This isn't some trick where I sign my soul away, right?" I checked, nervously walking up to the pedestal.

"That would not be possible, as I would clearly require some of your blood if I wanted to do that," Verana jokingly smiled, giving me a wink and handing me the quill.

Realizing she was clearly teasing me, I relaxed and grabbed the quill from her; then as I placed my hand on the book, a menu for it popped up.

Founders' Registry

Legendary

Originally written during the Primordial Dark Age, the Names recorded within its pages are those who banded together in assisting the first Elven king and the young talented prince in prevailing against the Primordial God who once ruled and presided over the Land Of Trees.

In Range – Ven'Thyl Saga Part I

"Strange, a Legendary item that doesn't seem to do anything…" While I pondered if I was missing something, I glanced at the seemingly endless number of Elven names written inside, and couldn't believe they were all Heads of the House or from this 'Primordial Dark Age'; so I questioned, "Verana, why are there so many names in here? I thought only the Head of the House was allowed inside the house treasury?"

"Well, my Lord, that was not always the case," Verana elaborated. "The simple explanation for it is that there was a time when every member was allowed inside the treasury; but after a mind control incident 500 or so years ago, when almost everything inside got stolen, the new rule was implemented so only the Head of the House could enter the house treasury."

"That doesn't sound good. Can that happen to us? Or anyone else in the house for that matter?" I asked, slightly worried at the thought of any of the house turning against me.

"As a requirement to control another's mind, one must be more powerful than the one they are controlling; meaning it would be very unlikely for Odelia, Aelthar, or I to be controlled. However, you, Shurtyrr, and Amariina would likely be susceptible to the control." She then tried to assure me, "Though worry not, my lord. Mind control is an extremely rare Skill to have, one that I can easily dispel if needed to."

"That's good to know," I said, feeling relieved. I signed my name 'Eyes Thalion Ven'Thyl' directly under Verana's, and a surprising surge of magic erupted from the book's pages.

Travelling down through the pedestal, the magic struck the chamber floor and scattered in all directions. The entire place began to shake, igniting runes that were hidden all along the walls, ground, and ceiling. Shortly after, the magic came back, gathering at the base of the pedestal and rising back into the book. The shaking seemed to have completely stopped, and I watched my name be solidified with magic in the pages of the book.

You have gained the Title: [Historic Archaeologist]

Fables of J

> **Historic Archaeologist:** Discovering an ancient artifact directly related to the time of the Primordial Dark Age of Novus, your mind begins to develop a deep desire to discover more about that time and truth it holds about the world. +100 Intelligence.

"What the—" My head began to spin, and my thoughts were filled with questions I had no answer to. *"What was the Primordial Dark Age? When was the Primordial Dark Age? Where can I find more information about the Primordial Dark Age? Why is the Primordial Dark Age important? What truth can the Primordial Dark Age hold about the world? Who was that Primordial God in the Primordial Dark Age? How did the Primordial Dark Age end?"*

"It is done, my Lord. The Founders' Registry will now forever remember your name in its storied pages." Verana had the happiest expression on her beautiful aged face, but it quickly faded away as she suddenly turned sideways in my eyes, and saw my body uncontrollably collapse to the floor.

"Lord Eyes! Lord Eyes....! Lord..."

Chapter 67
Partial News and Trinity Ritual

A NOTE FROM FABLES OF J
First new Chapter after a year long hiatus!

Not being able to stay for the whole tattoo, the other members eventually left for their jobs; but before Shurtyrr left, I inquired about some questionably legal items I wanted to obtain from the black market.

"Would those be hard to find?" I asked him.

"Quite the opposite actually," I was happy to hear that, but Shurtyrr mentioned, "though the price could greatly differ depending on the quality, rarity, condition, and type; as well as if others are currently in the market for them."

"I'm okay with that," I told him, not having an issue with the price, "I'll make plenty of coin when I'm done learning the styles and find work at the Adventurer's Guild."

"Then I shall go to see what I can find currently in the market. I will even reach out to my contacts in the other kingdoms to locate some." Shurtyrr gave a smile and bow. "Now if you will excuse me, Lord Eyes, I will take my leave." Then he quietly left the room.

"You have some odd interests, my lord," Odelia commented, continuing to hammer the ink into my skin.

"Quite odd indeed," Verana agreed, sipping her tea while she stayed to watch.

Ignoring their judgments, I asked, "How much longer did you say this was gonna take, Odelia?"

"Around eight more hours," Odelia reminded me.

"Ugrhhh…" I groaned, already extremely bored from just laying down for 2 hours

Fables of J

"I told you creating the foundation always takes the longest—not to mention I am also creating the Magic Style you already learned; so please bear with me, my lord," Odelia said, clearly working hard to push herself to completing the tattoo as fast and as perfectly as possible.

Acknowledging her efforts, I settled down and thought, *"Well, I guess if I'm stuck like this for eight more hours, I should catch up with what the other Players are doing."*

Scrolling through the past messages in World Chat, I learned in the last few days all the surrounding areas around Asheton were already completely turned into a dangerous zombie-filled forest. Everything from the animals to the monsters, to the unknowing NPCs and the careless Players; they all became undead wandering zombies of themselves. However, thanks to Global following my instructions to use my name, Asheton was generally safe and free of most of the danger.

Captain Dayla was able to warn the guards and townspeople before anyone was unknowingly infected—heavily increasing the security at the gates and the walls. The Guild's Branch Manager, Thaddeus Crane, was able to get a message to the Guild's Headquarters about the ongoing circumstances, and he not only received early permission to authorize Iron and Silver-Rank Requests to exterminate the zombies, but the news also drew in other adventurers from other towns and cities looking for work. And finally with the knowledge that any Healer Class with the Cleanse Skill could cure anyone infected, those Players who could became coveted and invaluable to Asheton and the other Players.

World Chat

Fi
Can't believe my party was actually about to leave this town, think about all the Exp we would've missed with all these zombies around.

Oscar Ottin
Looking for Cleanse Healer to fill our Party!

In Range – Ven'Thyl Saga Part I

> **Jo Mama**
> We were about to leave too. Glad we didn't.
>
> **Carol**
> Ya but u better watch out 4 the Zombie Players 1 of them was almost enough to kill 3 of my members so we would've died if there were 2 of them
>
> **Gugu**
> LF Cleanse Healer! 2 people in my party got infected!
>
> **Nessa Locksley**
> <—Cleanse Healer for hire (1 Gold per Cleanse or 5 Gold per joined Request).

"Looks like the Players might be settling in Asheton for a while." But after scrolling back a little more, I did learn a few hundred Players had already left Asheton days ago; some left for the capitals, others for smaller or remote towns, and a few who simply wanted to explore the new world.

> **Declan**
> Doesn't finding a hidden oasis in the desert sound awesome? Any1 wanna join me?
>
> **IRL Troll**
> No but u shud definitely go by urself
>
> **Capulet**
> I'm not particularly fond of the thought of dealing with sand and the desert heat, so I think I'll have to pass.
>
> **Simp**
> U obviously just heard a rumour and ur gonna die if u leave the starting town at our Levels

Fables of J

> **Zipporah**
> I wouldn't mind joining you, Declan.
>
> **Declan**
> Yes! Any1 Else?
>
> **Sayonara**
> I have a Quest to deliver something to the city of Sya, so if we stop by there first I'll join you.
>
> **Declan**
> Of course, we'll need 2 get supplies anyway!
>
> **A1**
> If my boy Brutus can join we'll come along
>
> **Declan**
> Hell yeah! Let's meet in front of the Sleeping Forest Inn to talk details!

    Only judging the Players by the messages I read, I found that a majority of them were only trying to get by or get stronger, unsure what to expect or prepare for in this new world—these were the Players below the Top 5000. On the other hand, Players above the Top 5,000 seemed to be more driven and ambitious, not afraid of anything and ready to jump into the unexpected and unknown world.

    A majority of these Top 5,000 Players also seemed to be associated in some way with the 3 big Player Guild Factions; Deicide, Elseworld, and The Guided. The only exceptions being people who were kicked out, people who didn't care for them, and any of the tutorial Top 10. Though apparently there was a lot of drama circling around the Deicide and Elseworld Factions for allowing known Player Killers to join them; but I couldn't be bothered reading that crap.

    Moving on from the Players, I read Mako's message and she told me that Mr.Hensley and his wife were both safe, as well as everyone from the Sleeping Forest Inn. Mako also mentioned after she teleported back to Castle Creedmor, she and Gryphon did check up on the goblin corpses Goblex disposed of, but that they were completely untouched, leaving no explanation as to how the zombie infection could have spread. However, Gryphon theorized an animal may have been infected before the formation of the dungeon and barrier, but ultimately, that fact didn't matter since the infection had already spread, and out of caution Gryphon incinerated all the corpses anyway.

Mako Nomura

Mako
Hey, this castle of yours isn't half bad.

Oh yeah, it's your first time there, right?

Mako
Yup, and I think with another few days of Goblex cleaning it up, it'll only look like a cleaned ruined castle.

Yeah, I don't know what to do with it, it's just a broken down mess I own.

Mako
Well you know, there's a mysterious Player going around constructing and rebuilding almost all the houses and buildings that were burned down during the night of the Goblin Attack, so maybe you could get her to rebuild your castle?

There's a Player actually building houses? Why?

Mako
Who knows, but what's weirder is the Players I've talked to all think she's the reason there's moving murals depicting all the events that have happened so far to the

Fables of J

> Players and the World, since a lot of them are painted near the houses she constructs.
>
> What? Moving murals?
>
> **Mako**
> Yeah, they're absolutely beautiful to behold, and you should definitely see them for yourself when you come back.
>
> Wait, what was this Player's name?
>
> **Mako**
> No one has seen her face, but all the NPCs have told the curious Players that her name is Da Vinci. And now that I think about it, wasn't she also in the Top 10 of the Tutorial, like you?
>
> Oooh, she definitely was.

I smiled, thinking, *"So that's what she's been doing, building houses and painting murals, huh? Sounds like she's taking her Subclass and name to heart then."* I then decided to send her a message.

> **Da Vinci**
> Hey, Da Vinci. I hear you've been rebuilding the burned down buildings around Asheton, but what do you think about rebuilding a ruined castle in the middle of a lake surrounded by mountains?
>
> **Da Vinci**
> \(?_?)/

7 hours later...

"And... that should do it," Odelia said, finishing with a last tap of the hammer on my back. "I am done tattooing for now, Lord Eyes."

In Range – Ven'Thyl Saga Part I

"Huh?" Half asleep with my head down, I realized what Odelia just said and immediately sat myself up. "Wait, really?! You're done?!"

"For now at least," Odelia replied, setting her tools aside.

"Okay, what now then?" I tried to touch the tattoo on my back, but Odelia swatted my hand away. "Ouch. Isn't the tattoo supposed to do something though, 'cause I don't feel like it is, is it?"

"Of course not, we have yet to finish, my lord," she said, explaining to me, "that was simply the Magic Ink which becomes the conduit for the Pure Essence to be permanently imbued within your body and forcefully awakening one of your dormant Magic Cores to be drawn upon at will."

"W-W-Wait, what? You lost me. What about a Magic Core?" I asked, completely clueless to what she was talking about.

Odelia sighed, "Lord Eyes, how did you even learn Wield Mana and the Elemental-Type Arrows without fully grasping and understanding what I told you about Magic Cores? In fact, were you even listening to me when I explained them in the first place?"

"Uhhh… look, I'm more of a visual learner, and I only really paid attention to your demonstrations," I said, justifying myself. "And to be honest, what you were going on and on about was really boring compared to all the new Skills I wanted to learn in my mind at the time."

Odelia gave me an intimidating glare, and I couldn't help but nervously laugh.

Though distracting the both of us, Verana entered the room again and said, "Oh, I see you finished an hour early! You have not finished the First Trinity Ritual already, have you Odelia? I was really looking forward to witnessing it once again."

Odelia let out another sigh, "No… we were about to start if you would like to take a seat." And as Verana took a seat, Odelia told me, "I will lecture you again about Magic Cores another time, Lord Eyes. For now how about we begin your First Trinity Ritual."

"Sure thing, but I don't have to learn this too, do I?" I inquired whether I should be paying attention or not.

"Those who choose to learn the Trinity Ritual are those who wish to teach and pass on their knowledge," Odelia stated, while grabbing 2

Fables of J

bottles of the essences she searched all over town for. "But no, it is not necessary to learn if you do not wish to."

I only witnessed her buy the Pure Magic Essence yesterday, but ever since I saw the mesmerizing glowing liquid inside the bottles, I was very curious about them. And indulging my curiosity now, I grabbed one of each three different types of essence on the table—from the nine total bottles—and saw the Stats for them.

Bottle Of Abyssal Dark Essence	Bottle Of Pure Magic Essence	Bottle Of Tempest Wind Essence
Unique	*Unique*	*Unique*
Harnessed and extracted from a pure source of Darkness, the essence contained within holds the properties of the Endless Abyss itself.	*Harnessed and extracted from a pure source of Magic, the essence contained within holds the properties of both Magic and Mana itself.*	*Harnessed and extracted from a pure source of Wind, the essence contained within holds the properties of the Ravaging Tempest itself.*
Craftable	*Craftable*	*Craftable*

"*Interesting. And I can see where the colour of the tattoo comes from,*" *I thought,* noting that Pure Essence was blue, Dark Essence was violet, and Wind Essence was green. I then asked, "Are you sure I shouldn't reimburse you for these, Odelia? I know the three bottles of Pure Essence alone was 6000 Gold when you haggled it down, but I can't imagine how much the other six would add to the cost."

In Range – Ven'Thyl Saga Part I

"You are too kind, my lord. But as I told you yesterday, it is completely alright," Odelia smiled, telling me, "It has always been my custom to take upon the price of the Trinity Ritual for my students, as my Master once did for me. And I will always choose to uphold that principle in his memory."

"Though endearing it may be, I would not worry about Odelia's coin, Lord Eyes," Verana chimed in, "10 million of what you saw in the treasury was her's after all."

"Huh?! 10 million?! Who are you people!?" I exclaimed, shocked by the amount.

"Oh, has it gone down that much since I gave up teaching?" Odelia acted surprised to hear it was that low.

"Well, that is what a century of accepting only odd jobs and spending coins to search for clues will do to someone," Verana stated, looking slightly disappointed in Odelia.

"Ah, do not look at me like that, Verana," Odelia averted her eyes and mentioned. "Zebey has already offered 100 thousand a year for teaching young lady Myeyl privately, and even offered a bonus 10 million if I can help her become a Trinity Archer before she turns 110 in age."

Verana relaxed her gaze.

"100k a year!? What the hell is this house? Who knew they'd be this loaded!" I exclaimed to myself.

"Okay, now back to the matter at hand. Lay back on your stomach, Lord Eyes, and I will begin the ritual," Odelia instructed me, holding a bottle of Pure Essence in each hand; and following her instructions, I lay back down and turned my head a little to watch what she was doing.

Uncorking one bottle with her mouth, Odelia brought it towards my back and began slowly pouring the glowing viscous liquid out of it; then the moment the essence made contact with my back, I instantly felt a strange sensation of something exploding as an intense blue and red magic burst out and illuminated the entire room—causing me to look away.

Health: 1,624/5,595

Fables of J

> Mana: 1,809/4,140

"Huh!? Why the hell did I just lose more than half my health and mana!?" I then asked Odelia, "Hey, what the hell just happened?" I noticed the shock and blood on her face, as well as Verana standing in concern.

"Uhhh... here is the good news, my lord; thanks to Verana's earlier nullification, you are not feeling any of the pain you should definitely be feeling right now," Odelia nervously informed me, unable to look away from my back.

"What? What does that even mean? Did something happen? What's that blood on your face?" I questioned, now getting slightly worried from their reactions.

"Well, to put it simply—"

"Save the explanation for later, Odelia," Verana calmly interrupted in Elvish. "Go get me my staff just in case while I take care of Lord Eyes' grievous wound."

Odelia didn't question Verana and immediately sped out of the room.

"Verana, what's going...on?" When I turned my head a little more to see what happened for myself, I saw an enormous splatter of blood directly behind me and on the walls, with my back being a red mess illuminated by the blue magic.

"Wh-wh-what..." My head suddenly became light and my sight began to blur.

"Lord Eyes, the essence exploding inside you has caused you to have lost a lot of blood all at once, so please refrain from moving or you will pass out very soon." Verana carefully laid me back down and assured me, "Do not worry, my Lord. I promise on the house you will be completely alright."

My eyes began to close as Verana raised her arms and appeared to glow herself. "The astral heavens, hear my call! **2-Star Constellation, Absolute Restoring Regeneration!**"

In Range – Ven'Thyl Saga Part I

I began to hear Odelia's voice reciting something, "I Odelia Ven'Thyl, the master who taught you the Magic-Wielding Archery Style, have instilled in you my student, Eyes Ven'Thyl, the knowledge instilled in me by my own master, Iliveyl Fre'Nddare..." My eyes slightly opened to a blue magic enveloping my entire torso. "May this piece of my power help guide you on your own path to becoming a Trinity..." I could feel magic slowly seeping into my skin and body, filling me with an incredible surge of energy.

> **You have forcefully awakened your Mana Magic Core, and have greatly increased your Magic and Mana by 33% of its base Stats.**

> **Magic-Wielding Archery proficiency increased by 25 Levels.**

> **Magical Arrows increased by 2 Levels.**

"Though to ensure the balance of your Magic Cores stays intact, so that one does not overwhelm the dormant others, I activate the **Trinity Seal!**" The surge of energy I felt completely disappeared all of a sudden.

You have been affected by the Status Debuff: [Multi-layered Seal].	You have been affected by the Status Debuff: [Sealed Magic Core].	You have been affected by the Status Debuff: [Sealed Skill].

"Urghhh... what the hell is happening now, Odelia?" I asked, slowly waking myself up from the bed.

"Oh! Have you already awakened, Lord Eyes?" Odelia asked in surprise, helping me sit up.

"Yeah, but what exactly happened? Did you mess up the ritual or something?" I questioned, looking around to see the almost dried blood on the bed and walls. "And is Verana alright?" I asked, seeing her sleeping on the couch with a large staff wrapped in cloth and chains beside her—glowing brightly in my eyes.

"Verana is fine, she is simply resting from spending the last three hours using her incredible Skills to fully restore your body."

Hearing that relieved me.

"And about what happened... I should have told you earlier, though you probably would not have cared either way, but there has always been a small chance for one's body to reject the essence entirely and inflict a great amount of internal damage to the recipient," Odelia revealed, "except I have never witnessed such a devastating rejection before, as you almost outright died from the essence reacting and exploding inside your body—it is likely due to your young age and your body being severely underdeveloped still."

"You're right, I would've taken the risk regardless, but what was all that stuff you were saying just now? I thought the ritual failed after my body rejected the essence?" I asked, curiously reading the notifications.

> **Multi-layered Seal:** The basis for placing multiple seals on anything, a seal placed on top becomes connected and must be simultaneously broken to be fully unsealed.
>
> **Connected Seals:** Magic Core Seal, Skill Seal
>
> **Duration:** Indefinite

Sealed Magic Core: A powerful seal specifically targeting your 'Mana Core', restricting you from being able to utilize any part of the Core's benefits until the seal is dispelled or released. **Duration: Indefinite**	**Sealed Skill:** A powerful seal specifically targeting the Skill 'Magic-Wielding Archery', restricting you from being able to utilize any part of the Skill until the seal is dispelled or released. **Duration: Indefinite**

"The Natural Method for the ritual did fail, but the Forceful Method was a fantastic success!" Odelia happily expressed; then telling me, "I realized you would have hated it if I wasted any more time, so I decided to finish it while you were recovering instead of waiting until you were up."

"Great decision, but if the Forceful Method was such a 'fantastic' success, why didn't we do that one first instead?" I reasonably questioned.

"Well, besides it being terribly inefficient compared to the Natural Method, it also involves a very difficult process, even for me, of absorbing the essence myself and excruciatingly forcing the excess into you, then personally awakening your Magic Core with my own will. The pain you would have experienced would have been unbearable even compared to a failure from the Natural method. Though luckily Verana nullified that down side, or you would have felt like a hand was personally crushing your heart directly, to the point where it was just about to pop but never actually doing so., And that torture would repeat for another 2 hours or so."

"Oookay, that's horrifying to imagine." I changed the topic, and excitedly asked, "But that means we're done here, right? We can move on to my next style?"

"Well yes, but do you not want to see the first part of our Trinity Tattoo? Or at least rest a little more after you just recovered?" Odelia suggested.

"No offense, but no," I said, covering myself back up with my cloak and standing up from the bed. "We've already wasted two days on this Trinity Tattoo, and I'd rather not spend any more time needlessly doing nothing."

"You are relentless, my lord," Odelia grinned, "and the look in your eyes tells me there is no convincing you, so which style do you wish to do next?"

"Combat," I answered bluntly, feeling my body being extra rested and limber at the moment.

"If that's what you wish, Lord Eyes," Odelia said, walking to the door, "but be warned, the Combat Style is far more physically demanding than the other styles, and it is also my preferred personal style to use and teach."

"Oh? Bring it on then," I smiled confidently. "I'll learn it just as fast as I did with the Magic Style."

"Shall we go then?" Odelia gave me a mischievous smile and a sinister look.

Chapter 68
Hand-to-Hand and Swordsmanship

A NOTE FROM FABLES OF J
50,000 Total Views! Thanks for reading!

Being blitzed by another flurry of punches coming from all different angles, I couldn't keep up and was caught by another powerful punch directly in the gut. That one punch alone dealt **500** damage and sent me flying against the wall.

"Urgh…!" The impact was completely absorbed by the runes on the walls, and my body simply bounced off and came crashing onto the ground. Looking at my **Health**, I picked myself up.

`Health: 2,031/5,595`

"Damn, she did more than half my health in a single combo again."

Spitting out the blood from my mouth, I stared at Odelia smugly grinning in her unorthodox fighting stance.

"I can't dodge her attacks, and *I can't land a single hit. What do I do?"*

She waited for me to come at her again.

"This was only supposed to be hand-to-hand sparring to show her what I could do, but when it comes to actual fighting without a bow, I'm basically useless."

Casting **First Aid** to recover my **Health** a bit, I healed some of the big bruises and cracked bones I felt all over my body.

Then having enough being treated as a punching bag, I used **Wield Mana** to form myself a short bow to use. *"Since there's no way I'll ever* *beat Odelia in hand-to-hand combat with my terrible fighting skills, I might as well use this chance to see how effective my new Magic Style Skills actually are in combat."*

Seeing this, Odelia's smug grin grew wider and gestured for me to come at her.

Drawing the mana-bowstring, I focused and formed two mana-arrows fully nocked and ready to be shot; though before I did, I casted **Element Arrow** on both and chose **Lightning**—imbuing an erratic yellow electricity around each arrowhead. However, Odelia was unflinching as she allowed me to carefully aim and fire the arrows at her chest. Knowing that wouldn't be enough, I activated **Sprint** and quickly circled behind her as the arrows flew; forming and shooting one more arrow, this time casting **Ensnaring Arrow** on it and aiming directly for her ankles. I then readied my next arrow and Skill for her reaction, but when I saw Odelia was just standing her ground, I decided to quickly fire three high-arcing arrows above her.

The electrified arrows were just about to hit her in the chest, but with unbelievable ease, Odelia caught both of them in single motion and held the two arrows in her hands—absolutely unbothered by the electricity surging through her. Then when she turned around to face me, an arrow with two mana-strands—attached at the tip of the arrow—hit her left ankle and suddenly caused the strands to reach and wrap around her other ankle, magically tightening themselves and bringing her ankles together. Realizing now that one arrow wouldn't hold against someone as strong as Odelia, I quickly sent four more **Ensnaring Arrows**; one at her knees, one at her calves, and two more at her ankles.

Odelia acknowledged me, "You are quite fast, my lord." She looked to be amused. "Though surely you do not believe this is even close to being enough to hold me, right?" With the simple outward flex of her legs, Odelia instantly broke all five restraints wrapped around her and caused them to dissipate.

"I didn't think they would, but they did work pretty well as a distraction."

At that moment three round arrowheads fell directly on top of Odelia. "Kaboom…"

Odelia looked impressed. "Oooh, well played, Lord Eyes," she said as she brought her forearms up to cover her head. The three round arrowheads then made contact with her forearms and immediately exploded on impact, creating three separate small blue explosions and causing the dust in the chamber to be blown all around.

Coughing and waving the dust out of my face, I asked, "Did I get you?"

And appearing unscathed from the dust cloud, Odelia replied, "It was a good effort, Lord Eyes, but that amount of magic is still too weak to even really damage my armour," showing me that my Explosive Arrows barely singed her black leather bracers—though it did cause her braided hair to be a slight frizzy mess.

"Really? Maybe I shouldn't have held back so much then?" I said, releasing my focus and dissipating my short bow.

"I feel the same, my lord, as you can take quite the beating with that First Aid Skill you have—much more than even Combat Style masters."

"Thanks? I think?"

"Though with that being said, we should call it for training today. I think I have to really reassess how I should be training you in the Combat Style."

"What does that supposed mean?"

"Well, as you know, Myeyl is also training in the Combat Style. And seeing how you already excelled at the other Styles, I thought you were around her skill level and sparred you as such; though I quickly realized that was very much not the case."

"If you realized that, why didn't you go easier on me then?" I questioned, still feeling the pain from her heavy punches. "I cracked like 20 different bones, you know?"

"Besides the point of it being fun for me, you were quite resilient like I said, my lord," Odelia smiled, chuckling to herself a little. "And if I recall, did you not say something along the lines of 'bring it on' and that you would 'learn Combat just as fast as Magic?'" She quoted my words. "So how would you be able to do so if I went easy on you?"

"I guess you're right," I agreed with her. "Then let's train even harder tomorrow!" I said, determined to learn the Combat Style as fast as possible.

The next day, our training began as it always did. With Odelia lecturing me.

"Not every fight for an archer can always be done at range. Sometimes we are forced into unavoidable close-range encounters," she stated, pacing around while I was forced to sit down and actually pay attention to her lectures this time. "And for that reason alone, the Close-Combat Style was created and developed to utilize hand-to-hand or one-handed weapon combat whilst simultaneously wielding a bow, all to deal with those unavoidable close-range encounters."

She then went on and on about the history of the creator of the Close-Combat Style, explaining to me that he was the Head of House Baen'Mtor during the time of the Great King Ven'Thyl, and that only the House Baen'Mtor could truly harness one's full potential for the Close-Combat Style.

"If that's the case, shouldn't I be trying to learn the Style from their house then?" I questioned, wondering why Odelia never mentioned that before.

"Yes, that would be a good idea if it were not for the fact that many Trinity Archers were lost in the Second Trinity War a few centuries ago, including, sadly, the life of the last Master Trinity Archer of House Baen'Mtor, the only one who was capable of the task in their house," she informed me. "Trinity Archers used to be largely acknowledged as a Class only meant for the nobles and those they deemed worthy, but after all the loss during the war, that no longer became the case. And thanks to the younger Trinity Archers, like myself, wanting to preserve the knowledge of the dying Class, we openly began teaching it to anyone regardless of status."

"Wait, so are you saying you can bring out my 'full potential' like their house can?" I needed a clarification.

"As it currently stands, there are only two people left in the entire world who can guarantee unlocking a Trinity Archer's full potential.

And luckily for you my lord, it seems like they both are willing to help you do so," Odelia smiled brightly.

"Are you talking about you and Zebey? Does it have anything to do with the 'Tri-Fusion Ritual' Myeyl mentioned on the day we first arrived in Ven'Thyl?" I asked, briefly recalling that day.

"It most certainly does, but I would not worry about such a matter until after you mastered all the Styles," Odelia quickly changed the topic, and said, "Now, follow my exact movements or you will surely fail in learning the Combat Style."

She then began demonstrating the basics of how to punch and kick, and I immediately got up and tried to follow her movements.

After about three hours of horribly trying to keep up with Odelia's movements, her constantly adjusting and fixing my fighting stance and forms, and practicing basic punching and kicking on the training dummies; I finally felt more and more used to all the unfamiliar movements, which caused a new notification to appear.

> **You have learned the Proficiency: [Hand-to-hand].**

> **Hand-to-hand: Any form of fighting done using your body as your weapon. Increases Attack and Attack Speed of your Unarmed Strikes by 1% per Skill Level. Skill Level based on personal skill with fighting unarmed.**

While we took a break, I asked Odelia, "Learning how to fight without a bow is good and all, but why aren't you teaching me any of the Fundamental Combat Skills I need to learn for the Style?"

"Ah, well first off; you have already learned Rapid Shot on your own, so that is one down already," Odelia pointed out, "and second, the Combat Style is a little different from the others; only requiring the one Fundamental Skill and the two Required Feats of completing a chosen Combat Test and meeting the Master's expected level of fighting skill."

"That's it?" I reiterated in disbelief and Odelia nodded yes. "I mean I'm not gonna complain about needing to do less work, but what's the two Required Feats?"

"Depending on who is teaching you, and what they consider to be the expected level of a Combat Archer, each teacher's Combat Test will greatly vary in difficulty," she elaborated. "For example, most teachers are easygoing, simply allowing the winner of two equal or similar students fighting in actual combat to determine whether they pass their Combat Test or not. But on the other hand, there are a few very strict teachers that actually require you to beat an already acknowledged and handpicked Combat Archer for their test."

"Let me guess, you're the strict kind?" Though I already knew the answer as she gave me another mischievous grin.

After our break, we then moved on to learning with weapons, as Odelia brought down a pile of different, old and dull one-handed weapons from the storage room above. "You can choose any of these weapons, my lord. I am skilled enough with each of them to teach you to Mastery, regardless of your choice."

While I looked over the pile, Odelia added, "But if you would prefer another weapon not here, then you will need to learn how to fight with it on your own."

Picking up a longsword and a short sword to choose between, I said, "I can't help but notice that these are all one-handed weapons, and you only mentioned using one-handed weapons earlier; why?" I asked, looking over at the pile with axes, maces, hammers, daggers, and different other swords. "Is there a reason for it?"

"The reason is simple, Lord Eyes," Odelia said, forming a bow with her mana. "It is far easier to draw a bow with them."

She quickly drew her sword with her drawing hand, with the blade facing down, and then drew the bowstring back, "Using two-handed weapons would clearly make this much harder to do, especially in intense combat."

But then I remembered Myeyl's weapons and I had to ask, "What about Myeyl? Isn't she using her dual-blades?"

In Range – Ven'Thyl Saga Part I

"She is," Odelia confirmed. "Myeyl was stubbornly adamant on using them, which of course makes her one of the very few who choose not to use a one-handed weapon with the Combat Style, and she now spends all her current training developing a way to incorporate them whilst wielding a bow."

"From seeing your demonstration just now, I can't imagine not using a one-handed weapon. But out of curiosity, what else would someone use as a weapon?" I inquired curiously.

"Well besides Myeyl's dual-blades, Cyspar who you have already met does not use a one-handed weapon."

"He doesn't? What does he use then?"

"To be more accurate, he never uses weapons—along with almost all of House Baen'Mtor," Odelia revealed to me.

"What? They don't use weapons? What do they use then?" I questioned.

"Like I told you earlier, their house created the Close-Combat Style, which of course includes the most powerful and unique Fighting Style of the Abyss—which far exceeds ordinary hand-to-hand combat, and is even on par or greater than using some weapons."

"Huh, no wonder I didn't see a single weapon on Cyspar when we first met," I thought to myself, while listening to Odelia elaborate.

"To understand just how powerful the Abyssal Fighting Style is, know that 5 out of the 10 current Guard Captains are members of House Baen'Mtor who have rightfully earned their positions through combat. And that is not even including the Head Captain who is also the current heir to House Baen'Mtor and the strongest of all the Guard Captains."

"Woah, it's that strong?"

Odelia nodded yes, and I thought, *"Well, I better avoid making trouble with their house then, I wouldn't want to get arrested."*

Refocusing back to training, I picked the longsword to train with for now, and Odelia began showing me the basics of how to wield it. And only taking an hour less than hand-to-hand, I also gained the proficiency for a sword.

> **You have learned the Proficiency: [Swordsmanship]**

Fables of J

> **Swordsmanship: Versed in the many arts of wielding a sword. Increases Attack, Accuracy, and Attack Speed of your Swords by 1% per Skill Level. Skill Level based on personal skill with wielding swords**

I tirelessly spent the next four days straight, on my own or with Odelia, practicing the basics of both hand-to-hand combat and swordsmanship—day in and day out. Though I quickly came to realize they were a whole lot harder to increase in Levels compared to my Archery Proficiency—as I was only able to increase **Hand-to-hand** to **Lv.7**, and **Swordsmanship** to **Lv.8** even after all the hours I spent training with them. Fully dreading my clear lack of inherent talent for fighting, I was able to gain Odelia's pity and convince her of revealing the days until the end of the month.

> **Time Limit: 4 Days, 12 Hours , 26 Minutes, 51 Seconds**

"Holy shit, Odelia! I only have four days left!?" I loudly exclaimed, taken by complete surprise of the time limit.

"Correct, my lord," she said, confirming her words, as she brought me a glass of water to refresh myself with. "I thought you best know after having watched you work so hard these last few days."

Tired from training all day, I gulped down all the water and said, "Thanks, I needed that."

"You are welcome," she said, taking the empty glass for me. "Now would you like the good news or the bad news first?" Odelia asked, avoiding direct eye contact with me.

"Good news, please."

"Well the good news is, considering how horrible you were only a few days ago—now only being slightly horrible—your growth with Combat Style is actually remarkable!" Odelia sounded genuinely impressed by that.

"I don't like how you just called me horrible, but I'll let that one slide."

Odelia gave me a cheeky smile and continued, "Jokes aside and apart from Myeyl, who is quickly turning out to be one of the most talented students I have ever taught the Combat Style to, your fighting skills are truly developing quite nicely compared to a lot of my previous students."

"Oh yeah? Then what's the bad news?"

"The bad news is, at your current level of skill, there is no way I can imagine you being able to pass my Combat Test by month's end, and will probably need another year or two of dedicated training to reach the level I expect," Odelia honestly stated; then pointed out the bright side, "Which is honestly not bad news at all when you think of someone learning a Style in only a year or two."

"Another year, huh? That won't do..." I said, then losing myself in thought, *"I really don't want to announce myself to the Kingdom yet, or at all if possible. I also really want that Legendary Crafting Material Odelia will give me if I complete the quest, but how am I gonna do it all in time?"*

"Do not worry, Lord Eyes, the house and I promise to protect you with our greatest abilities when you announce yourself to the kingdom in a few days' time. And I personally promise no harm will ever come to you as long as I am by your side." Odelia kneeled to show her dedication.

"That's the problem," I thought to myself, remembering the vision of Odelia somehow dying in my arms. Then a thought popped up in my head, and I said, "Wait, I know you're my Master and all, but how can you tell me that I won't pass a Combat Test that you haven't even told me anything about yet? I mean I could probably pass if I was ready for it... maybe."

"Remember when I said there were easy tests and hard tests?"

"More or less. Something about beating someone else in a fight, which I personally don't think is that hard at all," I said, feeling confident enough to easily beat anyone ten Levels above me thanks to all my bonus Stats.

Fables of J

"I very much agree, my Lord, and for that reason my Combat Test is quite different and much more deadly than the other teachers would require," she said, telling me, "I have even lost 30 or so students who have died attempting the test when they were not yet ready to do so."

I laughed at her trying to intimidate me, "Yeah right, you just don't want me to potentially win the challenge. But whatever the Combat Test is, I'm doing it! Even if you say I'll fail!" I thought to myself, *"Even if it is more deadly and I fail, there is no way she'll let me be killed anyway, so there's nothing to worry about."*

Odelia let out a great big sigh and explained her whole Combat Test to me, and when I found out what I was up against and what I needed to do to pass, I trained even harder than before to truly prepare myself for the daunting test.

Four days later in a blood-soaked forest...

Bloodied and surrounded by countless dead monsters, I was frozen in utter shock, barely able to get my apology out to her. "I... I... I'm sorry... Odelia..." I said, staring at the fatal wound in her chest. "This... this is all my fault... I knew this would happen... but I still decided to come here..." The blood rain drenched and covered our entire bodies in red crimson. "And in a few seconds... I won't even be here..." The feeling of being helpless again quickly boiled up inside and completely infuriated me.

"AAAAAHHHHHH!! AAAAHHHHH...!!! AAAHHHH—"

Chapter 69
Archers' Playground

Time Limit: 18 Hours, 51 Minutes, 47 Seconds

Done worrying about the time, I closed the Menu and asked Odelia, "So this is the place?", standing beside her on a small hill.

"Indeed it is, my lord," she replied. "Welcome to the Archers' Playground!"

From the top of the hill, I had the perfect view of an extremely long and wide grass clearing, with several dozens of different arranged targets placed throughout the open field. However, bordering the entire clearing was a rectangular makeshift wall made completely out of the huge fallen trees in the area—stacked up to be about four storeys high. And even though the trees in the area were nowhere near the heights of the ones in Ven'Thyl—being less than 100ft tall—they did have much more branches and foliage around them. So much so that there seemed to be some type of archery obstacle course built around the outside of the field clearing, as I noticed there were multiple different elves currently maneuvering through the treetops shooting swinging or stationary targets.

"You know Odelia, the shopkeeper yesterday told me quite the rumour about this place. Wanna hear it?" I asked, taking a second to enjoy the sights.

"Whatever she said, do not believe a single word of it, my lord," Odelia immediately shut down my offer.

But I just continued anyway, "She said that this place wasn't always a clearing. That it once was like every other part of the forest; filled with strong tall trees and beautiful overgrown foliage." Odelia nervously hummed. "Then one day, a very young but very angry girl came out here in the middle of nowhere to settle a score with another. Now at first I thought she was talking about you and Zebey, but when I heard only one person came back that day, leaving an unspeakable disaster in their wake, I thought otherwise."

Odelia let out a saddened sigh, admitting, "Yes… the story is about me, Lord Eyes, but I promise there was a good reason I killed that man."

"Oh, I think you're mistaken, Odelia," I corrected her. "I didn't bring up the story because you killed someone—I'm sure they got what they deserved—I brought it up because I now see the amazing disaster you caused, and I want to know how you did it."

"Excuse me? You want me to tell you how I destroyed the forest?" Odelia was baffled, trying to understand.

"Hell yeah, I do!" pointing out some of the old remnants of the battle in the area still remaining; from the large trees bordering the clearing that were obviously unnaturally destroyed by something, to the decades old holes and chunks missing from the still standing trees all around. "Was it like some sort of super powerful ultimate attack that did this much?" I imagined a huge charged arrow that exploded into a beam of light destroying everything. "Or was it more like several smaller powerful attacks that caused all this? But either way, mind teaching me exactly how you did it?"

Odelia suddenly bursted out in laughter, saying, "Wait, wait, wait. Let me get this straight. You only brought up a story where I killed someone in cold blood because you wanted me to teach you the Skill I used to destroy an entire section of the forest?"

"So it was just one powerful Skill! I knew it!" I became excited at the thought of learning it for myself/ "And yes I did do that."

Odelia continued to laugh as she began walking down the hill, "Hahaha… I cannot tell if you are just greedy for more power, my lord, or if you are just plain crazy about learning everything you can about the powers of a Trinity Archer!"

"What's wrong with being both?" I asked, following right behind her.

In Range – Ven'Thyl Saga Part I

When we reached the bottom of the hill, we found the closest gap in the tree border and entered inside. Passing through, I noted how there seemed to be more than a few shops inside these hollowed out tree trunks, selling mostly different kinds of archery supplies, but a few that sold basic provisions and needs. We received a few curious gazes from what looked to be the regulars, but seeing how we simply moved along, they ignored us as we exited out the other side.

We then arrived at the open field clearing I viewed from above, where there were several numbered sections painted in white on grass—all in ascending order from left to right, and starting at the number 20 all the way up to 500. Knowing where we needed to go, Odelia began heading straight for the farthest section to the right, and I realized the numbers represented distance, seeing as we came here to complete the Required Feat of shooting 500m for the Range Style.

I also noticed that although it was still very early in the morning, there were still plenty of people here practicing their archery in the different sections we passed by. It very much reminded me of all the very dedicated young archers during the day of a tournament; and not so different from when they all watched me shoot perfectly during those times, everyone in the area began watching in interest as we entered the 500m section—the only section that was currently empty.

"Now that we are here, Eyes," she said, changing how she addressed me in public. "Take your time, and try to ignore their gazes," she informed me. "This always happens when it looks like someone is trying to complete the 500m shot."

"Oh, don't you worry, Odelia. I'm more than used to people watching me shoot. Because I always win," I arrogantly stated, taking out Infinity from my Inventory and strapping it to my waist this time to simulate how quivers were worn during competitions.

"Eyes, there is no need to rush things..." Odelia tried to convince me as she massaged my shoulders. "Let us just stay here all day and practice shooting… Forget all about the other test…"

"Hah! In your dreams, Odelia!" laughing at her useless effort to deter me, I shrugged off her hands and took out Shame from my Inventory as well. "This will only take me 5 minutes, and then we're

217

going straight there next," I drew my bow, aimed the arrow, and fired at the target 500m away.

30 minutes later…

"Remember when you said 'this will only take me 5 minutes?' Can you tell how long it's been since then again?" Odelia teased, amused by my shot being 100m short.

"That joke is getting old, Odelia," I said, feeling slightly frustrated as I drew another arrow from Infinity and began to nock it.

She chuckled in amusement, "Sorry, Eyes, but it is hard to come up with new ones after spending 30 minutes making jokes already."

"Well, don't worry, this one is for sure it." When I fired my next arrow, I immediately knew I aimed it too high, and watched the wind blow it way off target. "That doesn't count."

Odelia laughed at me again, though after she finally calmed herself down, she said, "I know I could spend all day being thoroughly amused by your failure, but I also know you really wish to at least try your hand at my test before failing my challenge." She then grabbed Shame from me, saying, "You clearly do not know about this, so let me show you a little trick Shame can do."

"A trick?" I asked, confused by what she meant.

"Well, as I have been telling you the last few days, Shame is not powerful enough to make the 500m shot, which is why I told you to buy a stronger bow yesterday," Odelia reminded me again. "Too bad your needless affection for that shameful bow of mine, and your stubbornness to buy any of the bows I suggested yesterday, are all combining to add to your current failure to make the shot."

"Hey, you saw the bows at the shop you showed me yesterday; all the ones better than Shame were too high a level for me, and the ones you did suggest didn't feel right when I tried them out and compared them to Shame," I justified, standing by my decision.

"Ooor, you are just too picky, Eyes," she said, calling me out while she rummaged through the satchel she brought along with her.

"Hmmm… so I've heard," I said, knowing I have a very particular taste about my bows

"Though luckily for you, I knew this would happen, and prepared as such," she pulled out four medium-sized vials of red liquids from her satchel.

"What's that? A healing potion?" I asked enthusiastically, somehow not seeing one in the world yet.

Odelia chuckled and began unstringing Shame, "It really impresses me how little you know of the world, Eyes." When she finished removing the bowstring, she lightly dug one end of the bow into the ground and made it stand on its own. "And no, these are not healing potions," she said, uncorking all four vials with her mouth, and putting a vial in front of my nose. "Have a smell. Take a guess what it is."

Taking a whiff, I immediately identified the slightly metallic smell of the red liquid, "It's blood. But what are you doing with it?" I asked, curiously.

"I asked Shurtyrr to procure some knowing that you would most likely be failing with Shame today."

"Hey!" I protested, but I let it slide. "So what's it for then?"

"For Shame of course," she stated. "It will allow you to temporarily increase its overall strength, making it just about powerful enough to land the shot."

Odelia then poured each vial of blood, one after another onto the standing unstrung bow, and we watched as the blood slowly dripped down the grains of the black wood.

Watching closely, the wood began to move and creak on its own; shortly after, the blood strangely seeped into the grains it dripped down, and caused the bow to unexpectedly grow in size, "Woah, what just happened? What kind of blood was that?" I questioned, continuing to watch all the blood seep into the bow.

"The blood was ordinary. What you are really asking about is the wood," she explained, "specifically Blood Wood—or Vampire Wood for you younger generations—and its unique property of drinking any blood it touches to temporarily grow in size and strengthen itself." When Odelia saw all the blood gone, she quickly strung the bow again. "Now

Fables of J

this should give you about 5 minutes before it reverts back to its dried out state, so I suggest you make your shots count—unless you wish to feed some of your own blood to it," she said, presenting the bow back to me.

"If it needed that much blood for just five minutes, I don't think I want to be feeding it my own blood."

As soon as I grabbed the now noticeably larger and heavier bow, the new Stats for it appeared.

Bloody Shame (4 Minutes, 27 Seconds)

Rare

Attack: 375
+25 Strength

Effect: Increases damage by 1% the closer you are to the target, up to 30%.

Requirement: Lv.20, Str 150

"Woah, besides changing the name and showing a timer, I think it's attack increased by 50%! But this is like the time with the crown; an item having a hidden effect not written in the Stats," I noted to myself. *"I'll have to remember to ask Odelia later if there's a way to find out if an item has hidden effects."*

Then not wanting to waste the four minutes I was given, I drew an arrow from my quiver, positioned myself back in front of the target, nocked the arrow, pulled the bowstring back, took a deep breath, and aimed carefully. When I finished taking account of the minor wind, I released the arrow to my liking, and the loud echoing sound of Shame firing was the loudest I've ever heard it. With the sound being so

In Range – Ven'Thyl Saga Part I

surprisingly loud, I noticed a few people in the area amusingly jump and flinch out of caution, as they all turned their attention back to me.

"Oh, how I loathe the sound of that bow," Odelia commented, her disdain clearly showing on her face. Regardless of how she felt, we watched the arrow fly 100m, then 200m, 300m, 400m, and then just barely hit the bottom of the target 500m away.

> **Archery proficiency increased by 1 Level.**

"Damn! So close. I should've aimed higher," I said, already preparing and aiming another shot.

However Odelia suddenly applauded, complimenting me, "Eyes, you are amazing! I thought you may have been able to do it if you had the time and a powerful enough bow, but to think you are doing so with only using that shameful bow is truly something else!"

"I told you, Shame was good enough, but just give me 3 more minutes, and I'll hit a perfect bullseye." I confidently proclaimed.

"I now do not doubt you will, though once you have learned Sniper Shot Skill, demonstrate it to me and I will acknowledge you reaching the level of a Long-Range Archer."

"You got it!" And only taking 9 more shots and less than 3 minutes, with each shot increasingly closer to the bullseyes, the arrow finally landed perfectly in the dead center of the target.

Archery proficiency increased by 1 Level.	**You have learned the Skill: [Sniper Shot].**

> **Sniper Shot: A long distance shot that deals more damage the further it has traveled. Cost 150 Stamina. Damage based on Distance Traveled, Skill Level, and Strength.**

Smirking widely, I immediately used **Sniper Shot**; and without even needing to account for the great distance and arrow drop, I watched the arrow fly straight and true, piercing more than halfway through the target. "What'd you think? That was it, right?" I asked, finally noticing that more people were drawn to the area by my extremely loud bow—bringing a lot of attention to my display of archery.

"Eyes… you are something else," Odelia smiled proudly at me, but her expression quickly changed when she saw something in another section, and said, "though before I congratulate you properly, let us leave Archer's Playground first, alright?"

"Uh, I guess if we're done here, then yeah." But with Odelia oddly pushing me to move already, I questioned, "Hey, what's with rush, Odelia? Aren't I supposed to be the one rushing you?"

Odelia nervously laughed and explained herself, "Aside from many curious eyes currently watching us, I just noticed two very unsavoury individuals arriving here—ones I particularly want to avoid ever meeting again."

"Like a Myeyl-way where you actually secretly like them? Or another way where you don't?"

"The latter. Now let us—"

"Well, well, well!" Hearing the man's loud voice caused Odelia to click her tongue in annoyance. "If it isn't Odelia Ven'Thyl, the Murderous Dwarf Fucker!"

"She's here? Where?" a woman asked.

"Ignore them," Odelia whispered, quickly pushing me forward towards the exit. However, two hooded individuals suddenly moved with incredible speed and stood directly in our way.

"Leaving so soon without even greeting me?" the hooded woman asked. "That's not like you, Master Odelia. Why don't we at least catch up first?" Removing her hood, a young woman with long golden blonde hair and sapphire-coloured eyes made herself known.

"Sorry Minra, but we've little time to catch up," Odelia coldly responded, grabbing me by the arm and trying to move past them.

But putting a hand on Odelia's shoulder, the hooded man asked, "Who said you could go, murderer?"

Odelia sighed, "What do you want, Sol? Still angry I killed your father here?"

In Range – Ven'Thyl Saga Part I

"You even openly admit it?! You little whoreson bitch!" The man angrily removed his hood and thrusted forwards to stare directly into Odelia's cold unflinching eyes.

I expected someone was about to throw a punch, but cutting all the tension completely was an exhausted voice running towards us. "Milady! Sir Sol! Please stop leaving me behind!" It was a brown-haired elven woman who was wearing very similar robes to Jhan, and even had a very similar crescent shape staff on her back.

At that moment everyone got distracted by her, and I took that split second to check their names; the exhausted woman was **Lv.72 Ker Ilzt**, the angry man was **Lv.70 Sol Alea'Tlar**, and the one who called Odelia Master was **Lv.65 Minra Helvi'Ett**.

"Woah, these are some high levels," I thought to myself, pulling my hood down a little more.

"Oh, Lady Odelia! I didn't expect to be seeing you here, it's been a long time hasn't it?" Ker greeted Odelia politely.

"Indeed it has, Ker," Odelia smiled nicely towards her.

"So what brings you here? Is Lady Myeyl and my little brother coming here to practice today too?" she asked, already looking around to see if they were here.

Though before Odelia could answer her, Minra said, "I think he's what brings her here," pointing directly at me trying my best to hide from their attention.

"Oh, I did not see you there. Please excuse my rudeness." Ker then formally introduced herself, "My name is Ker Ilzt, from the Noble Protectors of House Ilzt, and currently a vassal in the noble house of Helvi'Ett, but you may simply call me Ker. Nice to meet you." She then held her hand out for a handshake.

Not wanting to make this awkward, I shook her hand and introduced myself, "Nice to meet you, Ker. My name's Eyes… newly joined member of House Ven'Thyl."

"Someone actually joined that pathetic excuse for a house? How laughable!" While Sol forced himself to laugh, Odelia and I both held ourselves back from doing something rash.

"I hear you've finally taken up teaching again, Master Odelia," Minra spoke with an annoying, condescending arrogance to her voice. "And here I thought I would've gotten the honour of being your last student."

"So Odelia killed that guy's father, and this girl was the reason Odelia quit teaching? No wonder she wanted to avoid them," I thought, understanding why she rushed me to leave.

"Like I told you before, Minra, we've little time to catch up," Odelia repeated herself, grabbing me by the arm again and trying to move past them again.

But putting a hand back on her shoulder again, Sol said, "I'll say it again too. Who said you could go, murderous bitch?"

Odelia loudly exhaled, clearly being frustrated by Minra and Sol's presence alone, so I decided to step in. "Hey, I know you obviously have a problem with Odelia, but are you sure this is the place to settle it?"

"I don't know who the fuck you are kid, but I've been dying to meet Odelia outside the city like this—where we are doesn't matter." Sol tightened and squeezed his grip on Odelia's shoulder, but she didn't seem bothered by it at all.

"What about you then?" I asked Minra. "Are you sure your noble house will be okay hearing that you're gonna be involved in this?"

"Did he just refer to me as 'you?'" Minra laughingly scoffed. "How can a mere commoner refer to a noble as 'you?'" she asked Ker, not even acknowledging me directly.

"I'm sorry, but maybe if you introduced yourself I wouldn't need to call you that, Lady…?" I prompted, still trying to act cordial towards her.

Ker nervously interjected, "Milady, Sir Sol, please. You both know how much trouble we'll all be in if you cause a scene here with everyone watching." She pointed out all the eyes currently watching us. She then spoke to Sol with a more serious tone, "And Sir Sol, I shouldn't have to remind you of the last time a battle was fought here. No matter how great you delude yourself to think that you can take revenge on Lady Odelia, know that you will never be in her league."

Sol angrily growled at Ker's words, but ultimately decided to remove his hand from Odelia's shoulder.

"Thank you, Ker. We'll be on our way now," Odelia said, bringing me along as we finally walked past them.

"It was nice seeing you again, Master Odelia!" Minra shouted and waved. "I hope we can meet again soon!" The more she spoke, the more I felt Odelia's anger

"And send your husband my regards!"

With those last words, I saw the scariest expression I have ever seen appearing on Odelia's infuriated face.

Chapter 70
The Millennium Dungeon of Blood

While we sped through the forest towards our next destination, Odelia asked, "Are you not going to question me about Minra and Sol, Lord Eyes?"

"Do you want me to?" I replied back.

"Not particularly."

"Then I guess I won't."

"Is that because you are respecting me by not prying? Or do you simply not care?" Odelia genuinely questioned.

"A bit of both," I answered truthfully, elaborating, "I know I wouldn't want you or others to pry on my sad past, so why would I pry on yours if you don't want me to? And honestly, I couldn't care less about those two assholes. I was even tempted to give you permission to beat the shit out of them after hearing how they talked to you, and how that Sol guy laughed at the house earlier."

"Well, I hope you know I could have, and would have taken both of them down if you did ask me to," Odelia confidently assured me.

"And I would've loved to watch that, but I know time isn't my friend today," I said, as I decided to read the notification I ignored earlier.

> **'Bloody Shame'** has been reverted back into **'Odelia's Shame'**

"Interesting, so the blood counted as a modification?" I noted to myself. *"I wonder what other strange modifications I can discover?"*

"Time surely is not, but know that I am a friend, Lord Eyes," Odelia told me while we continued through the forest. "And now that there are

In Range – Ven'Thyl Saga Part I

no longer any peering eyes and curious ears around us, this friend would like to congratulate you on reaching a level equivalent to a Long-Range Archer—but seeing how this will be the second style you've learned, I should rather congratulate you on being equivalent to a Dual-Style Archer instead." Then like before with the Magic Style, a large message appeared as I ran—causing me to stumble a little.

Class Change

Meeting both the required conditions to become a 'Long-Range Archer' Class or 'Dual-Style Archer' Class, you are now eligible to change your current 'Magic Archer' Class to one with equal or higher potential.

Which Class do you choose:

Your next potential Class Progression Choice will greatly change depending on your chosen Class.

[Dual-Style Archer] or [Magic Archer] or [Long-Range Archer]

You have learned the Skill: [Deadly Range].

"It's nice to have options, but obviously I'm picking the one with more potential," I thought, choosing the **Dual-Style Archer**.

Congratulations, you have changed your current Class to 'Dual-Style Archer'!

You have gained the Title: [A True Long-Range Archer]	You have learned the Proficiency: [Long-Range Archery]
You have learned the Skill: [Archer's Duality]	You have learned the Skill: [Deadly Range]

| Long-Range Archery proficiency increased by 33 Levels. | Deadly Range increased by 3 Levels. |

"Nice, I still got all the stuff related to Long-Range! Maybe it's because I'm both a Magic Archer and a Long-Range Archer?" I figured, reading all the descriptions.

> **A True Long-Range Archer:** Learning the Long-Range Archery Style from someone who's already fully mastered it, you obtained the power with your own ability and effort, and are acknowledged as a true Long-Range Archer. +33 Endurance and Sense.

> **Long-Range Archery:** One of the three pinnacle styles of Elven archery; Long-Range provides the range, accuracy, and precision needed to become a Trinity Archer. Complete mastery is required for combining the styles, but unbalanced mastery will result in overwhelming the others and erasing their progress. Skill Level based on Skill Levels of the Long-Range Style.

> **Archer's Duality:** No longer limiting yourself to one target, your mind and body becomes truly capable of focusing on two things at once, and is free of natural preference.

In Range – Ven'Thyl Saga Part I

> **Deadly Range:** All the arrows you shoot now become increasingly deadlier the further they travel, dealing an additional 1% Damage per 100 meters that the arrow travels. Percentile damage increases by 1% per Skill Level, Skill Level based on Long-Range Archery Level.

When I finished reading it all, I asked Odelia, "Exactly how far is this Dungeon again?"

"It should be roughly about 15 hours away at our current pace," Odelia estimated.

"That only leaves me 3 hours to beat the Combat Test, but who knows what I could come across there..." Quickly deciding, I said, "Okay, let's really pick up the pace then," as I then activated **Sprint** and raced straight through the overgrown parts of the forest—remembering the conversation I had with Odelia four days ago.

Four days earlier...

"What? All I need to do is beat a single monster in a Dungeon?" I repeated Odelia's surprisingly simple Combat Test; thinking, *"It's too good to be true."*

"It may sound simple enough, but remember, you may only use the Combat Style to do so—or otherwise forfeit the monster and try again with another," Odelia specifically stated.

"But you did say it could be any monster, right? It doesn't have to be a Dungeon Boss?" I asked, making sure I heard her right.

"Apologies my lord, but I do not think I have correctly conveyed the severity of my Combat Test to you, so allow me to explain again," Odelia's face became serious. "I truly have lost many students who underestimated or did not properly prepare themselves for the difficulty of my Combat Test. And although we will only be fighting the monsters on the outskirts of the Dungeon, know that if we do come across any of the Bosses inside, you must immediately run outside of the Dungeon; for even I am unsure if I can survive a battle alone with one inside that bloody, crimson place."

Fables of J

"Wait, you're serious," I said, finally heeding Odelia's words. "Just what kind of place are we going to? And what do you mean 'Bosses?' There's more than one?" I felt my concern grow.

"It is a place of old. One which has yet to fall in the last ten centuries; and is fittingly named the Millennium Dungeon of Blood..."

Abruptly hitting my nose, an intense horrid stench of fresh and drying blood—reeking of metallic iron—began to fill the surrounding air ahead of us. I already felt slightly dazed, dreading my selfish and greedy choice of knowingly coming to a very dangerous Dungeon supposedly made out of blood. Odelia on the other hand was completely unfazed, continuing to lead me forward for a few more minutes, until we finally reached our destination; the Millennium Dungeon of Blood.

The beautiful forest of emerald green trees unnaturally changed ahead of us; and almost as if a perfectly clean line was drawn onto the ground, the grass turned from a fresh green to a deep crimson. Growing on top of this crimson grass was the very same type of trees I saw in House Baen'Mtor's orchard; with the same black spiky bark, the same crimson leaf tops, and the same oozing red sap dripping out of them—now knowing it's blood and not sap. However since these were unkept, their appearance was much wilder, having multiple large protruding spikes all along the trunks of the trees.

"Are you sure you want to enter, my lord?" Odelia asked in concern, already gripping her bow with a hand on the hilt of her sword. "We can still return to the city and simply prepare for tomorrow's festival, you know? You do not have to do the Combat Test on this day—in fact I highly implore you do otherwise."

Taking my time to tightly wrap the simple cloth I bought the other day around my lower face to cover my mouth and nose, I said, "I'm not too psyched about all this blood, but unless you're planning to forfeit your challenge, I'm winning it today. So, what'll it be?" She thought about it for a second, but ultimately shook her head no. "That's what I thought. Now let's go find me a monster to fight."

And as we crossed onto the damp crimson grass, the Dungeon messages appeared.

In Range – Ven'Thyl Saga Part I

> **You are now entering a Lv.10(Max) Open Dungeon**

> **Your regeneration is now halved**

But before I could even question what that Dungeon Level meant, Odelia and I both heard screams of pain and cries for help in the distance; and with a simple acknowledgement to each other, we ran in the direction the voices were coming from.

Passing by stumps of cut down and burnt trees, we arrived at a scene with two partial bloodied armoured people—a man and a woman—protecting two other bloodied people on the ground—a woman screaming out in pain from what looked like a freshly torn off leg, and a man trying his best to heal the grievous wound. They were all surrounded by four large jaguar-like monsters, with another one to the right gnawing on what I assumed was the missing leg of the woman, and one more to the left ravaging through the insides of an already dead man.

"Blood Stalkers. Though if that many came out of hiding just to hunt them down, that must mean those adventurers have some pretty tasty smelling blood," she said, watching the armoured people barely fend off the attacks from the four circling monsters.

Intrigued by the monsters' appearance, I took note of their strange, skinless and bone faces; exposing their head's frontal bone structure, their orange coloured eyeballs, their solid black pupils, and displaying their several long and jagged sharp teeth. The rest of their body however had leathery hide, being the same crimson red as the leaves and the grass in the area, and had multiple bone spikes protruding down their back and spine—stopping just before their long, thick tails. I also noticed that their tails and back had some crimson hair that looked exactly like the grass on the ground. And as they circled around those injured people on all fours, I admired their strong and powerful looking legs as they cautiously attacked with their long sharp bone claws.

"So what do you think, Eyes? Still think you can take one down for my test?"

But before I answered, I took a look at the monsters' levels and saw they all had different levels—each being one level higher than the other, and the highest being a **Lv.55 Blood Stalker**.

Although I was nervous about my chances only using the Combat Style and the huge level difference, I still said, "Of course I do, but I want that one first." I pointed to the **Lv.50** gnawing on the woman's leg.

"Looks like you can already accurately identify the weakest enemy out of the bunch. You have some great instincts, Eyes. I am impressed." Odelia then formed herself four arrows. "Now, just give me a moment to capture all of them. Oh, and take this." She handed me the satchel she brought. "There are six Greater Healing Potions in there if you want to help those adventurers out, though you can always save them for yourself in case you get injured later."

Being overwhelmed, the armoured man—who wielded a strange looking two-handed battle-axe—got pincered on both sides by the two Blood Stalkers he was fending off. He was barely able to dodge the two attacks coming from the front, but not the two coming from the back. The Blood Stalker's sharp claws cleanly tore through the metal of his armour, leaving a huge bloody ten-clawed gash on the man's back, and causing him to scream out in excruciating pain.

The same thing was about to happen to the armoured woman, but she yelled out, "**Safeguard!**" and a visible blue aura surrounded her armour and shield. She then blocked the front attacks with her shield, and countered with a hammer strike to the side of the Blood Stalkers's face; however the attacks from behind did strike her back, but unlike the armoured man who wore the simliar looking armour, these claw attacks only left huge scratches on the armour instead of tearing through it. Though knowing that they wouldn't last for much longer, Odelia rushed towards them, and I followed—choosing to help.

Leaping over the monsters and the people with a single jump, Odelia immediately shot four consecutive mana-arrows at each of the Blood Stalkers surrounding the people. But not recognizing the arrows, I took special notice of the ten mana-rings around the shaft of the arrow, and watched as three of them hit the backs of the slow reacting **Lv.51**, **Lv.52**, and **Lv.53 Blood Stalker**; the fourth arrow however was noticed

In Range – Ven'Thyl Saga Part I

and avoided by the Lv.54 Blood Stalker. Then, as Odelia landed back onto the ground, the mana-rings around the hit arrows suddenly enlarged and began binding each of the hit Blood Stalkers—four rings binding the arms, four rings binding the legs, and the last two binding their wrists and ankles together. And in an instant, three Lv.50 monsters were helplessly bound and struggling to break free on the ground.

I smirked and admired Odelia, *"Man, she's so cool. And it looks like she's been hiding a better version of Ensnaring Arrow from me."* Then as I reached the adventurers, they were all surprised and relieved to see us, and I said, "Here. Drink this," quickly handing each of them a Greater Healing Potion.

Greater Healing Potion

Uncommon

Consume: Restores 30% of your Health over 60 seconds.

Craftable

Gulping the potion down, the armoured man collapsed to his knees, saying, "Oh, thank God people heard us... I really thought we were gonna be goners there..." while crawling himself next to the woman who lost her leg.

Struggling to uncork the potion, the one-legged woman shouted in irritation, "God damnit, Dig! There's still more of those Blood Stalkers around us, why are you acting so relaxed!" She slapped the still bloodied gash on the man's back.

"Fuuuckk!" he screamed out in pain. "What the hell, Hive!?" He sat up and turned his back away from her. "I know you lost your leg, but I didn't think you lost your senses too! Can't you tell these NPCs are clearly stronger than us?" he said, pointing to Odelia who was drawing all the attention of the remaining Blood Stalkers and trying to capture them unharmed.

Fables of J

"Wait, NPCs? These guys are Players?" I was taken by surprise. *"I got so distracted by seeing new monsters that I didn't even bother to check their names and levels."*

Quickly checking all of them now, I saw that the armoured man was **Lv.32 How Do I Get Home**; he was a human with dark brown skin, a completely bald head, and a black scruffy beard. The one-legged woman was also human, with simple tied up brown hair, and slightly tanned skin; wearing a mage looking robe, and had **Lv.32 Ahhhhh** above her head. And currently trying his best to still heal their injuries was **Lv.31 Curly**, appearing to be the only different Race in their Party—a High Elf with short curly blonde hair. Then lastly, the armoured woman wearing an open-faced helmet was named **Lv.33 Jane Doe**—I presumed she was also human as she was too short to be an elf.

"Damn, Players are already in the Level 30's? I better finish up learning the styles so I can level again too, or I'll really end up falling behind everybody else. But leveling must be pretty hard if they only got to the early 30's in the last two weeks. Though maybe these guys just haven't leveled a lot compared to the other Players," I thought, taking a note to check out the Rankings later.

"Dig, shut up! If you and Fletch didn't insist on collecting more wood than the request asked for, then we wouldn't be in this situation right now, and that greedy idiot would still be alive and I wouldn't have lost my leg!" The woman's eyes began to tear up.

"I know you're in a lot of pain, Hive, but don't blame Dig. You know it was a Party decision to keep going further into the Dungeon," Curly said, continuing to slowly heal the leg wound into a stump at the woman's thigh.

"I know, Curly..." the woman sounded so exhausted and defeated as she finally opened the potion and drank it.

"If you really want to blame someone, blame me, Hive," Jane spoke up. "I'm the Party Leader. I should've noticed the two Blood Stalkers hiding under the ground. And I should've protected both you and Fletch." She tightly gripped her shield and hammer in regret.

"It's no one's fault," Curly told them; reasoning, "If Fletch, who had the highest Sense out of us didn't notice, how would any of us have been able to?"

"Do not feel bad about not noticing the Blood Stalkers," Odelia suddenly mentioned. "They do specialize in hiding in the terrain after all," she said, dragging behind her the six Blood Stalkers struggling to break free of her bindings—angrily growling at each and every one of us.

Chapter 71
Combat Test Part 1

Instinctively their whole Party backed away, but they all relaxed after they realized Odelia had complete control over the restrained Blood Stalkers—as she had even muzzled them with mana to prevent them from biting. Sighing in relief, their Party Leader Jane said, "I don't know who you two are, but thank you for saving us. We really don't know what we would've done if you didn't show up."

"Yeah, no problem," I replied. "It was all her anyway." I gestured to Odelia.

"Don't count yourself out, stranger. The potion you gave us looks like it really helped Dig out." Jane pointed out how the armoured man's wound was practically healed.

"Oh, shit! Nice!" Dig just noticed it himself. "Thanks, man!"

"So, what do we call you two?" Jane asked, resting her hammer and shield down.

Odelia gestured for me to answer, and I thought, *"They shouldn't know I'm a Player, so why don't I keep it that way. But I shouldn't mention Odelia's name either; they could look for her in the city, and that could lead them to the house."* Trying to think of some aliases to use, I said the first names I thought of. "Jude… and this is my friend… Rosalie." Odelia smiled and nodded as she went along with it.

"Jude and Rosalie, huh? Well the name's Jane, and these are my Party members: Curly, Dig, and Hive. And now that we've all met, I hope we can be very good friends in the future. We'd love to repay you back for saving our lives—the both of you." She made sure Odelia was included. "You just name it, and we'll do whatever you need done." The Party all nodded in agreement.

In Range – Ven'Thyl Saga Part I

"I can't believe these guys are trying to get a Quest out of us in the state they're in. They must be Top Players for sure," I figured, *"but I guess I wouldn't be any different."* Then playing along, I acted if I was thinking of something I needed them to do, and said, "I'll tell you what, we don't need anything from you right now, but when we do, I'll contact you later, alright?"

"That's better than nothing, but how are you gonna know where to contact us?" Jane questioned. "Because we'll probably be leaving the city of Ven'Thyl in a week, and we're not even sure where we'll be heading next."

"Don't worry, I have my ways," I assured her. "Just promise me you'll do whatever favour I ask you guys when the time comes, alright?"

"You can count on it." Jane took me by the hand and shook it in agreement.

"I'll have to take a mental note of their names so I can message them if I ever need a favour done," I thought, generally memorizing their simple names.

"Pssst, Curly," Dig whispered, not wanting to interrupt, "now that you're done with Hive's leg, can you finish healing my back? I don't want it to scar."

"Sorry, Dig, but I ran out of mana. You'll have to wait a bit for me to regen," Cure replied quietly.

"Oh, if you guys still need healing, I can help with that." I then spent the next 3 minutes using **First Aid** on each of them until they were no longer injured.

> **First Aid increased by 1 Level.**

After that, we protected them while they buried what remained of their friend's body, and then we personally escorted them out of the Dungeon in case they ran into other monsters; but luckily we didn't come across any. We said our goodbyes and they all left for the direction of the city.

Once they were out of sight, I asked Odelia, "How wrong would it be if I desecrated their friend's grave?"

Fables of J

"Uhhh, what? Why would you do that?" Odelia was puzzled by such an unexpected question.

"Well, I was carefully watching them while they buried their friend, but I'm pretty sure none of them bothered to search the guy's body."

"What exactly would they search, my lord? The man only had his torso left?"

"I'm not really hearing you say no to the idea," I said, starting to make my way back to the grave and the Blood Stalkers we left tied to a tree with mana.

"That is because they did not even properly bury him and pray to the Goddesses," Odelia reasoned. "I mean how could they leave the body of their 'friend' in a Dungeon where it is more likely to be resurrected into undead?"

"They probably didn't know," I began to dig up the shallow grave.

"How could they not know, everyone knows?" Odelia stated, helping me dig.

"Maybe they're not everyone?" I shrugged, then as I saw a little bit of the man's chest, I reached down and caused his Inventory to pop up. *"Aww, besides the good amount of money, he doesn't have anything but arrows in here. I guess not being able to stack items really fucks a Ranger's Inventory."*

I took all of his arrows and stored them in Infinity; and with the 10% bonus I get from the 1% Title, I added a total of 319 Gold, 73 Silver, and 66 Copper into my Inventory. Though since they buried his Lv.30 bow with him, I also took that too.

"You are shameless, my lord," Odelia judged, helping me bury the grave again.

"What? Why would I let a perfectly good bow rot in a grave?" I defended myself, feeling no shame in taking his stuff as we finished refilling his grave. And getting back to business, I checked the Time Limit again.

Time Limit: 4 Hours, 42 Minutes, 11 Seconds

In Range – Ven'Thyl Saga Part I

"Damn, maybe I should've just made Odelia carry me here. We would've saved so much time," I thought, slightly regretting my choice not to; then notifying her, "Okay, Odelia, I think I'm ready to start the Combat Test now."

"Alright, but remember that you can only use the Close-Combat Style during the test, or you will have to try again with another Blood Stalker," Odelia reminded me, while she separated the **Lv.50 Blood Stalker** from the others tied to the tree. "If I see you use a hint of another style other than Combat, you will not pass even if you kill the Blood Stalker using the Combat Style, and you will have to try again with another one if you wish to pass my test," she reiterated again, dragging the Lv.50 to the center of the clearing.

"Yes, yes, I understand the rules. You don't have to repeat it a third time," I replied, following her to the center. "But one thing."

"Yes?"

"Do I have to kill it?"

"Of course. Why would you not?"

"Because this one doesn't seem that bad to me," I admitted, pointing out how this Blood Stalker wasn't struggling to get free, and that wasn't angrily growling at us like the rest of them.

"It likely tired itself out from struggling earlier, or it is waiting for its chance to strike," Odelia reasoned, unsure why I was being so reluctant.

Though deciding to kneel down, I stared directly into the Blood Stalker's eyes, and saw they had a strange calm and accepting feel to them. Then as it suddenly broke our eye contact and closed its eyes, it exposed its neck to us and looked to have almost accepted its imminent death. *"Interesting, it's smart enough to understand the situation it's in."*

Smiling, I said, "Release all your bindings, Odelia. I want to talk to it without any restraint."

"Talk to it? I do not know if you know this, Lord Eyes, but Blood Stalkers are unintelligible monsters—meaning they only communicate through growls and roars, and solely live only on their instincts and

Fables of J

hungering thirst for blood," she warned me. "It will surely attack you once I release it."

"Maybe you can't understand them, but I've understood these guys the whole entire time."

I directed my attention to the Blood Stalkers by the tree.

Still muzzled by mana, with drying blood on its skinless bone face, the Lv.55 growled, "Elf blood, good taste, more want!" It slobbered excessively as it stared at us from a distance.

The Lv.54 on the other hand struggled the hardest to break free of the bindings, angrily growling, "Break! Breaaak! Breaaaaak!" It looked to be the largest and strongest of the six Blood Stalkers. The other three Blood Stalkers also growled about breaking free, killing us, and eating our blood; all in their different simple words of choosing.

"If you were not you, I would not humour such an outlandish claim, but this is not the first time you would surprise me," Odelia said, backing away to the other Blood Stalkers. "Now, if you are truly ready to start the Combat Test, where is the new armour and sword you bought yesterday?" she pointed out.

"Oh, right! I almost forgot to equip them," I opened up my Inventory and equipped an almost full set of elven plate armour—except for the helmet that I didn't buy because I knew the crown prevented me from equipping anything else.

Elven Plate Pauldrons	Elven Plate Chestplate	Elven Plate Gauntlets
Uncommon	Uncommon	Uncommon
+4% Physical Damage Reduction +10 Strength	+10% Physical Damage Reduction +10 Vitality	+3% Physical Damage Reduction +10 Strength
Requirements: Lv.24, Str 100	Requirements: Lv.24, Str 100	Requirements: Lv.24, Str 100

Elven Plate Chausses	Elven Plate Greaves
Uncommon	Uncommon
+5% Physical Damage Reduction	+3% Physical Damage Reduction
+10 Vitality	+10 Strength
Requirements: Lv.24, Str 100	Requirements: Lv.24, Str 100

After being armourless for weeks now, I noticed the heavy weight of the armour weigh on my body. Though compared to the heavier, bulky looking armour Jane and Dig wore, this armour overall had a much lighter and slim look to it, but it did have large gauntlets and greave boots. The armour was also better designed, having a layer of chainmail and dark underclothes underneath the plate, making the darkish green border outlines of the armour pieces really stand out well.

Then, not wanting to get any of my cloaks ruined in what will surely be a tough battle, I decided to go cloakless today and put away the Cloak Of Colour in my Inventory, exposing the crown on my head. However, I still wore the cloth I had wrapped around my lower face to minimize the stench of blood.

"I know elven plate is lighter than regular plate armour, but are you sure you want to fight in that, Lord Eyes?" Odelia questioned in concern. "It is unusual to see an archer wear such heavy and restrictive armour, unless they are the city guards or it is wartime."

"Yeah, I'm sure. I just have to get used to moving in it is all," I said, rotating my arms and shoulders, and lifting up my knees and legs. Then after briefly getting used to the movement, I lastly took out the sword I bought.

Fables of J

Silverthorn II
Uncommon
Attack: 222
Effect: Deal an additional 22% more damage against Monsters weak to Silver.
Requirement: Lv.22, Str 100, Agi 78

Strapping it to the right side of my waist, I drew the sword from its black leather sheath and held it, blade side down, along my forearm. I took a second to admire its straight and thin double-edged silver blade, its guardless and finely wrapped black leather hilt, and the long silver spike pommel at the top.

Looking back to Odelia, I asked, "You said this sword works on monsters in this Dungeon, right?"

"That is what I said," Odelia confirmed. "Though only about half the monsters in here have a weakness to silver, and lucky for you, the Blood Stalkers are one of them."

"Good to know." Drawing my bow from my back, I said, "Okay, now I'm ready. Release your bindings." I held my bow in my left hand and my sword in the other—standing 5ft away from the Blood Stalker.

"Alright, here you go. But do try to be careful, Lord Eyes," she cautioned. And with a snap of her fingers, Odelia released all the mana-bindings around the Blood Stalker, but it didn't react at all and just laid there.

A moment passed, but it continued to lay still with its eyes closed, so I said to it, "Hey, Blood Stalker. You can understand me, right?"

Hearing me speak to it caused the Blood Stalker's body to twitch for a moment, but it went back to its stillness a moment later.

"Why are you just laying there and playing dead? Are you waiting to surprise attack me or something?" There was no response this time. "I can tell you're at least a little bit smarter than your friends over there, so why don't you wake up and talk to me, and maybe I'll let you go?"

In Range – Ven'Thyl Saga Part I

As I took a single step closer, the Blood Stalker instantly opened its eyes, quickly got up, and pounced towards me with its large, open boney maw attempting to bite me. Though having already prepared myself for the surprise attack, I performed a back handspring right before it reached me, and landed a clean kick right under its jaw. I subsequently landed poorly from the handspring as I wasn't used to acrobatic movement with the extra weight of the armour yet.

Shaking its head from the daze of my attack and being completely undamaged by it, the Blood Stalker growled, "Me miss..." It then started pacing back and forth in front of me, waiting for another chance to attack.

"And it speaks," I said, picking myself up from my poor landing. "So, what do you say? Wanna talk?" Putting both my weapons up in the air to show I meant no harm.

"Me talk, free me go?" the Blood Stalker growled, slowing its pacing back and forth.

"Yeah, I promise," I sheathed my weapons to prove it. "Now can you tell me about the Bosses in this Dungeon and what's hidden inside? My friend over there won't tell me anything because she thinks I'll want to clear it if I know." I secretly pointed to Odelia who looked shocked to see me actually communicating to the Blood Stalker.

"Many Bosses here, all danger. But never meet Big Boss, too scary danger," the Blood Stalker answered, stopping its pacing and sitting itself down.

"Big Boss? Is that the Dungeon Boss?" I inquired curiously. "Do you know where Big Boss is?"

It excessively shook its head no, "No! All know run from lake, too scary danger. Big Boss and Blood Water too strong!"

"Big Boss? Blood Water? What kind of monsters are they?" I wondered to myself, then asked the Blood Stalker, "Do you happen to know where this lake is?"

"Far here," it turned and pointed its bone nose in the direction Odelia guarded. "But elf go, elf die. Like all."

I chuckled, "Thanks for the warning, and the info," I said, telling the Blood Stalker, "you're free to go now."

243

Fables of J

The Blood Stalker tilted its head at me, "Free go?" it wagged its long thick leathery tail for a moment.

"Yeah, you can go. I promised. And you don't seem as dangerous as the others," I allowed it to go freely.

"No, me danger! They no danger!" the Blood Stalker growled aggressively, trying to puff its body bigger than the others.

"Okay, okay, you danger, they not danger."

It gave me a toothy grin, and slowly and carefully walked in the opposite direction of Odelia, all while keeping an eye on me for a surprise attack. I waved it goodbye, but it stopped only just outside of the clearing and began digging a hole with its claws.

Once it finished digging, it laid itself inside and made the hole look completely filled in, with the red hair on its back and its crimson hide blending perfectly into the ground—only having its bone face on the surface creepily staring at me.

"Must be how they hide themselves and wait for prey," I figured, walking back over to Odelia. "I want… this one next," I said, picking out the **Lv.51**.

"Lord Eyes, those growls were surely unintelligible, so where did you learn to communicate with Blood Stalkers?" Odelia questioned, separating the Lv.51 from the others, "I mean after all, Blood Stalkers are only native to this Blood Forest, and you told me you have never been to the Kingdom before, right?"

"Uhhh… I guess you could say I learnt it from Oros—he taught me how to speak to other monsters," I said, helping Odelia drag the angry Lv51 to the center of the clearing while it continued to growl about killing and eating us.

"That does not make sense, my Lord. Cyclops' only speak Giant or Common, Dwarvish too in Oros' case, so how could he teach you to speak to other monsters?" Odelia tried to understand the possibility.

"I guess that's just another one of my secrets," I gave her a wink, leaving her clueless. "Now release it." I readied my weapons again.

The instant Odelia released her mana-bindings, this Blood Stalker, without hesitation, pounced towards me with its sharp claws first. And barely stepping out of the way in time, I countered with a horizontal slash to its body with my sword as it passed by; but the blade didn't cut as deep as I thought it would, and only left a small graze on the Blood Stalker's leathery hide. *"Did I not use enough force, or is their skin just that hard?"*

Even though it was a small cut, the Blood Stalker roared in anger, "Elf dead!" as it charged towards me at incredible speeds.

Using **Rapid Shot**, I pulled four arrows from my quiver and rapidly fired them all consecutively—aiming for its eyes. Though reacting to the incoming arrows, the Blood Stalker brought its body to an immediate stop, whipping its long tail towards me, and causing the arrows to shallowly pierce its side. The tail whipped with such surprising speed that I couldn't react to it in time, landing a direct hit into my armoured stomach and knocking me backwards about 10ft.

Grasping my stomach from the pain, I felt a huge dent in the armour made by the powerful tail attack, but quickly stood myself up as the Blood Stalker began charging again. When it threw a downward claw strike towards me, I first dodged to the side, and then using as much strength as I could, I stabbed my sword straight into Blood Stalker's open side. But even after using all my strength, only half the blade went through before I couldn't push the sword any deeper. However the blade did cause a strange searing sound to be heard inside the Blood Stalker's body.

The Blood Stalker roared even louder than before, "ELF!" And knowing I needed to get away, I tried to quickly pull out the sword, though it just wouldn't budge from its body. Immediately deciding to let it go, I was about to use Archer's Dash to make some distance, but two claws quickly pierced into each side of my pauldrons, reaching down into my flesh, and bringing me down to my knees with the heavy weight of the Blood Stalker weighing over my shoulders and body.

"Aaahhhh!" I screamed out in excruciating pain, and using as much strength as I could, I barely held up the Blood Stalker from pinning me down onto the ground.

The Blood Stalker's bone face grinned widely, staring at me like I was delicious food while growling, "Blood good smell, want taste!" It opened its large boney maw and sunk all of its jagged teeth deep into my collarbone, shoulder, and a part of my neck.

Hearing the armour being crushed in its maw, feeling the warm blood gushing out of my body, and seeing its hungry eyes made it feel like all the pain was being tripled as I screamed out even louder than before.

"AAAAAHHHHHHHH!"

Chapter 72
Combat Test Part 2

"Lord Eyes!" Odelia yelled out, quickly drawing her bow and aiming directly at the Blood Stalker.

"Wait! Don't!" I shouted, bearing the incredible pain of the sharp teeth and the two claws digging into me. "I can... still do this! Aaahhh...!"

Clenching my teeth in pain, I focused all my strength into prying the claws out of my shoulders; though the moment I did, the Blood Stalker countered by biting down even harder into my neck and shoulder, causing me to drop my bow and move my hands to each side of its mouth to keep the jagged teeth from going even deeper inside me. And without my hands pushing them back, the claws freely dug back into my shoulders and I yelled out in even more pain.

"Aaahhhh!"

Then all of a sudden a notification appeared.

> **You have been affected by the Status Debuff: [Bleeding]**

Right after, my already halved **Health** began rapidly ticking down.

> **Health: 2,883/5,895**

> **Health: 2,824/5,895**

> **Health: 2,765/5,895**

"Shit, this isn't good! My health is going down way too fast! At this rate I'll be dead in no time if I don't think of something now!" I panicked, trying to quickly brainstorm how to escape. *"Think, Eyes! Think!"* I thought, still holding back the Blood Stalker's mouth and trying my best to ignore as much of the pain as possible.

"Lord Eyes, it is over! I am ending this!" Odelia shouted, fully drawing a mana-arrow aimed directly at the Blood Stalker's skull.

"Fuck, this sucks! I really wanted to pass on my first try, but I guess I don't have a choice if I want to survive—except I should at least finish this on my own."

Before Odelia could shoot, I let go of the Blood Stalkers mouth, and quickly formed eight mana-arrows—one in my left hand, and seven in my right hand. Ignoring the increased pain of the bite, I held the one arrow in front of the Blood Stalker's face, and waited for the opportunity to use the others. Then feeling that the Blood Stalker was about to tear open my neck and shoulder, I closed my eyes and slightly turned my head away from the left arrow and immediately casted **Element Arrow (Light)**.

An intense burst of blinding light instantly erupted from the arrowhead, and I could hear Odelia shout "Ahhh, Lord Eyes! Stop! I cannot see where to aim!"

At the same time, I felt the Blood Stalker's bite loosen as it growled, "Graahh! No see!"

Using that opening, I cast **Explosive Arrow** on all seven arrows in my right hand at once, and immediately struck them against the Blood Stalker's face. Simultaneously all seven arrows exploded on contact, creating a powerful cluster of seven explosions between the Blood Stalker and me, and producing so much unexpected force that I was sent tumbling out of the clearing.

Explosive Arrow increased by 1 Level

In Range – Ven'Thyl Saga Part I

    Impacting hard against one of the trees, my armour luckily broke off all the protruding spikes on its trunk, and I simply found myself on the ground trying to shake off the daze from the explosion. Struggling to pick myself up, I jumped in pain as I used my right hand to help me—just realizing the explosion had completely destroyed my right gauntlet, and left my hand and forearm a shredded and blackened mess.

    "If this was my only injury… it would probably hurt like hell right now… But with the wounds from the claws and the bite… I barely even feel it compared to them..."

    Groaning loudly, I pushed myself to get up regardless of the pain. "I should also never do that again… Explosive Arrow will only get more powerful as I level… and next time it might just do more than hurt my hand…" Giant waves of pain rippled through my entire body. Then, as I took a step forward, I felt my head begin to spin—causing me to stumble a little.

> **Due to having extreme blood loss, you have temporarily gained the Status Debuff 'Dazed', which cannot be removed until either your body has completely recovered the lost blood or your Health returns back to full.**

> **You have been affected by the Status Debuff: [Dazed]**

    I tried taking another step forward but I stumbled and almost fell to the ground. "Hmph… I can't even walk straight… I wonder how long it'll take to recover..."

    I looked at my current **Health**.

> **Health: 310/5,895**

> **Health: 251/5,895**

Fables of J

> **Health: 192/5,895**

"Holy shit!" I exclaimed, quickly casting **First Aid** on myself.

> **You are no longer affected by the Status Debuff: [Bleeding]**

"Fuck, that was close… I can't believe I was almost about to die there… And if I remembered First Aid could do that… I would've done it earlier..." I groaned to myself, feeling only slightly less woozy from the blood loss. "Well I better get rid of this Status… before I fight another one of those Blood Stalkers..." Taking my second to last Greater Healing Potion from my Inventory, I used my teeth to uncork it and I happily gulped down all the shimmering red liquid inside the bottle. To my surprise, it had a really pleasant and slightly sweet taste to it as it smoothly travelling down my throat.

With First Aid and the Greater Healing Potion's durations running, I watched as the huge open wound on my shoulder, collarbone, and neck slowly began to heal and close itself slightly. My blackened and shredded right hand also started to slowly magically repair the skin tissue back to normal—all while I kept an eye on my **Health** going up.

> **Health: 297/5,895**

> **Health: 372/5,895**

> **Health: 448/5,895**

Though before I could take out my last potion and drink it, I suddenly heard a loud roar "See elf!" as I then saw the blurry figure of the Blood Stalker charging towards me; now having a large crack in its face, scorch marks from the multiple mana-explosions, and my fresh blood heavily dripping from its mouth.

In Range – Ven'Thyl Saga Part I

"Damn, I should've known it wasn't dead." Instinctively reaching for a bow on my back, I realized that nothing was there, and remembered that I was forced to drop it to hold back the bite.

"Shit!"

Seeing the Blood Stalker getting closer, I tried to imagine a bow in my hand, but nothing formed, "Fuck, my head's too dizzy to concentrate my mana properly!" Still feeling off and woozy, I decided, "Reaching my bow it is then."

Awkwardly running and stumbling back towards the clearing and the Blood Stalker, I activated **Sprint** to increase my speed, but I immediately tripped over an unnoticed stump and fell forward onto the ground. Pouncing at me, the Blood Stalker roared, "Elf dead!" Panicking, I rolled and used **Archer's Dash**, barely making it out of the way.

Deciding it was best to avoid and ignore the Blood Stalker until I got my bow, I quickly dashed and stumbled my way back to the clearing, and saw that Odelia was still blinded and rubbing her eyes excessively from the earlier arrow. "Lord Eyes, are you alright? Where are you?" she continued to yell out. "Just wait a little longer, my sight will recover soon!"

"I'm okay, Odelia!" I replied, trying to relieve her concern. "And don't worry about saving me, I need to know if I can do this on my own!"

Quickly spotting my bow, I stumbled over to pick it up.

Turning around and holding the bow from a kneeling position, I grimaced in pain as my shoulder wound wasn't fully healed yet, and as my torn skin on my right hand drew an arrow and pulled the bowstring back. Aiming the arrow directly at the charging Blood Stalker, a wave of dizziness suddenly hit me and my usual steady aim wobbled and strayed from my intended target. Knowing that I was most likely gonna miss like this, I aimed directly above the path the Blood Stalker was moving in and used **Arrow Shower** instead. I then watched the single arrow fly in a high arc above, multiplying into a total of 22 arrows once it reached the apex, and all shower directly downwards onto the Blood Stalker.

Noticing the arrows late, the Blood Stalker still tried to get out of the area but was struck by more than half of them—the arrows each piercing different parts of its body. Though unfazed by the arrows sticking out of its hide, the Blood Stalker growled, "Weak elf!" It laughingly grinned at me and announced, "**Blood Heal!**" Its whole body then strangely began oozing blood all over, causing the stuck arrows to be slowly pushed out by the strong flow of the blood, along with my sword still stuck in its side.

"What the hell?" I noticed how all the previous wounds I made, slowly closed up and healed into scars—even causing the large crack on its face to slowly heal back to normal.

"We call that Blood Healing!" Odelia informed me with her sight back to normal and wih an arrow aimed at the Blood Stalker again.

"It just said Blood Heal, so I think your naming's slightly off," I told her.

"Huh, go figure," she said, explaining. "Anyway, Blood-Type monsters have the innate ability to use the blood they consume and store inside their bodies to heal themselves. It is what makes them so difficult to deal with in extended battles, and is likely one of the worst monsters you could have chosen in here to fight for your Combat Test—especially in a Dungeon full of blood such as this."

"Wow! You know that info would've been really nice to know before we started!"

"Who was it again who told me to release the Blood Stalker?" Odelia smirked at me but I just replied with a huff.

Turning my attention back to the Blood Stalker, I saw my arrows and my sword all be ejected out of its body as it fully healed. Speaking to the Blood Stalker, I said, "You're not the only one who can heal." casting **First Aid** on myself two more times, and deciding to save my last Greater Healing Potion for later.

"Good! More tasty blood!" the Blood Stalker growled with a laugh, circling around me. "**Bloodthirst!**" It was a small detail, but I suddenly noticed the Blood Stalker's orange eyeballs with round black pupils turn into red eyeballs with sharp slit-shaped pupils; all subsequently causing blood to drip from its eyes, veins to become prominent on its limbs, its

In Range – Ven'Thyl Saga Part I

body to slightly grow and enlarge, its claws to extend into the grass, and its tail to excitedly slam against the ground back and forth.

"Lord Eyes, do not get bitten again! The Blood Frenzy you are witnessing now means all its physical strength has doubled, and it is no longer going to be playing with its food anymore!" Odelia heavily warned me.

The moment I tried to reply to Odelia, I heard the Blood Stalker take its chance and try to attack me from behind; but already expecting that, I used a few **Archer's Dashes** to dodge out of the way and countered with a **Power Shot** to its side. However, relentlessly coming after me, the pouncing Blood Stalker forced me to use a few more dashes to keep my distance.

"Woah, it's moving way faster than before," I thought, focusing only on avoiding its pounces, bites, and claw attacks. While I continued to avoid and dodge the relentless attacks, I tried to cast **Charged Arrow** but it also didn't work.

"Damn, I can't even use Charged Arrow," I opened the Menu to get a glance of the Status.

> **Dazed: Unable to properly think and concentrate on things, you find your mind and body unable to function to their best capacity.**
>
> ***Physical and Magic-Type Skills that require concentration cannot be used while affected by this Status.***
>
> **Duration: Until the adequate amount of blood is regained or Health is recovered back to full.**

"Well I guess I'll just have to stall until this Status goes away then," I decided, keeping an eye on my Health while I used **First Aid** one more time.

Health: 3,566/5,895

Fables of J

Avoiding using any more of my mana, I started instead using all my stamina-based Skills as I easily dodged the now familiar attack pattern of the Blood Stalker. Prioritizing avoiding and dodging the attacks, I waited for openings and countered with alternating Skills from: **Power Shot**, **Spread Shot**, **Rapid Shot**, **Leap Shot**, and **Sniper Shot**. I was actually dealing significant amounts of damage to the Blood Stalker, even after missing half of the Skills because of the dizziness; but as soon as I dealt too much damage to it, the Blood Stalker healed all of it away with its Blood Heal, and I had to deal the damage all over again.

Pacing myself, the battle continued for another 20 or so minutes, until almost all my Stamina was drained; leaving the Blood Stalker injured just before the damage threshold I noticed it preferred to heal itself—timing it exactly when I recovered back to full Health.

> Health: 5,895/5,895

> **Fully recovering back to full Health, you are no longer affected by the Status Debuff: [Dazed].**

Seeing absolutely clearly and feeling my mind sharply focus, I smugly smirked while I faced the injured and exhausted Blood Stalker who was no longer in a frenzy.

"Thanks for leveling my Skills up, but I think it's about time I end this. Catch me if you can, you overgrown cat!" I taunted, sticking my tongue out at it and running away while using **Charged Arrow** with the arrow in my hand.

"Grahhh, elf! **Bloodthirst!**" the Blood Stalker roared, chasing right after me.

Focusing on charging my arrow as fast as possible, I kept an eye on the close bites and claw attacks from the Blood Stalker. Then using the last bit of my Stamina on **Sprint** and **Leap Shot**, I jumped high up into the air.

In Range – Ven'Thyl Saga Part I

Stamina: 0/3,930

The Blood Stalker stopped in place staring up at me, "Fall elf!" angrily growling while it waited for me to land.

"I will! But first, you die!" I said, as I finished charging the last bit of my full **Mana** into the arrow.

Mana: 0/4,140

The arrow looked almost completely normal, except for a visible mana-aura surrounding it, but the instant I nocked it to the bowstring, it drastically changed. Expanding into an enormous 15ft-long mana-arrow, it looked absolutely absurd with the mana-fletching forming way past the bow's bowstring, and the mana-arrowhead forming way past the bow's grip; and the small, in comparison, physical arrow floating in the center between the two points. Then as I strained to draw back the heavy mana-arrow, I could already feel its incredibly potent power waiting to be released.

Smiling wickedly, I aimed the massive arrow directly at the Blood Stalker who looked to be frozen in fear, and feeling it was only right to announce, I shouted, "**Maximum Charged Arrow!**"

Though at the same time, Odelia could be heard shouting, "No! That's too much power!"

As soon as the arrow left the bowstring, the sheer incredible force of the wind pressure it caused pushed me slightly higher up into the air. And in less than half a second, the arrow traveled and pierced the center of the Blood Stalker's back, completely destroying all of it and leaving no remains whatsoever; then disappearing from sight as it dug a giant sinkhole into the bloody crimson ground. However, without even realizing exactly when it broke, I saw that I was only holding the small grip of Shame—spotting the rest of shattered pieces being blown away by the resulting updraft created by the arrow.

Congratulations, you have Leveled Up 6 Levels! All Stats have increased by 12, and you gained 60 Available Points.

Chapter 73
Calm Before the Moon

"Maybe that was a little overkill," I laughed to myself as I safely landed back on the ground—staring at the large sinkhole I created. And feeling thoroughly refreshed after the Level Up, I decided to check out my Character Menu that I've completely ignored for weeks now. After noting how I lost 5 Strength from losing my right gauntlet, I moved onto the Stats side.

Stats
Name: Eyes Thalion Ven'Thyl Race: Wood Elf Level: 30 Class: Dual-Style Archer [Titles]: 28
Health: 6,120 (10% Regen/hr) Mana: 4,290 (5.5% Regen/min) Stamina: 4,080 (5.5% Regen/min)
Vitality: 408(+20)[78] Magic: 429[86] Strength: 425(+25)[80] Agility: 438[88] Intelligence: 546[109] Endurance: 421[84] Sense: 435[87] Luck: 313[63] Available Points: 100
Statuses: [Multi-layered Seal], [Sealed Magic Core], [Sealed Skill] Bonuses: 25 Strength, 20 Vitality, 25% Physical Damage Reduction +25% of Base Stats, +10% to Base Regeneration

"Wow! My Stats are looking great!" I exclaimed to myself. *"But those are just the Total Stats, what's the actual Stats at?"* I hovered my finger over Vitality to find out.

In Range – Ven'Thyl Saga Part I

Vitality: Increases amount of Health and Stamina. 408(Total)= 330(Base Stat)+ 77.5(25% of Base Stat)+ 20(Armour)

"330, huh? The 25% Stat Bonus from the crown really inflates the numbers up, but I guess it's all the better for me though."

Then noticing all the notifications I ignored during battle, I read through them next.

Archery proficiency increased by 2 Levels.	Archer's Confidence increased by 1 Level.
Power Shot increased by 1 Level, and has reached the current Max Level of Skills.	Dodge increased by 1 Level, and has reached the current Max Level of Skills.
Dodge increased by 1 Level, and has reached the current Max Level of Skills.	Archer's Dash increased by 1 Level, and has reached the current Max Level of Skills.

"Current Max Level? Does that mean there'll be a higher level later then?" I wondered, continuing to read the rest.

Arrow Shower increased by 1 Level.	Leaping Shot increased by 3 Levels.
Rapid Shot increased by 2 Levels.	Spread Shot increased by 2 Levels.

Fables of J

Sniper Shot increased by 2 Levels.	Charged Arrow increased by 1 Level.
Long-Range Archery proficiency increased by 8 Levels.	Deadly Range increased by 1 Level.

I also got a new Skill from just Leveling Up to Lv.30.

> You have learned the Skill: [Ranged Advantage]

> Ranged Advantage increases by 4 Levels

> Ranged Advantage: Projectiles you shoot gain a 5% increase to Range, Flight Speed, Damage, and Penetration. Percentage increases by 5% per Skill Level, Skill Level based on highest Ranged Proficiency Level.

"That's another Skill added to the list, I'm starting to lose track of them all. I wonder if the other Players are having the same problem?" I thought, opening up the Skills Menu.

	Skills
	[Sort]
Class Actives:	[Archer's Dash Lv.10(Max)], [Arrow Shower Lv.8], [Charged Arrow Lv.9], [Element Arrow Lv.1], [Ensnaring Arrow Lv.1], [Explosive Arrow Lv.2], [First Aid Lv.7], [Leaping Shot Lv.9], [Power Shot Lv.10(Max)], [Rapid Shot Lv.9], [Sniper Shot Lv.3], [Spread Shot Lv.9], [Turning Arrow Lv.6], [Twin Arrow Lv.7]

In Range – Ven'Thyl Saga Part I

Class Passive:	[Archer's Confidence Lv.4], [Archer's Duality Lv.Max], [Archer's Stride Lv.Max], [Deadly Range Lv.5], [Magic Arrows Lv.2], [Ranged Advantage Lv.1]
Subclass Active:	[Seer's Eye Sacrifice Lv.2]
Subclass Passives:	[Eyes Of A Seer Lv.6], [Seer's Eye Collection(15,274) Lv.6] [Seer's Visions Lv.6]
Active:	[Sprint Lv.10(Max)]
Passives:	[Dodge Lv.10(Max)], [Fitness Lv.6], [Natural Tracker Lv.1], [Sneak Lv.5], [Perception Lv.9]
Race Passives:	[Elven Physiology Lv.Max], [Keen-Sighted Lv.Max]
Class Proficiency:	[Long-Range Archery Lv.42], [Magic-Wielding Archery Lv.14(Sealed)]
Weapon Proficiency:	[Archery Lv.40], [Hand-to-hand Lv.10], [Swordsmanship Lv.12], [Wield Mana Lv.15]
Crafting Proficiency:	[Bowyer Lv.1], [Creature Harvest Lv.2], [Fletcher Lv.1]

Satisfied with my Stats and Skills, I closed the Menus and saw Odelia picking up my sword from the ground and carrying it over to me.

"You know that did not count, right?" Odelia asked, presenting Silverthorn II to me.

"Yeah, I know," I said, grabbing the sword from her and sheathing it back in its sheath.

"And I am sorry about my shameful bow. I should have warned you the moment I saw the Charged Arrow expand to such a size."

"Don't be sorry. It was an amazing bow. Nothing was shameful about it at all," I told her, making her smile. "I only had it for less than a month, but without it, I don't think I'd be standing here right now."

"Your adulation for my bow is unnecessary, my lord," Odelia humbly bowed, "but thank you for your kind words nevertheless."

"No problem. But where am I ever gonna find a bow like that again?"

"Well, seeing how you were quite picky about the bows in the city, I could always teach you how to make your own, you know?" Odelia openly suggested.

"Really!? That'd be so awesome!" I said, excited at the thought of making my own bow, as I had only previously bought them whole or in parts in the previous world.

"Then we can start the day after tomorrow's festival," Odelia gladly stated.

I pumped my fist in excitement, but I decided to bring something up. "Before I forget, I saw your face when I was fighting, Odelia," I said, remembering how she was so ready to end my Combat Test. "Tell me the truth; you didn't actually believe I could kill a monster from this Dungeon at all, now did you?"

"I did not," Odelia answered matter-of-factly. "In truth, I only brought you here so you would understand the difference in strength between you and the monsters on just the outskirts of the Millennium Dungeon. I could have never imagined you actually killing a monster here by yourself, let alone in such a devastating manner, even if you freely used the other Styles." She genuinely sounded to have believed that.

"I appreciate the honesty, but have a little faith in your student, Odelia. It is me after all," I said, feeling slightly offended by her disbelief in me.

"Apologies, Lord Eyes. But allow me to tell you it was truly an incredible and astonishing sight to behold the power you already have at your young age," Odelia apologetically praised. "Nevertheless, like I have been telling you for days now, you are not yet ready for my Combat

Test, my lord—landing a single cut in the entirety of the battle is simply not good enough."

"Actually it was two..." I counted my first shallow cut as one.

"Okay, two cuts is simply not good enough," she corrected her statement. "And now that you have seen and experienced what it takes to pass my test, I will gladly accept your surrender to my challenge, and will be looking forward to you announcing yourself to the kingdom at the eve of tomorrow's Five Heroes Festival."

I bursted out into laughter, "Haha... In your dreams, Odelia! There's no way I'm giving up now! Besides, this only helped prove to myself that I can pass your Combat Test. I just need some time to think about how to do it."

Odelia shook her head and sighed, ominously saying, "I would advise you to hurry your thoughts then, my lord. You may have much less time than you think." She looked deeply up at the huge full moon brightly illuminating the whole crimson forest in a whitish-blue moonlight.

Confused and unsure by what she meant, I opened up the Quest to see exactly how much time I had left.

> **Time Limit: 4 Hours, 1 Minutes, 56 Seconds**

"Less time than I think? But I still have 4 hours? Does she think I'll need more than an hour each for these Blood Stalkers?" I thought, staring at the remaining four tied up to the tree.

I noticed the slightly smaller Lv.52 and the Lv.53 Blood Stalkers stopped growling at us and they both looked scared of me, but the largest Lv.54 was still angrily growling, "Kill strong elf, make me strong!"

On the other hand, the Lv.55 slobbered more than before as it stared at me, growling, "Smell tasty blood, me want..."

Ignoring them, I spent the next few minutes thinking of different ideas to pass the Combat Test; from simply trying to use my poor Hand-to-hand and Swordsmanship to somehow beat them with brute force, to others like kiting them out with basic archery until they got exhausted and I could finish them off with close-range attacks. But I knew all of those ideas would drain me both physically and mentally if I couldn't

Fables of J

beat one of them and had to face another—even if I took into account recovering from the possible Level Ups. Then making up my mind to go all or nothing, I came up with one last idea.

"The actual thing that'll determine if I pass this test or not isn't whether I can actually kill a Blood Stalker with the Combat Style, but in fact whether I can display enough combat skill to convince Odelia I'm at a level of a Combat Archer," I thought, clearly remembering that as the Second Required Feat of the Style, *"and to safely do something like that, I need Stats—one's I don't have yet, but I will soon."*

"It's a gamble, but if I kill 3 of the 4 Blood Stalkers now, I can probably get to Lv.40 and make things so much easier," I thought, though I already knew the problems in that idea. *"But that would only leave me with one chance to pass, meaning if I fail then, I'd probably have to go find another monster in the Dungeon—which could also lead me to failing if I get taken by surprise by an unfamiliar monster and need to use another Style to kill it too. But this is also probably my best shot at succeeding."*

Recalling the earlier battle, I started to think, *"When the Blood Stalker said 'Bloodthirst' and got stronger and faster, we were about the same speed, which means my Agility is already good enough. But when I stabbed my sword into its hide, I had to use all my strength just to get the sword half way through, and I wasn't even able to take it out after that. Well, I guess I know where I should dump all my Available Points in then."* I decided to spend **90 Available Points** into Strength, and put the remaining **10** into **Agility** for a little more speed.

> **Strength: 537(+25)[103] Agility: 450[90]**

Almost instantly I felt my entire body becoming significantly stronger, causing the armour I wore to be slightly tight as my muscles grew and flexed inside it.

> **Fitness increased by 1 Level**

Clenching my fist, I said aloud, "I just need a little bit more."

In Range – Ven'Thyl Saga Part I

"Huh? Did you say something, Lord Eyes?" Odelia asked, strangely not paying attention to me as she had both her bow and sword drawn—carefully surveying the area around us with her eyes.

"No, I was just talking to myself," I told her, "but what are you looking for? Did you sense something dangerous in the area? Is it a Boss?" I eagerly asked, wanting to see what a Boss looked like in this Millennium Dungeon.

"I did not see or sense anything yet—and as for a Boss, you would not want to see one, especially not tonight on the night before the Five Heroes Festival," she stated ominously again, continuing to survey the area.

Still unsure by what she meant, I simply moved on and thought, *"I could probably just kill the three Blood Stalkers with a single Maximum Charged Arrow and be done with it, but I still have 4 hours left, and I should definitely use them to practice the Combat Style and Level Up as many other Skills to the Max Levels as I can. I'll just have to remember to save the last hour for only the Combat Test."*

Having decided, I grabbed the Lv.53 and brought it to the center of the clearing, using this as a perfect time to also see a Monster's Menu for the first time. I switched to the **Eyes Of A Seer**.

Monster Info
Name: None
Species: Blood Stalker
Age: 12
Gender: Male
Class: None
Title: None
Level: 53
Vitality: 310 Magic: 35
Strength: 364 Agility: 392
Intelligence: 25 Endurance: 286
Sense: 403

Fables of J

> **Innate Skills:** Lv.Max Blood Hunger, Lv.9 Blood Heal, Lv.8 Blood Instincts, Lv.7 Bloodthirst
> **Acquired Skills:** None
> **Status:** None
> **Weakness:** Silver

"Interesting... I'm not quite sure how useful knowing any of this will ever be, considering it doesn't even show me the Health or the descriptions of the Skills, but it's cool to see," I thought, switching back to my preferred **Eyes of a Wood Elf**.

Feeling ready to start, I asked Odelia, "Can you release the bindings please? And don't worry, I'll be fighting this one with the other Styles so I won't get as injured as earlier."

Unsure what I was planning, Odelia simply nodded and released the bindings.

And although this one looked scared of me earlier, as soon as he felt the feeling of being freed, the Blood Stalker jumped to his feet and bared his teeth at me, growling, "Dumb elf, dead now!"

"We'll see about that," I smirked, drawing Silverthorn II and taking out the Lv.30 bow I stole earlier.

> ### Fleet-footed
> **Uncommon**
> **Attack: 350**
> **+30 Agility**
> **Requirement: Lv.30, Agi 100, Str 80**

Not feeling threatened at all by this Blood Stalker, I used **Sprint** and rushed straight towards him with my sword in hand. Caught off guard by the sudden burst of speed, the Blood Stalker was slow to react, and I got a free horizontal slice straight along his body—leaving a long clean gash on the side of its leathery hide. I smiled, feeling just how worth it it was to invest into Strength.

In Range – Ven'Thyl Saga Part I

The Blood Stalker roared in pain, "**Blood Heal!**" causing the gash to rapidly heal and close itself significantly faster than the last Blood Stalker I faced.

"Weak Elf!" he snickered.

Ticked off by the way he was laughing at me, I swiftly drew four arrows and shot two **Ensnaring Arrows** at his left legs, and two more at his right legs. Then, as four arrows struck each of the separate legs, the Blood Stalker snickered again after the arrows barely even hurt him. Ignoring the laughter, I watched as the long mana-strands moved with surprising quickness and power, wrapping around the legs and pulling them together by force, and causing the unsuspecting Blood Stalker to tip over and fall onto the ground.

> **Ensnaring Arrow increased by 1 Level**

Smugly looking down on him, I didn't bother to speak and simply unleashed an unending barrage of different **Element Arrows**, **Rapid Shots**, **Spread Shots**, and **Twin Arrows** to his face—not giving it a chance to heal.

> | **Rapid Shot increased by 1 Level, and has reached the current Max Level of Skills** | **Spread Shot increased by 1 Level, and has reached the current Max Level of Skills** |

> | **Element Arrow increased by 1 Level** | **Twin Arrow increased by 1 Level** | **Element Arrow increased by 1 Level** |

Until finally the sudden burst of golden light rejuvenated my body and the Level Up message appeared.

Fables of J

> **Congratulations, you have Leveled Up 3 Levels! All Stats have increased by 6, and you gained 30 Available Points.**

Wasting no time, I brought the large Lv.54 to the center right away, and asked Odelia to release the bindings again. She did exactly that, however I noticed an ever growing cautious look of concern on her face as she still continued to carefully survey the surrounding area. Though, trusting Odelia to deal with whatever came attacking us or to warn me if it were a Boss, I refocused my attention back to the large Blood Stalker.

Deciding not to use Ensnaring Arrow, in fear of making the fight too easy, I spent the next several minutes kiting and evading the attacks of the Blood Stalker—using every other Skill that needed to be leveled to the max. And thanks to the Blood Stalker's Blood Heal, it made it easy to do.

> **Congratulations, you have Leveled Up 2 Levels! All Stats have increased by 4, and you gained 20 Available Points.**

Arrow Shower increased by 1 Level, and has reached the current Max Level of Skills.	Charged Arrow increased by 1 Level, and has reached the current Max Level of Skills.	Leaping Shot increased by 1 Level, and has reached the current Max Level of Skills.

Twin Arrow increased by 1 Level.	Turning Arrow increased by 1 Level.

In Range – Ven'Thyl Saga Part I

Time Limit: 2 Hours, 10 Seconds

When I saw I still had 1 hour left until I really had to start the Combat Test, I let myself relax and walked over to the unnerved looking Odelia. I was about to say some remark about if she was nervous because of me, but suddenly in the blink of an eye, the whitish-blue moonlight that illuminated the crimson forest completely disappeared. And if it weren't for my eyes that could see well in the dark, I would actually believe that the forest and night was shrouded in complete darkness, as we did not even have the pleasure of seeing the stars of the night sky.

Just when I was about to pose a question to Odelia of what was happening, in another blink of an eye the forest and the night was illuminated in moonlight again; however not with the whitish-blue moonlight I expected, but instead with a blood red moonlight that painted everything it touched a dark red.

Immediately I looked up to see the huge, full moon brightly floating in the sky; now bathed in a deep bloody crimson. The grim sight helped me understand what Odelia's earlier words meant.

"Tonight's a Blood Moon..."

Chapter 74
Crimson Moonlight

As if I was looking at a picture with a filter on, everything I could see was truly painted in crimson; from the shine of my elven plate armour, to the silver blade of my sword, everything was illuminated by the huge Blood Moon in the sky.

At that moment, the natural stench of blood coming from the Dungeon became a pungent odor, intensifying and overwhelming all the air around us. I began pinching my nose to reduce the smell, but the pungent odor already seeped into my nostrils and put my mind in a daze again. And quickly following, the trees around us no longer oozed droplets of blood, but instead began endlessly raining down blood from its branches and leaves.

"Why didn't you tell me…"

Unexpectedly, the sounds from a certain night in the hospital momentarily flashed in my ears, and I immediately covered them and shook my head of that memory. Though losing my balance while I heavily tried to forget, I found my feet slipping and being soaked through as the wet, crimson ground created several pools of blood throughout the entire area.

"Woah!" Odelia said, catching and supporting me with her shoulder. "Are you alright, Lord Eyes?"

"I'm… fine," I said, trying to regain my senses, "but why didn't you mention the Blood Moon earlier?"

"My lord, you cannot be serious?" Odelia looked at me in disbelief. "You should more than know that this happens every year on the night before the Five Heroes Festival—when the God of Monsters casts his crimson blessings on the moon. Why do you think I was so hesitant to allow you to come here today?"

In Range – Ven'Thyl Saga Part I

"I thought you just didn't want me to win," I confessed, but wanting to know more, I asked, "What exactly is the blessing again? And is there a reason this 'God of Monsters' does it?"

"Maybe I really should teach you some history?" Odelia jokingly chuckled; then informed me, "As you should know, a natural Blood Moon is a rare occasion when the moon turns a lightish-red colour—unlike the darker colour one we have tonight—and empowers and strengthens the monsters, causing them to go on a rampage in most cases."

I nodded in understanding, knowing at least that much about Blood Moons from games, books, and other fantasies.

She continued, "However, the Blood Moon we have tonight is unnatural—blessed by the God of Monsters himself to create more chaos, and to oversee everything bathed in its crimson moonlight glow. And also unlike a natural Blood Moon, this one affects even monsters who do not look directly in its light; not only empowering and strengthening them more than a natural one, but also invigorates them for breeding, making even the most infertile monsters fertile for the duration of the Blood Moon."

Surprising me, the two remaining Blood Stalkers attempted to break free from the mana-bindings again, but while I watched them fail to do so, I noted how they unnaturally grew in size and widened the unbreakable bindings for the first time. Becoming curious, I briefly used the **Eyes Of A Seer** and saw their Levels had changed by 5 Levels; to a **Lv.57 Blood Stalker** and **Lv.60 Blood Stalker**.

"Does the Blood Moon have a similar effect as my crown?" I wondered to myself, noticing that their eyes changed again. Unlike their natural orange eyeballs or their red eyeballs after using Bloodthirst, these new ones were black as night, and had black slit-shaped pupils with detailed crimson irises—ones that exactly mirrored the perfect image of the Blood Moon above.

The Blood Stalkers both then angrily growled the same thing, "Kill elves! Breed! Kill elves! Breed!" Uncomfortable by how much they were moving, Odelia shot a few more arrows at them and reinforced the previous bindings—fully restraining them again and giving me a thumbs up.

"So basically tonight's like a super aggressive mating season for the monsters then, right?" I simplified what she explained

She laughed in amusement, "I have never thought of it like that, but to put it simply, I guess it would be."

"If this occurs every year, you must have a name for it, yeah?" I inquired.

"Not really. Older Elves simply refer to it as the Last Moon, but I have heard the younger generation, like Shur and Ama, call it Gom's Blood Moon."

"Gom?" I repeated, remembering that name from somewhere.

"God of Monsters," Odelia revealed.

"You keep saying that, but doesn't he have an actual name you can tell me? I know the Twin Goddesses do," I said, remembering them as Luci'El the Goddess of Life and Noxi'El, a.k.a 13, the Goddess of Death.

"Oh my goodness, Lord Eyes. No wonder you were born gifted with such talent, it helps balance your incredible amount of ignorance. Shall I start teaching you as if you were five years of age, because even children know that?" Odelia chuckled to herself.

"Very funny. So, the name?" I repeated, still wanting to know.

Sighing at me again, Odelia said, "Lord Eyes, I or anyone else cannot speak the name aloud, for it has long been forbidden to do so. It has been that way since the Beginning."

"This sounds like a 'He who must not be named' situation, but what's the Beginning?" I wondered, then asked, "Why?"

"Because invoking the name of the God of Monsters could possibly summon it directly to you," she answered seriously.

"Possibly? If it's only a possibility to summon and not a guarantee, why is it forbidden?" I reasonably questioned.

"It is because the God of Monsters will always bring with it a great catastrophic calamity," Odelia stated, "though lucky for us it cares not to be summoned wastefully; only choosing to appear when it finds something that has piqued its interest, or if it is in the midst of great

In Range – Ven'Thyl Saga Part I

chaos. And if you were wondering, I believe its last known appearance was the Second Trinity War, where it single-handedly ended the war by destroying half of each kingdoms' armies and forcing the rest to retreat from it."

"The God of Monsters sounds powerful, but I guess that should be expected from a God. However, if he's anything like the Twin Goddesses, I don't know how the Players are gonna kill him."

"Anyway, it is time for us to head back now. We would not want to run into monsters frantically searching the Dungeon for a mate," Odelia said, already walking in the direction out of the Dungeon.

Stopping her, I said, "Woah, woah, woah. What are you talking about? I have plenty of time before the month is over, meaning I still have a chance to pass your Combat Test."

She tiredly sighed, "Lord Eyes, were you even listening to anything I said about the Blood Moon?"

"Of course I was, and who cares if they're a little bit stronger, I can still pass the test in time," I said, feeling so sure I could.

"After watching you earlier and seeing you only get stronger from each battle, I am not worried about you not being able to kill a measly Blood Stalker anymore, but I am worried it will take too long if you only use the Combat Style," she clarified, warning me, "During your Combat Test, other monsters will surely find their way to this area; whether it be because they are searching for a mate, or running away from the inevitable rampages of stronger monsters deeper inside the Dungeon. And in the best case scenario, I can imagine we would be surrounded by hundreds of Lv.50-60 monsters, all of which we would need to fight to simply escape."

"And the worst case?"

"A Boss shows up and I possibly sacrifice myself for you to escape."

A sinking feeling filled my stomach and the memories of my previous vision raced through my mind. *"This is it, isn't it?"* I now clearly remembered holding Odelia's body in my blood-soaked arms, in a crimson forest exactly like this one. *"This is the place she—No! It can't be! I won't let that happen! If I can see the future, I must be able to change it, right?"* But I couldn't entirely trust myself that I was able to.

"Lord Eyes? What are you waiting for?" Odelia asked, waiting for me to follow.

"Ughhh... I can't give up just on the Combat Test yet," I groaned, scratching my head out of irritation. "Odelia, is there any way you would leave this Dungeon and teleport back to the house without me?"

"Huh? Absolutely not! I cannot leave you alone in a Dungeon such as this!" she adamantly refused.

"I thought so..." Then I thought, *"Is completing this Quest more important than Odelia's life—not even close. But if I know how this will end up, maybe I can still prevent it from ever happening and get both things I want?"*

Feeling frustrated with myself for knowing what the right thing to do was, but being too selfishly greedy to plainly choose it, I angrily picked up the Lv.60 Blood Stalker and tossed it across the clearing. Then walking over to it growling at me, I told the Blood Stalker, "I'm sorry you didn't get a chance to fight for your life, but I need to end this as soon as possible," as I rapidly began charging up an arrow with mana.

Though while I was in the midst of charging, my eyes unexpectedly bursted with golden light as ten ethereal tendrils appeared from them. Confused why they decided to come out, I tried bringing them back into me, but they all refused to listen and immediately started branching outwards. And noticing four tendrils moving towards Odelia and the Lv.57, I specifically focused on those four and forcefully willed them to return to me.

"Lord Eyes, what are you doing right now? What are those things?" Odelia questioned, justifiably worrying at the unusual sight of me.

"It's hard to explain. Just keep your distance," I told her, "they'll come after you if you get too close." She reluctantly listened as she watched me carefully.

The Blood Stalker I stood over then began writhing and growling in pain as the tendrils savagely wrapped around each of its eyes and pulsated intensely. "Grahhh! Hurts! Hurts! Stop!" Meanwhile, the remaining four tendrils moved to the already dead bodies of Blood Stalkers I killed earlier. Only taking them a few seconds, they quickly wrapped themselves around the eyeballs, rapidly syphoning each of them, and causing a familiar notification to pop up.

> **You have collected the [Eyes of a Blood Stalker]**

> **Eyes of a Blood Stalker: Sight naturally developed for hunting down bloodied prey, your eyes distinguish even minuscule amounts of blood traces from one another and accurately track them accordingly. Gain the 'Bloodthirst' Skill**

"The Blood Stalker Skill?" I thought, receiving the notification for it soon after.

> **You have learned the Skill: [Bloodthirst]**

> **Bloodthirst: Forcefully bleeding through your eyes, your body enters into a bloodthirsty, frenzied state and becomes physically stronger the more blood you lose. Gain the 'Bleeding' Status as long as this Skill is 'Active' and lose 1% of your Health per second, but increase All Physical Stats by 0.25% for every percentage of Health missing. Removing the 'Bleeding' Status will end this Skill immediately. Physical Stat Percentage increases by 0.25% per Skill Level.**

And before I could even fully grasp what I just read, all my tendrils came back to me, and a group of notifications popped up.

Fables of J

You have collected the [Eyes of Eicio's Blood Moon].	Seer's Eye Collection increased by 1 Level.
Eyes Of A Seer increased by 1 Level, and you now have vision of an NPC's Menu.	Seer's Visions increased by 1 Level, and you can now see even more of the Visions.

Eyes of Eicio's Blood Moon: Possessing the blessed gift the God of Limbo casted onto the moon, your entire being is empowered and enthralled by the immense godly power it bestows, temporarily losing yourself if you succumb to the divine blessing. Gain 25% to All Base Stats while empowered by the eyes, but potentially enter into an uncontrollable altered state.

"What the hell is this? Eicio's Blood Moon? Is it not the God of Monster's Blood Moon? And does this mean this 'Eicio' guy is the God of Limbo?" My mind raced with all sorts of questions, but interrupting my thoughts was a sudden loud rumble shaking the ground, and faint screams of dying monsters deeper in the forest.

Heavily concerned after hearing the noises, Odelia insisted, "Lord Eyes, I really must urge for us to be leaving now. I believe those were High Orcs and Minotaurs dying just now, and considering they average around the Lv.70-80s, it is not a very good sign to have heard that many dying at once."

"Okay, okay, okay, okay. Just... just 10 minutes," I frantically told her.

"For?"

"The Combat Test."

"Lord Eyes—"

"I know, but... just 10 minutes. That's all I need," I begged. "Please?"

In Range – Ven'Thyl Saga Part I

She shook her head and sighed at my stubbornness. "You will be the death of me, my lord; but fine, you can have your 10 minutes," she reluctantly agreed.

"Thank you, but don't say stuff like that." I was already worried that I would be.

Turning my attention back to the now blinded Blood Stalker I stood over, I nocked the arrow to the bowstring and caused the **Charged Arrow** to largely expand again—though having only used half my **Mana** this time to not break my bow again. Then aiming diagonally down at the **Lv.60 Blood Stalker**, I released the large arrow and heavily strained my new bow. However, it was made well enough to just withstand the power of the maxed leveled Skill. Though what couldn't withstand the maxed leveled Skill was the Blood Stalker, witnessing the arrow easily pierce through its bone face, killing it in one shot, and digging a small diagonal tunnel into the blood soaked ground.

> **Congratulations, you have Leveled Up 3 Levels! All Stats have increased by 6, and you gained 30 Available Points.**

"I do mean to rush you, my lord, but your ten minutes have already begun," Odelia stated, carefully keeping guard with her bow and sword in hand.

"Yeah, I know. I'll make this quick." I drew Silverthorn II as Odelia already released the last **Lv.57 Blood Stalker** angrily empowered by the crimson moonlight.

Chapter 75
Combat Test Part 3

A NOTE FROM FABLES OF J

Thanks for all the Good Ratings lately; besides it cancelling out the few 0.5-2.5 Troll Ratings, it really helps me get a full grasp of how Good/Bad you readers think my story is. :)

Expecting the large, empowered Blood Stalker to angrily charge at me, I prepared to shoot it with Rapid Shot when it came close; but rather than charging, it unexpectedly began drinking from the ever-growing pools of blood on the ground instead. Quickly realizing it was trying to store blood for healing, I immediately ran towards it and activated a maximum 12 arrow **Rapid Shot**—blood splashing in the air as I took each step.

Then allowing the Skill to control my movement, I grabbed all 12 arrows at once—holding them in my draw hand—before rapidly and efficiently shooting each of them in quick succession with systematic perfection. Though hastily reacting to the barrage of incoming arrows, the Blood Stalker turned its large body and used it to take the piercing impact of each of the arrows. However with its empowered body, the arrows didn't seem to pierce its leathery hide as well as it did with the previous Blood Stalkers.

Grinning at me, it roared, "**Bloodthirst!**" As blood flowed from its eyes, its veins prominently appeared on its limbs, and its already large size increased even further—now appearing to stand 8ft in height while on all fours.

"Well, unlucky for you, two can play at that game," I said, activating my own **Bloodthirst**.

> You have been affected by the Status Debuff: [Bleeding]

In Range – Ven'Thyl Saga Part I

Forced to halt myself in place, a sudden throbbing and agonizing pain surged through my entire body, causing me to drop to my hands and knees, screaming in pain.

"Aaahhhhhh...!"

I could feel my pulse rapidly increasing as it thumped loudly in my head, and caused all the blood vessels in my muscles and body to be filled with a rushing flow of blood. But soon after, the blood vessels in my eyes abruptly popped, and blood came falling down out of them onto each side of my face. With my eyes seeing red, not only did an overwhelming need for bloodshed fill my mind, but also a thirsting appetite for the pools of blood surrounding us—parching my mouth the longer I stared at them.

Hearing the splashing of the blood on the ground, I looked up to see the Blood Stalker fiercely charging towards me. Then powerfully leaping into the air, it pointed its elongated razor sharp claws directly at me, as it aimed to pounce on top of me and crush me with its giant, heavy body.

As I frantically rolled out of the way—covering my entire body in blood in the process—the Blood Stalker landed onto the bloodied, wet ground and caused all the blood in the area to splash high up into the air. As the splashing blood accidentally created a momentary cover for me, I took that chance to strike before the blood splash could fall back down.

Simultaneously using my arms to propel myself and my legs to kick off the wet ground, I activated **Sprint** and easily slid straight under the Blood Stalker's belly, slicing a deep gashing wound while I passed underneath. Though overwhelmed by the need to see more of its blood shed, I relentlessly attacked with my increased speed; leaping over the Blood Stalker while slicing its back and cutting into several inner and outer sections of its legs, and to top it all off, severing its thick tail clean off.

The Blood Stalker roared in a frustrated and pained rage, "Grahhh! Weak elf! Red Moon make me strong!" It blindly swiped its claws and attempted to bite me while it profusely bled from all over its body. Suffering too much damage, it growled, **"Blood Heal!"** causing the

Fables of J

numerous cuts and slashes to rapidly heal. Even its tail slowly began growing back, as it then began drinking more blood from the ground again.

"Tick-tock, tick-tock..." Odelia amusingly smiled, pressuring me with the time.

Ignoring her, I started to think, *"This is gonna be more annoying than I thought. And with all these blood pools around, the Blood Stalker can basically always have Bloodthirst on and heal whenever it wants—all without having to worry about finding a source of blood to drink from,"* I thought, casting **First Aid** to heal the Health I lost from the bleed, and deactivating **Bloodthirst** at the same time.

You are no longer affected by the Status Debuff: [Bleeding]	Removing the 'Bleeding' Status has immediately ended the 'Bloodthrist' Skill

Then it hit me, *"Wait, if First Aid can end the Skill, maybe I can surprise the Blood Stalker by turning off Bloodthrist while it's not expecting!"*

Finishing drinking blood from the ground, the Blood Stalker grinned and angrily bared its jagged teeth at me, *"I'll have to injure it to the point of needing to heal again and wait for an opportunity to surprise it."* Then I thought of a backup plan. *"I'll save Eicio's Blood Moon eyes as a last resort if I can't kill it in time,"* I thought, as I prepared myself for the charging Blood Stalker again.

Still slightly faster than the Blood Stalker, even without using Sprint or Bloodthrist, I easily dodged and evaded all of its familiar bites and claw attacks, and countered each of them with slashes across the different parts of its body again; but dealing too much damage to it, the Blood Stalker frustratingly healed it all away again too.

Continuing the battle like that for three minutes, I made sure to never allow it a chance to refill on blood from the pools, which resulted in the blood it was oozing out from Blood Heal to lessen, and pushed me to keep up my relentless slashes on its body. However, as I was about to dodge another double clawed attack, my foot suddenly got caught in

In Range – Ven'Thyl Saga Part I

something which momentarily stopped me from moving. Leaving me no choice, I raised my arms to guard from the incoming attacks, and felt each of the razor sharp claws dig deep into my armoured and unarmoured forearms—causing me to tumble back from the sheer heavy force behind both attacks.

> **Health: 4,195/6,420**

Not tumbling far, I realized I was strangely being pulled back towards the Blood Stalker, and looked down to see that the Blood Stalkher has used the pools of blood as cover to sneak its tail around my ankle. *"Actually pretty smart,"* I thought, impressed by the Blood Stalker's use of the terrain, *"but it shouldn't have any more blood to heal with, so I think it's about time I end this."*

Activating **Bloodthirst** again, I felt myself already getting accustomed to the intense pain, as my eyes started to bleed and my body grew increasingly stronger.

> **You have been affected by the Status Debuff: [Bleeding]**

Allowing the overwhelming bloodthirsty instincts to take over, my body knew exactly what to do, as I reached down to touch its tail and cast **First Aid** on it first. Instantly the Blood Stalker's giant body shrunk, and without a moment of hesitation, I pushed myself up to my feet and used all my strength to slice down onto its tail—severing it once again and freeing my ankle.

The Blood Stalker roared out in pain, recoiling back from its blood-spurting tails. At the same time, I took advantage of its pained reaction as I held Silverthorn with both hands, brought it over and behind my head, and forcefully flung it straight forwards at the Blood Stalker's head. Then, flying and spinning with incredible speeds, the sword landed perfectly blade first into the Blood Stalker's bone face—in the space slightly above its eyes—piercing halfway into its skull. Though somehow still alive, the Blood Stalker swayed back and forth, completely disoriented with a sword stuck in its head.

Knowing I had to finish it, I activated **Sprint** again and ran head first towards the clueless Blood Stalker with full speed. Then as I approached, I lowered my body, grabbed the hilt from underneath, and pushed my arm straight upwards to the sky. With the sword rotating inside of its head to point downwards, the top of the Blood Stalker's skull split with a geyser of blood spraying up into the air, and its entire body collapsed. Yet even still, with a sword in its head, and its skull split in two at the top, the Blooder Stalker was still somehow alive.

Faintly breathing, it let out a blood curdling growl, "...Blood...**Blood Heal**..."

"Wow, you can heal even after that?" I watched its split skull heal extremely slowly. "I admire you Blood Stalkers for being so resilient, but you're not making it out of this alive." Pulling Silverthorn out of its head, I positioned myself standing over top of it, and fully winding my sword back, I struck a heavy finishing slash straight across the back of the Blood Stalker's neck—cleanly beheading and killing the monster in one fell swoop.

> **Congratulations, you have Leveled Up 2 Levels! All Stats have increased by 4, and you gained 20 Available Points**

Swordsmanship increased by 1 Level.	You have learned the Skill: [Archer's Fury].

> **Archer's Fury: Temporarily entering into a perfect Flow State, you unleash an inner fury reflecting the calm, deliberate, and patient nature of an Archer. Duration: 1 Hour. Cooldown: 24 Hours.**

"*Oooh, a Cooldown Skill!*" I excitedly exclaimed to myself. "*I can't wait to try it out!*"

After deactivating **Bloodthrist**, I directed my attention to Odelia, and saw she was currently fending off a hoard of thirty **Lv.55-65** monsters.

In Range – Ven'Thyl Saga Part I

Having already killed around twenty that were severed into countless scattered pieces on the blood-soaked ground, Odelia faced off against a majority of monsters I was already familiar with; from more Blood Stalkers, to Trolls and Orcs, and even a few large Ogres; but there were also a few monsters I haven't seen before.

The eight **Lv.55-58 Aciks** for example; small red goblin-sized creatures that looked to have no eyes, ears, or noses. But even with their deficiencies, they were still accurately spitting a barrage of acid in Odelia's direction using their large jagged teeth maws—which made up most of their round heads.

There were also four **Lv.59-62 Nalkas**; grey-skinned humanoid creatures with large, red beady eyes and a body that was thin to the bone. Moving the fastest out of all the monsters, it used its four abnormally long arms and its two long legs to crawl quickly across the bloodied ground, with a long, skinny, and spiked tail dragging behind it.

The last unfamiliar monster was a **Lv.62 Blood Scorpion**, which looked to simply be a giant red scorpion, with blood dripping all over its body, giant pincers big enough to grab an entire person, and two large, blackened stinger tails.

Regardless of how the odds look to be stacked against her, Odelia didn't appear to be concerned about these particular monsters at all, disposing of each of them with such ease. And while I observed her truly fight for the first time, I realized just how big the difference in our combat ability was. Other than her incredible speed, she freely moved around as if gravity affected her differently; gracefully spinning and leaping all around while precisely slashing through each monster she passed, while calmly assessing and dodging the countless attacks directed at her at the same time.

"I've got a pretty amazing teacher," I thought to myself, simply in awe of Odelia's skills. But after keenly noticing her using Swordsmanship and Hand-to-hand Skills I haven't seen before, I wondered, *"Why didn't she teach me any of those? They would've made the Combat Test so much easier,"* as I watched her jump directly over a **Lv.65 Blood Ogre**, use an unknown Skill to emit a purple aura around her feet, and then suddenly plummet with unnatural speed on top of the

Fables of J

ogre's skull—utterly obliterating it on contact and killing the large ogre in a single kick.

"I so need to get her to teach me that!" I thought. However, noticing more monsters arriving from all directions of the Dungeon, I shouted, "Odelia! I did it! We can leave now!"

Continuing to slay the nearby monsters, Odelia shouted back, "I know! I saw! You truly are remarkable, Lord Eyes! Congra—" Her eyes widened and she pointed behind me, shouting, "Lord Eyes, watch out!" But before I could turn around, an unbelievably loud screech echoed directly behind me, and too focused on covering my ears from the deafening sound, I found my feet suddenly lifted from the ground as two giant taloned feet pierced into my armour and shoulders—causing me to lose two thirds of my **Health** in an instant.

Health: 2,127/6,495

"AAAHHHHHH!!" I screamed out, feeling the taloned grip tightening the further away we got from the ground. Struggling to look up, I saw an enormous bird creature with the name **Lv.80 Vulcrin**.

"A Lv.80?! What the fuck is this?!"

Panicking, I tried to raise my arm to slice at the feet with my sword, but the moment I started to move, the talons only tightened further around my shoulders, causing me to scream out in agonizing pain again.

Health: 1,729/6,495

Through the pain, I heard Odelia shouting something from way below, and when I looked down to see what she was on about, I was completely surprised by three giant mana-arrowheads spinning like crazy and coming straight towards me.

Hearing the sound of the giant incoming arrowheads, the Vulcrin looked down and noticed them too, but simply tilting and flying to the left, it dodged every single one of them. But for some reason, it suddenly screeched out in immense pain, heavily wobbling as it flew, and drenching me in a layer of its thick blood.

"What the—"

In Range – Ven'Thyl Saga Part I

At that moment, I watched as a giant spinning arrowhead drilled straight through the Vulcrin's left wing; and right after the first one came, another one drilled straight through a different part of the wing, and then another soon after that. Following the arrowheads with my eyes, I watched as they magically turned their way back towards us, and pierced straight through the Vulcrin's body again. Each time they should be flying away, they instead turned themselves back around towards us, and came in for another attack—relentlessly homing onto the Vulcrin specifically.

No matter how hard the Vulcrin tried to avoid the arrowheads, they always found a way to strike its giant body and drill numerous bloodied holes all over, subsequently ending with it falling limp in the air—causing the three mana-arrowheads to abruptly stop and dissipate into nothing.

"It continued until the monster was dead? What the hell was that Skill?" Though I quickly shook my head at that unimportant thought right now. *"No, I gotta focus. I can't be under this thing when we crash, or I'll die too at my current Health."*

Ripping the loosened talon grip out of my shoulders, I held on to the dead Vulcrin's foot and quickly healed myself with **First Aid** as a precaution. Recognizing we were well above 500ft in the air, I truly understood the unbelievably massive scope of the Millennium Dungeon from up here, but quickly moved on and tried to climb my way up on top of the Vulcrin's falling body.

However, while we fell closer and closer to the ground, I suddenly heard Odelia clearly shout "Let go!" Not knowing where she was or what she had planned, but knowing that I could fully trust in her words, I gave up climbing and simply let go.

Free falling, I closed my eyes in trust, and a few seconds after the point when I knew I should've hit the ground, I smiled at the realization that I was no longer falling. Opening my eyes, I found myself perfectly caught in a large mana-net 50ft above the ground—tethered to the trees in the area—with Odelia smiling in relief right underneath it.

Snapping her fingers, the net dissipated into thin air and Odelia caught me.

"I got you," she said before letting me down and checking my injuries. "Are you alright, my lord? I am so sorry I did not kill the Vulcrin faster, you must have been so frightened."

"What are you talking about? That was amazing, Odelia! You saved my life!" I expressed wholeheartedly, feeling very grateful for her. "Thank you!"

"It is simply my duty to protect you as your master and personal guard, Lord Eyes. There is no need for thanks, for I will always be there to save you when I am needed," Odelia proudly declared, deeply bowing to me.

"That's what I'm worried about," I thought, then I excitedly asked her, "Odelia, what was that awesome Skill you just used? How did you make those arrows perfectly track the monster like that?" as I used **First Aid** on myself again.

"Not now, my lord. We are deeper inside the Dungeon than I would ever prefer, and the monsters I left behind should be catching up any moment now," Odelia stated, already having six mana-arrows nocked to her bowstring.

"Right, you're right," I agreed, holding back my ever-growing curiosity about the Skills Odelia hadn't taught me yet. "Oh, but why don't we just teleport out of here?" Holding Odelia's arm, I activated **Return Home**, but a sudden notification appeared.

> **You are unable to use Teleportation Magic within this particular Dungeon.**

"I'll forgive you for not knowing this one, my lord, but Teleportation Magic does not work in the Millennium Dungeons—regardless if they are a Closed or Open Dungeon," Odelia informed me.

"Aww, shit..." I thought to myself, telling Odelia, "Okay, well at least let me heal you before we fight our way out." I noticed the several wounds that weren't there before I got taken by the Vulcrin. "You look like you got injured trying to save me."

"I accept, although you look like you could use some healing yourself, my lord." Odelia pointed out my heavily injured shoulders.

"I'll be fine," I assured her, casting **First Aid** on her wounds first. "I still have this after all."

I pulled out my last Greater Healing Potion and drank it right away—also using **First Aid** on myself one more time.

> **First Aid increased by 1 Level**

Though while we were in the middle of healing our wounds, unnaturally large, dark clouds completely blocked out the crimson moonlight, and everything was once again shrouded in darkness. It was almost silent for a moment, then all of a sudden countless amounts of monsters could be heard frantically approaching from every direction. As they slowly appeared in the darkness around us, they displayed their collection of mesmerizing glowing Blood Moon eyes.

Pressing my back against Odelia's and drawing my weapons, the large dark clouds passed, and the crimson moonlight returned to illuminate the entire forest again. But what it showed us was something no one would ever want to see; for hundreds and thousands of high-level monsters completely and utterly surrounded just the two of us.

"Do not worry, I will protect you, Lord Eyes," Odelia claimed, drawing and aiming her bow, "and luckily for us, I do not see a Boss amongst them yet."

"You must be stronger than I already think you are, if you really think you can take on all of these monsters by yourself while protecting me," I said, looking at the horde of monsters ranging from **Lv.55** all the way up to **Lv.75**.

"Oh, you have no idea, Lord Eyes," Odelia chuckled to herself.

"Although I'd love to see you go all out, why don't I take the ones under Lv.65? You can take the ones over Lv.65, okay?" I suggested, worried she would push herself too much otherwise.

"Alright, but I will be slowly carving a path out of the Dungeon, so follow close behind, understand?" Odelia then consecutively fired the six arrows she had already nocked in different directions, causing six enormous explosions that disoriented the entire horde.

Fables of J

Following Odelia's lead, I thought, *"Desperate times, calls for desperate measures, and I can't hold anything back if I want to keep Odelia safe and prevent my Vision from happening."* I decided to use both **Archery's Fury** and the **Eyes of Eicio's Blood Moon** at the same time.

Instantly I felt myself enter into a tranquil fury; perfectly feeling my slowed and stabilized breath as my mind cleared—absolutely sure of what I could and needed to do—simply waiting for every perfect opportunity to strike. Yet capturing my gaze, my eyes were completely drawn in and enthralled by the beautiful crimson moon; filling my entire being with its overwhelming and empowering divine glow.

A wicked smile grew widely on my face, as my mind revelled in the tranquil fury, as my body bathed in the divine moonlight, and as something inside of me knew I was simply unstoppable.

Chapter 76
Limbo

Not knowing when it happened, I found myself stranded in a boundless sea of darkness, of which there was no end in sight. Blindly searching around for any semblance of a light source, I asked myself, "Where am I? And how did I get here?" truly finding nothing but blinding darkness.

I recalled my last memory, "The last thing I remember was fighting alongside Odelia to escape the Dungeon…" Though my memory seemed to be heavily clouded after that. "But why can't I remember what happened after that?"

Looking around one more time and seeing nothing, I decided to crouch down and try to feel for the ground; but strangely, I felt nothing there, as I simply reached below the point my feet met the supposed 'ground' it stood on.

"Huh? What's going on? What is this place?"

Trying to figure out if I was affected by some sort of weird status effect, I tried opening up my Character Menu to see, but nothing happened; not a single Menu would appear.

"I can't even open the Menus? Now I know something is wrong," I said, openly talking to myself, as opposed to my usual thinking.

"Hello! Anybody out there!" I called out, desperately hoping to hear a response. "I'll even take a monster if you can hear me!" My voice echoed in the nothingness. "Odelia, are you here? Can you hear me? Where are you!"

But I got no response.

Wandering the boundless darkness for any signs of life, I continued to call out for anybody when a sudden loud and disembodied distorted voice echoed throughout the nothingness.

Fables of J

"Ooooh? What do we have here?" The voice sounded surprised, and I immediately looked around to see where it was coming from, but there was nothing around. "There seems to be a lot more commotion in Xull's and Vas' Dungeon this year, I wonder why? I better get a closer look to find out."

"Hey, voice! Can you hear me?" I fearlessly called out, needing some answers.

However, not acknowledging me at all, the voice said, "Huh? What is this? How is it possible for an ordinary elf to be affected by my blessing?"

"Can you really not hear me? And wait, your blessing? Does that mean you're Eicio, the God of Limbo?" Then it made all too much sense. "Oooohh, I must be in Limbo right now, that's what this place is," I concluded, "but if I'm the elf you're talking about, then I must not be dead, right?" Though, as expected, the disembodied voice didn't respond to any of what I just said.

"Looks perfectly normal... No signs of any progressing Types of Monsterification... So did those two specifically remove their blessing from him? And if so, how atrocious of an act did this elf commit against them? It must've been something majorly significant if they did remove their blessing."

"Hey! Wanna explain more? What blessing? And what do you mean 'Types of Monsterification?'" I openly inquired.

"Strange, the elf seems to be getting significantly stronger and fully recovering every couple of kills. Does he have some sort of Unique Skill that allows him to do so?" the voice questioned, still ignoring me. "Well regardless, what a unique little elf I've found here tonight. It almost even makes me want to meet with him in person, hmmm..." It hummed in contemplation.

"Hey, if you're watching me fighting but I'm here, who's controlling my body then?" I reasonably questioned. "And what happened to my Dark Elf friend? Is she alright?"

The voice then randomly shouted in frustration, "Gaaahhhh! I know we should always be role-playing and staying in character, but I'm literally just talking to myself like a crazy person! I've even grown a habit of it now! And I can't imagine what the others with even lonelier characters feel like!"

"A Guide?! Well I guess I shouldn't be surprised since the Goddesses were also Guides, but still..." I listened to him continue speaking.

"I mean even if I break character and these NPCs hear me, it's not like they'll acknowledge me as anything other than Eicio or the God of Limbo!" he vented out his frustration.

"So you are Eicio!" I said, confirming my earlier question.

"And who the hell's Player is this? The Level Cap should still be set to Lv.50 until later, so how is he already fighting against monsters in the Lv.60s and 70s on his own?" Eicio questioned.

"Wait, there's a Level Cap? And why is it so low?" I was slightly saddened to be capped at Lv.50

"Is he 1's Player, or maybe 32's? I know those two were really bragging earlier about how their best Players were gonna finish 1st and 2nd in the Level Rankings—except I don't remember them mentioning Eye Thalion Ven'Thyl earlier, but that name seems familiar though..." After a quick pause Eicio remembered. "Ahhh! His name changed a little, but I think he was one of the Players who finished in the Top 10 in the Tutorial; now which Player belongs to which Guide again?"

"You're a god and you can't even remember ten pairs of people?" I was starting to question these Guides reliability.

"Oh, forget it. I'll just check later at the Meeting," Eicio stated, moving on. "But what's with this guy? The Player starting Races are all affected by the Goddesses' Blessing, meaning my Blessing shouldn't be able to affect him unless they stripped away theirs first—which I doubt they did—or if he somehow found a way to change into a Monstrous Race—which he clearly hasn't. So am I missing something?"

"Did you just say we can change Races again? And to Mountrous ones at that? There isn't anything better than a Wood Elf, is there?" I wondered, only half-heartedly entertaining the thought of changing from a Wood Elf.

"Damnit, Nulla! I can't even figure out how it's happening because you restricted our powers so we could stick to role-playing our characters!" he angrily shouted. "You hear me, you smug bastard! Don't think you can tell me what to do just because you were chosen by the Creator to be the Admin!"

"Seems like you Guides have your own internal issues and problems with each other. You should really talk it out," I said, listening to Eicio shout more.

"Hey, Nulla! Come down here and fight me for your character! If you lose we switch, and if I lose... well I won't lose!" Eicio loudly demanded.

Then all of a sudden a different echoing voice spoke, "100, you temperamental idiot. Stop talking and get back into character."

"So, you actually decided to show yourself after all, Nulla!" Eicio sounded extremely thrilled by the fact. "And if you're already calling me names, you must really wanna fight me, huh?"

"I didn't come here to fight, you idiot. I came here to tell you to use your brain and remember what happens when an intelligent creature is affected by Eicio's Blood Moon for the first time—because you clearly forgot something so important of your own creation, that you blatantly started spouting information you know you shouldn't be revealing to Players." Nulla sounded so done dealing with Eicio.

"Huh? What are you—"

"How the Creator ever chose you to become the God of Limbo I have no idea—maybe the Creator simply felt sorry for creating you last," Nulla savagely stated.

"Okay, that's it, I've had it up to here with your high and mighty attitude—Wait! An intelligent creature affected for the first time!?" Eicio sounded absolutely shocked.

"Ahhhh, so the idiot finally realized his own mistake," Nulla smugly said.

"Oh shit, oh shit, oh shit! I didn't even consider the possibility that a Player could invoke themselves to be in my presence so early on, and already be in my Limbo waiting for my response!" Eicio mentioned, worried.

In Range – Ven'Thyl Saga Part I

"Well, aside from simply looking inside your Limbo for once, you really should've realized it the moment you saw Eyes Thalion Ven'Thyl mindlessly being affected by your Blood Moon."

Eicio only hummed in response, knowing it was his fault.

"But what's done is done, and since I'm here anyway, why don't we have a little chat with Eyes Thalion Ven'Thyl?"

"Why would we do that? Let's just erase his memory and be done with it," Eicio suggested.

"Well, I did think about that after you were revealing too much, but then I thought, who else would remember how much of an idiot you are?"

"Hey!" Eicio took offense to that.

"So are you coming with me or not?" Nulla asked.

"Fine, but we're fighting later," Eicio agreed.

"Wait, they're not really coming in here to erase my memory are they?" I worried that they actually were.

Quickly looking for a place to hide, I found nothing but more boundless darkness, as two figures made of pure light suddenly descended from the darkness above me. One appeared with the word 'Nulla' written across its nonexistent face, while the other appeared with the simple letter 'C' written in the center of its chest—also having a nonexistent face. And although they both emitted an illuminating light, I still couldn't see a thing in here, including my hand reaching out to their light. Then as they approached me, I decided to avoid thinking to myself as much as possible here, for whatever reason it was, I knew I would just blurt whatever it is I'm thinking to them.

The figure with the 'C' on its chest looked over its body in surprise, "Hey, what gives, Nulla? Why do we look like this?"

"Oh, come on, 100, have some integrity," Nulla replied, reasoning, "Why would I ruin the great significance of his actual first meeting with our particular characters? Now with us looking like this, the spectacle and authenticity of the interaction will be maintained."

Fables of J

"God, I hate you so much all the time," 100 openly expressed. "And why are we even here? You can achieve the same result by erasing his memory, you know?

"Well, depending on how I feel after our conversation, I might just be inclined to do otherwise," he said, as I watched the word 'Nulla' on his face reform into a smile.

"I don't really care what you're planning, Nulla, but if the others find out you're playing favourites and interfering again... well you know how we are," 100 reminded Nulla.

"Hey, I have every right to participate like everybody else—why can't I play?"

"Because you're the Admin, stupid? How are you gonna justify the fairness in that?"

"Hmmm... I can't, although that's why you're gonna keep this little meeting a secret, right?" Nulla put a friendly hand on 100's shoulder.

Though quickly shrugging the hand off, 100 said, "You kept calling me an idiot earlier, why would I agree to that?"

"First of all, you are an idiot. And second, if you keep this meeting between us... I'll allow you to revive any one already Dead Player of your choosing, regardless of their original Guide," Nulla said. "Of course we would need to change some of the records to prevent the others from knowing, but how's that sound for a deal?"

"Oooh, now that's tempting..." 100 quickly pondered the idea, and said, "You're lucky all my remaining Players are useless trash so far, so I guess I'll take the deal—but only on the condition I can make two Egos for my Revived Player."

"Two!? How is that any more fair than me participating?" Nulla exclaimed. "And didn't you already create an Ego for one of your current Players like everybody else?"

"Actually, I didn't. For none of my trash Players were good enough in the Tutorial to warrant me making them one," 100 grumbled. "But now that I can decide which Dead Player with the most potential I can revive, I thought I might as well make them their own Ego, plus one more for keeping my silence about this secret meeting of course."

"Urgh, you're unbelievable, 100," Nulla shook his head at him, but reluctantly agreed anyway. "Fine. I agree to your terms. I'll just have to deal with the others whining about a Player owning two Egos when they come across them."

"Glad we came to an agreement."

While they shook their hands to seal the deal, even with a nonexistent face, I could tell 100 was happily grinning as he did so.

Then finally directing their attention to me, Nulla said, "Now, Eyes Thalion Ven'Thyl, thank you for patiently waiting for us to finish our conversation. I know you must have a lot of questions after everything you just heard from us."

"Maybe a few, but are you gonna answer any of them? Or are you just gonna erase my memory like 100 suggested?" I asked, being wary of this situation.

Nulla chuckled, "Like I said earlier, I might be convinced otherwise—though if it makes you feel better, how about I answer one of your questions now?"

"Any question?" I asked, wanting confirmation.

"Maybe, although why don't you ask one and find out?" The word 'Nulla' turned into a smile again.

"That means not any question," I assumed, and while I thought about possible questions, my thoughts came out verbally into words. "I doubt he'll answer any questions about the Creator and the Guides, or why they brought us to this world, so maybe I should ask 'how do I get out of here?'"

They chuckled in amusement at hearing my thoughts, and 100 apologized, "Sorry about that; my Realm of Limbo is a place where thoughts cannot be kept hidden, and where the deepest of secrets will always reveal themselves to us—though I'm sure you'll find out when we truly meet in person."

I had no response to that, so Nulla asked, "Was that the question, 'how do I get out here?'"

"Yeah. Wait, no! Maybe?" I panicked, unsure what I wanted to ask anymore.

Fables of J

Nulla chuckled in amusement again and then explained, "Well, either way, since it is your first time experiencing Eicio's Blood Moon and you invoked yourself to be in his presence, I believe you are stuck here until Eicio himself decides to confer with you, or until the Blood Moon ends.

"What!? How long is that gonna take?" I questioned in concern, "Isn't my body still out there fighting? What if I die?"

"That would be tragic. But don't worry, from what I've observed, you'll definitely at least make it to midnight," Nulla confidently assured me. "Although if you really are worried, you could always ask 100 here to let you go—a simple acknowledgement in his true form would suffice."

Though before I could ask, 100 unexpectedly shouted, "Ahhh, I think I know how you were affected by Blood Moon now! You're 13's Player, the one who received the Seer Subclass, yeah? Meaning you must've stolen some eyes affected by the Blood Moon, right?"

"Well yeah, that's all true, but can we talk about letting me out of here first?" I asked, tired of being unable to see anything but them.

"Now why would I do that when all of the Players are getting teleported back to the Hub at midnight anyway?" 100 immediately covered his own nonexistent mouth. "Ooooh, I shouldn't have said that."

"Wait, what? We're going back to the Waiting Hub?" I was caught completely off guard by that reveal.

Nulla sighed, "You truly are an idiot, 100. How can you allow yourself to be affected by your own Limbo?"

"Okay, I'll take responsibility for revealing that one, but the earlier stuff was an accident, I promise," 100 said, trying to excuse himself.

"We'll see what the others think at the Meeting later," Nulla mischievously smirked.

Interjecting, I said, "Knowing I'll be safe is great and all, but can we get back to letting me out of this place?" I reminded them, saying, "I know you guys might not care, but I have a friend in the Dungeon I have to protect no matter what, because she might end up dying tonight."

"A friend in the Dungeon? I didn't see any one, did you Nulla?" 100 sounded unsure who I was referring to.

"I think he's referring to the dead Dark Elf his body was instinctively trying to protect," Nulla replied.

Hearing those words sent me in complete shock, "W-What... what do you mean dead?"

"Oh, that Dark Elf woman was your friend?" 100 asked, curiously.

"WHAT DO YOU MEAN DEAD!" I demanded to know.

"Woah, calm down. I or Nulla didn't do anything to her," 100 surprisingly reacted calmly. "She was already dead on the ground when I arrived at the Dungeon."

"Then how the hell is she dead!" I still angrily yelled out, "There's no way I'd still be alive if something was strong enough to kill her! So tell me exactly how the FUCK she could ever end up dead while I'm still alive here standing!"

"I don't know..." 100 sincerely replied.

"However, we are in the perfect place to find out, now aren't we 100?" Nulla gestured to the entire space.

"That we are," 100 agreed, telling me, "You've clearly already suppressed your memories of what happened, but my Realm of Limbo will always reveal one's secrets."

All of a sudden, the pure dark boundless nothingness began to distort and change, and the bloody crimson forest slowly appeared all around us. Then at that very moment, all the memories came rushing back into me, and before anything else was even shown to us, I already knew exactly what happened.

"I killed Odelia..."

Chapter 77
Remorse and Guilt

A NOTE FROM FABLES OF J
The last Chapter and official end of Part 1 of the Ven'Thyl Saga.

My mind was clear and decisive, my movement exact and powerful, and my arrows accurate and deadly. I feared nothing, for nothing could stand in my way. And assuredly, everything I did ultimately became fearlessly reckless because of my own stupid arrogance. Odelia was even forced to push me out of the way from attacks I didn't view as threatening but that she apparently did, as always prioritized my safety first above all else.

Focusing mostly on the lower-level monsters flanking from the sides and back, I sent an array of arrows to keep the horde at bay, while Odelia focused on the higher-level monsters and still pushed ahead in the direction out of the Dungeon. However, no matter how many we killed, stronger and stronger monsters were simply drawn in by the noticeably loud ruckus our seemingly endless escape created, and it became increasingly difficult to fight through the countless numbers of the horde.

"You guys were surrounded, but you were still killing enough to make progress in escaping the Dungeon, so what went wrong?" 100 asked, observing my memory being displayed throughout his Limbo.

"I did…" I quietly admitted, knowing it was all my fault.

"Will you stop talking for once, 100? I'm watching here," Nulla said, intently watching my memory as well.

"Fine," 100 agreed, shutting his nonexistent mouth.

In Range – Ven'Thyl Saga Part I

"Lord Eyes, are you sure you are alright?" Odelia worriedly asked, swiftly dismembering 20 Nalkas at once. "Those are eyes affected by the Gom's Blood Moon, are they not?"

Diving out of the way of a thrown log from an Ogre, I countered with an **Element Arrow (Ice)** straight to the Weak Point I could now always visually see on the Ogre's bare chest—piercing straight into the heart and causing it to collapse in shock.

"I told you, stop worrying about me! Focus on yourself and escaping!" I shouted to her, rapidly shooting and slowing down a few incoming flying Blood Wings—large bat-like monsters with saber-teeth and long claws.

"I am simply asking because you have not been acting yourself, my lord!" Odelia pointed out, leading a charge towards a herd of armed Minotaurs blocking our way.

Following her and sending five **Explosive Arrows** behind us, I asked, "What are you talking about? I've never felt stronger!" I slid under a pouncing Blood Stalker, grabbed its tail as it passed, pulled it straight towards me with my sheer strength, and thrusted Silverthorn down into its skull before tossing what was left into the horde. "See what I'm talking about?"

"I do not think we are seeing the same thing…" Odelia sounded and appeared uneasy about my current state, but tried her best to focus on escaping for now.

Then as Odelia and I continued to slowly push through the horde, it became obviously clear to me I was having way too much fun mindlessly killing the countless monsters. Each time I leveled up and recovered all my Stats worsened the desire, driving me to pick up the pace and continue without even the least bit of rest.

That increase of pace wasn't a problem for Odelia at first, but needing to do more and kill faster to keep me safe, it eventually caught up to her. And for the first time since I met her, Odelia began displaying slight signs of exhaustion through her heavy breathing and visible sweat. Yet determined to keep me safe, she pushed through her exhaustion, and looked to have come to a decision.

Fables of J

"Lord Eyes, I did not want us to use our most powerful Skills to avoid the attention of the Bosses, and to not be exhausted if one were to appear..." She paused, strangely clutching her stomach. "But I think we are close enough to the outskirts that it will be alright..." Odelia tiredly mentioned, moving and swinging her sword much slower now.

"Really? Then can I use a Maximum Charge Arrow?" I excitedly asked, wanting to see how much destruction I could cause.

Though before I knew it, Odelia suddenly picked me up and threw me over her back, saying, "No. Save your energy for escaping. I'll take care of the rest..." Getting into an extremely low crouch, Odelia took a deep breath in, and as she exhaled out, her legs fully extended and we instantly skyrocketed up into the sky.

"Holy shit!" I exclaimed, barely holding onto Odelia's body from the resulting intense air pressure pushing down onto me.

Then as we reached the apex of her otherworldly jump, Odelia strangely spoke in Elvish, telling me, "I may not be there to teach you my Earth Piercer… so make sure you pay close attention… my king."

But before I could respond, an explosion of purple aura erupted from Odelia's back and enveloped her entire body.

Holding her bow in her right hand and her sword in her left, I watched as the aura split in two, traveled through and down her arms, and imbued itself into both her bow and sword. Once all the aura was infused into her weapons, Odelia used her sword as if it were an arrow, drew both it and the bowstring back, and aimed it directly at the horde of monsters below us. And as she smoothly released a perfectly aimed shot, the sword flew right off the bowstring, causing two extremely loud echoing booms; first simply being the bowstring snapping forward and breaking off the bow, and second being a deafening sonic boom created by the sword unexpectedly breaking the sound barrier.

Almost instantly piercing straight into the ground, the sheer impact of the attack caused a terrain-altering earthquake to ripple throughout an entire kilometer radius below us; uprooting and toppling the trees in the area, shattering and splitting the bloodied ground into countless rubble chunks, and causing all the pooled blood to be lifted and sent flying up into the air.

In Range – Ven'Thyl Saga Part I

Impressed, 100 whistled and acknowledged Odelia's attack. "That was some attack! It might've even been strong enough to scratch our characters, don't you think Nulla?"

"You just can't help talking, can you? But I'm sure she would've done more damage if she wasn't so poisoned," Nulla commented, noticing Odelia's condition.

"She's poisoned? When? Where?" 100 asked, not noticing when it happened earlier either.

"She hid it from me so I wouldn't worry…" I answered, now feeling so stupid for not noticing earlier.

Landing on the unstable rubble ground of the forest, Odelia suddenly collapsed onto the floor; and before I could ask her what was wrong, I finally noticed a black ichor profusely secreting from her lower abdomen, along with blackened veins appearing on the surface of her grey skin. Her body trembled uncontrollably shortly after, and as she began to cough in pain, black bloodied ichor spewed from her mouth.

Still speaking in Elvish, Odelia softly spoke to me, "My king… this is your opportunity to escape… Please leave before more monsters come…"

Ignoring her wish, I grabbed her dropped bow and stored it in Infinity; and walking over to her sword deeply embedded into the ground, I stored it in Infinity too. Then walking back over to her, I forced her weakened, reluctant self onto my back and began carrying her in the direction out of the Dungeon.

"My king… please leave me… I'll only slow you down…" she weakly pleaded, informing me, "This is Blood-Altering Poison… I don't know how it'll affect me… and I can't risk affecting you too..." Odelia tried to push herself off my back, but I held her on as I continued running.

"You know, Odelia, I lost my Uncle Thalion because I was doing something as stupid as fighting a Combat Test during a Blood Moon," I said, sharing my past with her for the first time.

"My king…"

"He died after an accident I basically caused myself…"

"My injuries aren't your fault, my king…" Odelia tried to assure me.

"No… but I am the reason they happened..." When she didn't answer, I kept talking, "I couldn't save my Uncle Thalion, and I couldn't save…" Shaking my head, I promised her, "I will save you, Odelia, no matter what!"

"You can't save me… now get away!" Then all of a sudden Odelia's body began shaking abnormally fast on my back, and in an instant I found myself tumbling forward as she forcefully pushed herself off my back.

Quickly recovering from the tumble, I shouted, "Odelia, I'm not leaving—" I was completely shocked and silenced by the sight of Odelia's body unnaturally contorting in horrifying ways.

Tilting her head back and to the side, her entire appearance somehow changed to be frighteningly gaunt. Blackened veins greatly protruded all along her neck and face, black ichor spilled from her mouth, her cheeks became ghastly hollow, dark circles appeared around her eyes, and I watched as Odelia's eyeballs blackened and her irises became the reflection of the Blood Moon.

"My king… LEAVEEEEEEE!" A long ear-shattering scream erupted from Odelia's mouth—knocking me back from the force of the sound alone.

"O-Odelia!" I desperately called out to her, being just enough to stop her from deafening me completely.

"Y-You can't escape from me now..." she stammered, holding herself back while her limbs horrifyingly contorted. "Y-You have to KILL me!"

"What!? No!" I adamantly refused.

"I-I will KILL you otherwise..." she gasped, showing me the long sharp nails now ripping through her leather gloves.

"But you can't die! I have to save you! There has to be another way!" I said, refusing that to be the only choice.

"Y-You want to save me? T-Then… KILL ME!" No longer able to hold herself back, her body lunged forwards with incredible speeds,

In Range – Ven'Thyl Saga Part I

grabbing me by the neck, and choke slamming me straight into the ground—shattering the rubbled ground further.

"O...de...li...a..." I choked, barely able to speak as her hand clasped tighter and tighter around my throat.

"M-My king... do it!" Even in her state, Odelia pleaded for her death, and as I stared into her completely changed eyes, I still saw the real Odelia inside.

"**Blood...thirst!**" And with that activation, I reached for Infinity, pulled out an arrow, and immediately casted **Element Arrow (Light)**. Instantly, Odelia screamed out in blinding pain, releasing her death grip around my neck as she stumbled back, covering her eyes. Gasping for air, I rolled over and pulled out my sheathed sword, and then stood over the still blinded Odelia. But as I raised my sword to strike her down, I just couldn't bring myself to do it, regardless of my overwhelming bloodlust at that moment.

"I'm sorry, Odelia...I can't kill you..." I lowered my sword.

Then as the light from the arrow dissipated, Odelia unexpectedly recovered faster than before. Though surprising me entirely, she warmly smiled and said, "T-That's okay... I'll do it for you."

In a single moment, Odelia savagely lunged towards me again, and all the basic swordsmanship instincts she taught me reactively caused me to raise my sword, unintentionally driving the blade straight through her chest and into her heart. In utter shock, I couldn't move, but Odelia approached and dug the blade even deeper inside her, until her entire body was thoroughly impaled by the blade of my sword.

Catching her as she leaned her dying body against mine, I had no words but her name to speak, "Odelia..."

"I-I never got to tell you, my king..." She wheezed as she faintly spoke, "C-Congratulations... you're now equivalent to a Combat Archer..."

Fables of J

> ### Class Change
>
> **Meeting both the required conditions to become a 'Combat Archer' Class or 'Tri-Style Archer' Class, you are now eligible to change your current 'Dual-Style Archer' Class to one with equal or higher potential.**
>
> **Which Class do you choose:**
>
> ***Your next potential Class Progression Choice will greatly change depending on your chosen Class.***
>
> **[Tri-Style Archer] or [Dual-Style Archer] or [Combat Archer]**

Feeling her body lose consciousness and fall limp in my arms, I sobbed while pleading, "Odelia, stay with me! You can't die yet! Tell me how I can save you!" And like that, the dreadful Vision I foresaw finally fulfilled itself.

"Oh, boy. You did kill her," Nulla reiterated, "and seeing how much you're crying, she must've meant a lot to you, didn't she?"

"He didn't kill her," 100 objected, stating, "she clearly killed herself, and now he's just blaming himself."

"He may not have thrusted the sword, but he did raise it up; and therefore, he killed her—although only partly," Nulla reasoned.

"So if I shoot an energy blast and you happen to be in the way and die from it, does that mean I killed you?" 100 openly questioned.

"Yes. And I dare you to try," Nulla said, trying to instigate a fight, but even 100 didn't fall for it.

However, trying to avoid getting caught up with reliving Odelia's death, I instead focused on clearing my still hazy memory of how exactly I got here.

"It's not over yet! I can still save her!" I told myself, wiping the tears and blood from my face. Then taking a second to logically think, I

In Range – Ven'Thyl Saga Part I

listed the three most important things I needed to do. *"First, I need to escape this Dungeon. Second, I need to teleport back to the House. And third, I need to get Verana's help to save Odelia. In the worst case scenario, I still have the Tear of an Elder Cyclops that can revive her, but I have absolutely no clue what'll become of her after that."*

Suddenly hearing the ground rumbling, I looked around and saw another horde of incoming monsters in every direction. Quickly carrying Odelia in my arms, I began running in the direction out of the Dungeon again, but ultimately being surrounded by the horde, I had to stand my ground and fight to clear a path. Knowing I needed to be stronger to deal with this alone, I haphazardly increased my Stats with the unused Available Points—mostly focusing on Agility—and accepted the **Tri-Style Archer** as my Class Change.

Congratulations, you have changed your current Class to 'Tri-Style Archer'!	

You have gained the Title: [A True Combat Archer]	You have learned the Proficiency: [Close-Combat Archery]
You have learned the Skill: [Combat Aura]	'Archer's Duality' has been proactively developed into the Skill: [Archer's Triality]

Close-Combat Archery proficiency increased by 33 Levels.	Combat Aura increased by 3 Levels.

Feeling an exhilarating rush of power, I activated **Bloodthirst** to increase the rush further, and allowed myself to be filled with an overwhelming vengeful bloodlust. Then sending a **Maximum Charged**

303

Fables of J

Arrow to one side of the horde, I utterly obliterated an entire half of the endless horde.

> **Congratulations, you have Leveled Up 3 Levels! All Stats have increased by 6, and you gained 30 Available Points**

Not having time to cast another one, I **Sprinted** over to Odelia and beheaded a group of Aciks trying to drag her body away into the horde. Being split between both protecting Odelia's body and clearing out a path, I felt myself being overwhelmed in only a few minutes; and only worsening the endless battle, **Archer's Fury** finally ended.

> **'Archer's Fury' is now on Cooldown (23 Hours, 59 Minutes, 59 Seconds)**

Then all of a sudden, I completely lost control over my entire body, as a heavy club from a **Lv.70 High Orc** struck me right across the head. However, strangely unfazed by the attack, my body simply moved on its own, creating a visible blue aura around my fist, and upper-cutting the High Orc right under its jaw—knocking the lights out of it with a single punch.

My mind subsequently became extremely clouded, as I began moving much more instinctively rather than intellectually; and on top of the overwhelming bloodthirsty instincts of Bloodthirst, I became more like the monsters I was ruthlessly slaughtering, as opposed to the person I was just a moment ago. Finding an instance of space from the now slightly fearful horde, I found myself gazing back up at the enthralling Blood Moon, and began speaking to it without volition.

"The God of Limbo, he who does not reject and accepts all! I invoke your name, Eicio, and request an audience at your godly leisure!" And in an instant, everything became a dark boundless void.

"Why did I say that?" I questioned, confused why I knew those words.

"Oh, sorry again," 100 apologized, telling me, "If a creature affected by my Blessing is intelligent enough to properly invoke my

In Range – Ven'Thyl Saga Part I

name, they will always request for my presence, for I can—you know what, why don't you find out on your own if you dare, Seer..."

"Okay, it's about time we end this," Nulla interjected, "we only have 2 minutes until the Recall starts."

"Already? Wow, time sure does fly in here, doesn't it?" 100 commented.

"Wait! I can't go yet!" I adamantly stated. "I can't just leave Odelia dead in the Dungeon, I still have to save her!"

"Well there isn't much you can do with the time remaining, the Recall is scheduled to happen regardless of what you or the other Players want," Nulla informed me. "Not to mention, I haven't even brought up what I came here to discuss with you yet."

But ignoring his words, I desperately pleaded, "Revive her! You're gods, right? I'll do anything, just save Odelia!"

"Ooooh, careful what you wish for, Eyes Thalion Ven'Thyl," Nulla smiled widely. "Though you may think us 'gods', I, the Administrator, and 100, a Guide, are not allowed to directly affect anything that happens in Novus—or it will result in us being severely punished by the Creator."

"Says the guy who's planning to do exactly that with me," 100 called him out.

"You know Players are the fun exceptions," Nulla replied with a smile.

"That they are," 100 agreed with a laugh.

"So both of you won't do a thing?" I asked, and they both shook their heads. "Can you at least release me from this place before I get recalled or whatever? I at least want to say goodbye..."

"Well, I don't mind saving our discussion for a later date where you'll be more open and inclined to listen," Nulla shrugged.

"And I guess I can grant you your request. After all, you are ultimately the reason I'm getting an additional Player," 100 said, holding his left index finger out. Nulla then tapped the finger, revealing from under 100's light an abnormally large and long red-furred finger. Walking over to me, he placed the finger on presumably my forehead, and said, "Return when there is no place else who will accept you..."

In an instant, I found myself standing back in the crimson forest, surrounded by countless corpses of monsters I seemed to have savagely slaughtered on my own, and noticed the unusual collection of crimson clouds raining down blood throughout the entire area.

Finding Odelia's body, I was frozen with guilt when I saw it again, barely even able to get my apology out to her.

"I... I... I'm sorry, Odelia..." I stared at the fatal wound I created in her chest. "This... this is all my fault... I knew this would happen... but I still decided to come here..." The blood rain drenched and covered our entire bodies in crimson. "And in a few seconds... I won't even be here..." The feeling of being helpless again quickly boiled up inside and completely infuriated me.

"AAAAAHHHHHH!! AAAAHHHHH...!!! AAAHHHH—"

A loud and echoing sound suddenly exploded in my ears, and appearing in the sky was the giant, multipart magic circle that first teleported us to this world. And as the different parts of the magic circle began to turn and move, it became brighter and brighter, but all I did was stare at yet another person who died because of

Glossary

AOE – abbreviation for area of effect. (In a video game) an attack or defense, such as a spell or special skill, that affects all characters within a specified range of the target place or character, rather than affecting only a targeted character

Broken - a term used in many games to describe characters, techniques, or other elements or combinations of elements so overpowered that they make the game stop functioning as intended and/or severely skew the game's balance in a player's favor, making alternatives nearly irrelevant by comparison

Common - unspecified common language spoken by majority of races

Zerg - slang term for a group of low-level gamers who depend on overwhelming numbers to achieve victory, rather than relying on technique or strategy

Kiting - a popular method of killing monsters or other players by staying at a distance, using ranged attacks, and running whenever the enemy comes near

NPC- stands for non-playable character and is any character in a game that is not controlled by a player

PKers – abbreviation of player killers

Spam - in the context of video games, refers to the repeated use of the same item or action

TLDR – abbreviation of too long didn't read. A briefly expressed main point or key message that summarizes a longer discussion or explanation

Made in the USA
Columbia, SC
28 August 2024

1903c957-0b6e-4a64-8b25-dbbbd76d9151R01